JORDYN ELLERY

Redemption

To blossom, means to grow

Copyright © 2023 by Jordyn Ellery

All rights reserved. No part of this publication may be reproduced, stored or transmitted in any form or by any means, electronic, mechanical, photocopying, recording, scanning, or otherwise without written permission from the publisher. It is illegal to copy this book, post it to a website, or distribute it by any other means without permission.

This novel is entirely a work of fiction. The names, characters and incidents portrayed in it are the work of the author's imagination. Any resemblance to actual persons, living or dead, events or localities is entirely coincidental.

Jordyn Ellery asserts the moral right to be identified as the author of this work.

Jordyn Ellery has no responsibility for the persistence or accuracy of URLs for external or third-party Internet Websites referred to in this publication and does not guarantee that any content on such Websites is, or will remain, accurate or appropriate.

Designations used by companies to distinguish their products are often claimed as trademarks. All brand names and product names used in this book and on its cover are trade names, service marks, trademarks and registered trademarks of their respective owners. The publishers and the book are not associated with any product or vendor mentioned in this book. None of the companies referenced within the book have endorsed the book.

Trigger Warnings for this book are as follows: graphic violence, profanity, sexual violence, kidnapping, torture, suicide, graphic sexual scenes, choking, breath play, mental health issues, eating disorders, fertility issues, death, gun violence, war, physical health issues, trauma, bound, gas lighting, family trauma, drugs, alcohol, addiction, cheating, mental abuse, PTSD, borderline personality disorder, PD, self harm, grief.

First edition

This book was professionally typeset on Reedsy.
Find out more at reedsy.com

*For those who dream of a knight in shining armor rescuing them from the confines of a castle.
Except our knight is muscular, masked and fucks like a God.*

Contents

Acknowledgement	iv
Playlist	1
Chapter 1	3
Chapter 2	7
Chapter 3	13
Chapter 4	25
Chapter 5	39
Chapter 6	52
Chapter 7	59
Chapter 8	69
Chapter 9	75
Chapter 10	82
Chapter 11	88
Chapter 12	91
Chapter 13	96
Chapter 14	99
Chapter 15	105
Chapter 16	112
Chapter 17	117
Chapter 18	122
Chapter 19	128
Chapter 20	138
Chapter 21	143
Chapter 22	149

Chapter 23	154
Chapter 24	158
Chapter 25	164
Chapter 26	172
Chapter 27	177
Chapter 28	185
Chapter 29	194
Chapter 30	198
Chapter 31	202
Chapter 32	207
Chapter 33	212
Chapter 34	217
Chapter 35	224
Chapter 36	229
Chapter 37	233
Chapter 38	238
Chapter 39	247
Chapter 40	252
Chapter 41	258
Chapter 42	264
Chapter 43	272
Chapter 44	277
Chapter 45	284
Chapter 46	289
Chapter 47	295
Chapter 48	302
Chapter 49	313
Chapter 50	322
Chapter 51	329
Chapter 52	334
Chapter 53	342

Chapter 54	343
Chapter 55	347
Chapter 56	356
Chapter 57	365
Chapter 58	371
Chapter 59	373
Chapter 60	377
Chapter 61	381
Chapter 62	387
Chapter 63	392
Epilogue	403
A huge thank you!	413
About the Author	414

Acknowledgement

Okay first things first, Mam. The word 'cunt' is not used to describe a pussy, so I suppose you can read this one now. Other than that, I hope you enjoy the book! (Can't guarantee this for future books–sorry :/)

To the fam – as always, thank you so much for your continuous support and having faith in me even though my books are not safe to leave lying around children. I appreciate every one of you who have purchased a copy of my books and I hope I continue to impress you!

To my twin flame – where would I even be with my number one hype woman? Courtney, you've listened and worked with me to figure out the star signs for every single character in the Billy Boys universe, looked at every pinterest board I've sent you and listened to numerous readings of my WIP. I think you deserve at least a few bottles of wine on me– *minimum*. Thank you for always being there. x

To my amazing Jelly Squad, you girls are amazing! You support me in every way and honestly you guys have been my rock, thank you. Each of you have been incredible and keep me motivated in the best ways possible. You all will always hold a special place in my heart. x

To my magnificent street team, it's been an absolute pleasure having your continuous support with all things social media! Literally, so many readers wouldn't know about little old me and my books if it wasn't for you guys! Thank you! x

To my phenomenal ARC readers, your role has been so significant in my journey and push me to continue doing what I do. Being able to see your reactions, to see your reviews and ratings is one of my most favorite parts of being an author. Thank you so much to every single one of you!

And huge thank you to all of the beautiful readers out there who have read any of my books – you guys are literally the star of the show. I do this all for you and if you enjoy it, it's the icing on the cake. Thank you! x

Playlist

Hostage – Billie Eilish
Wicked Game – Jessie Villa
Sink or Swim - Artemas
Gilded Lily (Slowed & Reverb) – Cults
Sex, drugs, etc. - Beach Weather
Take a moment to breathe – normal the kid
Idea 22 – Gibran Alcocer
Desire - Meg Myers
Valentine, Texas - Mitski
Come Find Me (feat. Lykke Li & Romy) – Emile Haynie
Love Will Tear Us Apart – Nerina Pallot
My Cell – The Lumineers
Dynasty - Miia
Cravin' - Stileto & Kendyle Paige
Keeping You Around - Nothing But Thieves
Paradise Circus – Massive Attack

Apocalypse – Cigarettes After Sex
Push it Down - L Devine
Crazy in Love - Sofia Karlberg
Hurt for Me - SYML
Easy to Love - Bryce Savage
Slowly - NewDad
Right Now - Gracie Abrams (Chapter 61)
Everything I Do Is For You - Amira Elfeky
Afterlife - Nothing But Thieves

Chapter 1

Rhea

One. Two. Three. Four. Five. Six. *Seven?*
No that can't be right.
One. Two. Three. Four. Five. Six. Seven. There is seven after all.

I place the towel around Gemini to give her some warmth whilst placing each of the kittens closer to her, she looks exhausted. I mean, I couldn't imagine giving birth to one, let alone seven.

I gently stroke her head and pull her water bowl closer as she rubs her ears into the palm of my hand, closing her eyes.

"Oh Gemini, you're a momma now." I purse my lips and stare at the kittens in adoration as Gemini begins to lick them clean of their birthing coat.

It's her first litter, which happened completely accidentally, she seems to have a better luck with love than I do. The apartment door opens and I glance up to see Felicity waltzing in, shopping bags in tow.

"It's time!" she squeals, dropping the bags and rushing over to us.

"You're a little late, Fizzy." I gesture to the kittens that are now suckling on Gemini. She crouches down and gives Gemini a little pat on the head and then looks back up at me.

"How did she do? Did she struggle?" Her face etches with concern.

"It went as well as it could have I suppose, I mean I don't think either of us expected seven of them, but she powered through like the tough kitty she is." I smile down at her.

"Oh gosh, I'm going to have to get some extra organic cat food, she deserves it. My strong little kitty." She pushes off the floor to stand back up. Delving into the sofa, she props her feet up onto the coffee table.

"How'd the job interview go?" I ask.

"Oh yeah! So basically, I didn't technically have a job interview, well I did, but like I kind of just… had a walk in?" she cringes.

"Hm, and what exactly does that entail?" I cock an eyebrow at her.

"I seen the ad, and you know how I feel about Indie Thorne, she's like my idol, so I kind of just swung by, offered my services and she literally offered me the job on the spot!" She claps her hands together with delight.

"You're joking?" My jaw is dropped open.

"Nope." she says, popping the P.

"You are the luckiest girl ever Fizz, I've never known anyone strike it as lucky as you have it." I shake my head, laughing and joining her on the couch.

"Says you! Little miss 'I'm going to the clouds', over here." She nudges me in the side.

"Look, I've been in flight school for years, it's not luck, it's skill." I say strongly.

Chapter 1

"Maybe so, but you've still landed an internship with that agency, I've heard some of the best pilots work there. Hm, maybe they're cute too?" I roll my eyes and pick up the purple daisy pillow from behind me and throw it at her face.

Because of our close proximity, she has no time to dodge so it hits her exactly where I wanted it to.

"Hey! I'm just saying." She raises her hands defensively, earning another eye roll.

"Moving on from the topic, did you get the seeds I asked you to grab?" I gesture to the shopping bags.

"Seeds? Seeds. Oh, um. No I forgot, but... big but here. I did grab you a stunning bottle of champagne, to celebrate my new job!" she grins at me.

"You bought *me*... a bottle of champagne... to celebrate *your* new job?" I ask slowly, trying to break it down for her to understand what she's just said.

"Okay, okay fine. Guilty as charged, I forgot the seeds and I wanted to try and make it up to you by saying that I got you something, but I didn't. The champagne was for me, sorry, Rhea." She looks down.

"I gathered that, Fizz." I chuckle.

She pulls out her phone and begins scrolling.

"So, whose popping the champagne then?" I question. She looks up at me and shakes her head with a smile on her face.

"Looks like it's gonna be me." She stands up and gathers her bags, placing them on the kitchen counter.

Our place is pretty quaint, a little bit on the rough side, could do with a few licks of paint on the baby blue walls, but it's affordable. That's the important part for two people who are practically unemployed, well, until now.

As I've just found out, Fizzy has a new job working for a prestige ballet company and I, well I'm about to begin my official pilot training with Titan Agency, but at the moment I'm not doing anything.

Most of our furniture was already here when we moved in, except our accessories and the TV. We replaced the mattresses as the old ones looked like someone had died in them (they probably had). The kitchen is definitely the same kitchen that has been here since the eighties, but we tried to run with it. We've added a lot of boho style decor, to make it all blend in and look entirely intentional, something out of an interior design magazine. Or, that's what I tell myself anyways.

The real selling point for me was the tiny terrace outside of my bedroom, connected with large glass double doors, single-glazed of course. This meant that I was able to keep my plants alive, giving them the perfect spot to flourish under the sunlight. I have a lot of indoor plants too, but it wouldn't be the same if I couldn't keep my heliotropes or hibiscus'. My goal for the end of the year is to have the entire terrace filled to the brim with all kinds of flowers and plants that passers-by will be able to look up and see the beautification of my tiny garden.

"Do you want a petite lady-like flute of champagne, or shall we be normal and have it in a mug?" Fizz asks, holding up both options.

"Go for the mug." I wink and laugh.

Chapter 2

Devon

I pull away from Reed's house, confident I've done my good deed for the day, or evening I suppose. I hope he takes me up on my offer to be his sponsor, I know all too well what it's like to be in his position, in the same dark envelope of life. The one where we can't quite figure out which is the right way up, so we end up spinning in circles until eventually we lose our balance.

Ten months clean. The chip in my pocket seems to heat up whenever I think about it, whenever I think about her.

Isabelle (Bella) Hudson.

She's been gone for ten months and I really thought it'd get easier by now, but the guilt is just as present as the morning of.

I swing the car onto the gravel at the side of the road as the tears begin to cloud my vision. *Fuck Devon.* You were doing so well, you haven't felt this upset in so long, why now? Why was it so difficult to talk about her tonight?

I grit my teeth and punch the steering wheel over and over to let out the pent up emotions inside of me, turning them from hurt to anger as I remember that night.

* * *

The bass floods throughout my entire body, the drinks are flowing, people are dancing and sweating.

I drink the last of my red cup and part through the crowd to get to the kitchen for a refill. People are crowded around a table playing beer pong, some are chatting away, some are tongue-deep into each other. Either way, everyone is busy meaning I have free reign of the selection.

Whiskey? Nah.

Vodka? Nah.

Absinthe? Bingo.

Anything to drown out the misery of my life, the memories, the warfare and death. I fill the cup halfway and top the rest of it up with lemonade, but turn my nose up at the unbranded version.

"Devon! Are you on drinks duty?" Kai raises his cup at me, shouting to be heard over the thumping of the music.

"Like hell I am." I raise my cup back at him and take a drink, walking off with satisfaction. I've came to this deadbeat party to enjoy myself, not to work a shift in the kitchen. If I'm honest, no idea whose birthday it is. All I heard was it was free alcohol and some big-name DJ was playing, so I came straight here after landing from New York.

I rejoin the crowd, taking another sip and wincing at the disgusting taste of it, but I can't tell if it's the absinthe or the lemonade. Probably the lemonade.

Chapter 2

The crowd in the huge living room bounces along to the beat and my head buzzes with delight, the music filling all of the empty holes inside of me, eradicating the missing pieces. I bob to the beat, drinking the last of the cup. Whoa. I'm pretty drunk now.

Downside of drinking a lot? It takes you a lot more alcohol to get drunk, maybe from now on I just have to drink this stuff, it seems to be the only thing that works. I feel a light hand brush mine and I turn, my eyes taking a few seconds to focus on the short blonde in front of me.

"Hey baby," she purrs. I smile down at her, not sure if I'm even making eye contact to be honest.

"Have we met before?" she asks in her high pitch whiny voice.

"Nah, I think I'd remember that pretty face anywhere," I slur, internally rolling my eyes. It works every time.

"Oh stop." She bats my chest and giggles. Bore.

"You are like, drop dead gorgeous baby." She rubs her hand up and down my arm. If that's her way of trying to impress me, I am not impressed. I say better things to myself staring in the mirror.

"Thank you sweet." I lean down and peck her cheek, but she grips my face and pulls me onto her lips. Eager.

I kiss her for a while as she fists my shirt, moaning into my mouth. I pull away, the alcohol causing my head to spin a little.

"Let's take this upstairs." She grabs my hand and I find myself following after her, her heels strutting in front. It's only now that I even notice she's wearing barely anything, a tiny mini skirt and something that resembles a bra.

She pulls me up the stairs and pushes open a door, leading us inside. She closes the door and the room is virtually black, the sound from downstairs sucked away and the only evidence of it is the bass beneath our feet.

I stumble back as she practically jumps me, my head hits off what I assume to be the wall, as she tries to part my lips with her tongue. I haven't even had chance to catch my breath and she's pulling at the belt on my jeans.

"Oh baby, you feel so big, you're so hard for me," she moans. I'm pretty sure I'm flaccid. The only thing I feel right now is absolutely mortal. If I could see, the room would be spinning.

The room lights up and I realize my phone has fallen out of my pocket from the actions of this horny bitch that's currently on her knees in front of me.

I squint my eyes and can make out what I think, is Bella's name. I sigh, not tonight Bells, I'm trying to enjoy myself. I don't know how much longer I can deal with her antics if I'm honest.

I'm sucked away from my thoughts by the wet, warmth of her mouth.

"Ohh." I breathe. Do I even know what's going on? Whatever she's doing, feels okay. I think I'm slightly paralyzed from the waist down, this poor girl is giving it all she's got and the least I could do is get hard for her.

The phone lights up again, igniting the room. Bella, kindly fuck off. I shut my eyes and concentrate on some kind of porn I'd watched recently. I think as hard as I can, come on Devon. Let yourself feel something. For fucks sake, why is it not working?

I let out a breath and grab onto her hair, forcing myself deeper into her mouth. The hair in my hands makes me think of her, of Bella. I visualize Bella on her knees in front of me, her pretty blue eyes looking up at me, filled with tears as she takes me further than she thought possible.

There he is.

I thrust in and out of her mouth, the lack of female touch I've had begins to explode around my body, lifting me to the clouds above as I keep picturing her sweet face in front of me. My balls tighten and I pick up my pace, chasing the release.

"Fuck, Bella," I moan as I spurt into her mouth, and she quickly pulls away.

"Bella? Who the fuck is Bella? My name is Chloe." She spits, rising up onto her feet.

Chapter 2

I'm still dazed from my orgasm as she throws something at me and I think she says something along the lines of 'you're an asshole' and she disappears. Where did she go?

I tuck myself back into my boxers and feel my head swim, overwhelming me. Fuck, I need to sleep or I'm going to throw up.

I shakily walk over to the bed on the other side of the room and dive into it, not caring where I am or whose bed this is. I tuck the pillow underneath me and fall asleep, her face still plaguing my mind. Fucking Bella.

The sun beams onto my face and I try to cover it up with my hand, but it doesn't work. The sound of my phone vibrating in the distance draws me back to reality, too much alcohol, some random chick and passing out. An event I'm all too familiar with.

I peel myself out of the bed and sway slightly, the after-effects of absinthe still very much with me. I spot my phone near to the closed door and pick it up. The phone stops vibrating the second I pick it up, typical. I swipe down the notifications and see that I have numerous missed calls from Bella and a voicemail, then multiple calls from Tommy and my mom.

I dial my mom back.

"Hey mom, sorry I had a bit of a wild–"

"Devon," *she sniffles.*

"Mom? What's wrong?" *I begin to panic, my mother never sheds a tear, let alone cries.*

"I'm so sorry, I am so so sorry," *she cries, my heart beginning to clench.*

"Sorry for what, Mom? You're not making any sense." *I grip my phone tighter as my mind begins to race.*

"It's Bella." *My heart sinks.*

"Which hospital is she at mom? I'll be right there." *My mind instantly clears up and I think of the missed calls last night. If I'd have known she was in such a bad place again, of course I would have picked up, I'm such an idiot. Bella has struggled for years now with depression, she's taken numerous overdoses and luckily, each time she's failed because we managed to get her medical attention, fast.*

"Mom?" *I ask again, her silence beginning to grate me.*

"She hung herself Devon."

Her screams drown out as I drop the phone to my feet and sink to my knees as my heart completely breaks, shatters and explodes into thousands of pieces.

Chapter 3

Rhea

I took extra time this morning to make myself look presentable. I ironed my uniform – again.

I wear my 'Co-Pilot' badge with pride, as a reminder of the hard work it's taken for me to get to this point, to have the privilege to work for a company as prestigious as *Titan*. My hair is pulled back into a low, tight bun and I readjust my aviation cap, the embroidery of the gold *Titan* logo contrasts with the navy blue of the rest of the uniform. I sport a white shirt, navy blue tie and my two-stripe epaulets.

My thirteen-hundred hours of flying means I'm only two hundred hours away from obtaining my third stripe, which I'm sure is what won my position. Being only twenty-five, it's rare to obtain so many hours flying, but I made sure to opt for any overtime and long-haul flights during my initial training.

I pull along my small carry-on and wait at the gate for the captain.

I'm bursting full of nerves, excitement and anticipation. It feels completely surreal that I'm about to begin my journey with *Titan* and obtain my official 'First Officer' title with them. It is as if all of my dreams have come true.

A packet of orchid seeds sits comfortably within my pocket, a reminder of all things good in life, a good luck charm as some may say.

Checking my watch again, I glance around at the bustling airport. We were supposed to be on the flight six minutes ago to begin our checks, and of course, have our formal introduction.

That's when I see him, the Captain. He strides towards me, his cap held under his left arm and his double-breasted blazer pristine, the gold buttons glowing under the lighting. My body begins to shake.

As he nears, I stand up my carry-on independently and offer out my hand.

"Morning Captain, I'm Rhea, your new–"

The breeze that swamps me nearly knocks me off my feet as he surpasses me.

Did he just? *Yup*.

Pulling my hand back, I rub it on my trousers, looking around to see if anyone else witnessed my embarrassment. Great, so my first day is already off to a bad start. The Captain clearly has a rocket stuck up his ass, but nothing is going to deter me from claiming what is rightfully mine. I deserve to be here just as much as him, just because he has more flying hours does not make him too high of a rank to shake his co-pilots hand. Whatever.

Gripping my carry-on, I begin to walk down the tunnel towards the plane.

"Good Morning Ma'am," the male flight attendant nods to me and reaches out to take my bag.

"Good Morning James, a lovely morning it is." I chirp, earning a large smile from him, taking pride in the fact I don't treat anyone as if they are lesser than, unlike some (grumpy Captain). It doesn't cost anything to be polite, nice even. Clearly, some people need to take a lesson in the 'common manners' department.

Entering the cockpit, he sits with his head down, one of the pre-flight notebooks claiming his interest.

"You're late," he grits.

Is he serious right now? I was waiting for *him*. I got here before he did, wanting to make our introductions before flying. In fact, he was the one that was late. I don't want to get off on the wrong footing, so I let it slide.

"Apologies, Captain." I take a seat in the co-pilot seat and pick up my own checklist.

"I'm Rhea by the way, Rhea Jensen," I try again, offering out my hand towards him.

"Captain Stark." He says firmly, not looking up from his checklist.

Great, so we can't even be on first name basis, well these next few weeks of flights are going to be… interesting.

"The weather?" He grunts.

"Oh, sorry yes. It's a clear run, no forecast for any rain or storms. Were not expected to run into anything out of the ordinary."

"Passengers?"

"Two-four-eight, Sir."

"Crew?"

"We have six crew on board with us today, Sir."

He continues jotting down the information. In some way, I feel as if this is some sort of test, to see if I actually studied our pre-flight information. To my satisfaction, the lack of comments from him feels like a win.

We proceed to complete the rest of the checks in silence, the only sounds are the bustle of the passengers beginning to board the flight and the crew members escorting people to their correct seats.

Stark puts on his headset, I take it as my cue to do the same.

"Hey, Tom. Yeah, this is Stark, flight A4820, how is the traffic looking?" I hear his voice through the headset, his voice deep and serious.

"We have you aligned for take off in forty minutes, you can taxi in around twenty to runway three."

"That's perfect, thank you, Tom." I respond.

His head shift beside me, turning to face me. I keep my head down, into my notebook. Don't tell me he's one of those captains that demands he be the only one to speak with air traffic control, I am just as vital a component in this equation as he is. I won't allow his ego to get in the way of my usual role, I will carry out my duty as I normally would, even if it means earning a few dirty looks from the guy with his head in the clouds.

"Tom, can we not squeeze in the gap between flight R349 and D624? Runway two?" he asks.

"Well yeah you could, but you'd have to taxi within the next four minutes." Tom replies.

He shifts beside me.

"Call the flight crew, see if we can begin to taxi." He's really beginning to grate on me, he is the one sat closest to the phone line. But, kill them with kindness.

"Of course Captain." I take my headset off and get up to the phone. I press the call button and place it to my ear.

"Hi Captain, Hannah speaking." Her high-pitch voice speaks through the phone.

"Oh sorry it's Rhea, co-pilot. Captain wants to know if we are ready to taxi?" I ask.

"Well, we still have two passengers who are to come to the gate, we've made our final call for boarding but we wanted to give them an extra five minutes." I then relay the information to Captain Stark.

"They had their chance, tell them to lock up the door so we can do our pressure checks and then taxi to runway two." He says firmly.

"But were not actually scheduled to leave yet, could we not just hang on until our original slot?" I question.

"No." His voice clips.

I roll my eyes. "The Captain has ordered for the cabin to be closed off, commencing all cabin pressure checks." I reiterate to Hannah and she chuckles, I'm sure she must be aware of Captain Stark's impatience.

"No problem Rhea, sealing all cabin doors immediately."

"Thank you, Hannah." I put the phone back on the wall and take my seat.

"Preparing to taxi in the next two minutes Tom," he says, beginning to flick all of the switches as the engine roars louder.

"We could have just waited a little longer." I state, unsure why he is in such a rush.

"The world waits for no one, Reign." he doesn't even look at me.

"It's Rhea." I respond, annoyed he hasn't even bothered to remember my name.

"Yeah," he responds, as if he didn't say my name wrong in the first place.

I proceed to double check all of the stats of the flight, fuel level and pressure.

"Preparing to taxi now." he says through the mic.

"All pre-flight checks completed and sufficient." I say and I swear he looks up at me again, I am not going to be hushed unfortunately, Captain Stark.

I lock my seat belts in place and watch as the plane begins to move backwards, away from the terminal. The ground crew scurry around, directing the plane towards the correct runway.

Captain Stark stares straight ahead and takes control of the plane, the engine volume increasing. I assumed he would take control of the take-off, but I'm going to insist on him letting me land, it's only fair.

We remain in silence as we wait for flight R349 to take off, their plane already aligned and waiting to go.

"Stark here, waiting in queue of R349."

"Nice work Stark, you have been given the approval for take off subsequent of R349's departure." Tom confirms.

I watch as flight R349 begins to race down the runway, vibrations of the jet can be felt through our own plane.

I do another check over the controls, checking the pressure again, temperature of engines, now optimal, and the flaps of the plane are the correct position.

We align up on the run way, the nose the plane perfect with the central line.

"Flight A4820 preparing for take-off." Stark says.

"Cleared for take-off flight A4820." Tom responds.

Stark proceeds to initiate the jet engines and pushes the lever forward, the sound intensifying immediately. During this time, it's quite hard to hear anything but the engines.

He releases the parking brake and we begin to charge forward at speed, the sounds of the wheels rushing down the runway as we gain momentum.

"Speed at one-eighty km/hr, Captain." I watch the speed gauge rise quickly.

"Speed at two-hundred km/hr, Captain."

"Speed at two-twenty km/hr, Captain."

"Speed at two-sixty km/hr, Captain."

"Speed at two-eighty km/hr Captain." He begins to pull up, the thundering noise of the wheels on the tarmac suddenly ceases as the aircraft begins to power through the air. I keep my eyes fixated on the panels in front of me, ensuring everything is as it should be.

"Climbing altitude of one-thousand feet." He says to air traffic control.

We continue like this until we reach thirty-five thousand feet.

"Initiating cruise control." He confirms, placing cruise control on, the flight pathway flashes up on the screen showing us our intended route to Washington.

He remains sat there, staring straight ahead and I don't know whether or not to try and break the ice again. I take the moment to take in his appearance, his mysterious and dark features, his sharp jaw, his virtually black stubble that is trimmed to perfection. His hair is slightly wispy under his cap, it looks like the kind of hair that once it's wet, it pulls up into little curls.

"Can I help you?" He says to me, his gaze still fixated straight ahead.

I clear my throat. "Sorry, I'm afraid we've got off on the wrong foot, now that we're going to be working together for the foreseeable I thought–"

"Working together?" he turns to me, his eyes squinted.

"Yeah…" I shift in my seat, his gaze burning into me and turning the cockpit into a pit of flames.

"You're the fill in for Locke, I don't need to waste my time with getting to know temporary staff." His voice is completely uninterested in this conversation.

"I'm afraid not, Captain. I'm here on something slightly more permanent, a full-time job." I smile at him sheepishly, not trying to come across as obnoxious but more that I'm trying to explain it to him.

He unbuckles his seat belt harness and stands up.

"I'm afraid you're mistaken, Riley. Your business with me is temporary. If you'll excuse me I need to use the bathroom." He buttons up his blazer and leaves me in my own head.

Well he's persistent, I'll give him that. He knows my name by now, I mean it even says it on my badge, he is purposely trying not to acknowledge me for whatever reason. Unfortunately for him, and probably me, I've been assigned to be his co-pilot for the first six months of my training, until I get my official fifteen-hundred hours of flying under my belt. Titan praised him as if he spewed gold from his mouth, but instead it turns out to be abuse. Apparently, he is one of the best pilots they've got so they thought I could be their prodigy, learn from the best and hopefully become the best alongside him. How this is going to work? *That*, I'm not sure of.

I'm trying hard not to take any of this personally, I know some people can just be grumpier than others. Maybe he had a bad night sleep, or a bad day, some bad news or something? Either way, I'm here to stay, to learn and thrive. I won't let a little bit of sour attitude deter me, if anyone can do this, it's me.

He returns from the bathroom with a coffee in his hand, his other hand empty. Ah.

I offer him a slight smile and he looks straight through me, taking his seat again.

"I'll just be off to the bathroom too, try not to crash without me." I joke, giggling slightly. He takes a sip of his coffee, his face stone cold. Okay, can't take jokes, noted.

I unbuckle myself and exit the cockpit, Hannah is currently in the bay where the trolleys are stored.

"Hey Rhea, how's your first day going?" she grins at me.

"Really well actually, a really good start" I grin back, enthusiasm in my voice.

"Are you sure? With Mr. Grumps in there?" she pops her hand on her hip and tilts her head towards the cockpit. I laugh a little and take in a hasty breath.

Chapter 3

"He's fine, nothing I can't handle. Would you mind making me a green tea whilst I pop to the bathroom, I'm seriously about to burst." I jig a little, the need becoming unbearable.

"Oh, absolutely, you got it!" She winks and turns away whilst I slip off into the bathroom. I relieve myself and flush, washing my hands after. I grip the edges of the sink and lean over to look at myself in the mirror.

"You've got this, Rhea." I chant to myself, giving myself a little motivation.

"Nothing you can't handle, you said." I pull my lips into a tight line, then grin at myself, adjusting my face till it looks completely natural. *There you go.*

I straighten out my blazer and hear a crumple. What is – Oh. I reach my hand into my blazer pocket and pull out the packet of orchid seeds. *Perfect.*

I slide them back into my pocket and exit the bathroom, grabbing my green tea from Hannah with a 'thank you', and slip back inside of the cockpit.

"Hey, I got you something," I begin, slightly nervous how he's going to take it.

I sit down in my seat and pop my green tea into the cup holder, pulling out the packet of seeds.

He still doesn't look at me. "I'm not hungry." He states firmly.

"No silly, I got you a gift, as like… I don't know, a good luck for the flight?" I chirp. He turns to me now, his eyebrows furrowed and his already dark brown eyes, somehow darker.

"A gift?"

"Yeah, it's nothing expensive or fancy, it's not like I put much thought into it or anything, I just had them with me and thought that you could use a little pick-me-up, you know? I totally get it if you don't want to acc–"

"Just give me the damn gift, Rhea." He holds out his hand and rolls his eyes. *Rhea*. He said my name, finally.

"So, you do know my name?" I smirk, to which he rolls his eyes once again and flexes his hand.

"Here you go." I beam at him and place the packet of seeds in his hand. Confusion lines his face as he flips it over, then shakes it.

"Seeds?" He sounds disappointed.

"Not just any seeds, silly. They're orchids, dendrobium to be precise. They symbolize strength. I brought them as my good luck charm today, but now you have them. So, it can be your good luck charm for the flight?" The last of what my words grow higher in pitch as my nerves begin to take over. I don't know why I keep rambling so much, it's not like he cares anyway.

"Great…" He drags and then places the seeds at the side of him, next to his coffee.

I pull my lips into a tight line and take a sip of my tea, hoping to curb my increasing anxiety at the moment. Shit, did I take my tablets this morning? Yeah, yeah of course I did. I bounce my left leg up and down, looking at the control panel and trying to fixate on something else.

"Are you normally this chirpy? This… hyper?" He asks, his voice monotone.

Yeah Rhea, he totally thinks your a freak, way to go.

"I'm just happy to be here." I confirm, not really wanting to have to explain my personality to him.

I almost want to counteract with, "*are you normally such a dick?*", but, I decide against it. I need to make this work for both of our sake, even if he won't admit it to himself.

For the rest of the flight, we mostly sit in silence. The flight is only fairly short as it's my first in a while. Titan also thought it would be better to put me on a few shorter journeys to get to know the protocols, the crew and *him*.

"Can I take the landing?" I ask, as we are at the point we need to begin our descent.

He throws his coffee in the trash and glances up at me, the sunlight behind me beams down on his face, igniting his eyes. Under the rays of the sun, his eyes have turned from a deep brown to a light hazel, highlighting the slight green flecks that can't normally be seen. His eyes are framed with thick long lashes, his face slightly rough and crows feet around his eyes. He looks around thirty, maybe thirty-one but I can't be sure.

"Have you ever landed an A330-200 before?" he says, condescendingly.

The *audacity*.

"Of course I have, what kind of question is that?" I bite then instantly regretting it.

Don't allow yourself to be triggered Rhea, he isn't *him*. You're better than that, remember.

He smirks at me. "Then, go ahead."

He offers his hand to the steering controls. I nod my head and place the headset back on my head, connecting to the Dulles air traffic control.

"This is flight A4820 from ATL, we are beginning to descend, preparing for landing. We are forecast for landing at exactly ten-forty-three, can we receive confirmation that the runway will be clear" I speak.

"This is Dulles air traffic control center, flight A4820 is cleared for landing on runway three at ten-forty-three." The male voice responds.

I press the button to alert the cabin to put their seat belts on. I adjust the frequency of my headset to in-flight mode and reiterate that we are beginning our preparations for landing and if everyone can be seated.

We decrease altitude gradually, the cruise control doing most of the work for us. We reduce the throttle and fully extend the flaps, releasing the landing gear.

"This is flight A4820, preparing to land on runway three, altitude is seven hundred feet, we are on our final approach, commencing to touch down on the tarmac at ten-forty-three." I take hold of the steering controls as the nose of the plane aligns with the landing strip.

I concentrate fully, doing another check over all of the control systems. Everything is in order.

The plane flies over trees and houses and I prepare to initiate the brakes the second we touch the tarmac. I touch down and pull back on the thrust reversers, the rumble of the plane is deafening as I keep a firm grip of the steering controls. We race down the runway, the speed decreasing rapidly. As we pass the halfway point I nearly have the plane down to fifty km/hr, my most perfect landing yet.

I reduce the speed enough so that we can taxi the rest of the way, turning off to the correct terminal. I turn to my left to see Stark with a glum look on his face.

"What'd ya think?" I ask him, trying to hide my smugness from one of the best landings I've completed.

"It was fine." He deadpans.

That's probably the most I'll ever get from him, but I'll take it.

Chapter 4

Devon

"Hey mom, yes I'm home. No mom, I'm sorry for worrying you. I've had back to back flights all day but yes, I'm safe." I speak down the phone, her texts have blown up my phone since I got back from New York.

It's been a long day, Atlanta to Washington to New York, and then back to Atlanta. All accompanied by some golden retriever dressed in a co-pilot outfit.

My head hurts.

"I've had the news on all day! I was waiting to receive the worst phone call of my life, Devon, you normally keep me updated." Her voice is filled with worry and concern.

"Mom, I'm truly sorry. I'll do better." I reassure her.

Ever since we lost Bella, she's been terrified of the thought of losing me, so much so she insists I call her every time I land safely, no matter what time it is or time-zone differences. She means well, but it can be a pain in the ass when I have a day like I've had today.

"Okay love, now you get some well deserved rest. Are you still coming for lunch tomorrow with Tommy?" she asks, knowing that I can't say no to her.

"Of course, Mom." I grit through my teeth, though she can't tell.

"Perfect, it'll be nice to see you both together for once!" She chirps. I roll my eyes.

"Night Mom, I love you."

"I love you too darling." I disconnect the phone call and push open the entrance to my house.

I flick on the lights and the hallway comes to life, the pristine glossy floors reflect the chandelier above. I lock the door behind me and throw the keys into the bowl on the side table.

Dropping my bag, I stroll into the darkness of the kitchen, opening the refrigerator to grab a bottled water. I pop it open and gulp it until it's empty, throwing it in the trash. Aside from sodas and bottles of water, the refrigerator is empty. With it only being me here, and I'm never here, I don't have time to do any kind of grocery shopping. Besides, it would just end up being expired by the time I got back. I tend to be away for days, sometimes weeks.

I suppose this is the lonely aspect of being a single guy, not having your partner being the one to keep your house, a home. Instead, it's my shell, my shelter, without the meaning. I enter this house, sleep in this house, but nothing about it is a home.

I mean, Christ, the pictures on the wall are still the stock pictures of families I don't know. But, it offers some sort of familiarity, despite the fact they're strangers. I come home and see the same faces on the wall each time, offering me their hand to guide me and invite me inside of these walls. All I want is regularity, if this is my normal, I'm happy.

The fact I have no groceries, my bed is still made, the trash is empty and it's all symbolism of the fact I've come this far, on my own.

My mom is a beautiful human being, she is considerate, kind and wears her heart on her sleeve. It's everything I aspire to be, but circumstances changed that. Bella, changed that.

I thought I could help. I thought I was her savior. I thought I was everything she needed… until I wasn't.

She needed me in a moment that was so crucial, so tender and weak that I disregarded her. I let her down, in so many ways. Ways that I will never forgive myself for. She needed me in her most vulnerable moment, I shunned her away. She needed help, all I offered her was my silence in excuse of my own selfishness.

Oh, Bella. My sweet, sweet Isabelle. The things I would trade to take back that night, to take back your suffering, to take back my actions. *Fuck*.

To be there for you.

I find myself heaving over the kitchen sink, her face swallows me, brings me down with her beneath the water, unable to breath.

My magnificent Isabelle, my love, my reason for my existence, is no longer here. She's six-feet under and no longer shares the same breath with me. The oxygen does not keep her body alive, she is *gone*.

Nothing I can do now changes that, no matter how hard I try. I want to be everything for her that I wasn't. I want to be the compassionate, loving and sweet, the man she always saw in me. The man I can't seem to find.

I love you Isabelle, I've loved you since we first played together on our front lawns and I stole your Frisbee, claiming it as my own. And our mothers, they were inseparable. Until, your mom faced the most difficult encounter of her life, her breast cancer. It truly, truly broke you. You were never the same, you tried so hard to carry on without her, you wanted to prove to her you had more to give.

Oh my sweet Isabelle, I am so sorry. I focused on myself, I focused on my career, I was so incredibly selfish. Isabelle, my love. Come back to me, I beg you.

"Come back to me." I pour out, my chest clenching as I grip onto the kitchen counter.

"Isabelle, come back to me." I cry out, my heart aches and my voice is strained as I try to hold back my tears. Please.

I bow my head and fist my hands, furious and upset all at the same time.

I need her. She needed me. I failed her just as she showed me, how much she needed me.

My sweet, sweet Isabelle.

The visual of her five-year-old self fills my mind, her innocence, her sweetness, her candor. Until it evaporated before me.

She became sour, insufferable, indescribable.

"Isabelle." I whisper, the tears beginning to pour.

It's moments like this, I need my pathetic addiction. My only escape from reality, but then all I need to do is think of her, think of how I put her second for that one time only. And it cost me her.

Never, never again.

"Please Bella, Bella I need you. I can't do this without you." My legs grow weak as my voice comes out as barely a whisper.

It hurts, it fucking hurts. *So much.*

Nothing about this is okay.

Nothing about this is normal.

Nothing about this is right.

I try to breathe, I try to take in the only thing that had kept her alive, until my chest refuses. Just like she was restricted.

What if she regretted it?

What if the second she stepped away from the chair, she wanted her second chance?

What if I was the only way she could have had that, and I ignored her?

I should have been there.

I should have answered her phone call.

I should have realized her persistence. But, I only realized once it was too late.

I stand back up to my full height and grip the glass with a shaky hand, trying to fill it with water but, I can't grasp it. It drops to the sink with a clatter and I see the million different shrapnel of glass, representative of my soul this past year.

"Come back to me." I cry, my chest heaves and aches all at the same time.

I can't let her go. I will never let her go. She is the missing piece of my puzzle, the only reason I needed, the epitome of my existence.

And she's *gone*.

"Argh!" I cry out as I sweep the draining board full of clean crockery, I can't hold it in, it needs to come out.

I sink to the floor, my head in my hands as I curl up into a tight ball. The crinkle of something in my pocket jolts me away from this pit, from the self-destructive tendencies. I reach into my pocket and pull out the packet of orchids.

"Strength, you say?" I hiss, tossing the seeds to the floor. I shake my head and cup my arms around my legs as I allow the pity tears to fall.

"Where were the orchids when you needed them Bella?" I shout into the abyss, the silence giving me nothing in return.

"Fuck!" I scream, gripping onto my hair as if it's her. Her hair, her scent and her fucking body. FUCK.

The fucking body I will never touch again, FUCK!

BELLA.

Silence.

Unanswered.

Another lonely night. Without her warmth.

My hunger is gone, my inner self is gone, she is gone.

I shake my head as I wrap my arms around myself, trying to substitute for the missing piece in my life, the one person who made me whole and the one fucking person I took for fucking granted!

I can't fucking fathom the fact anything came before her, and now *after* her.

"SHE FUCKING NEEDED ME!" I cry out in pain, as I lay on the floor and tears stream down my face. I will forever, and ever and ever, blame myself. I'd saved her before, why couldn't I save her this time, the time that mattered.

The marks on her neck cause me to heave and throw up, my nonexistent presence plays the scene over and over.

I'm stood in the corner of the room, seeing her distraught and crying. The tear-stained cheeks that are red just as her nose, that will soon turn to gray, surrenders to her darkest thoughts. Her chest thumping, her body heaving and her heart hurting. The heart that will soon stop beating.

But I'm here, emotionless, helpless and frozen in time. Isabelle my love, listen. Save yourself, save your future, fuck.

SAVE ME TOO.

I don't even know how long I've laid here on this cold tile. The pain in my chest, my veins and my brain, seem to subsidize any other kind of unpleasantry. My brain is the only thing that keeps her alive, everyone else has moved on, forgotten perhaps. But I haven't, and I never will.

"ISABELLE!" I shout, my voice now practically inaudible.

"Bella," I whisper, clutching onto my shirt around my heart as I curl up tighter, the images of her divine smile invade my thoughts, lulling me to sleep.

I dream and I dream, of the life we could have had, the life we were never offered, the life that we had stolen.

Chapter 4

* * *

I knock twice, a bottle of Merlot in my hands and a bouquet of lilies, my moms favorite. I hear her dainty footsteps nearing the door and she pulls it open with the biggest smile on her face.

"Devon, my darling boy." She reaches forward and takes my face in her hands, her thumb sweeping across my cheekbones.

"Mom." I smile, leaning into her hand.

"These are for you." I push forward the gifts.

"Oh darling, you didn't have to." But she takes them anyway, her coyness is pleasant despite the fact I bring her something every time I come here for lunch.

I follow her inside, into the home that holds so many memories, the evidence littering the hallway. There is probably a hundred pictures in this corridor alone, all different shapes and sizes, some singular and some collages. I avoid looking at one part of the wall, knowing the pictures it holds. It's of me and Bella.

We were neighbors growing up, our mom's were best friends and eventually, we fell into the same. We were inseparable, everything we did had to be together, we had each other's backs completely. Bella is – *was* only two weeks younger than me. We celebrated every birthday in the week after my birthday and the week before hers, we had joint parties, matching presents and God, even matching clothes at one point. The memory almost makes me smile, until I remember when everything changed.

Their family was similar to ours, no father involved and a doting mother that wanted the best lives for their children. But I have a younger brother, Tommy whereas she was an only child. I entered the military and gained most of my flying experience through them, I became an Officer. That was until I got medically discharged after

I had been shot down whilst I was in Afghanistan, it seemed I was suffering with tell-tale signs of PTSD. I felt like a failure, felt like I'd given up and wanted to carry on. It was only when I returned to normal life, I realized how warped my sense of reality was. How I was crippled with anxiety and completely distraught over the fact people walked around defenseless. When you've seen the things I had, it made me realize just how bitter and evil the world can be, the hidden poison among us.

Around seven years ago, Sarah, Bella's mom, was diagnosed with breast cancer. My mom and Sarah kept it hidden from us for months, until it became too noticeable and we started asking questions. Sarah became frail, her skin was mottled, she was always wearing thick jumpers in the middle of summer and when her hair began to thin, we took it upon ourselves to find out. We searched through the entire house for any letters, medical notes or tell-tale signs that something was going on. We couldn't find anything at all and on our way out of the house, the phone rang. We didn't answer but the voicemail played aloud, it was a nurse from the local hospice and were asking for a call back. It was then we decided to confront them and everything fell apart, we fell apart and Bella was completely ruined.

Not even three weeks later, Sarah had passed away. In some ways, we lost Bella that day too. She was never the same, she withdrew herself from our family, she lost any sense of her true self and she was completely closed off. We all tried to help her, she struggled with addiction to cocaine and alcohol, mixing the two and having toxic dosages. We got her clean, I paid for her rehab stays (multiple of) and she began therapy sessions to deal with her grief, to learn how to live again without her crutch on substances.

She was doing well, we had hope again. She wanted to be in a relationship with me, to which I told her I wasn't good enough for her, I couldn't give her what she needed. I was freshly employed with

Chapter 4

Titan and had just earned my four stripes, I just simply didn't have the time to thrust myself into a fully-fledged relationship with her when I knew she was already a fragile girl.

One night, we had one of our usual movie nights at my place, but something about her was different. I couldn't put a finger on it until she snuggled into me, and then I could smell it. She'd been drinking again.

We got into a huge fight, she was throwing things at me and I couldn't understand why she was self-sabotaging again. I begged and begged her to not give in, to not give up, she'd come so far I didn't want her to fall back into her deep depression. I told her how much she meant to me, how much it hurt me to see her struggling and I wanted to be there for her.

Then she kissed me.

And I kissed her back.

It was a strange feeling, a confusing feeling, it felt like I was encapsulated in a swirl of different emotions, none of them making sense anymore.

"Are you coming through Devon?" My mom calls from the kitchen.

"Coming!" I shout in response, pulling my mind away from the universe of the past.

I enter the kitchen and mom is serving up a hearty casserole with green beans and mashed potato.

"Smells amazing, as always mom." I smile at her as she rushes around in her red plaid apron, her hair tucked up into loose bun. Her hair is almost fully white now, her skin is leathery and her own body is frail.

She had me and my brother when she was in her thirties, with a man she presumed was the love of her life. She'd waited all that time thinking that she was doing the smart thing, she didn't get knocked up as a teenager. She studied hard at school, graduated and became a journalist, she traveled and had the best memories, until she met my father.

William Reynolds.

He was a sorry excuse for a man, despite him being successful in some sort of business trade, I don't really care to remember. He left when I was three and Tommy was a newborn.

"Are you not going to go and say hello?" My mom stops shoveling the green beans and looks at me through her aging eyes. Inside, I want to scream that I want nothing to do with him, but on the outside I'm nodding.

I take in a deep breath and leave the kitchen, towards the living area. I can see the back of his dark curls above the sofa edge, he's watching something on TV and hasn't bothered to engage in my presence.

I walk around the sofa and take a seat in the worn armchair, it's too comfy to let go of. Once I'm seated I look over at him and notice he's thinner than the last time I seen him, his attention still focused elsewhere.

The tension between us swarms around the room and the air grows thin, my breath becoming slightly harsher to compensate.

It's been over six months since we last spoke, and it didn't end well. We got into an argument about his finances, he'd been borrowing money from mom, but we both knew he had no intention of paying it back.

So, I called him out on it.

Mom has a sufficient amount of money, we grew up fine and never went without, but now that she's retired and she's slowly been renovating the house, her stack of cash is slowly dwindling away. In the end, I gave him four thousand dollars, to cover whatever it was he needed it for. He of course, hasn't paid me back but I could afford to do it anyway.

"Hey Tommy." I break the silence.

"Devon." he nods his head at me and his gaze gives me a once over before turning back to TV.

"How's work?" I ask, trying to make some sort of 'normal' conversation.

"Fine." he doesn't even bother to look at me now.

I shake my head and stand up, leaving him alone. I'm not going to keep putting my energy into him when all he does is reject it.

"Mom, need any help?" I shout and return to the kitchen, grabbing the cutlery to set the table.

"Thank you sweetie, Tommy! Lunch is ready." She wipes her hands on her apron and looks around the kitchen before making sure we have everything on our plates that she intended.

She carries them through to the dining room, the same large wooden table, with farmhouse style chairs, sits central. I've noticed over the years she only uses these special plates when we all come over as a family, usually she uses the plain, cheap ones for herself.

I love how much my mom appreciates our company, she must get real lonely sometimes. I visit as much as I can, especially now.

I finish setting the cutlery around the allocated spaces, the same ones we've always had. Mom at the top of the table and me and Tommy either side of her. When we were younger, me and Tommy used to kick each other's shins under the table, enough so mom would separate us sometimes.

I take a seat and Tommy comes into the dining room, taking a seat across from me. He's always been a smaller frame than me, but he was taller. I'm a comfortable six-three and he is at least three inches taller than me.

"Shall we say grace?" Mom pats down her clothes and reaches for our hands.

We nod and I take hold of Tommy's hand, cold to the touch. I bow my head and close my eyes.

"Bless us our Lord, we are thankful for the food you have given us and the roof over our head. We thank you for the family between us and all things good. Thank you my Lord, let's eat." She finishes and I give her hand a little squeeze, before releasing it.

I've never been religious myself, but I think in some ways its helped my mom get through her hardest times, and I will always respect that. If she wants to say grace? I say grace.

"Thank you, mom." I nod at her and begin to dig into my plate of goodness.

"So Tommy, are you going to tell Devon the good news?" She prompts him, but his head is down as he eats. I raise an eyebrow.

"What good news?" I slowly chew my food.

"Tommy?" Mom looks at him patiently. Tommy just shrugs and continues to eat.

"I'm going to be a Grandma!" Mom claps her hands. My fork clatters to my plate as my eyes bulge out of my head.

"With who?" I ask, staring intently at him.

"Why does it matter?" he says quietly. I laugh and shake my head.

"Why does it matter?" I repeat, not able to contain my laughs. He looks up at me, his eyes squinted.

"It's with Annie. You know Annie, right, Devon?" He says, a smirk written across his face. My face drains of color.

"Annie." I say, my voice cold and unnerving.

"Yeah, Annie Sweeney" He says, smiling at me as he shovels some mashed potato in his mouth.

Annie fucking Sweeney.

She's the girl that was torturous towards Bella throughout high school, and thereafter. She took every opportunity she had to embarrass Bella, framed her, set her up and filmed her.

The worst one was when she stole her clothes from her locker after she had been in the shower post gym-class. It wasn't what you thought, it's not like anything about Bella's body was embarrassing, her body was fucking incredible and I swear Annie was just jealous.

But, it was the fact that Bella had been self-harming, she had tried to conceal it by going in the shower after everyone else, hoping everyone would have left by the time she had to get changed. Instead, it was the polar opposite. They all filmed her crying, distraught and broken, then sent it to every one in the school. It was the most disgusting act I'd ever seen and the second I found out who planned it all, I wanted to rip her fucking head off myself.

"That's fucking low Tommy, even for you." I spit, the anger beginning to burst it's seems.

"Language!" My mother shouts, looking at me appalled.

"What's that supposed to mean?" Tommy cocks his head at me, scowling.

"We all know your moral judgment isn't your strong point Tom, but you knew exactly what you were doing by sleeping with the enemy."

I crinkle my nose and look back down at my plate, trying to let the anger subside for my mom's sake.

"Look, Devon. Sorry to break it to you but she can't be the enemy if the person you're fighting for is no longer here." My breath hitches, my hand clenches around my knife in my hand.

"Tommy! That's enough" Mom shouts, she knows just how much that sentence will hurt me.

"Watch your fucking mouth." I growl, keeping my eyes on my plate before I do something I'll regret. Or not.

"Devon! I have said that's enough!" My mom shouts, slamming her hands down on the table and rising up.

"You're just jealous, Devon. Just because you can't have kids with your girl doesn't mean I can't have them with mine." He chuckles, leaning back.

RED.

R
E
D

I jump up from the table and reach over, grabbing him by the scuff of his collar and slamming his face down into the middle of the table. Mom screams beside me and shouts at us to stop.

"If you ever think I'd be jealous of you, I suggest you book yourself into a fucking mental facility, you deluded fuck." I spit into his ear and slam his head back down onto the table before releasing him. Mom screams again.

"Mom, I'm sorry, truly. Don't invite me for lunch again if he is going to be here." I grasp her hand and kiss the top of it, sparing one last glance at a smug looking Tommy. He makes me feel physically sick.

I begin to walk down the corridor to the front entrance, past the wall filled with a better time in life.

I look down to see Reed calling me, I exit the house and pick up, the anger still seeping out of me.

Chapter 5

Rhea

"Have you posted the advertisement for the kittens yet?" I shout to Fizzy from my room. I'm in the middle of watering the plants on my terrace, exhausted from a long night of partying. It was our friend Freya's birthday, so we were up till God knows what time, I don't even remember what time I rolled back into our apartment.

"Not yet, but I will. What date will they be eight weeks old?" She shouts back. I roll my eyes.

"Do I look like a calendar to you?" I laugh and wince at the pounding sensation in my head.

I swear I didn't get hangovers like this when I first turned twenty one. I hear Fizzy laughing from the living room and I carry on watering my plants. I have a long haul flight tonight to London and we're staying over and flying back tomorrow afternoon.

I would be lying if I said I was looking forward to sharing eight hours in a cockpit with Mr. Grumps, I could barely manage it for the short time on our last flight.

On the upside, I get a few hours in London tomorrow to do a bit of exploring, but I'll have to work out the time-zone difference.

I have to finish packing my bag and get a shower before I leave for the airport. Fizzy is taking me today so I don't have to pay for extortionate airport parking prices.

My plants are thriving, blossoming in the summer heat, they look beautiful. My favorite at the minute is my peach colored Chrysanthemums. They contrast with most of the bolder colors as they're pastel and lighter in comparison.

Oh shit. That reminds me, I have my therapy session soon. I finish watering the plants and throw on an over-sized jumper and some leggings, not bothering to have a shower for this.

I grab my phone and keys and walk out of my room.

"Almost forgot I've got my meeting with Ezra, I have to rush or I'll be late, don't forget to post the ad, we also need more toilet paper, thanks Fizz, love you" I rush out before slamming the door behind me.

I pull up in front of the huge office building, dashing out of the car and through the wide double doors. I press the elevator button and tap my foot impatiently, gripping my keys.

The doors open and I almost fly straight into someone's chest as my eager self rushes inside.

"Sorry." I cringe, his large expanse covering my pathway.

"Rhea?" he says.

I look up and meet his eyes.

"Oh, hi, um... Captain Stark." I don't actually know his first name so this sounds way more professional than it probably needs to be.

"Are you always late to things?" he asks, peering down at me with a slight glimmer in his eyes.

There are red rings around them and they stand out against his darkness.

"No, I'm not late, well kind of, but I wasn't late, the other day I mean." I ramble.

He lets out a dry laugh and the depth of it sends vibrations down my spine.

"Sure." he says and steps out of the elevator, offering a two-finger salute to me.

I stand there watching as he walks away, his attire completely different from his usual work uniform. The tight, white t-shirt grips to his biceps and as he walks I can see the muscles in his back pull and flex. Jeez, Rhea you need to get laid if your drooling over some guys back muscles.

I shake my head and step face first into the closed elevator doors. My eyes sting from the connection of the metal with my nose, I grip onto it and squeeze my eyes tight.

"You've got to be kidding me." I wince and sigh, pressing the button for the elevator again and pressing my nose in different places to make sure I haven't just broken it.

Seems fine to me.

I run into the receptionist area on the fourteenth level, barely acknowledging the receptionist and storming through his door.

"Ezra, I'm so sorry I'm late, I know your a busy man and I almost forgot entirely but I tried to get here as fast as I could." I speak breathlessly.

"Rhea, it's fine. Relax." He chuckles at me as he sits in his usual leather chair with one hand on his ankle that's sat in his lap.

I sit on the couch across from him and lean my head back over the back of it, so I'm looking up at the ceiling. My chest rises and falls as I try to catch my breath again before I begin speaking.

"Tough day?" Ezra asks, picking up his notebook.

"It's been okay, not great but okay." I confess.

"How are things looking? Have you grown any new plants?"

"Well no, but I've been looking after the ones I've got well. Oh! Gemini had her babies! Seven of them, can you believe it?" I lift my head up with a big smile.

"Seven wow, I bet they're a handful."

"Just a little." I smile fondly.

"How is the new job? I know you can sometimes struggle with the big changes." He questions, writing in his book.

I think about his question for a moment before answering.

"It's good, like you know, good for my mind. I like keeping busy." I tighten my lips.

"Just… good?" he asks.

I nod slightly, rolling my bottom lip between my teeth.

"How are your colleagues? Have you met them yet?"

"Yeah, well he's a tough nut to crack. Quite distant, not really in touch with his emotions. I've tried my usual methods but he doesn't seem to be taking to them, I've tried to stay positive." I clasp my hands together in my lap and twiddle with my thumb nails.

"How does that make you feel?" he pries.

I swallow.

I'm unsure.

How *does* it make me feel?

I suppose the biggest thing is that I want to be the one to break through his barriers, I want him to see me. He treats me like I'm nothing, like I have no importance, that I'm lesser than him.

"Weak." I say, my voice clipped.

"Can you explain that a little?" he continues.

"I feel powerless when I'm around him, like I'm invisible. It's like I'm an empty shell, like I don't matter." I explain, my throat growing tighter the more I think about how it makes me feel.

"Is there anything you could do, to change that?" his pen is scribbling away in his notebook and I find myself glancing around his office.

He displays an array of basketball memorabilia in a cabinet behind his desk, the windows are large giving the office immense amounts of light and the carpet between us is fluffy. Fluffy enough that I want to lay in it, snuggle it and melt away from the world.

"Rhea?" He has stopped writing.

"Oh, um. Well, I'm just going to stay positive, you know? I don't want to change myself to suit someone else. I am confident in myself, I don't need to rely on his opinion of me." I emphasize my words and feel them slowly sinking into me deeper.

"Exactly Rhea, be confident. You know your own capabilities, don't let anybody's energy influence yours. You are strong Rhea. Not weak. Look how far you've come." He offers me a grin and I nod, blushing slightly.

Ezra is only slightly older than me, and he's also easy on the eyes. I'm sure most women would say that their reason for choosing him would be for that reason alone, but I wanted someone younger. Not for those reasons, but for the fact I thought they were more understandable, easier to connect with and aren't oblivious to modern day struggles. So far, I've been proven right. Ezra has been great and he's the only therapist I've stayed with for longer than six months, we're coming up two years soon.

"Have you had many thoughts about the past?" his question is sensitive to avoid any triggers.

"A little." I clench my jaw and place my hands either side of me on the sofa, digging my fingers in slightly to avoid the tension.

"How often?" he returns to his book.

I scrunch my nose up and look out of the window. "Nearly every day." I breathe.

"Okay, and what have you being doing to curb those thoughts Rhea? Have you been using any specific techniques?" he asks.

I blow out a breath and feel uncomfortable to have to talk about it out loud. Despite being in therapy for years now, it still doesn't get any easier.

"Listing a type of flower for each letter of the alphabet, using my stress ball, reading." I say.

"That's amazing Rhea, truly. You've managed to turn it around and deflect, not letting it win. You are winning Rhea, you're flourishing right before my eyes." He smirks knowing he's just described me like a flower, the calmness washing over me.

We continue the rest of the session like this, opening up and talking through it all, figuring out how to balance everything.

"Thank you Ezra, I'll be back next week." I smile at him and exit his office, feeling a lot lighter than when I walked in there.

Life is subjective, each person that exists has their own perception on it, different experiences and opposite lifestyles. The most important thing I've learned is that life *is* subjective, which means I can make it entirely my own, it's in my control and I can direct it exactly where I want it to go.

* * *

"Fizzy! Come on, I need to go, like now!" I shout from the doorway, my travel case beside me and my blazer tucked neatly over it. She rushes through the kitchen, grabbing a slice of toast from the countertop.

"Sorry sorry, I just had to grab this…" She dangles a key chain in

Chapter 5

front of me and I furrow my brows.

"What is that?" I inspect it, the key and a sparkly cherry key ring hangs on it.

"It's a key, to the studio!" she beams at me and I turn my head to the side, not quite understanding he excitement.

"Indie gave me a key to the studio, meaning I get to open and close the studio whilst she's a little busy. That means she trusts me!" She tries to clap her hands together but her slice of toast gets in the way.

"Oh, amazing." I smile at her but beckon my hand for us to leave.

We climb into her car, my case on the backseat. She puts the key in the ignition and the engine makes a strange clicking noise.

"Fizz?" I turn to her to see her face turned up in confusion.

"Just give it a sec, this happens all the time, don't worry your little self." She laughs dryly, twisting the key again and getting the same response.

She chews her lip and slumps in the chair.

"You've got to be kidding me" she sighs and continues to try the engine.

"When was the last time you checked the oil levels in this?" I ask her.

"The tank is half full, it shouldn't be that." She messes around with some buttons on the steering wheel.

"No Fizzy, the oil?" She looks at me like I've grown two heads.

Jesus Christ. How is this girl even still alive, I swear she has a death wish.

"Pop open the bonnet, I'll check it." I unstrap my seat belt and climb out of the car, lifting up the bonnet and propping it onto the catch.

I pull up the oil dipstick and a long, stringy goop of oil falls off the end. I lean forward and try to look inside of the hole, scanning to see if there is any more clumps. The engine splutters again and I wince as it spurts out black oil all over me.

"FELICITY!" I scream in fury.

I hear the slam of a car door as I keep my eyes squeezed tightly shut, the feeling of the slippery substance sliding down my face. All I can hear is her giggling.

"Oh Rhea, Rhea I'm so sorry." She can't stop laughing and honestly if she wasn't who she was, I'd have been cussing at her right now.

"Lead me back upstairs, please," I try to speak with my mouth shut to avoid any oil from entering into my mouth.

I can't believe this, I'm going to be so late.

Once we enter the apartment I throw off my clothes and dive straight into the shower, scrubbing my body vigorously to get rid of the slimy substance that coats me. I even have to wash my hair but I have no time to dry it so I'm going to have to tie it into a tight bun whilst its still wet and then take it out once I'm in the cockpit.

I climb out and throw a fresh change of uniform on, struggling to find my balance as I hop into the skirt that is definitely too small for me now. I much prefer to wear my navy trousers but this tight mini-skirt is going to have to do for today with a pair of nude tights. I slip on a pair of simple black heels and grab my car keys from the counter.

"We can just take my car," I grumble, Fizzy waits outside of the apartment for me.

"Come on, lets go!" I lock the apartment door behind me and we rush down the elevator to the parking lot, *again*.

"I'm so so late." I cringe and Fizzy climbs into the drivers side.

I get into the passenger side and we try to make it to the airport in record time.

I rush through security and it's only then I'm cursing myself yet again, I've left my case on Fizzy's backseat. But I don't have any time to stop. I run as fast as I can to the gate, seeing that the plane is already on final boarding. *Shit, shit, shit.*

The passengers have already boarded the plane and here I am, being tardy. The flight crew let me aboard straight away and my face is dripping with sweat and anxiety.

"I'm so sorry I'm late Mr. Stark, I had a bit of car trouble and -"

"Seems to be a bit of a habit of yours." He states, the pre-flight checklist in his hand and he's leaned over my side, completing my usual tasks.

I cringe and walk slowly over to my seat, embarrassment spread across my face.

"Not great to harness a habit like that in a career where time is of the essence," He says, chewing the top of his pen.

I can't even fight him on this one, this is completely unacceptable.

"It won't happen again." I falter.

It's now that he looks up at me, his eyes trailing from my flushed face, down over my breasts and following downwards along the expanse of my exposed legs.

"Interesting attire," he mocks, before placing his headset on.

I blush once again and quickly climb into my seat. I place my own headset on and buckle myself in, checking over all of the necessary components. Everything is in order

"This is flight T8294, we are ready to begin taxi to runway four" he confirms and I don't even bother to be sarcastic this time as I sit silently.

I keep myself reserved and concentrate on the task at hand. I wanted so badly to do the take off myself, but I feel like my actions have betrayed me, and I don't think my concentration levels are there just yet, so I let him have it.

***

We reach cruising altitude and I slouch a little more in my chair, the tenseness loosening now that we have got the hardest part out of the way.

I pull at the hair tie and let my blonde hair cascade around my shoulders, the dampness still evident. My hair has fallen into loose curls from being twisted into a bun whilst still wet, the coldness of it sending shivers across my skin. I look down and see my nipples poking through my white shirt – *Christ*.

No bra, seriously? Did I even arrive here dressed at all?

I have no overnight case with me, I'm in a skirt that is far too short for me and as far as I'm aware, England is *cold*. I practically shiver from the thought of me having to step off this flight, knowing I have no other means of clothing apart from what I have on right now.

I'm going to have to go straight into London and purchase something more suitable to wear, it's going to look obnoxious to walk around in my uniform in the middle of the day.

"Cold?" Captain Stark asks and I turn my gaze to him, his eyes fixated on my face.

Oh god, he didn't see them, did he? I bite my lip and reach for my blazer to put it on. I swing it over me and pop my arms inside, the crinkle of something draws my attention. Perfect icebreaker.

"I got you a gift." I say and he rolls his eyes at me.

"What is it this time? A newspaper?" his tone is full of sarcasm.

"Very funny Mr. Stark, but no." I pull out the packet of seeds from my inner pocket, still in there from earlier.

"They're white rose seeds." I smile down at them before offering them to him.

"More... seeds?" he questions, retrieving the packet from me.

"Yup, it's great isn't it." I chirp.

"Well, they're seeds." He deadpans.

"They're only seeds until you grow them Mr. Stark, then the real

Chapter 5

beauty begins." I smile fondly.

He only shakes his head and places them to the side. I return my gaze to the window and focus on the infinity of clouds below us, the calming sensation beginning to filter through me.

There's something about being thirty thousand feet in the air, a kind of serenity, to be able to ignore the world beneath the clouds and the only worries you have are with you inside of this tiny room.

* * *

I land perfectly, once again. Stark didn't really acknowledge me for the rest of the flight, his usual from what I'm beginning to learn. He's not one for conversation, but at least that means he can keep his snide remarks to himself.

Now that were back on the ground, all of my anxiety has returned along with gravity.

I need clothes ASAP.

"Welcome to London Luton, the local time here is 5.46a.m." Stark says.

My eyes widen as I turn to him.

"What?" I practically shout at him, he flinches at the sudden volume.

"Is there any stores open around here? Like clothing stores or something?" I try to explain my concerns.

"How should I know?" He shrugs and directs the plane as we become lined up with the jet bridge.

I huff and fold my arms.

I can't believe this. I'm just going to have to go straight to the hotel room and sleep, and hope that when I wake I will have enough time to figure out the clothing situation.

We place the plane into standby mode, the jets shutting down and waiting for the passengers to leave the plane before us.

"Are you always so uptight?"

My jaw drops as I unbuckle my seat belt.

"Are you always such an overcritical cunt?" I bite.

Oh Rhea, *why*?

He lets out a hearty laugh, one that I've not heard in the numerous hours I've spent with him.

After all of my efforts to crack him, *this* is what does it?

"What?" I sigh, rolling my eyes.

"It's just nice to see there is more to you than a bland appearance and garden seeds." He smirks.

Ouch.

Bland.

That's a new one and quite frankly, painful. I've been called a lot of things in my twenty-five years, but bland has never been one of them. Especially coming from someone like him, someone who is meant to be my boss.

"I don't think HR would appreciate said comments." I don't even want to repeat the words he's just said to me, they still sting.

"Ah, you're a tattle-tale too?" He stands up from his chair, grabbing his blazer from his seat.

I can literally feel the steam exploding out of my ears right now; how dare he?

He hasn't taken a single second to get to know me, he could barely even acknowledge my name.

But now, *now* he wants to cast judgment on me?

"See you this afternoon, Rebecca." He salutes me and I literally want to throttle him.

Chapter 5

I grit my teeth and stare at his back as he exits the cockpit, leaving me to drown in my own world of self pity and fury.

Chapter 6

Devon

Ah, the relaxation of fresh and crisp hotel sheets, the smell of room service and the peacefulness of being alone.

These are definitely some of the perks of being a Pilot, the endless days and nights inside of a hotel room, leaving your troubles behind and binge-watching some *Netflix*.

I flick through the options and eat some fries. I've already changed into an over-sized tee and joggers, perfect nap material.

I put on *The Office* and see it's already on season four, but I've already watched it a hundred times so I continue watching from where its at.

I readjust the pillows and lean back with my hands behind my head, stretching out on the full expanse of the bed.

My phone buzzes and I take a quick glance at it to see it's from Reed.

Chapter 6

When you get back tonight, we need to discuss things. Things just got a whole lot more intense.

Honestly, that guy needs to stop worrying so much, everything will be managed and under control, especially if I have something to do with it.

My attention shifts to the quiet knocking on my door.

I thought I hung the 'Do not disturb' sign on the handle.

I roll my eyes and pull myself off of the bed, already annoyed at being interrupted from the minimal amount of sleep I can have.

Pulling the door open, I take a step back.

"What are you doing here?" I ask Rhea, who is stood at my door, still dressed in her uniform.

"Look, I already know you don't like me and like it's not that I don't like you, but I don't like, like you. If you know what I mean?" I cut her off.

"Just answer the question, Rhea." I sigh and lean against the door, folding my arms over my chest and crossing my ankles.

"I'm sorry, what I'm here for is like, um. I kind of don't have a room booked under my name and gosh. This is really embarrassing but I haven't received my paycheck yet and I'm swamped with bills at my place and I kind of don't have any money to book somewhere else." I raise an eyebrow at her.

"And?" I question.

She frowns at me and looks around the corridor before turning back to me again.

"You want to stay with me?" My lips part.

"No, god no." She rushes, becoming flustered.

I shake my head. "Then what? You want some money?" I laugh dryly, but she doesn't.

"I can pay you it straight back I promise, well, not straight away but as soon as I get my first paycheck, I'll pay you it all plus interest." She begs.

I rub my fingers over my jaw and look up at the ceiling as if I'm contemplating it.

"Hm, I'm not too sure, Rhea. I mean, I don't even know you." I just want to see her sweat.

"Please Mr. Stark, I don't have any other options, I've tried to ask my best friend but with the time zo-"

"Jeez, if you stop calling me that, I'll give you the money, you make me sound like I'm an O.A.P," I cringe.

"What else am I supposed to call you?" she questions and it's then I realize she hasn't been calling me that to keep things formal, it's because she genuinely doesn't know my name.

I feel like an idiot now.

That was the reason I kept calling her by the wrong name, because I thought she was doing it to piss me off, so I did the same back.

"It's Devon." I say and disappear from the doorway to grab my wallet from my pilot jacket.

I pull out my credit card and walk back over to the door.

"Take this." I go to close the door after she takes it from me and I'm interrupted by her.

"Thank you, Devon." She offers a slight smile and her cheeks have turned to a rosy pink, her hair is wild and curly around her face, she carries this 'innocent' look.

"Just don't lose it." I say and close the door.

I walk back over to the bed and throw myself face down onto it. My back aches slightly and I grab a pillow, pulling it into me to snuggle.

What? A man can't appreciate a little comfort from an inanimate object?

I close my eyes and listen along to Michael Scott arguing with Dwight until I finally get some rest.

Chapter 6

* * *

"I got you something." She turns to me, she looks a little fresher than she did earlier, I'll admit that.

She holds out my credit card and behind it is another packet. Is she kidding me right now? More seeds.

"Brilliant, thanks. I'm actually running pretty low on seeds at the moment, you're such a lifesaver. What would I do without you?" I shake my head.

"Wow, he can speak more than a few words in a sentence." she snaps back.

I roll my eyes and return my attention to the runway in front of us.

"You sure you can take off in such a big plane like this?" I tease, earning a scowl from her.

"Watch and learn, Mr. Stark" she grins, initiating the jet engines to full throttle.

I grit my teeth and watch as she proves me wrong, again.

* * *

I literally want to bash my head against the panel in front of me as Rhea tries to play some sort of '21 questions' with me. I am not one for small talk, in any circumstances, never mind with some chirpy newbie.

"What made you want to become a pilot?" She asks, chewing on a *Snickers* bar, courtesy of the UK.

"Are girls meant to be eating things like that?" I point at the chocolate bar in her hands and she slowly stops chewing, looking at me through squinted eyes.

As if it was some kind of challenge, she shoves the rest of the chocolate bar into her mouth, it barely being able to fit in.

I watch as she tries to clamp her lips around it and I feel a sudden rush of heat to my groin. Swallowing harshly, I look away, confused and annoyed that her lips had that sort of effect on me.

"Any siblings?" She asks, and for once I'm thankful for the ultimate turn-off.

"Brother."

"Is he named after a place in England too?" She asks, genuine curiosity in her voice and not the mocking I expected.

"Nope." I fiddle around with my tie, adjusting it to perfection.

"What's with the seeds?" I ask her, catching her eyes but she looks away quickly, her eyes flitting around.

"Nothing, I'm just an avid gardener." She says quietly.

"I'm just going to the bathroom." She stands up quickly and pushes open the cockpit door, disappearing.

What did I say?

I only asked her about her weird obsession with seeds, I don't see what was so bad.

Whatever.

Only a few more hours of tolerating this, and I'll have a nice few days off. Well, off the radar I suppose. I've got a favor to do for Reed, a special request that needs to remain off the books, my specialty.

Rhea comes back into the cockpit and instead of plaguing me with her questions, she stays silent.

Now I really know something is up, from the few journeys I've shared with her she's barely ever managed to keep her mouth shut. I swear I go home and my ears ring from how much she's spoken to me, it's more than I've had in the last year.

"Did I say something wrong?" I try to offer an olive branch.

Chapter 6

"No, no it's fine." She sniffles.

Way to go Devon, you've made the poor girl cry.

"Hey, I'm sorry, I didn't mean to hurt your feelings." I soften my voice.

Yes I'm a dick most of the time, but the last thing I want is to genuinely upset someone.

"It's fine, Devon. Don't worry about it," She says and rubs her nose, her cheeks inflamed and a slight rash beginning to form on her neck.

"Here, let me grab you a tissue." I get up out of my seat and ask one of the flight crew to grab me a box of tissues from storage.

She brings them back quickly and I offer her a slight thanks, and hand them to Rhea. She takes them and uses it against her eyes and nose.

I'm not the best when it comes to dealing with girls who are upset, especially when I'm the one whose managed to cause it.

I reach my hand out and rest it against her arm, rubbing my thumb gently up and down, hoping to soothe her in some way.

Yup, probably part of the reason I'm still single, I'm about as affectionate as a traffic light.

"Lets just forget this ever happened? I don't want to discuss it anymore." She mumbles, setting the box of tissues down, holding her head up high and readjusting her hair.

I squeeze my lips into a tight line and nod, dropping my hand from her arm.

"I wanted to become a pilot because I was so tired of having to be grounded all of the time, I had to grow up far too young, I wanted some way to get away from it all, but do something for a good cause. So I got my pilots license and joined the military as a pilot. But I got discharged a few years back and well, now I'm here." I say in response to her earlier question that I refused to answer.

She blinks a few times and nods, then proceeds to check over the route schedule.

I bite the inside of my cheek, not actually realizing that even if I found her annoying, her conversations actually became something I'd grown used to.

The absence of them now feels foreign and uncomfortable.

* * *

The rest of the flight is like that, I mean jeez, I think I've even tried to make more conversation than she has.

And I'm not a conversationalist.

She doesn't even ask to have the landing. When I offer it to her, she declines with a shake of the head.

Once we land, she hurries up out of her seat and leaves the plane before the passengers have even finished leaving the plane, she claimed she 'wasn't feeling well'.

It's raised alarm bells in my head, all of this, for reasons that I wasn't consciously aware of, until now.

I was unaware just how much I'd grown attached to all these small parts of her, no matter how much they conflicted with my own interests, it was just how she is. And when she isn't like that, I don't like it. I want her to ask me her stupid questions, I want her to tell me weird facts about plants, I want her to tell me all about how much better she is at landing than I am.

But instead, she was empty.

A shell.

Something I said about the seeds triggered her, and I have absolutely no idea why.

But I will find out.

Chapter 7

Rhea

I've been absent for a week now. I've relapsed for the first time in two years. Not like some sort of addiction, or I suppose at this point it could almost be considered one. I've given up my mental battle and I'm stuck again. Stuck in this abyss of depression, the one that swallows me whole, digs it's claws into me and drains the life from me.

An old friend, some would say.

I don't even understand why I became so triggered, people have asked me questions like that before and it's never had that sort of effect from me. I think the build up to it, I'd been trying so hard to get him to like me so that my life wouldn't be difficult, added pressure to it.

Ezra warned me to tread carefully with the change, and I didn't listen. I thought I was doing so well and I jumped into the deep end with both feet blindly, stupidly.

Why did I think I was ready?

Now, I've screwed it all up and I never want to go back there, I am literally one email away from handing in my resignation. The same self-destructive thoughts swim around my head, stabbing at me with the harsh words.

Failure.

Disappointment.

Weak.

Coward.

Bland.

I feel incredibly nauseous, lost and broken. I know I need to see Ezra, he's the only one who can help me when I get like this, but I can't do it. I need help, but I can't ask for it.

I need saving, but I can't be saved.

Not when I'm like this.

It's ironic, in the times you need help the most, you can't reach out for it. There's some sort of shame that comes along with depression, the need to hide away from your problems, even if that means sitting inside of your own head and absorbing the worst parts of you.

I know how to help myself, but I can't. I'm trapped. In this darkness. Drowning. Suffocating. Bleeding.

I close my eyes and fist the covers around me, trying to give my self some kind of release, but the tears won't spill. It's numbing, tragic and lonely. I'm lost in my own head with no way out. I'm Alice, and I'm falling through the rabbit hole, deeper and further away from reality.

I'm entering into the void, clawing at the walls on my way down, trying to keep myself from succumbing.

"RHEA!" My body is being shaken, but my eyes are closed.

Chapter 7

I'm free-falling, I'm frozen, I'm burning, all at the same time. Everything is taking over me, I have lost all control over myself.

"RHEA! Rhea please!" A deep voice shouts. My eyes roll around in my head, lost in this state between consciousness and death. Limbo.

"Rhea, come on, wake up." The grip is firm on my shoulders and I can feel myself being pulled into their arms, the warmth a foreign feeling compared to my heart, that is completely surrounded with ice.

I fight against it, charging through and I feel myself coming back, climbing the walls to the anchor of light at the top.

My eyes flutter open and the sudden burn of the light overwhelms me a little, my eyes squint in correspondence.

"Rhea, God, you're okay." I turn to the deep voice and realize that I'm peering straight into his honey brown eyes, his lashes fluttering quickly as he scans the entirety of my face.

But then I tense, and realize what the hell has happened. I pull myself up and away from him, yanking my blankets with me seeing as though I'm only in a strappy top and pajama shorts.

"What are you doing here?" I exhale, my chest loosening.

"You've not been in work for a week, I was worried. I thought, God I don't know what I thought." He runs a frustrated hand through his hair and tugging a little.

"You were just really upset the last time I saw you, and I wanted to make sure you were okay. I don't know why but I just had the urge to check up on you. Are you okay? You don't seem it." His voice is strained, to the point it sounds painful for him to speak.

"I'll be fine, I'm fine." I try to reassure him but my voice is definitely not convincing.

"Look, this is going to come across as weird. Really weird. But, you can talk to me, you know? I know you don't really know me but I made a promise to someone, a promise I never got to fulfill. And, I just got this feeling, that you weren't okay. And you're clearly not." He speaks, but keeping his eyes fixated on the floor.

In what universe have I fallen into?

Devon Stark is perched on the end of my bed, I'm in some sort of insane, wacko dream right now. I thought the random sex dream about him was one off, but now this is just strange.

I'm not obsessed with him, am I? I reach out a shaky finger and jab it into his arm, nope he feels pretty solid.

He looks at me confused as his eyes flit between my hand and my face, trying to figure out what I'm doing.

"Where did you come from?" I ask quietly, pulling my knees up to my chest.

"As in my mother, or state?" He teases.

Suppressing a laugh, I raise an eyebrow at him expectantly.

"Okay, fine. Yes, I breached company policy to get your address, but I'm truly sorry about the door, I don't understand why you don't have a spare key like everyone else."

"I've watched far too many true crime documentaries to be stupid enough to leave a door key under the door mat, or plant pot or whatever. Wait, what about the door?" My eyes fire to the entrance of my bedroom, it seems fine to me.

He looks away and then back at me, his shoulders slouching slightly.

"Um, obviously I knocked. But there was no answer and, shit. A lot of bad thoughts ran through my mind and I panicked and just sort of… kicked it down instead."

"You *what?*" I scream at him, scrambling from the bed and out of my room.

The first thing I check is to see where the kittens are, they're notorious for trying to escape, without access to an open doorway. I don't see them. I begin to panic.

Chapter 7

"Kitties." I whistle to try and gauge their attention.

Devon appears at my bedroom door frame and watches me running around frantically.

"When I first came in they tried to dash, so I grabbed them all, they're in the bathroom." He confirms and instantly my body sags.

"Thank God." I throw myself onto the sofa with a hand on my chest, the rise and fall of it harsh from not actually leaving the bed for an entire week.

I feel quite dizzy actually, I don't remember the last time I ate.

Fizzy has been super busy with the ballet studio, so when she returns at night my bedroom door is always closed, I don't even think she knows I'm here. She probably assumes I'm on back to back flights.

I glance at the broken door and close my eyes, stressed at how much that is going to cost me to replace, especially with the money that I owe Devon and the fact I'll be a week short of pay now.

"Don't worry, I've got it covered, I've just called a guy." He slips his phone into his pocket and keeps his hands tucked into them.

Well, I suppose that's one less thing to worry about on my never-ending list. What I can't wrap my head around is, why he's here? The last time we spoke it was like we were finally acknowledging each other and now, he's in my apartment, which he kicked the door down of, and stole my address and breached company policy.

"Were you really missing me *that* much?" I sigh.

"Look, there is nothing wrong with a colleague checking up on another colleague for their welfare"

"Oh, so we're colleagues now are we?" I let a smirk play on my lips, seeing his temper begin to rise I kind of enjoy seeing him get so worked up over the fact he cared enough to check up on me.

"Rhea," his voice warns, he knows I'm pushing him.

"Well you've checked up on me, I'm still alive, why are you still here in my apartment?" I bait.

He lets out a breath through his nostrils, causing them to flare aggressively. He unfolds his arms and walks over to the couch.

"You look like absolute shit, and you're carrying a vile odor." He says to me, scrunching up his face.

"Nobody asked for your opinion, or your presence for that matter." I turn my head away from him to see the plants through my bedroom, a few of them starting to turn from their vibrant green, to a mellow yellow.

"Fine, I'll leave." He turns to walk away, but stops, placing his clenched fist in his mouth and biting down on it.

"Fuck, why are you being this difficult?"

He still doesn't look at me.

"Me? What do you mean difficult? Like I said, I didn't ask for you to come here and I really don't appreciate you adding to all of *this*." I flap my arms, gesturing to the rest of the room.

He shakes his head and turns it towards me, "What is wrong with you?"

"What do you mean? I'm just sick." I cough a few times, trying to emphasize it, but he's clearly not buying it judging by the look on his face.

"How did you know I was absent anyway? I thought you had your 'private matters' to deal with?" I say, making the air quotations and pulling a face.

Hoisting myself up from the couch, using far too much energy than I would like to admit, I walk to the refrigerator to grab a water bottle. Now that I've been rudely pulled from my pit, the dehydration is quickly catching up.

"Yeah, I did. And I came back. And you weren't there."

"You really sound like a big boy, explaining things like that in so much detail." I roll my eyes.

Chapter 7

I open my water and begin to drink it.

"I can assure you, I feel like a big boy too." The water I'm mid-swallowing goes down the wrong way and I begin to cough and splutter, my eyes watering as I try to get my breathing back on track.

"You, *what?*" I turn to him, the water soaking my tank top across the front.

His eyes flit downwards and then back up at my face again.

"Nothing." He smirks.

I blink a few times as I stare at the wall in front of me, my body still frozen in shock and absorbing his words. His words that make me think about him in other ways, ways I most certainly should not be thinking of.

"Ahem," a gruff voice interrupts us.

I jump slightly. I have been without social interaction for a week, give me a break.

"Ah, Rob you made it, perfect timing." Devon slaps the man on his back and looks over at me, giving me a thumbs up.

"So, er, this door I'm assuming?" Rob points towards the door that is in pieces.

Coming to think of it, how the hell did he manage to kick down a door with that width? Is he some sort of Clark Kent, with hidden super powers and living a double life?

"Did you bring the door I specifically requested?" Devon says to him and the guy mutters something about the weight of it and the flight of stairs.

I watch as Devon disappears and I'm left alone in my apartment with this random guy.

"I always thought that kid had anger issues." The elderly man shakes his head as he begins to take out his tools from his bag.

"Is that so?" I push.

"I'm always cleaning up some sort of mess he's left behind." His voice is muffled as he fiddles around in his bag, but I'm intrigued. Especially now that this offers me some insight into his life, behind the front he holds at work.

"Yeah, it's terrible isn't it, I bet you're worked off your feet." I try to play into his narrative.

"I just want to stay retired, you know? And all he does is keep bringing me back out to sort out shit like this." He gestures to the door and I nod in agreement.

"Surely, you can just say no." I furrow my brows, confused with his annoyance.

He holds his breath and places his hands on his knees as he's crouched over the door. He stays silent and seems deep in thought, he looks pained and stressed, something I can relate to far too much.

He lets out a sigh. "I don't-"

"I've got it." Devon practically runs down the hallway with what looks to be at least a three-hundred-pound metal door.

"What is that monstrosity?" I cringe at the sight of it.

"That, my darling, is safety." He places it down, leaning it against the corridor wall as he admires the expanse of it.

Is he actually insane?

"Look, sorry to be the bearer of bad news here but that is not getting attached to these hinges." I pop a hand on my hip in an attempt to appear confident and stern.

"Hm, Rob how long do you think it will take?" he completely blanks me.

"Hey! Devon, this is my apartment and it is not going up." I huff.

"I can get it done and dusted in about fifteen minutes sir." Are these guys for real? Do they really think they can just completely disregard me?

"Devon. That door is staying put." I hiss at him, and he waves me off.

Chapter 7

He literally brings out the demons in me that I try so hard to push down. I haven't felt the anger emotion in a long time, and he knows just exactly how to press my buttons, like I'm his puppet and he gets to pull all the strings.

Rob is currently unscrewing the old door and Devon is tapping away on his phone. What am I even meant to do here? I'm a one-hundred-and-thirty pound woman and these men combined has to be at least 400 pounds, I wouldn't stand a chance at trying to fight them off. I can't even slam my door in their face.

I fold my arms across my chest and stomp my way back to my bedroom like a moody teenager.

Flopping onto the bed, I think of ways I can stop that chamber-looking door from being put up. I roll over and stare up at the ceiling, defeat washing over me. How am I meant to explain this to Fizzy, let alone our landlord? Christ, we're definitely losing our safety deposit on this place.

My gaze blurs slightly from not blinking but that's when I see it, the fire alarm. Oh Rhea, you absolute *genius*. I may not to be able to move them by force, but I can move them by building policy.

I climb off the bed and pull open my top drawer with my tea lights, the candle lighter sitting there casually, as if it is not about to be my saving grace.

Finding some paper from my desk, I light the corner or it, the flame igniting the paper as it ripples along the crisp edge, pulling and folding away.

Working quickly, I pull my desk chair to the middle of the room, heaving myself up onto it and holding up the paper so it is just beneath the fire alarm, the smoke trail floating upwards and into the flashing beacon.

A few seconds later, chaos erupts and the entire building begins to sing a siren. I wave the paper about to diffuse the flame, but it persists and continues to burn away. *Shit.*

There isn't much paper left until it reaches my fingers so I do the one thing that is going to give away my plan. I bolt out of my bedroom, directly into the kitchen and throw it into the sink, firing on the faucet. The paper shrivels up and the flame ceases as my chest heaves up and down from the adrenaline rush. I grip the counter and lean over it, the sound of the alarms chanting away.

"Clever." A husky whisper trails across my neck.

My breath hitches and my heart beat increases rapidly, sending an array of goosebumps across my skin. I slowly turn, to see Devon stood far too close behind me. I glance to the door to see that the new ugly door is fully fixed to the frame and closed. Great. So this was all for nothing.

"Looks like we're going to have to head downstairs now." His deep undertones send vibrations across my surface. My mouth is dry as my lips part and I just nod my head, as if I'm in some sort of trance.

"I've done what I came to do, so I'll be seeing you, Rhea." He dips his head and for a moment I think he's swooping in for a kiss, but he holds my gaze with a finger under my chin, tilting my head upwards.

I just stand there, nodding and dazed. He drops my chin and walks over to the apartment *barricade,* and I follow after him as the voices of the apartment janitors knock on each and every door to escort people outside.

I don't know what the *hell* Devon has just done to me, the way his breath caressed my every wound and lapped at them with the desire to fix me, but it wasn't something that I didn't enjoy.

Chapter 8

Devon

Have you gone a little crazy, Devon?
   Maybe.
   Was the steel door necessary?
Not in the slightest.
Do you care?
Not at all.
Sometimes, I get a little over-protective. Okay, *very*. But, you can never be *too* safe. I managed to get into her apartment with ease so surely, anyone else could too.

I don't know what exactly has been happening inside of me over the past week without her, but it's something that is making me act out irrationally. It drove me insane with worry, not knowing if she was okay or not. Especially because of the last time we spoke, her coldness, acting completely out of character and rushing off the way she did. And then, *poof*. She disappears.

"Devon man, you're spaced." Everett shouts to me from across the gym hall.

I look up at him and then realize I haven't punched the boxing bag in a while. I grit my teeth and begin to aggressively throw my gloves at the bag in front of me, the burn in my biceps reminding me of the reason I'm doing this. The grueling military training flashes through my mind, the faces of my comrades that seem to become transparent before me and disappearing completely.

I translate the pain into adrenaline, firing shots at the bag with all of my strength.

"Hey, hey. You okay man?" Everett jogs over to me, his hands tied up in his own boxing gloves.

"Perfect" I spit out the build up of saliva in my mouth.

The sweat beads down my forehead as I pant. I wipe my forearm across my forehead, trying to push my hair and sweat out of my eyes.

"I haven't seen you this worked up in a while, what's up?" he stands beside me, scanning my face concernedly.

"I said, I'm fine." I inhale through my nose deeply, wanting this conversation to be shut down.

I am not one to talk about my feelings, least of all with the boys. They're my only escape from this treacherous life, the only thing good I have, aside from my mother.

"Look, I'm one of your boys, okay? Just, if you need to talk, then talk. You know, mental health for men and all that?"

I let out a low chuckle and nudge his side playfully. If there's one person who can add humor to the situation, it's Ever.

"You're such an ass." I shake my head, grinning.

"Oh come on, Devon. You're the biggest ass of us all." He turns away, laughing to himself. *Such an ass.*

Chapter 8

* * *

I begin my pre-flight checklist, Rhea beside me.

"I have something for you." she says sweetly. I attach my eyes to hers, genuine interest piquing.

"What seeds is it this time?" I offer her a smile and she reaches into her pocket, pulling out my new flight ritual.

"These, are yellow roses." She hands them over to me, her face full of confidence, her eyes full of life.

"And, what do these symbolize?" I question, letting her know I'm now familiar with the routine.

"Friendship, happiness and new beginnings" She offers a toothy grin afterwards, pleased with herself.

"Friendship, you say?" I raise an eyebrow at her.

"Yes Devon, friendship. I think that's the least you can offer me after the commotion you caused in my apartment" She shakes her head before lowering her attention to her own checklist.

"The least?" I push.

She turns to me with wide eyes, her cheeks glowing pink.

"No, I just mean, like, ugh!" she crosses her arms across her chest in a huff. I love that I have this effect on her.

"I don't know why you always have to make things so awkward!" she frowns, pouting her full lips.

I keep my gaze on them for a moment too long, she notices. Her pout instantly drops and she lets out a big sigh.

"You are *such* a guy." She whispers to herself, but I hear her anyway.

"Is that so?" I continue to taunt her, knowing she is getting so worked up.

"Oh, my, God!" She groans, closing her eyes and looking up to the ceiling as her neck becomes exposed to me.

It's then I notice the tiny tattoo on her neck, near to her hairline and beneath her ear. It appears to be in the shape of a rose, but the flower itself is not actually a flower at all. It's a bud.

"Nice tat." I state simply.

She rubs her hands down her face and leans forward again, her eyes squinted at mine.

"Thanks." She rolls her eyes.

Our attention is interrupted as the cockpit phone begins to ring out. I hop up immediately and grab it.

"Hey Captain, we just wanted to know what the hold up is?" One of the flight attendants asks.

I pull my arm forward, uncovering my watch from beneath my blazer. *Shit*. We're behind schedule.

"Oh, just a few technical difficulties, we'll begin to taxi in five." I put the phone back on its holder and turn to see Rhea looking at me quizzically.

"Well, seems your bickering has taken us behind schedule, late *again*." I sigh, pulling my lips tight.

"Devon I swear, I am about to become violent if you don't shut up about the non-existent tardiness." she growls at me, her eyebrows furrowed as she tries to give me her 'toughest' look.

I've seen angrier goldfish.

"What will we do with you? Your feedback from me isn't looking great so far." I turn away from her to hide my smirk.

"Oh, Devon. You're really going to get it." She mutters, whilst finishing her checks.

"Oh, go on then, you can be the one to take-off" I say, kicking back on the chair with my arms behind my head, letting out an obnoxious 'Ah'.

The air is knocked out of me as she launches the checklist into my stomach and I keel forward, groaning.

"Don't say I didn't warn you." She smirks, placing on her headset.

In all honesty, it was worth it. There isn't a second of this conversation I haven't enjoyed. For the first time in a while, I feel *happy*. It seems that those seeds may mean something after all.

* * *

"Like really, how have you never watched *The Happy Place*?" She asks me, genuine shock in her voice.

"I don't have time for things like movies." I state.

"It's a series, and what do you mean you don't have time? You're not in the sky *all* of the time." she argues.

"I have a wife and three children to attend to, my life is pretty preoccupied at home." I sigh, trying to seem genuine.

"What?" She barks at me, her eyes wide.

"What? You've never asked me anything about my personal life" I reply.

She stays silent for a moment and then her gaze shifts to my bare fingers.

"You're one of those." Her face pulls up in disgust.

"One of what?"

"When you're not with your wife, you don't wear your wedding ring." She grimaces.

This is when I really begin to laugh, full on giggle. It's been so long since I've felt this way, to feel relaxed and comfortable enough to let loose.

She stares at me with shock on her face, not understanding my reaction.

"Devon?"

"I'm sorry" I continue to laugh, completely hysterical.

She looks like she's getting annoyed again, judging from the raised eyebrow and screwed up eyes.

"Sorry, I was joking, baby." My laughter begins to cease.

"So you don't have a wife, or kids?" She asks with confusion.

"Nah, I was just messing with you. I'm as single as the sky is blue." I grin proudly.

She seems to just nod and returns her attention to the map, only an hour till we begin our descent.

"What about you, huh?"

"What about me?" She replies.

"Are you, like dating anyone?" My voice grows deep and husky, without any intention behind it.

"No, far too mentally unstable for that kind of thing" she chuckles to herself awkwardly.

I don't really know what to respond to her confession. If anything, I relate to it a little too much.

"Well, we can be mentally unstable together." I offer a lazy smile and sit back in my seat, the sun beginning to set in the distance.

Chapter 9

Rhea

The last few weeks of flying have been a learning curve for both me and Devon, it's been pleasant. I'm pretty sure Devon has enough seeds to grow an entire greenhouse of flowers and plants. I'd love to see it, but my mind can entertain itself with its own visuals.

"Do you always wear your hair like that?" Devon begins a new conversation after hours of us bickering over the necessity of having pets. Of course, my opinion is that having a pet is better than having a boyfriend, at least you know they won't be out in the middle of the night cheating on you or ruining your life.

He didn't take too kindly to my comments and insisted that I was 'weird' and that he doesn't understand why people spend so much time looking after something that's destined to die within our lifetime. He stopped when I shed a tear, thinking of the few years I have left with Gemini. Regardless of the fact I know it's coming, it doesn't make it any easier to hear.

"What do you mean?" I respond, confused at his interest in my hair.

"In that, twisty thing." He points to the bun at the base of my head, his inaccuracy of describing it has me giggling.

"No, not all the time. Believe it or not, I have a life outside of being in this cockpit, with you."

"You're kidding? You mean, there are people other than me, who you spend your time with? I'm deeply hurt." He pouts his bottom lip and pretends to shed a tear.

"Shut up, you big baby. Unfortunately, you have to share me with *all* of my other friends." The sarcasm drips from my words, knowing that the majority of my time is spent with either Fizzy or Gemini, and the kittens.

"Something about this doesn't feel right, it's not fair that I don't get to have you all to myself. Surely, I'm the only person who makes you laugh." He plays along with my narrative.

"Oh, Devon. No one could make me laugh as much as you do, everyone else is so boring!" I half-lie, he really does have me belly-laughing more than most.

He grins at me, his cheek apples bunching up as his perfect teeth bare his feelings.

I think that I would happily sit here forever, with him. Laughing and joking together, without a care in the world, all to earn that glamorous smile from him. My stomach flutters slightly, his eyes meeting mine as I analyze his creases around his eyes.

Devon is older than me, I know that for sure. He's got a very… masculine body. The kind that you don't get until later in life, he's built stocky and broad, most would find him intimidating. I did, kind of. In my defense, he did nearly knock me off my feet when we first 'met'.

That reminds me, "Why did you ignore me on my first day?" I

Chapter 9

interrogate him, not caring if it makes him uncomfortable.

His smile drops as the sour, detached Devon enters the room.

"I didn't." He tries to deflect.

"You did." I push.

"I didn't see you." He counteracts.

"You did." I cross my arms over my chest as I stare him down.

His gaze leaves mine, focusing straight ahead as his jaw flexes, displaying the tension.

"Just–just drop it." He deadpans, the switch in the atmosphere has the temperature dropping to the point my arms have erupted in goosebumps.

"Sure." I falter, not wanting to push an answer that must be so damning, he can't say the words to me, now that we're practically considered friends.

Returning my attention to the flight path, I count down the remaining hour of the journey, wishing I'd hadn't put my foot in it.

* * *

Fizzy has been so busy lately that we felt the need to organize a night out, to let our hair down and party together. I've truly missed her, our movie nights and our girly chats.

The kittens begin to leave in three weeks and honestly, I'm so sad about it. I've grown so attached to them, each of their own personalities.

One night, me and Fizzy sat down and named them all based on the names of the dwarves from *Snow White*. It made sense, with their being seven of them and honestly, it suited them so well. Grumpy,

Sneezy, Bashful, Dopey, Sleepy, Happy and Doc.

I have a soft spot for Sleepy because she's the most snugly of them all. She hops up onto my bed whilst I'm sleeping and settles herself into the crevice of my neck, curling her tail around my jaw. I am definitely going to struggle to let her go, we've both grown attached to each other. But, I just simply don't have the time for her with my schedule. Gemini is a lot older and requires less attention, she potters around the apartment and disappears throughout the night, bringing back whatever new toy she finds.

But with Sleepy, she craves the physical touch, the snuggles and the scratches. I am hoping her new owner is able to give her just that, if not more. I advertised her as needing an owner that is willing to give her the attention and love she needs.

Even now, she's tiptoeing in and around my legs whilst I do my makeup, brushing herself up against my skin. Her light gray coat and her striking blue eyes make her irresistible, if she wants my attention, she's got it.

"Rhea, do you want a top up?" Fizz shouts from the kitchen. I eye up my gin and tonic and see it's running low.

"Please" I respond, applying a nude liner around the outline of my lips.

I finish off the rest of the glass before she comes in to get it.

"Damn girl, you look so hot" she drops her jaw, eyeing me from head to toe.

I opted for a black blazer dress, it's low cut to reveal too much of my cleavage, but simple enough not to draw too much attention. Black heels and a clutch compliment the outfit well, a thin gold necklace to add to my bare chest.

"Come on I thought tonight was about letting our hair down, though? You can't do that with your hair tied up!" Fizzy chuckles.

Chapter 9

I roll my eyes and look at myself in the mirror, my light-blonde hair pulled back into a bun. Yeah, maybe down would be better.

My hair is slightly curled from the twist of the bun, meaning I don't have to do much with it. I grab two butterfly clips and twist each side of my hair parting, gripping it back with the clips. The last thing I want is to be shaking my ass in the club and have my hair sticking to my forehead.

Taking hold of my clutch, I shout Fizzy back in to get some pictures before we go out.

"Coming, here– grab your drink." She hands me my gin glass, shimmying so that her dress falls a little further over her ass.

She opted for a sparkly gold dress, that compliments her fiery red hair and her tan skin (fake of course).

I pull open the camera and we pose in my full length mirror. Some pictures are pouts, some laughing, some serious and some pulling funny faces at each other. I flick through them, taking a drink and clicking on one of us smiling at each other. The phone is central and our heads are above it, the light reflects off our grins and our legs are positioned perfectly. That's the one.

I post the picture to Instagram with the caption 'Letting our hair down', tagging Fizzy in it and adding a champagne glasses emoji.

"Uber's here, party time baby!" Fizz cheers, swinging her hip into mine.

I try and drink as much of my drink as possible before we exit the apartment and trying to avoid spilling it all over me whilst I walked.

* * *

"Vodka and diet coke!" I shout over the bass of the club, for the fourth time.

The bartender looks at me and shrugs again, my throat burns from singing along all night and have to shout my drink orders repeatedly.

"VODKA," I shout again and he nods finally, spinning around to grab a glass. Thank God.

I wait for my drink, swaying slightly from my intoxicated state. I glance around and see a guy at the bar, sat on the stool and peering over at me with a serious stare. I look away and try to distract myself but my eyes wander all the way back to him, his gaze still burning into mine. I can't tell if it's the alcohol heating my cheeks or if I'm blushing. Either way, they're heated.

He beckons the bartender over and I watch as he says something to them and then pointing over to me, the bartender nodding in response. I look behind me and don't see anyone else, he definitely pointed at me.

A blue cocktail is pushed in front of me, alongside a vodka on ice. Great, straight vodka.

I open my clutch to grab my credit card when the bartender shakes his head and gestures a thumb to the guy who is staring intently at me.

Oh, he's paid for my drinks? *Nice.* I mouth a 'thank you' over to him and he smirks at me, taking a sip of his drink. I tip the straight vodka into the cocktail, not caring that I'm mix the two. I wasn't going to drink it straight, I'm not *that* idiotic.

I drink some of my cocktail and place it back down, offering a thumbs up to the guy and nodding my head. He gives me a lazy smile and shrugs. I like him.

Deciding to leave my station at the bar, I go looking for Fizzy, I need to make sure she's not swinging from a chandelier somewhere. She's a little crazy and reckless when she parties.

I weave in and out of the crowd, trying to spot the familiar red-head in the crowd, but I can't see her. Pushing my way through sweaty and stumbling bodies to the bathroom, a bunch of girls hover around the entrance.

"Anyone seen a red head, hot as fuck and shines like an *Oscar* award?" I slur, becoming aware of how drunk I am.

"No sorry, babe. We'll keep a look out for her though." One of them responds and I nod my head.

I drink a little more of my cocktail and begin to feel as if the room is getting further away. The music seems to drown out, the bass being the only thing I can feel.

My throat feels dry and my vision blurs, I take another sip of my drink to try and eradicate the chalky feeling. My pulse thrums in my neck and I can hear it *so* loud, over anything else, the sweat beginning to bead down the side of my head.

I hold onto the wall for support, dropping my glass as it becomes difficult to function and stay in control of my own limbs.

An arm snakes around my waist and I lean on them for support, rolling my neck as my hair falls forward, restricting my vision. Everything disappears, the feeling of my legs, the beat of my heart, and my consciousness…

Chapter 10

Devon

I scroll though the most recent update on our forum, our next target. *Banks Steele*. The notorious Banks, CEO of *Steele Arms Weaponry*, who happens to sell his lethal weapons to the wrong side. The enemies. The ones who kill our own. The ones who killed some of my closest friends.

Despite his high profile nature, he's been incredibly hard to track down.

When we began our vigilante group five years ago, we came up with a hit list. We added some of the most infamous traitors, *Lukas De Ramorez, Frank Weston, Emilio Santiago, Cruz Busquets, Zoltan Baranov and of course, Banks Steele.*

We've spent years tracking down each of them, using our own forces to eliminate them and donate all of their funds to charities that help women and children flee from war in the countries affected.

Luckily for us, our mission is almost complete with Banks being our final and only target. His father was the originator of his company, Viktor Steele, but when he passed, Banks took it on himself. Somehow, he's even worse than his father. I get it, he's young and all he sees is the dollar signs. But, it's cost far too many lives than I want to admit.

Weapons of mass destruction are unfortunately a reality of this world and people around the world sell them to the highest bidder. A guy like Banks doesn't have morals, he doesn't give a shit who he's selling the weapons to, as long as they pay well. It's people like him who encourage war, provoke it and ramp up the stakes.

My team and I have all experienced the vile and inhumane actions of war, the torture, the pain and destruction. Banks lives his life, traveling the world, living in luxurious apartments and profits from the cost of innocent lives.

My second phone rings out and I answer it immediately, waiting for the update on Banks' whereabouts.

"He knows." Locke says.

"What do you mean he knows?" I grit.

"He made a move."

"Okay, where?" I don't understand his concern.

"Atlanta." He responds and I freeze.

"Are you kidding?"

"Nope, he landed a few hours ago. But we've all spoken and we think it's bait, a trap of some sort." I nod, agreeing.

"Yeah for sure, he doesn't live his secret lifestyle and then place himself out in the open for us to find him, there is some ulterior motive here." I respond, trying to gauge his next steps.

"We've got eyes out on him, but we can't be too careful that he's not planning on eliminating each and every one of us." Locke's tone is full of worry.

I think Banks has known for a long time that we're onto him, with us removing the other CEO's from their companies, we have to have crossed his radar at some point. But my concern now is, why is he baiting us like this?

He knows the risk we impose, our intentions, and it's like he doesn't care. He's trying to prove that we don't intimidate him and that he has the control. But, what he doesn't realize is that we're ambush predators, we take our time and wait for the right moment. It's how we've managed to be this successful so far, we don't act out irrationally. Everything we do is planned so intricately that we figure out every possible scenario and a solution to it, so we are always expecting and never surprised.

We rarely ever stray away from our original purpose, but a number of people have crossed paths with us that we couldn't turn down. Like, Reed's psycho ex-wife and sister.

One thing that me and my guys agreed to when beginning this group was that we keep one specific quality about us, to avoid getting caught up in it all. It's that we only kill people when it is an absolute last resort, a necessity and we've tried all other methods prior.

Judging from our killings, none of them have conversed with us, each of them completely self-obsessed and protective over their money that they don't agree to stop supplying war. They died protecting the money that we so generously use to support anyone affected by war, and it is an incredible feeling. It's justice, served and delivered by ourselves.

I lost all faith in the true intentions of government long ago. They are just as sad and bitter as the rest. But, the last thing we want is to be on their radar, if we're not already. Articles have been published, suspecting that there is a vigilante group going after the CEO's of companies that produce weaponry. Their theory aligns more with the fact were anti-gun violence, rather than anti-war. Either way, we aren't too bothered as the result is both the same, the elimination of bad people in the world.

"We've organized a meeting in the warehouse, the industrial estate just outside of town." Locke says.

"Okay, when?"

"Tonight, if you're busy it's fine we can bring you up to speed once you're back."

"No, no–I'm free. I'll be there around nine." I agree with him and end the phone call, locking the phone and laptop back away in my desk.

The house echoes from my every movement, bouncing from one wall to the other, reminding me of how alone I am.

* * *

"Okay, everyone welcome." Pete stands next to the whiteboard on wheels, the rest of us sat around the table with our laptops in front of us.

If anyone came across us, they would just assume this was just a normal business meeting, without the sinister topics.

"Banks Steele, twenty-six years old, born and raised in Washington, CEO of Steele Arms Weaponry, known for supplying weapons to Afghanistan, Israel, South Korea and Saudi Arabia." He begins to point to the other board beside him, Banks' face central, unfortunately wearing a smug grin.

His dark hair and green eyes taunt me and irritate me. I might need to borrow his picture for shooting practice, I'm sure my aim would be phenomenal.

"As you all know, we've been tracking this man for years now and he's incredibly difficult to trace. But, we have confirmation of his location, and it's right here in Atlanta." A few of the guys begin speaking to each other, concern in their faces.

"Now, we don't know if he knows about us but we have to presume he does. We need to act very carefully from now on, no sudden rash decisions, think everything through and report anything suspicious" He continues.

Pete leans down and our laptop screens all flash with the image from the CCTV in Atlanta airport, my workplace.

"He came in on a private plane around six hours ago, we don't know his intentions here. But, one thing I know for sure is he's not here for a holiday. We have to assume the worst, that he's here for us, for business purposes."

"Pete, where is he now?" Locke says.

"Glad you asked, well the last record we have on CCTV is him entering St. Regis hotel downtown. I've initiated the facial recognition software so that we'll be sent immediate notification when he leaves." We nod and proceed to watch the video of him entering the hotel, wearing casual clothes and a leather jacket.

Strangely enough, it doesn't seem to me like he's here for us. This seems different. A guy who was here to take down a vigilante group wouldn't be interested in spending his time in some random hotel in the middle of Atlanta, when he has access to every other place in the world.

"Something about this feels specific, personal I suppose?" I say, running my finger over my bottom lip.

"Hm, yeah. I can see that." Dan agrees.

"Any theories?" Pete nods to us both and my brain kicks into overdrive, trying to make sense of his actions and why he's come out of the dark.

Chapter 10

"We'll just keep track of his movements tonight, see if it leads us anywhere."

None of this sits right with me, something about it, has my stomach in knots.

Chapter 11

Rhea

My throat feels like it's had acid poured down it, the burn and dryness of it makes it too painful to swallow.

My head pounds with pain, bouncing from the front of my skull to the back, and then circulating all over.

I groan and wince at my attempt to move, the stiffness overriding my joints.

"She's waking up!" A male voice shouts.

The sound alone is enough to make me shiver as the sensation in my head worsens. I feel fragile and injured but I have no idea why.

"Go and get him." A different voice says.

I swear they're barely whispering but to me they may as well me screaming directly into my ear drum.

Using all of my strength, I start to open my eyes, the darkness of the room making it slightly easier. I blink slowly, staring at the wall beside me. I try to sit up as I'm laid on my front. It's then I realize, the reason my body is aching is because my hands are tied behind my back and attached to my feet, in some sort of hog-tie.

What the fuck?

All at once, my senses come alive, like someone inside my head has just pressed the 'panic' button.

Where. The. Fuck. Am. I?

I do the only thing that I think I can, I scream. Or so I thought, all that comes out is a muffled sound. I clench my teeth and end up biting down on some sort of spongy texture. I attempt to push against it with my tongue but its fixated in there with, what I assume to be, a gag.

Struggling, I turn my head to see behind me, to see the rest of the room, but it proves to be incredibly difficult. My eyes are wide with fear and they flit around the expanse of the room that I can see, I notice the gold detailing on the bed that say 'St. Regis'.

So I'm still in town?

Who the fuck has brought me here?

I twist and pull against the restraints, the rope burning my skin as I push and writhe, hoping to loosen them somehow.

"Stop, your only going to make yourself sore." A deep voice says from behind me.

I attempt to respond with a 'fuck you', but it doesn't translate with the obstruction in my mouth.

Groaning, I choose to ignore him and continue to give it my best shot against the rope. Now it makes sense, when people in movies break their wrists to get out of restraints, with the adrenaline coursing through my system.

I'm definitely considering it as an option.

Whatever the hell these guys want with me is beyond comprehensible right now, all I know is that I need to get out, to escape.

"I said stop." the voice grows nearer and I twist my head at an awkward angle and that's when I see the familiarity.

The guy from the bar, the one who ordered me the drink. For Christ's sake, why was the one guy that shown an interest in me a total psycho?

Closing my eyes, I use all of my strength to shimmy off the bed. Right now, even rolling away feels like an option.

His hand grips my face, pushing my cheeks inwards to the point of it being painful. He brings his face down closer, his blue eyes fighting with mine.

"He wants her sedated." A different voice says.

I somehow widen my eyes even more and begin fighting against him, panic and fear washing over me.

"Grab her." The other voice says.

The guy from the bar pulls me backwards by my tied limbs, I'm desperate to get away but I'm so useless right now I don't know how. I feel a sharp pain in my arm and I cry out as best as I can, the dread of what he's just injected into me takes over.

Trying to fight against it, I plead for my body to somehow overpower whatever drug it was. Of course, it's inevitable.

My eyes grow heavy and the tenseness in my body begins to loosen as I fall back down into the darkness.

Chapter 12

Devon

"So as far as we're aware, he hasn't left the hotel?" Locke says to Pete.

It's day two of us monitoring Banks' movements.

"Nope, we've gained access to the hotel cameras too, no trace of him" Pete responds.

I've got a flight in a few hours so I can't sit monitoring, but the guys are going to track everything whilst I'm gone.

"Did you manage to find out what room he's in?" Locke asks Dan, our best hacker.

"Judging from the footage, it's roughly room two-four-eight or two-fifty." I nod and begin to re-watch the video from last night.

"He traveled alone did you say?" I ask, watching as two men exit one of the potential rooms.

I continue to track their movements throughout the hotel, until they disappear out of the front entrance. They raise my suspicion.

"What about these guys?" The men gather around my laptop and I replay the video for them.

"Hm, can we run a facial recognition on these two please?" Pete asks Killian.

"On it."

I chew my lip anxiously, an agonizing feeling gnawing at me. They're here with him, I know it.

"Got a match." Killian says.

He flips his laptop around and two profiles are pulled up, side by side.

"I knew I recognized him." I growl.

Jesse Wolfe

The bastard who is known for his criminal activity, the ruthless fucker who manages to get himself involved with far too many rich guys.

He's usually hired to carry out their dirty work, I've read and seen far too much about him for this to just be a coincidence. He was leaving one of the rooms we suspect is Banks' room and he's from Massachusetts, not Atlanta.

"Well I'll be damned, well done, Devon." Pete nods his head towards me.

Pete's like the operations manager, he is a lot older than us and has a lot more experience than any of us. He also has a background in the CIA, so he knows the tricks of the trade.

The other guy I'm not so familiar with, *Cruz Winchester*.

He's never flashed up on our system before and he's got a clean record, which is certainly alarming when he's accompanied by someone as dangerous as Jesse Wolfe.

"What business would require him to hire two guys, one of them being a high profile criminal, and bring them to Atlanta?" Killian

Chapter 12

questions.

"They haven't made contact with us, haven't attempted anything to raise the alarms, I suppose were just going to have to watch their next moves." Pete says.

"I'm going to have to head off, but keep me updated if anything changes." I nod my head towards the guys and stand up from the table, packing my laptop with me.

"Be safe, Devon" Pete warns.

"Always" I respond, before taking the elevator up to surface level.

* * *

"Captain Stark, is there any reason for the delay on flight R3411?" Tom speaks through the headset.

"We're just finishing up on final checks, I'll alert you when we are ready to taxi" I respond, my leg frittering up and down.

Rhea is late again, her habit is becoming uncontrolled. I don't want to drop her in it though, I know sometimes traffic can be terrible or she might be held up with security or something.

I stare straight ahead, every minute that passes feels like an hour, each second throwing worrying thoughts into my mind.

I don't even have her phone number so I can't call her to check if she's okay. If she's not here in the next five minutes I'm going to have to call it in.

The gut feeling that something has happened, swirls around. It doesn't sit right with me. She obviously hasn't called the airline like when she'd taken time off last time, or they'd have arranged for replacement staff and wouldn't be asking me what the hold up is.

Two more minutes.

I try to focus on my breathing as my rate picks up, anxiety chipping away at me. She's fine. She's just ill or something, surely. I purse my lips and run my hands down my thighs, my mind trying to convince myself of more positive reasons for her absence.

One more minute.

Okay, she's got to turn up. This isn't like her, she's obviously just had car trouble, or she has an important doctor's appointment or maybe her cat is sick?

"Captain Stark, we've received word that Rhea Jensen is taking a leave of absence, we have a temporary co-pilot on their way to you as soon as possible." Tom speaks.

Leave of absence? What the hell?

"Tom, what's going on?" I ask, flexing my jaw.

"I don't know man, I don't get specifics." I can imagine him shrugging based on his lazy tone.

I retrieve my phone from my bag and dial management, to then be placed in a hold queue to speak to someone.

I have so many bad thoughts running through my head, mostly irrational.

The cockpit door opens and a guy from our team walks in, looking chirpy and fresh. *Great.*

"Hi, Captain Stark, Johnny Gilmore, pleasure to be flying with you today." He offers his hand out to mine and I stare at it, his over-confidence grinding against me.

He retreats and rubs his hand on his pants and nods slightly, confusion lining his features. He sits in Rhea's seat, making himself comfortable. I have never wanted to rip someones head from their body more than I do right now. That, is Rhea's chair.

"I'm assuming that we've been rescheduled?" he asks.

I continue to hold the phone to my ear, the annoying violins playing obnoxiously, taunting me that no one has picked up.

Chapter 12

"Hi Tom, Gilmore flight R3411, can we have the new flight schedule please?" He doesn't let my ignorance phase him.

I mean he can't be blamed really, but someone is going to have to get the runt of my wrath.

"Did they tell you why she isn't here?" I grit my teeth.

"Who?" he responds, his nose deep in the checklist.

"Rhea, the pilot you have replaced." I roll my eyes at his denseness.

"Oh, no she's probably just pulled a sick day, happens all the time with newbies." He shakes his head as if he knows anything about her at all.

"She isn't new." I flex my jaw, becoming more irritated with his disregarding nature.

"Well yeah, you know what I mean" he waves me off, completely unconcerned.

"Flight R3411, prepared to taxi." Johnny says through the headset.

As much as I want to sit here and wait on the phone, to find out what's going on, we do still have a job to do.

I send a text message to Dan, asking him to find Rhea's phone number so I can call her as soon as we've landed. I need to know she's okay.

The plane begins to move backwards and I decide to take over the controls. The quicker we get to New York, the sooner I can contact her.

I grab my phone again to make sure I've placed it on flight mode, a text message coming through at the same time.

Pete: *Banks is on the move.*

Chapter 13

Rhea

I'm somewhere else.
Somewhere unfamiliar.
It's cold.

I shiver and crack my eyes open, a blanket of darkness coating my eyesight. It takes my eyes a few moments to adjust to the black abyss, barely making out the brick wall in front of me.

It's not the same hotel I was in earlier, it's a gloomy expanse, morbid even. No windows. Ancient-looking door. Cobbled floors.

I can hear the water drops further away and the creaking of old pipes. The air smells musty, each breath I inhale feels contaminated with a toxic element. Each time it penetrates my lungs it causes my chest to constrict, the urge to cough becoming unbearable.

The gag around my mouth has given me an intense jaw ache, I can't remember the last time I'd had a drink of water.

I remember the last time I had a drink, unfortunately, and it landed

Chapter 13

me here, with a group of psychotic men living out their wildest fantasies.

Footsteps echo along the walls and my body immediately tenses. My heart begins to thump with anxiety as my legs try to shake, but they're restricted. My nostrils flare as the sweat beads on the back of my neck, goosebumps spreading along my arms and the hair vertical.

The footsteps are nearing, surely whoever it is, is aiming for this room. To me.

Locks turn, each click making me flinch, like a traditional horror movie jump-scare. Except this is completely real. This is reality.

The door swings open and my eyes instinctively squeeze shut at the bursting stream of light. They burn and fill with water, it pains me that I can't rub them, my hands tied behind the chair, refusing me the luxury.

"Hi, Rosalie." His voice scrapes talons along my spine, splitting me open and rendering me paralyzed.

The sound of my first name coming out of his mouth chips into every part of me that I built up so strong. He chips away at it with his chisel and hammer, knocking me back down to beneath him. All of my confidence, all of my strength and courage I had, eradicated.

Stolen.

Shattered.

Slaughtered.

I don't even want to open my eyes. Maybe my subconscious offers me the mercy. Instinctively, they close and will not reopen, as if my body is trying to repel him. To save me.

"Oh, my love, it's been far too long." his laugh is dry, mocking.

I gulp as best I can, my breaths harsh and unforgiving, just like him.

This is surreal, it's torture served to me on a silver platter, like the God's curated together to serve me a punishment worse than death.

"Oh, come on, darling. Haven't you missed me?"

Every word that comes out of his mouth takes me back. Takes me to the place I swore I could never return to. Would never return to. But he's got me, he's captured me as he always said he would. I was his mouse, his toy, his prey.

My body begins to break out into shakes as I can feel him nearing, the air wrapping itself around my neck and squeezing any life I had left. I'll gladly allow it.

My eyes burst open when I feel his cold grip on my shoulder, his sinful hands.

I come face to face with the Prince of darkness.

Banks Steele.

Chapter 14

Devon

The second we hit the tarmac, I switch my phone back on. It buzzes continuously with alerts from the guys, but I don't get chance to read them.

"What's the deal with you, Stark? You've been giving me the cold shoulder the entire flight, your head is so far up your ass to even wait till we've docked to turn your cell back on?"

I whip my head to face him, "Nobody asked you to fly the plane *and* stick your nose in my private matters." I bark at him.

I don't have the patience for this guy at the minute. One wrong move and he is about the lose his ability to fucking breathe.

"What? Never heard of small talk–I'm guessing not. But honestly Stark, you can be such a chore to fly with." He rolls his eyes as the plane begins to line up with the jet bridge.

I blink a few times, giving him the opportunity to take it back. I pout my lips and sigh at his lack of correspondence.

"Alright then, Gilmore. You got an issue with me?" I scowl, my voice deepening as I bite my inner cheek.

"Me— Damn, Stark. You have an issue with just about everybody and you're asking me if I have an issue with *you*?" He laughs obnoxiously.

I inhale slowly, my body as still as a cat, hunting its prey.

"I don't think you know who you're speaking to, Gilmore." My voice is barely audible as my body seethes.

"I very much do, Stark. I'm tired of hearing how everyone wants to trade and swap shifts to avoid flying with you. Did you know I was the sixth pilot they called for a replacement? Why do you think they hired some untrained and incapable pilot to fly alongside you?" I swallow harshly, not daring to speak as I try to keep my anger at bay.

"Don't fucking speak a single word about her. She's more than capable, I've seen it. Dick."

He stands up and grabs his blazer from his chair, placing it over his arm.

"Try and be nice every once in a while. You'll be amazed how much better the world gets, Stark."

"It's Captain Stark" I grunt, not sure how to keep control of myself without saying or doing something that gets me suspended immediately.

"Good day, Captain Stark." He salutes me with two fingers to his forehead and ducks out of the room, leaving me to conjure what the fuck that was about.

People... Avoid me?

He was pilot number six?

I release a shallow breath and that's when I realize how badly my hands are shaking. Oh, fuck— *Not now*. I clench my teeth together and rub my hands up and down my thighs, trying to throw it off. I

Chapter 14

really need to request a change of anti-anxiety meds from Ezra.

Picking up my carry-on and phone, I finally find the courage to step off of the plane, the shakes beginning to subside.

I make my way through the airport and hail a cab to take me straight to my hotel. I don't fly back to Atlanta until tomorrow, so it gives me time to figure out what the fuck is going on with Rhea.

As soon as I'm in my suite, I get to work, opening up my laptop with the tech-ware fitted, graciously by Blake. He emphasizes how his job is boring and unimportant, but without him I wouldn't have had the first clue on how to get this business off of the ground.

I begin to search the database to find out any background information about her, mainly for other methods of contact. I'm not one of those psycho-stalker guys who holds files on people who aren't on my radar.

Unlike Reed.

I skip over any medical notes and directly target her occupation profile. It pulls up to her application form for Titan and I scan through it quickly, coming across her contact information.

I pin the number into my phone and dial. Voicemail.

This is bullshit.

Just as I'm about to put my phone back down, it rings out. I answer it immediately without checking the caller ID and to my disappointment, it's Pete.

"Stark, you good?"

"Yeah." I breathe, flexing my hand in front of me to relieve the building tension.

"You alone?" I nod at the same time as saying yes.

"I'm going to ping something over to you, and I need you to tell me what you see." I furrow my brows and grab my laptop from the hotel bed, placing it on the desk instead, pulling out the chair and sitting down.

"Go ahead." I reconnect to the VPN and open our private server.

A video file waits for me, the title of it encrypted. It's a one-time view video so it's completely eradicated once I've watched it.

"Stay on the phone with me."

I mutter in agreement and move my cursor over the file, the screen of my computer turns black for a moment. Then, an extremely grainy video flashes to life in black and white.

I look around the screen, numerous people dancing away in a club, some at the bar and some loitering in random open places. My eyes dart around the screen, looking for anything in particular. I scan each person, not seeing anything too suspicious.

I'm almost about to ask what the fuck I'm supposed to be seeing here, but that's when I can see him.

It's in the very top left of my laptop screen but I recognize the jacket immediately, even through the grainy footage. The same, beaten up, leather jacket.

Cruz.

"Cruz Winchester, at the bar." I confirm with Pete.

"Keep watching." His tone is dead.

I continue to watch, seeing him call the bartender over, whispering something in his ear. That's when some sort of exchange happens, but the quality is too poor to make out anything distinct.

"He's dealing?"

"Worse." Pete groans and I can just imagine him running his hands over his well kept beard.

The bartender walks away from Cruz and returns to his usual bartending duties. I flick my eyes back to Cruz and see him sipping away at his drink, his gaze fixated on someone at the bar.

A girl.

That's when everything pieces together. The bartender places two drinks in front of the blonde mystery woman and they engage in conversation for a few moments, before pointing over to Cruz.

She lifts her hand and gives him a thumbs up, accepting the drink. *Bit weird, no?*

"She gave him a thumbs up?" I retort.

"Christ, Stark, pay attention."

I watch as she tips her drinks into one glass, taking a drink. She pushes away from the bar and heads over to the other side of the room.

Cruz hops down from his stool and follows after her, but keeping his distance to an extent.

That's when I see his accomplice, Jesse.

The girl talks to a few people before seemingly morphing into Bambi as she stumbles into others. Cruz and Jesse nudge into each other and come up behind her, snaking their arms around her waist.

I flex my jaw as I realize exactly what they'd done.

They fucking roofied her.

They begin to walk out of shot and at the last glimpse, she is fully relying on them for support.

How much did they fucking give her?

This is so fucked up.

"They fucking roofied a girl and took her back to the hotel, no doubt to commit the most disgusting acts possible." I grimace.

"They had targeted her from the second she'd walked in that place," he confirms.

"Where was this?"

"Havana Roomz, just off Baker Street." I've been there a few times, I'm surprised I didn't recognize it from the video.

"Any idea who the girl is? We could get in contact with her, offer her a deal. Trade of evidence and ensure that they get their due diligence?" I ask him.

"See, that's the thing, Devon." I stop and listen intently.

"We have footage of her entering the hotel, but none of her leaving."

"What are you saying?" My eyes grow wide. They–

"Banks left the hotel this morning, Tweedledee and Tweedledum in tow. No sign of the girl. We called the hotel as soon as we discovered the footage and they have already cleared the room out, she wasn't there." His words send chills along my spine.

"So… She just, disappeared?" I glance around the hotel room, my brain running the possibilities.

"We ran facial recognition on her. We got a positive match"

Well, that's a relief.

"Her name is Rosalie Rhea Rivers. She was romantically involved with Banks for a number of years. As far as media can tell, it has been since they were teenagers. So this attack, is very much personal. Whatever happened between them, has obviously rubbed Banks the wrong way. Enough so, he's taken action."

This is insane, but not unusual for control-freak psychopaths, like Banks Steele.

"We have theories. They were carrying with them an extra suitcase during their departure. We've struggled to pinpoint where they went after that, Dan is on it. We know they haven't left the state via their jet, so they're still close by."

Trying to limit my worries about Rhea, I sigh.

"What do you need me to do?"

Chapter 15

Rhea

"You always were stubborn, Rosie."

I cringe at the use of my old nickname from when we were kids.

I try and do anything *but* look at him.

His tantalizing appearance detonates every single bomb I had tried so hard to protect.

All of my work for the past three years has been unraveled. He's here to hurt me for the last time, finish what he started.

"Banks," I sob as I shake my head.

He looks down at me through his blue eyes, scanning over the entirety of my face. It's hard to believe, but before he inherited his father's company, we were in love. We were completely inseparable, we were *soulmates*. He was the most tender, sweet boy. Banks and I had plans for the future, including marriage and children. Everything was white picket fence, perfect and pristine.

The day his father died, the earth shifted on its axis. Everything began to fall apart. Banks was thrust into a world he'd tried so hard to escape from. He grew distant and shut me out, he began to keep secrets and our relationship had taken a huge curve ball.

From my perspective? Yeah, I thought we were infinite, nothing could break us. Until, the night of. The first time.

Everything had been up in the air, he disregarded me completely. Our time together lessened and his time with them grew. He became angry, futile and coldhearted.

He wasn't the same guy I'd loved all of my life. He wasn't the guy who saved me the last of his bagel, the guy who bought me every gelato flavor possible when I had my first period, the guy who paid the fairground attendant extra so that we could take in the view for longer. That moment is one I treasure, or did.

That was when he asked me to be his girlfriend, we were only fourteen at the time. So much has happened since then, so much has changed.

I tried. I tried so fucking hard to keep him grounded, to remind him of the good things that life had to offer a man as magnificent as him.

The first time, was the worst.

The first time I'd said too much, acted too stubborn and underestimated him. That night, I realized he wasn't Banks anymore, he was Steele.

I close my eyes and replay the moment over in my head, taking the backseat row and watching it all play out in front of me.

Shock. Trauma. Pain.

I'd never been hit before in my life, never had to endure such cruelty and bitterness. I spent the entire night, curled up in the tub with the bathroom door locked, sobbing my heart out and caressing my skin, trying to smooth it all away.

It took me a long time to realize that he wasn't going to stop, it was only going to get worse. The freshly bought wardrobe of turtle-necks, long-sleeves and scarves.

I was wearing full-length trousers in the middle of summer and I couldn't visit the beach anymore.

I lost myself entirely, shrinking away into my own pit of misery and guilt. I blamed myself for so long for not leaving sooner, for not seeing what was right in front of me the entire time.

I suffered for so long in silence, alone and desperate.

My mind traveled to the darkest places, places that still haunt me now. It has never left, it will always be there.

I found a level of strength eventually, enough to escape. Banks underestimated me.

He seen me as a timid bunny, his obedient and gullible partner. He didn't expect me to be able to flee the way I did, but for once, he came in useful. Banks had so many connections that it was almost too easy to find someone willing to forge entire new documents under a new alias.

I wanted to keep a small part of me, so I chose my middle name 'Rhea' as my first name and a generic last name.

Banks always used his scare tactics to keep me within his grasp, he closed me off from the outside world entirely so that the only person I had was him.

When I moved to Atlanta, it didn't feel like I was leaving anything behind, I was getting my overdue, fresh start. Until he caught up with me.

It's only taken him three years. I had three years of freedom. Three years of living again.

Now, I'm set for a lifetime of pain.

He sinks to his knees in front of me, his hand resting on my thigh. The action alone is enough to cause goosebumps to litter across my body, my throat closing up and my eyes brimming with tears.

"Rosalie, I've come to take you home."

What—Why does he sound like that? Why is he looking at me like that? Like... *before*.

I shake my head slowly, a tear escaping my control. Reaching up with his free hand, he uses his thumb to caress my cheek, the tear soaking up onto his skin. I swallow at the proximity of his touch, the torture in feeling his hands on me again. Fire ants surround my body, nipping away at my skin and igniting around his thumb.

He's—

He's *touching* me.

"Please my love, please forgive me. I have done so much wrong to you, I have been lost without you. Each morning that I wake up without you by my side, is a day that I don't want to face. The only reason I'm still here is because I had the hope of finding you again and bring you back to me, where you belong." His thumb rubs over my cheek slowly as the tears continue to cascade down my face, my inner strength faulting.

This isn't fair. This is purgatory. I am battling against the demons of my conscience, trying to shut out all of the unforgettable memories his voice brings.

I startle at the sound of his pen knife popping open, my entire body stills and my mouth dries.

"Banks, *no*." I whisper, my voice hoarse and pained.

He looks deep into my eyes, studying me. He leans forward and my eyes are drilled into the blade, completely stunned and fearful of what he's going to do with it. My heart drums loudly, enough to drown out the screaming sirens in my head.

The sound of slicing jolts my body, expecting to feel some hot, searing pain in my body. But it never arrives. My arms drop limply at my sides and I slouch forward, hours of sitting in the same position, finally being allowed to release into my muscles.

He wraps his arms around me and pulls me forward.

I don't have any strength in me to resist, I don't think I have anything in my body right now, but the ability to barely function. He cradles me and sinks his face into my hair as I grow completely numb, wanting to shrink away into non-existence.

Every movement he makes seems to spin my senses into oblivion as I hyper-analyze everything he's doing.

"I've got you baby, come home with me."

His words taunt me, offering me something he threw to the dogs.

It's a brutal game he's playing, knowing what he's done and still using every weakness of mine, to his advantage.

"I can't," I whisper, barely audible.

He pulls back and places both hands on either side of my face, his eyes warm and inviting.

"Rosalie, I've never regretted anything so much in my life. I'm so fucking sorry, baby. I'm here to make things right, to get us back on track to where we were. We can have our home, our family and our dreams. Please, Rosie my love, I will show you the world, I've changed– It's *me*. It's *your*, Banks." His face screws up, frustration bubbling over.

"I have a life, Banks, I have friends and a home and a job, that I love so much– I can't. I can't just throw that all away, I've worked so *damn* hard for it." I don't even know why I'm considering it.

The unlocked trauma is really beginning to overtake me, a serious case of Stockholm Syndrome right now.

His hot breath fans over my face, a contrast to the icy surroundings. I'm sat here in my tattered dress, from the club, my psycho-ex is in front of me, begging for my forgiveness.

"Why–why did you do all of this? Banks, if you wanted me to forgive you, this is not the way it's going to happen– This is the exact behavior I was talking about!" The end of my sentence breaks off into a cry as I become infuriated at the circumstances.

None of this was necessary, everything about him is backwards. He drugged and abducted me, kept me tied up for days, just so he could ask for my forgiveness and take me home. No. This, this is his power play. His control. Still.

"Rosie– Fuck, I'm sorry. This was completely wrong, it wasn't meant to be like this. I just, I didn't know how to approach you, to get the chance to speak to you."

"So, you abducted me, instead? That was your genius idea?" My eyes are wide and my lungs struggle to inflate from the impending explosion that is oncoming.

I shake my head and try to pull away from him, but he grips my wrists. Hard.

"You belong with me, we were perfect together. Yes, I fucked up and did some stupid things but it's always been Rosalie and Banks against the world. Baby you need to come home."

"I belong exactly where I choose. I belong with my friends, my home, my job. You blew your chance, Banks– no. You beat your chance out of me." I spit at him, finally conjuring up the confidence to expose my feelings.

His eyes squint as I try to pull away from his grip, the burning sensation heightening as he fights my strength.

"You know, I really have tried to be nice about this. I don't want you to hate me, I love you." He pulls me by my wrists towards him and I stumble onto him.

He uses the opportunity to bring his lips to mine, the soft touch of them brings back so many memories, so much happiness.

It's so difficult to disregard the ten years of joy and love for the year of his downfall. His evil. He was everything to me, we grew up together. We were each other's person, we were *it*.

Chapter 15

The kiss deepens and his tongue slides across my lips, begging for entry. My eyes roll in my head at the familiar feeling and I grant him access. Our tongues meet and playfully lap at each other as I fist his shirt, the buried emotions arising through the surface. This is so fucking wrong, but it's Banks.

He pulls away and rests his forehead on mine, our breathing in sync as we pant.

"Fuck, I've missed you so much," he sighs and closes his eyes.

I am so weak, I'm like putty in his hands the second he treats me like before. This is why it was so hard to leave, why I put up with the pain for so long. He wasn't always evil, he was sweet mostly but just... so angry.

"This can't happen." I bump my nose against his and my eyes flutter closed.

The smell of his skin reminds me of home, a mixture of eucalyptus and citrus. *Eucalyptus.*

Plants. Seeds. Devon. Home.

I pull away abruptly, blinking a few times to reevaluate what the fuck is going on. This man– He hurt me. He isn't the man I fell in love with, the man I loved would never do this. I hurt myself because he hurt me, the years of therapy, the healing and the constant battle.

The overwhelming sensation of claustrophobia overtakes me and the urge to escape breaks.

I push against Banks, standing up.

I bolt.

Chapter 16

Two Weeks Later
Devon

When I tell you I'm going out of my goddamn mind– I'm fucking crazy. I can't sleep. I can't eat. My stomach churns at the thought of her, the missing goodbye.

It's crazy how in such a short space of time, she had this impact on me. I never thought I'd miss my hyper, plant-obsessed co-pilot.

She's like a hurricane. She came into my life and blew it apart, sucking everything out of me and taking it with her as she left. She breathed life into me, she made me see things differently, positively. She was like my addiction, I became dependent on her without realizing it, my body relied on her to function.

Spending hours on a plane together most days, she slowly wore down my barriers. I allowed her to enter, to see parts of me I've kept hidden for years. And now, she's *gone*.

Dropped everything to move back to wherever the hell she came from. No word to her friends apart from a pathetic, 'I'm sorry, it's what's best for me', text.

Radio silence for me.

I can't lie, the fact I wasn't on her radar for a good-bye, stings.

I've been contemplating tracking her down and demanding answers for her sudden change of attitude. Who uproots their life like that?

But, yes. I've been wallowing in my own self pity for two weeks. Enough so, the boys have dragged me out to Billy's, to 'cheer' me up.

So far it's been Everett and Blake chewing the ears off me and Reed.

"Nah, come on man. That sucks! You're telling me you prefer the UK version of *The Office* to the US? You sicken me, Blake"

"What– I like it, big deal." Blake rolls his eyes and drinks his beer whilst Everett is about to burst out of his seat.

"Guys, come on, let's vote. UK or US?" he tips his beer bottle towards Reed and I.

"US" I say bluntly and take a sip of my lemon water.

"US, easy" Reed responds at the same time as Ever jumps up out of his seat hysterical and pointing at Blake.

"See! What did I tell you, weirdo." He starts doing a little dance and raising his hands in the air, shaking his ass in Blake's face.

I shake my head at their energy.

"Alright then, question for you all. Love Island UK or US?" Blake smirks and Ever shrinks back into his seat, his face turning serious.

"Blake, man, that's not fair." Ever pouts his lips at Blake and I look at them confused.

"Love what?" I question, earning bug-eyes from the rest of them.

"Love Island... Are you being for real right now?" Ever's jaw drops open.

"Do I look like the kind of guy that watches reality TV?" It's then I turn to Reed to see he's avoiding making eye contact.

"Oh, Reed. You watch that shit too?" I grimace and throw him a disappointed look.

"Nah, it's not like that I swear– Indie. Yeah, she watches it. I just, see it sometimes." He tries to counter.

"Whatever, Reed, we all know you love seeing hot chicks sat around a pool all day."

"Hey, I've got my perfect woman at home. And, she's carrying my daughter, I've got everything I need right there. Unlike the rest of you." He bites.

"We can't all bait someone into signing a contract to get married." I chuckle.

"Alright, alright. Shot taken." Reed raises his hands in defense as we all laugh together.

"Speaking of, I kind of have something to say." Blake begins, capturing our attention.

"I have some news. I fucked up"

We glance at each other, confused.

"The girl I met in here, a while back. I think it was the same night we met you, Reed." We nod.

"As it turns out… I'm kind of going to be a dad."

Not one of us moves. We blink a few times, waiting for him to follow up with his joke. But, the joke doesn't arrive.

"Wait, you're serious?" I say.

"Oh yeah, dead serious. She's due in like six months or something."

I scratch the back of my scalp whilst Reed offers him his congratulations and welcomes him to the 'fatherhood club'.

Ever is quiet, staring down at the table.

"I mean, are you sure it's yours?" I tighten my lips and chew on the inner of my cheek.

"Can't you just be happy for me, man." He huffs.

Chapter 16

"I'm just looking out for your dumb ass, someone's got to if your going to trail after some random chick, like a puppy for a bone."

"Yeah, well. I'm like seventy-five percent sure." Blake shrugs.

"Seventy-five!" we all scream in unison.

"Okay– Okay. Eighty." He tries to reason but it earns a groan from us all.

"So you… might be a dad?" Reed treads carefully, trying not to trigger him any further.

"Why do you think I hadn't said anything sooner, you guys are so judgmental. Let a guy live." Blake shakes his head and I glance towards Ever, who is still sitting, looking glum.

Blake excuses himself to the bathroom and I take the opportunity to ask what the fuck has gotten into him.

"Ever, what's up?"

"Me? Oh, nothing. Just thinking is all." He tries to shrug away my question but he doesn't hide his emotions very well.

Everett has always been the most in touch with his emotions. Me? Probably the least. He ruffles his blonde hair and readjusts it to put it back right.

"You know you can talk to us." I push.

"Yeah, I know." He mutters.

"Look, I gotta go. I'll see you guys around, I've got a big comp coming up so I might not be here for our weekly visits for a while. Don't have too much fun without me." He slides out of the booth and jets off, leaving me and Reed in bewilderment.

"What the fuck was that about?" Reed asks and I look directly at the back of Ever as he scurries out of the bar.

He was fine before Blake spoke about being a dad. Something is going on with him, and it's not this competition he's talking about.

I'm interrupted by my phone buzzing in my pocket. No. My *other* phone.

"Give me a second" I stand up and accept the call, walking towards the exit of the bar.

The sun is still setting, it's not yet dark. There are a few guys on motorcycles in the parking lot, so I slip down the side of the building.

"Devon, speaking" I say.

Silence.

"Hello?" I pull the phone away from my ear to check the caller ID, it's an unknown number.

"Who's there?" I grow impatient.

A quiet sniffle falls through the phone, gripping at my heart.

"Rhea? Is that you?" I ask before the line cuts off.

What the fuck?

I try and redial the number but it doesn't connect, meaning whoever called was on a cell like mine. They scramble the information to make the call untraceable. So surely, it can't have been Rhea, right? That wouldn't make sense. The whimper was definitely female, like she'd been crying.

Fuck.

I dial Pete.

"Hey Stark, everything okay?"

"No, I'm pretty certain that Rosalie has just called my cell."

Chapter 17

Rhea

I have discovered more in the past two weeks than I have in my entire life. Banks has kept me by his side throughout everything and if I'm being honest, I think I'm traumatized.

Hearing all the behind the scenes of his company only confirmed my darkest thoughts.

There is so much torture, destruction and animosity in the world that means this business is a fully fledged profitable market. It sickens me to think of the necessity of weaponized vehicles, guns and bombs. They are essential to keep the evil alive.

Banks told me that there is a group of people looking for me, asking if I'd got myself mixed up with some dangerous guys, which I obviously have not.

Or so I'd thought.

The first time I'd tried to escape, I managed to get as far as the corridor before I was jumped by two men. They pinned me to the floor with handcuffs, apparently expecting me to try and flee.

The second time I'd tried to escape, was in Banks' house. He allowed me my own bedroom, fully kitted out with jewels and sparkles.

To any other woman who hadn't witnessed what I had, it'd be dreamy. But instead, it was like my worst nightmare. Confirmation I was back there. With him.

I tore the curtains from the four poster bed and tied them together, attaching them to the marble pillars. I descended from the bedroom window, not realizing I was about to drop down by the main entrance.

It was perfect timing for them, they caught me the second that my feet hit the ground.

The third time, gave me hope. I'd been searching for keys in Banks' office, now that my windows are graciously locked, and ended up being trapped in the room with Banks and his security.

I hid within his coat store in the office, waiting for them to leave, but what I could hear was much more interesting.

My ears pricked at the sound of his name. Him, who I've been missing ever since. According to Jimmy (Banks' security), Devon Stark was part of a team that was set on looking for me, to save me. Of course, their concern was taking them down, eliminating them one by one. But, it gave me hope. It made me realize that Stark actually valued our friendship, he wanted to protect me and take me back.

I have no idea what any of my friends are thinking, I have no idea what 'loose ends' Banks has tied up in order to keep a missing persons report from going wild.

I don't have a phone anymore, I'm not allowed access to online and I can't leave the house unless it's with Banks himself or three of his guys. So, to avoid spending more time with Banks, I stay here, locked away.

It's oddly like a Rapunzel situation, being held captive and waiting for my Prince Charming to come and rescue me. But throw a few guns, torture and evil into the mix.

Once they'd left the office, I searched through the file that the security had left on the desk, I knew I was cutting it close. I flipped the pages until I came across his sweet, mysterious face.

They'd been breaking him down, discovering information about him. I didn't get chance to read over the profile fully, but the second I'd found a contact number on the form, I did what any sane person would do.

I called him.

What I didn't expect, was for me to get choked up about it.

Hearing his voice was so comforting, I'd forgotten what it'd felt like. To be laughing and joking alongside him, to bicker over who was taking the landing, to hear his questions about the symbolism of the seeds I gifted him every flight.

To others, we probably didn't seem that personally connected. We never had the opportunity to spend time together outside of work, but we'd sit together at breakfast at the hotels, eat lunch together and pass each other in the gym.

It was so minuscule, but to me it felt like a budding rose. Over time, the longer the sun shines, the repeated watering, the care and attention, we could have blossomed into something else entirely.

As you can probably tell, I haven't had much to think about these past few weeks other than what I'm missing out on, what I'd taken for granted. It's the butterfly effect, wondering if I hadn't gone out that night, would I be here? If I didn't take the job at Titan, would I be missing him? Would we have crossed paths either way? If we'd have had more time, would we have grown into something more?

Who knows.

That's the joy and devastation of life. Never being able to suspect what's going to happen next. Never being able to control it. Never knowing what could have happened.

Oh, how I'm struggling without my usual methods of relaxation. I hope my plants are still alive, I would hate to see them wither away, similarly to how I am now.

And now, I'm cooped up in this bedroom with no curtains surrounding my bed, no answers and nobody around the help me.

A soft knock on my door and I instantly know it's Lois, the house maid.

"Breakfast, deary." She says with her British accent.

Her warm eyes peer over at me, her hair swept beautifully into a bun, not a piece out of place. She wears an apron over her clothing, smeared with different colored substances. She continues watching me and I let out a sigh. She enters the room and closes my door behind her, her feet padding across the carpet as she nears.

She sinks down onto the bed beside me, smoothing my hair as I curl up into my pillow.

"Another hard day?" Her face is so genuinely sweet.

Her plump cheeks and warm complexion remind me so much of my grandmother. Her adoration and attention towards me have me spiraling into history, being a child and sitting in my grandmother's arms. The blanket of protection, the snuggles and forehead kisses. I miss her so much.

"Oh lovey, I know there isn't much I can do, but I decided to make you your favorite dish to accompany your breakfast." My ears prick at the sound of 'favorite dish'.

"Blueberry surprise?" My eyes grow wide and my mouth begins to salivate.

One thing I've struggled with is my eating, or lack thereof. The clothes provided for me fit comfortably when I arrived; now they hang off my hips.

"With extra whipped cream." She beams at me, placing her hand

Chapter 17

on my arm and rubbing it slightly.

"Lois, can I– Could I ask you something?" I hesitate.

Lois was around when me and Banks grew up, she served his father back then. It seems that Banks slipped straight into his father's shoes, and turned out to be even worse.

"Of course, deary." I ponder on my question for a few moments, unsure how to ask it.

"I just– I wanted to know if– If you think Banks could, has, changed?" I bite my lip and look down nervously.

"Oh, um, well, I don't really think it's my place to–"

"No, of course. That was wrong of me. I'm sorry to put you in an awkward situation." I smile sheepishly, beginning to rise from the bed.

"But, as a mother myself, my unbiased opinion would be that I would not want my daughter anywhere near a guy like Banks." She nods her head at me and stands up.

I eye her cautiously and nod my head knowingly. She may not be my own mother, but her advice I would trust. Her opinion is worth a lot to me, she's seen the good, the bad and the ugly.

"Now let's go and get you some of that blueberry surprise, you're about to become all skin and bone!" She chuckles and links arms with me.

I squeeze her arm reassuringly. We both know so much, without having to say words. This conversation, stays between us.

Chapter 18

Devon

I've taken a leave of absence from work. I can't concentrate without her, I need to get my priorities figured out. I've been a pilot for over a decade and I spent almost two months with her and now I'm some sort of love-sick puppy.

It also made more sense to invest time into tracking down Banks again, there is a girl missing.

Strangely enough, there hasn't been a missing person's report filed anywhere. We've checked numerous police databases and nothing has flagged up, meaning she has no family or friends, or more than likely, he's covered his tracks.

We've sat for too long.

Not being able to take action and waiting is one of the hardest parts of this job. Knowing you have the resources to help, but biding the time until it's the right time to use them.

"Pete, I think I've found them!" Dan shouts up, capturing our attention.

The sounds of chairs scraping and feet shuffling fill the room as we gather around Dan.

"I managed to crack the server to find the closest radio signal to the phone call that Stark received. I reverse inputted the data and used the Lowell system, it brought me here." We watch his finger guide us over the page and onto the map with the red location marker.

"Then I reviewed nearby properties, ruling out possibilities. It was then I'd came across a property that was purchased by an LLC and I hacked into their accounts. It revealed Steele's headquarter address on the files, meaning that Steele owns this LLC, therefore, this property." He finishes, practically breathless.

I meet Pete's eyes to see him staring right back at me.

"We've got him." I say.

"We've got him." he responds, a smirk on his face.

* * *

Hours of planning, packing and conversations, meant that we were able to formulate our attack. We got hold of the blueprints of the property, staff lists and surrounding residents.

It seems that this is Banks' safe house. A place that none of his clients are aware of, his personal residence, I suppose.

It's in a quiet estate in Dallas, Texas, away from his turmoil and destruction that he causes around the world.

For us, we get to kill two birds with one stone. Well, save one and kill one.

There is nothing that compares to the pre-attack buzz. It's like being high on serotonin and adrenaline at the same time, the confidence within me is about to burst into a firework of catastrophe.

Let him fucking burn for everything he has done and let me be the one to light the flame.

"Men, do you have everything? Bulletproof vests, night vision goggles and helmets? Tyson has loaded the van with the weapons and ammo, you just each need to make sure you bring your own fitted, personal equipment. It's gonna be a long ride." Pete calls out.

I grab my backpack with my gear in, slipping my laptop into the opening. I double-check the front pocket to see if they're still there. Yup. My orchid seeds. My good luck charm.

I'd be lying if it doesn't torture me every day, knowing she's out there somewhere, living her life as if I'd never happened. I mean yeah, we kind of didn't really 'happen', but there was something there and I'm not a man who knows too much about feelings.

Sometimes people come into your life for a reason, even if it is for a short while. I'm glad I got to experience that with her, though. It was like she was this spiritual awakening in me, she sparked a joy in me that had remained untouched for years.

At this point, I feel like I'd give anything to have the universe draw us back together, to have our paths cross over again. The likelihood of it happening the first time was small enough, the chances of it happening again are next to none. I'd begun to hope, to imagine what life would be like if I shared it alongside someone else.

But not just anyone, with Rhea.

If I could turn back time, I'd have given it more effort. I'd have pushed myself to break down my barriers, to welcome her with open arms and give her a chance at seeing the real me.

None of it feels real, that one second she was beside me and we had months of training together and now, she's gone.

Maybe, I'm not worthy of a great love. Maybe, this was the universe's way of telling me that I will never be enough. Maybe, it was a big fat, *fuck you.*

I'd never wanted that life, never wanted the happy ending, I didn't care enough.

A drop of her was like I'd been swallowed by the oceans. A flicker of her sparked a fire in me, that continued burning long after she'd left. Still burning.

"Stark, you good?" Locke calls over to me.

"Yeah, man. Just prepping." I hold up my helmet in defense whilst he nods in response.

Fuck, I'm so up in my own head lately.

Swinging my backpack over my shoulder, I grab my hard case and wheel it to the exit. The guys are all shuffling in and out, separating us and the equipment into three vans.

We take our work very seriously, with no slip-ups available. Pete is incredible at what he does, he was ranked incredibly high in the military as an Operations Officer. Each one of us brings our expertise and each individual undergoes a specific training regime before being granted access to the team.

"Devon, you take the van with Locke, Smithy, Dan and Nate." Pete shouts over.

I look for their faces and make my way over the van, throwing my stuff in the open trunk.

"Nate's driving, I called shotgun" Smithy shoves my shoulder with his, displaying his missing teeth.

Smithy was discharged from the army after stepping on a landmine, losing his sight and hearing in the left side of his head. Despite his disability, he has impeccable composure and picks up on more than what we do with both. He says that it gave him the ability to hyper-focus and a level of concentration that can only be unlocked after losing some of your senses.

"Looks like we're in the back, Stark." Locke rolls his eyes and gestures his thumb to the back door.

"Oh, come on man. We're not *that* bad." Dan jokes, swinging his arm over Locke's shoulder.

"All I'm asking, is that you keep your weird questions about my wife to yourself, and then we'll be good." Locke folds his arms and peers back at Dan.

"It's not every day that a guy marries a guy, who then becomes his wife later on. I'm just intrigued, is all." Dan argues, trying to sound genuine.

"Dan, take your arm off my shoulders before I take it for good." He threatens.

Dan retaliates by pulling him in tighter and rubs his knuckles on the top of Locke's head, scuffing his hair. Locke pulls at him to try and get out of his headlock, swinging Dan around with him.

"Hey everyone look, I've got Locke in a headlock!" He shouts, laughing obnoxiously.

"Boys, boys! Stop it, you're drawing attention!" Pete bellows as they draw apart.

"You're dead meat, Dan." Locke scowls at him and then climbs into the van.

"It's probably best if I sit in the middle of you both." I huff and climb in, sliding into the middle.

"Thank you." Locke whispers and I offer a dry laugh in return.

"Okay boys, road trip time!" Dan cheers, slamming the van door shut.

We all grown in unison, knowing we have to put up with Dan for the next eleven hours.

Nate starts up the van and we follow behind Pete's truck, Killian's truck following ours.

I readjust myself in the seat to try and get comfortable, as much as I can in between two bulky, muscular men. I close my eyes, thinking

Chapter 18

about the only girl who seems to keep me grounded.

A loud gurgling sound breaks my train of thought and I open my eyes to find where it came from. We all turn to Dan.

"Ugh, sorry guys. I had Taco Bell before I came and I'm not feeling too good." He cups his stomach and closes his eyes.

This is going to be the longest journey of my life.

Chapter 19

Rhea

I've been allowed out into the garden, along with three unknown men.

I prefer to refer to them as Bubbles, Buttercup and Blossom. My own little fantasy of the *Power-puff Girls*.

It helps with the anxiety that comes with having huge men crowd over you whilst you plant your orchids.

It's been more peaceful than usual, Banks has been away on a business trip, meaning I've had a little more free reign than when he's home. But, that ends today. He's flying back home, no doubt full of anger and frustration.

I'm absolutely terrified.

He's been, how can I say this… fine. Yeah, *fine*.

He's also had no real work events though, and I know this one was a big deal.

The first couple of weeks were strange, he kept his distance as if to

Chapter 19

allow me time to 'settle in', even though I was essentially *stolen* from my life. He kind of gave me a little hope, a small amount, just enough to make it bearable to survive.

Without Lois, I wouldn't have been able to keep going.

Not having my therapist, Ezra, I've found writing in my journal to be the better way to express how I'm feeling. I keep the journal hidden under the mattress, a gift from Lois. She is the only one who changes my sheets so she's discreet about it, placing it right back where I'd left it. I don't even think I'd care if she'd read it. It was pretty embarrassing to have to reveal my bloody sheets and ask if there was any tampons, so I've broken that dignity seal with her.

"Ma'am, your two hours in the garden are up." A deep voice echoes from behind me.

I shovel some more soil around the flowerbed, ignoring him. This is the only time that I get, the only time I have to be me, truly me.

"Ma'am, I said your–"

"Yes, I heard you the first time." I groan, reaching for my mini rake.

Just as I'm about to grasp hold of it, a thick gloved hand wraps around my wrist, tearing me away from it. I gasp and whip my head around to him.

"That means, your time is up, Princess." he growls. I can't even see his face through his mask, but I can see his vile smirk.

"Listen, Buttercup. Take your fucking hands off me before I scream bloody murder!" I seethe with anger as his grip tightens. I pull back, trying to release myself from him.

"I'll put a bullet through your brain before you even get the chance, sunshine." His deep laugh ripples through me, causing the sweat to pool at my lower back.

"Jesse, that's enough." Blossom barks.

Buttercup turns his head towards the guy behind him, dragging my wrist with him, pulling me along with floor slightly. I wince at the pain and use it as my opportunity to break free, kicking him straight in the ankle as he lets out a howl.

I scramble to my feet and set off into a sprint towards the driveway.

I need to get out. I need to escape. Their footsteps are heavy behind me, curse words being thrown around like confetti.

My bare feet burn against the paving as the scorching Texan sun tortures me.

Oh, *fuck*.

Fuck. Fuck. Fuck.

The driveway is complete gravel, meaning it will destroy the soles of my feet and slow me down. Come on, Rhea, *think*.

I scan my surroundings, looking for an alternative.

The trellis.

I sprint off in the other direction, away from the driveway and closer to the tall brick wall. The trellis coats the majority of the wall and I throw myself at it, gripping onto the wooden particles as if my life depended on it.

My life *does* depend on it.

Clawing my way upwards, my heart races faster than my legs can move. I climb higher and my hand grips onto the concrete slab of the wall.

Yes, I'm here.

I prepare to swing my leg over the –

I'm yanked downwards by a fierce and painful grip on my ankle as I let out a blood-curdling scream. I tumble down and land on top of one of them, the reality of it sinking in. I swear, my heart hurts more than my ankle right now.

I was *so* close.

Too close.

My eyes fill with tears as the men rearrange their uniform, panting and relieved. I lay on the grass, my arms limp at my sides as I peer up

Chapter 19

at the clouds above. The clouds that I once flew in. The clouds that gave me the freedom, that I now don't have. The clouds that remind me of *him*.

Our clouds.

"And, what the fuck is going on here?" The voice demands.

I close my eyes, allowing the tears free reign. More free than I will ever be.

"Sir, she's an absolute nutcase. She just tried to climb that plant wall thing as if she was fucking Tarzan." Buttercup spits, peering down at me and then back at his boss.

"Rosalie?" he prompts, expecting an explanation from me.

I stay silent.

"Get her back up to her fucking room, I'll deal with you lot later." Banks shakes his head in disgust, storming away, back to his car.

"Get me in trouble again and I'll make you fucking pay." Buttercup yanks me up by my arm, barely giving me time to get my balance.

The other two stay silent as he marches me inside.

* * *

I pick at my food, shoving it around the plate with my fork. Banks sits across from me, nose deep in his phone. I let my eyes gaze upon him for a second too long.

"What?" He looks up at me, his eyes as cold as ice.

"Nothing." I drop my head and look into my lap, the grip on my fork faltering, causing it to clatter to my plate.

I startle and grab hold of it again.

"Is something the matter with you?" Banks scans my face, looking irritated.

"No." I mutter, picking at my food again.

"You know, I've tried to be really fucking nice to you. All you give me is hassle and one-word answers. This is not the Rosalie I remember, you used to be so full of life, you loved me." His voice catches at the end.

I meet his eyes and he stares at me. For a split second, he was my Banks. And then his eyes return to Steele.

"Fuck, Rosalie!" He shouts, slamming his hands down on the table and knocking his wine over in the process.

My body jolts as I cower, trying to shrink away from him, from this. My mind spins in all different directions, panic and terror swallows me.

He flexes his jaw as Lois comes rushing into the dining room, a horrified look on her face.

"Sir, let me grab a cloth for that." She rushes around the room as Banks is fixated on me, his skin shining under the chandelier.

"Just bring me another glass and a bottle of Domaine Leroy Chambertin Grand Cru." He speaks without moving his eyes from me.

I don't dare to look away from him, fearful that the second I do, he's going to pounce. Every hair on my body stands up straight, the sweat trailing down my spine.

Lois practically runs back into the dining room with a glass and the requested bottle of wine. She corks it open and begins filling it.

"Fill it all the way." He spits, the deathly evil sits comfortably behind his eyes.

I gulp heavily as my legs begin to shake with trepidation.

Lois leaves the bottle by his side and escapes the room, offering me one last glance of sympathy.

"Drink." He says, pushing the glass forward to me.

I shake my head.

"Drink the fucking wine." He grits, bearing his teeth.

"I'm not thirsty." I squeak, my voice betraying how utterly fucking terrified I am of him.

His chair scrapes back as he rises from it, my body erupting into shivers. I breathe deeply through my nostrils, the pace picking up to match my thumping heart.

He slowly walks around to my side of the table, but I'm unable to follow him. My eyes remain possessed by his chair. The fear of my fate being in his hands is too much to bare.

The wine glass is pushed further in front of me as he crouches down to his knees beside me, the strong scent of him confirming my worst nightmares.

"Drink the wine, Rosie." He deadpans.

I dare to glance at him, the veins in his neck piercing the surface. Allowing my strength to subside, I falter. Pick and choose your battles, Rhea.

Gripping the wine glass, I bring it up to my lips shakily, taking a sip of it, the richness and fruitiness, playfully caressing my tongue. I lower the glass, my eyes watering.

"All of it, peach." He smirks at me, watching the fear he inflicts on me fires him up.

He loves this. I stood up to him, which nobody does, so he thinks I've disrespected him. Now, he wants to reassert his dominance, prove who has the power here.

I close my eyes and gulp at the thick liquid, wishing that it would wash me away with it.

"Good girl." His hand presses into my thigh and I jump at the contact, spilling some of the wine onto his white shirt.

He looks downwards at the stain as it spreads wider, seeping into the material.

"Oh, Rosie, look at the mess you've made." He tuts, shaking his head. My eyes are wide with fear.

"I can't sit in this dirty shirt now, can I? How about you help me take it off?" He stands to his full height, towering over me.

Why? Why give him the excuse, Rhea?

"Come on, it's nothing you haven't seen before." Not that he'd ever let me forget.

Right now, I want to grab my dinner knife and plunge it straight into the wine stain on his chest. And I'm not a violent person.

He steps forward so his crotch is in my eye line, I shift my eyes upwards.

My hand shakes as I twist and reach forward, closer to his body. My pulse drums in my ear and every part of my body is coated with sweat as I make contact. I fumble with the buttons, trying to unbutton them as fast as possible to avoid his proximity for longer than necessary.

"Oof, easy tiger." He chuckles to himself, my inner being cowers at his obnoxious behavior.

The shirt parts, displaying his tanned and toned midriff, the same canvas of tattoos across his entire body. The same tattoos that I witnessed him get, the same body I used to caress with these hands. Now, two different universes apart.

He slips the shirt off, revealing the rest of the artwork. Each and every part intricately designed and stunning in their own way.

"Rosie." He whispers, running a hand through my hair. I look up at him, the softness of his face breaks my heart, again. His original scowl has eased, a gentle smile takes over.

"Kiss me." The lightness in his tone, strokes my ears.

My mouth dries, causing me to swallow harshly.

This is so beyond wrong, he's using my weaknesses against me. He knows me too well, which is the worst part. He knows exactly what I loved about him before, how to press my buttons and get whatever he wants out of me. It's not happening this time.

Chapter 19

He lowers his face to mine, his warm breath spreads across my cheeks.

"Mr Steele, we have an emergency– Oh. Shit. I'm sorry." A guy in a suit waltzes in through the dining room door. Saved by the fucking bell.

My body relaxes and I slump back in my chair as Banks collects his discarded shirt from the floor.

"Coming. Don't think I'm finished with you yet." He leans down and presses his lips against my temple, I flinch in response.

He steps away and follows after the man, leaving me alone in the dining room.

The air instantly thins, allowing me to breathe freely.

I reach forward and grab the bottle of wine, pouring it into my glass and taking large gulps of it.

I finish the glass and fill it up again, with whatever is left in the bottle. Banks may be a psychotic asshole but he does have a brilliant wine selection.

The alcohol buzzes through my system, taking quick action due to the lack of food I've been eating.

The door to the dining room pulls open and I freeze in my tracks, panicked that he's back.

One of the guards from earlier walks in, remaining by the door and keeping a watchful eye on me.

"Ah, Bubbles. I wondered when I'd get to enjoy your company again." I raise my glass to him, giggling to myself.

If this situation is the most depressing thing in my life, the least I can do is try and enjoy the little parts of it that can bring me joy.

Bubbles stays silent, his arms crossed as he leans against the wall, watching me drink away my sorrows.

"Cat got your tongue today, Bubbles?" I stand up, swaying slightly and sloshing the wine in my glass.

I swig the glass to my mouth and pour the rest of it, dribbling it slightly onto the plush carpets.

"Oops, poor Mr. Banks will have to get that cleaned up!" I laugh, placing the empty glass onto the table.

"Oh, Bubbles. Would you be ever so kind, and take me to my cell." I sigh, nearing him.

I can't tell if it's the wine or my lack of intimacy, but I'm kind of digging the cargo pants and military boots.

"You seem like a loyal servant, my sweet, Bubbles." I giggle and stand up in front of him, his height and frame surrounding me.

He takes a step forward and opens the door, allowing me to pass through first.

"Bubbles! Such a gentleman!" I dance past him, making my way towards the staircase. He follows after me, escorting me to my room.

"You know, I didn't ask for any of this, right?" I chat away whilst I'm walking.

"Girls don't ask to be kidnapped by their psycho abusive exes, it's not some horny fantasy that others may think it is. This is soul-destroying." I whine as we walk side by side along the corridor, to get to my wing.

We reach my room and I try to push the door open, failing dramatically.

"Help me, Bubbles." I pout my lips at him as he towers over me, his bulky arms swallowing me up. He smells incredible, a musky delight.

"What have we got under all of this armor?" I smirk, trailing my finger along the bulletproof vest.

I can't see his face, all that is visible is his mouth and his sharp jawline. His yummy-looking jawline. My finger follows upwards until it reaches his bare skin, the touch of it is silky smooth until I reach his dark stubble.

I swear, I don't know what has gotten into me, but I can't stop myself.

Bubbles stands there, deathly still. He appears to be staring down at me, his face stone cold and unresponsive.

The second my finger traces over his plump lips, he pins my arms above my head, forcing me backwards onto the door.

I lose my breath and pant helplessly. I can't ignore the sensation that has begun to take over my lower region.

My mouth salivates as he presses his body into mine, I can barely feel him through his layers but it only tempts me more.

His breath sweeps across my face, causing my eyes to flutter closed. He's enticing me to the point I want nothing more than for him to jump me right now.

He licks his lips, his tongue wetting them and inviting me for a taste.

I part my mouth and try my hardest to see through the glossy black windows that hide his eyes.

Within a second, he's opened my bedroom door and he's pushing me inside.

I gasp at the sudden movement and stumble backwards, unsure of what he's about to do. He retrieves the key for my bedroom out of his pocket and locks the door behind him, securing us inside.

Together.

What I didn't expect, was for him to remove his helmet.

What more I didn't expect, was who was beneath it.

Chapter 20

Devon

My heart races as I remove my helmet, revealing myself to her. She gasps in disbelief as I ruffle my hair. My face and hair are sweaty from being masked in it for the last few hours.

This, was not part of the plan. She, was not part of the plan. In all honesty, I don't have a fucking clue what is going on here.

We plan for everything, we rule out any possibilities and have solutions before the problems have arisen. This, her, is inconceivable. My brain feels like it's turned to mush. She, turns me into putty.

Did I think when we took out one of the guards and took his place, that I was going to come face to face with Rhea fucking Jensen. No. Or, whatever her name is, I don't fucking know anything anymore.

"Devon." Her voice speaks my name softly.

The second I set foot into the dining room, I wanted to bolt, or sweep her up into my arms and kiss her, I don't know. I'm struggling to understand the situation, all of the information that I've been given over the past few weeks, is actually... Rhea. Meaning, Banks is her ex, she is the one who was in the bar, she is the one who was roofied and kidnapped. *Fuck*, this is insane.

I can't tell you how much I wanted to burst out laughing at her crazy, chatty self. I've missed her so fucking much. I've missed everything about her, she's *everything*.

"Bubbles?" I raise an eyebrow at her and her eyes spill over with tears as she throws her arms around my neck, attaching to me like a koala.

I scoop her up and bury my face into her neck, smelling the sweetness of her hair. We squeeze each other tightly, afraid that if we let go, we will disappear.

"I can't believe you're here." She sobs into me.

I tear off my gloves and throw them to the floor, threading my hands into her hair and pulling her against me.

"Rhea, I've missed you, so fucking much." I whisper into her neck, closing my eyes.

Her body vibrates as she continues to cry into me. I have no clue what the hell has gone on here, but I don't want to imagine it right now.

Despite this being completely off plan, we still need to stick to the plan, which takes place tomorrow.

I loosen my grip on her and pull my face back as she lifts hers. Our eyes meet and we stare between us, my eyes flicking to and from each of hers. They glisten under the moonlight from the window, searching mine for something.

I flick my eyes to her lips, a slight red stain to them from the wine she's had. My nostrils flare as I alternate between her eyes and her lips, drawing me in as I'm desperate for a taste.

Before I even get a chance to consider what I want to do, she slams her lips against mine. My eyes roll to the back of my head as the softness of her lips push against mine, igniting a fire across my entire body.

She parts her lips as I dip my tongue into her mouth, the bitterness of the wine still fresh. I cup the back of her neck, bringing her deeper to me.

For years, I've been lost and until now, I didn't realize that she had been my lighthouse. She has given me my second chance at life, the opportunity to walk the right path and find my way back home.

A tear slips from the corner of my eye as we indulge in each other, tasting and teasing our tongues.

This is not a matter of battling, this is a matter of waving the white flag. We are conforming and joining together, a union of two souls, desperate to survive and only the fusion of us, grants us the opportunity to live.

I don't ever want to let go, she is addicting, rewarding and goddamn perfect.

She pulls away completely breathless, glancing at my face before she sighs and places her lips back on mine. I explore her body with my hands, one hand at her head and the other brushing her side.

I stagger forwards and push her up against the wall as she tries to wrap her legs tightly around me, my armor making it more difficult. I delve into her mouth again, fulfilling my every desire and implanting my love into her with every tender touch.

I pull away, but not too much, pressing my forehead to hers as we pant together.

"My God, Rhea." I sigh, her lashes fanning against my cheeks.

"Devon, there are some things you need to know–"

"I know baby, I know." I try to shush her by pressing another peck to her lips, barely being able to resist being away from them.

Chapter 20

"My name isn't—"

"I know, Rhea. I know." I kiss her lips again, the plush feeling of her silky lips against mine proves irresistible.

We stay like that for a while, staring into each other's eyes, sharing kisses and bumping noses. I can't get enough of her.

"How did this happen? How are you here?" She murmurs, lost in thought.

"There is too much to say right now, but I will tell you everything, as soon as were out of here." I nudge my nose against hers.

"When?" She breathes.

"Tomorrow, hang tight until tomorrow baby." I reply, hating the thought of having to part ways with her and not take her home right this second.

This is why we avoid getting involved in personal situations. If we'd have known it was her, they wouldn't have sent me in, they would have had Locke onto it. But if anything, I'm grateful that it was me, knowing I'm getting to share this moment with her.

"I have so much to say to you." I pant, my heart aching with the need to profess how I feel.

"Me too, so much." She presses her lips to mine, like pouring flammable liquid onto an, already burning, fire.

"You're strong, Rhea. So strong. Stay strong for me." I squeeze her tightly, finding it difficult to let go.

"Please, come back for me." She sobs, letting her mask slip.

"Of course, I'm going to be right here. I'll stay with you whilst you fall asleep, okay?" I nudge her nose again with mine and she nods her head eagerly.

I pull away from the wall, gripping onto her legs and waist as I back her onto the four-poster bed. I pull back the covers, allowing her to get comfortable. She settles herself in and I draw the blankets back over her.

I dip into the other side of the bed as she turns over to face me, reaching out to grab me. I lay on my back and grab a pillow to cover my armor, I can't imagine it to be the most comfortable thing to sleep on. She rests her head on top of the pillow on my chest and entwines her legs with mine, wrapping her arm around my waist.

I place my hand on her bare arm, brushing the skin softly and watching the goosebumps that arise in response. I smile to myself, feeling my heart fill with a burning passion to love her with all of my being.

"Thank you, Devon." Her voice barely audible as she drifts off into a sleep.

I already know that as soon as we leave this place, we have a whole entire new world to explore, and we're going to love every second of it.

Chapter 21

Rhea

I'm not surprised, but devastated, to wake up in my bed alone this morning.

This seems like some crazy fever dream that Devon was actually here.

Wait, he was, wasn't he? I wasn't conjuring up some mad fantasy about bubbles after too much wine, surely?

I rub my eyes and sit upright in the bed, the sheets pooling at my waist. I bring my fingers up to my lips and trace them carefully, knowing they hold my special secret of Devon Stark.

I can't stop the warm feeling that spreads throughout my body at the thought of him here, in this room with me. I didn't think that what I felt for him was, *this*.

The second I saw him, the urge to kiss him was too much to deny.

After suffering for weeks with Banks and his ways, it made me crave the affection and adoration that he couldn't offer.

I look like an idiot right now, with the huge grin across my face. I think it's the first time I've smiled and truly meant it.

I kissed Devon Stark, and I loved it.

"Rosalie dear, breakfast is ready!" Lois sings, tapping at my door gently.

"I'll be down in five, Lois!" I chirp, practically jumping out of bed with my newfound energy.

This is a completely different atmosphere as to what I've experienced since being here. For once, I'm filled with happiness and hope that there is still good in this world.

I pull a hoodie over my t-shirt and change into some comfortable sweats. My blonde hair is in desperate need of some TLC.

Practically skipping out of my room and down to the dining room, my body bursts with delight, prepared for what today will bring.

I stop in my tracks at the visual of Banks sitting at the table, a coffee in one hand and his phone in the other. He looks just as pristine as normal, his suit crisp and tailored to perfection.

He looks up, his eyes meeting mine.

"It's a fine morning isn't it, Rosalie?" He smirks at me and raises his brows, whilst sipping on his coffee.

My face drops and I feel myself retreating back to the person I was before Devon showed up. Lacking in all areas of confidence and afraid of him. I flit my eyes around the room, unsure why he's decided to have breakfast with me on this morning, of all mornings.

"Come, sit. We have big plans to discuss." He smiles lazily and gestures to the seat in front of him, an array of pleasantries litter the center of the table.

Poor, Lois. She must have been awake since the crack of dawn to prepare all of this.

I gingerly take a step forward, my body struggling to mask it's uncertainty. His eyes follow me like a hawk, the unease spreading throughout me. Something, is going on.

Pulling back the chair, it scrapes against the solid wood flooring and I sit myself down, my body stiff.

"Eat, indulge." He waves his hand at the food and returns to his phone, tapping away.

I scan the options before me, each piece sickeningly sweet and sinful. Shakily, I snatch a blueberry muffin, placing it on the plate before me, not interested in eating it at all. Right now, my stomach is churning and twisting with anxiety. 'Big plans', he said.

"You know, you used to adore when I would put all of this effort into having breakfast with you." He sighs, placing his phone down and leaning forward with his elbows propped up on the table.

He, put effort into this? This is Lois' hard work, not his. I hardly consider it an 'effort' to order someone around and show his face.

"That, was before." I retort.

The door opens behind me and Buttercup, Blossom and Bubbles (Devon), line up along the wall, looking every bit as intimidating as they're meant to.

"Rosie, baby. I think I need to address the elephant in the room. Yes, some things happened between us that I'm not proud of, but you can't throw us away because of some silly mistakes. We have so much history, as well as an amazing future ahead of us. I can give you everything you could ever ask for, I'm the full package." He flexes his jaw and leans back, crossing his arms.

Is he being serious? Everything that he has just said has the sirens in my head screaming. That was nothing close to an apology, barely even an acknowledgment of the suffering and trauma he put me through. He thinks he can buy my affection as his way of covering up the abuse and turmoil of our relationship. I can barely string a sentence together, I'm stunned speechless.

"How can I make it up to you? I know you're weary with me but I want us to go back to how we were before. I miss you, I miss *us*."

"There is no 'us', Banks. I don't even want to be here, you abducted me against my will and have three bodyguards to ensure I can't escape. I am a prisoner. This is not some sort of sick relationship where you can convince me to love you. I want to go home." My heart aches, thinking of my bedroom and my cozy nights with Fizzy, the life I was stolen from.

The smile on his face only deepens, he's fucking laughing at me. My eyes threaten to spill tears, but I won't spare any at his expense.

"Rosie, you've always been a little feisty. It's one of the things I love about you. But, your not some sort of damsel in distress. There is no prince charming to come and rescue you from the big bad wolf." He claps his hands together, continuing to laugh at me.

I swallow harshly, distraught at his disregard for my feelings. He has always gas-lit me in the worst ways, making me feel completely inferior. But, I've escaped once, and I'll do it again.

"Besides, we have an amazing trip planned. A month long vacation on a private island in the Indian Ocean, mm I can smell the tropical beach already. It's the perfect opportunity for us to rekindle and right our wrongs."

"I'm sorry?" He's completely caught me off guard.

I hear one of the men behind me shift, I'm assuming it's Devon. Banks glances at them and then back at me, a murderous grin across his face.

"It's just going to be me and you, Rosie. And our defense squad of course." He waves his hand at the men behind me and my body begins to ease slightly, knowing that if our escape plan can't take place tonight, I won't be on my own.

"Banks, I appreciate the gesture but, no thank you." My voice is quiet and timid, I just want to be out of here to go back to my life, the life I chose.

Chapter 21

"I'm afraid it wasn't really a matter of asking, I was telling you what our plans are. Now, I'd appreciate it if you could return to your room and pack up your few belongings. I've had a private shopper pick out something a little more suited to the occasion. Oh, you are going to look so appetizing, Rosie." He licks his lips, leaning over the side of the table and scanning the expanse of my legs.

Everything feels like it's striking me at once. All of the anger, frustration and torment I've experienced in these weeks is beginning to bubble up to the surface. How much longer am I able to keep up this facade? All I'm doing is biding my time before he strikes, and he will. It's Banks, he may be a complete asshole but I'd never take him for being stupid.

"I'm not really feeling up to it, honestly." I shrug and begin to pull apart my muffin, not bothering to actually eat any of it.

"Oh, but I have so much planned. It will be the best vacation of your life, Rosalie. I promise you." Like his promises mean shit.

"May I be excused?" I dust off my hands on my legs and wait for his response.

"You may, as long as it's to go and pack." He laughs and reaches his hand forward to find mine.

I freeze as he interlocks his fingers with mine, the same dread filling me up from my toes to my head.

"Just give me a chance, okay?" His lips thin into a tight smile and he squeezes my fingers gently.

I peer up at him, feeling ten times smaller than his frame, his hand encapsulating mine.

Offering a curt nod, I realize I have absolutely no idea what I'm agreeing to. I know one thing is for certain, I need to get back to my room and I need Devon to come with me.

"Can I have someone help me pack? I just want to get a shower and freshen up." I lie through my teeth.

"Sure, of course. Lorenzo, do you mind?" His eyes are trained on the three men, but I can't pin point who he's asked.

I turn my head to look at them, Devon's height overpowering the other two. Nobody moves, silence.

"Lorenzo?" Banks asks again, his impatience wearing thin.

That's when Devon slowly nods, he obviously wasn't aware which one of the guards he had replaced and judging from the silence, it was Lorenzo.

"Brilliant, now run along, Rosie. Big plans, remember?" Banks beams at me, setting me free of his grasp.

I practically jump out of my chair and tuck it back in, scurrying out of the room with Devon in tow.

The second the door to the dining room closes, I rush into him. I wrap my arms around his bulletproof vest and rest my head against it, wishing I could hear his beating heart. I couldn't wait, I needed his comfort and his familiarity before I turn completely insane. He returns the embrace, but is quick to push me away.

"Not here." He whispers, grasping my hand and tugging me through the corridor towards the staircase.

We speed-walk to my room, slamming the door shut behind us. He removes his helmet and it reveals his divine face, his long lashes and dark features. I just want to caress his jaw with my thumb and taste his luscious lips again. I want to be wrapped within his arms without the fear of someone catching us, I want us to be free.

"What the fuck are we going to do?" I pant.

Chapter 22

Devon

I'm starting to doubt if we were even prepared at all for this mission. I've never encountered a single mishap, never mind two within the space of twelve hours. Banks is one sneaky motherfucker, that's for sure.

"Give me an hour, I'll have to try and speak with the rest of the team and see if we can bring the plans forward, try not to worry." I grasp hold of her small hand, caressing it with my thumb.

"Team? There's more of you?" She squeaks. I remember we haven't actually had *that* conversation, yet. I've never had to explain this to anyone, besides the boys. It's different to telling your friend, than to telling your love interest, it isn't like I've got a choice anyway.

"Yeah…" I scratch the back of my neck awkwardly, chewing on my lip.

"I'll ask questions later, we have a grand escape to plan." She chuckles, leaning into me.

The smell of her lavender scent envelopes me, consumes me. I want to bathe in it, allow it to overtake me and mix with my own masculine scent. She's always been so warm and comforting to be around. I don't even think she realizes the affect she has on the people around her, bringing out the best and offering a safe haven from the bigger issues in life.

I'm thankful in these moments that she isn't some emotional wreck, as most other people would be in her situation. The strength she has is unmatched.

"Hang on." I release her hand and begin to dig around in the pockets of my cargo trousers, looking for something that she needs right now.

I pull out the orchid seeds, the packet crumpled and barely readable anymore.

"Take this. Let this be your good luck charm from now on, it looks like you definitely need it." I laugh and gesture to the room, highlighting the situation she's in.

Her eyes are wide and her mouth gapes open at the sight of the packet in my palm.

"Rhea?" I lower my head to try and meet her height, searching her face for answers.

"I– Oh, God. I'm actually gonna cry right now." Her voice breaks at the end of the sentence as she brings her hand up to cover her mouth, to try and mask her sob.

Oh fuck, I didn't mean to upset her. Fuck, I don't know what to do with crying women, especially her. When I'm with her, I don't know which way is up, never mind how to comfort her.

"Shit, I'm sorry. I didn't mean to–"

"No, no. It's just… You kept them." She glances up at me through her water lined eyes.

"Of course I did, why would you think I wouldn't? I mean, it's the most bizarre gift I've ever received, but the most thoughtful too. I'm not into any of that horoscope shit or anything but having these as a little prompt to remain hopeful, is everything I didn't know I needed. *You*, are someone I didn't know I needed." I explain.

"I've never been so direct with anyone in my life, but my God, Devon Stark. I want to jump your bones right now." Her breath hitches as she takes a step closer to me, the pheromones from her body circulating me, torturous and tempting.

"You know, I quite like when you refer to me as your God." I smirk down at her, the adrenaline coursing through my veins.

"I will bow down before you, every… single… time…" She whispers seductively, her hand reaching out and teasing my belt.

I gulp harshly, feeling the rush of heat fill me, at the thought of her on her knees before me. This fucking woman.

She stands on her tiptoes, her hands creeping lower. Every slight graze, every small movement, every breath of hers, unforgiving.

She leans forward, her lips nearing my jaw. "I would worship you with every part of my soul, begging for mercy for the sinful acts I would commit." Her mouth is venom, a poisoned apple that I desperately need a bite of.

I will be praying to the fucking Gods myself if she makes me feel like this, without even encountering her touch.

I blow out a heavy breath, trying to contain myself. The effect she has on me is devastatingly obvious right now, it's so damn hard.

"You're killing me, Rhea." My voice is husky and deep.

"I think it's quite the opposite actually, Captain Stark. I'm offering you savior." She taunts.

Oh my holy *fuck*.

Who knew that such a sweet and innocent face, had such a filthy fucking mouth. If only she knew how badly I want to smear that mouth with my cum and give her something to feel dirty about.

I shift on my feet, the air suddenly not sufficient enough to give me the supply I need. My internal body temperature has catapulted, soaring through the skies whilst I melt into oblivion for flying too close to the sun.

The knock on the door has us scrambling apart as I practically throw my helmet back over my head, not getting chance to tie the chin strap. I suppose a perk of this over-the-top outfit is that my face is covered over, so the guilt and surprise I display is masked.

"Rosalie, dear. Would you like me to help– Oh. I'm sorry, I didn't realize you already had assistance." The lady from the kitchen eyes me, squinting them slightly.

I don't blame her, knowing how intimidating I appear and the morals of the late, Lorenzo. I keep my body faced away from her, knowing that if I turn to face her she doesn't need to see my face. The guilt is tented, heavily, in these pants.

"It's fine, Lois. I'm all good here, thank you though. I really appreciate it." Rhea leans around me, offering a reassuring smile.

"You give me a shout if you need anything, anything at all. Okay?" I don't even have to be looking at her to know she's referencing to me.

Rhea nods enthusiastically, trying to shoo her away. Once the door closes again, my shoulders slump and I groan at the pent up frustration, being so close to her and not being able to delve inside of her.

"We need to be careful, I can't imagine what Banks will do to you if he catches you." She whispers, concern etched in her brows.

"Oh, darling. You should be more worried about what I'm going to do to *him* when I get my opportunity." I smirk down at her, my ego playing out in full force.

"Is that so? Captain Stark is a silent assassin now, is he?" She taunts, the words slipping through her lips easily.

"As it turns out, I am. Darling." I suck my bottom lip behind my teeth as she undresses me with her eyes.

Chapter 22

"You see, Rhea. There may be things about you that you've kept hidden from me but, you don't know the secrets I've been keeping from you..." I bring my arm from my side and trace the lining of her jaw with my index finger, nearing her mouth.

"Once you come into my world, Rhea, you will never be able to leave." I whisper, aligning my face with hers.

"I wouldn't want to leave." She pants, her tongue wet and glistening.

I continue across her face with my index finger and pull her bottom lip down, revealing her teeth. Her tongue darts out, swiping across the tip of my finger. My eyes flutter closed at the sensation of the wetness, the glide of her soft and smooth tongue is only providing me with visuals of it being elsewhere.

"I'm crazy for you, Rhea." I breathe.

Chapter 23

Rhea

Can somebody wake me up from this insane situation? Actually, don't. If this is some wild fantasy of mine, I'll happily remain here until my eyes no longer open and my heart no longer beats.

Devon Stark has just opened my mind to a whole new language, and my feelings along with it.

This odd situation has sparked all kinds of emotions within me, he makes me almost thankful that I've been, tragically, abducted.

I'm the damsel in distress and he is my Prince charming.

Eat your words, Banks.

I can't help but feel completely smug as I'm packing away these clothes, knowing I'm a step ahead of Banks, that I'm already saved.

Devon has arranged to escort me to the gardens this afternoon, my final farewell to the plants that have kept me grounded throughout this state of affairs. It's then we will try to gain some alone time and

Chapter 23

discuss the new plans of my grand escape.

I'd be lying if I said I didn't feel the least bit giddy about it, feeling like I am a main character in a story and this is the role I have to play. I just beg that whoever is writing the story, allows me a happy ending.

Today, most of all, I've missed flying.

I've missed my freedom and the tranquility of being thirty-thousand feet above the rest of the world.

Knowing that I could be back on my original flight path as early as tomorrow has given me a skip in my step. I'm perplexed with positive feelings, each and every one pushing behind me, giving me the drive to keep going.

I shove the last of my clothes into the travel case, not bothering to fold them, it's not like I'll be needing them anyway.

I zip up the case, sitting on top of it to hold it down. I tuck my hair behind my ears, a slight sweat lining the sides of my face from the effort of closing it.

I stand up and place my hands on my hips, feeling triumphant. I saunter over to the dressing table, opening the drawer to reveal the packet of orchid seeds that Devon had given me earlier.

Bringing them out, I perch on the stool, gazing longingly at them.

The emotions that the seeds bring out, remind me of both the good and the bad. When I first found my passion for gardening, I was in such a dark place, alone and lost in the madness of the world. I gave these to Devon to provide him with the same love and support that I had received, and he kept them. Now, they've been returned to me during my time of need. I can't deny that I think this was an act of fate, a reward, some sort of repayment for my kindness.

Escaping from Banks the first time, could have impacted me in the way where I became bitter and angry at the world.

Instead, I used it to fuel me to be *better*, to be *greater* than he ever was. I would not allow what he did to me, shape who I am.

Devon spoke words to me that I've struggled to deal with myself, to truly believe. He told me I was, *strong*.

You know, most girls would swoon over being called beautiful, pretty and gorgeous. But to me, it's all far too generic. It's not personal. It holds no value.

Being told that you're strong is like no other. It screams that they see you, they know the recognition that gives you and their consideration for who you are as a person.

I think, in that moment, I fell in love.

* * *

"What do you mean?" I ask, panic filling my voice.

"We have to leave, now. I don't want any of your bratty behavior, it's essential that we leave now." Banks' stern tone beginning to scare me a little.

"Why now? Why is there a rush on the matter? I thought, this was just a pleasant trip away?"

It's then, I realize.

This isn't some sort of desperate, last attempt at winning my forgiveness. This has been carefully orchestrated to get Banks off the grid.

He used me, to make me feel like he was changing, that he cared about me. Truly, I don't know why I expected anything different, I didn't. It just seemed like another selfish Banks move, to win my affection, it's turned out to be not about me at all. I just happen to be an accomplice within the mix, a threat of some sort. He knows I could very easily give away his position, his whereabouts.

"Rosie, for once, I'm begging. Shut the fuck up." He groans, running

Chapter 23

a hand through his hair.

"Banks, what the fuck is going on?" I demand, realizing where my voice is.

Right now, he needs me more than I need him. I'm happy to step over my boundaries.

"Get in the fucking God damn car, before I throw you in myself." He fumes, his teeth bearing at me as he speaks.

"No. Not until you tell me what's going on." I retort, the confidence within me excelling.

"Nathan, just do it." He sighs, looking away.

I furrow my brows in confusion as I turn towards the three of them, Devon's beautiful stature capturing my eyesight.

I flinch as Nathan, a.k.a Buttercup, steps forward and grasps onto my upper arm.

"Ouch! Get your fucking hands off me!" I insist, his grip deathly as the pain demands a response from my fight or flight.

I try to pull my arm free, his fingers only burn into my skin further.

"Banks, come on!" I shout, whipping my head towards him and throwing daggers.

My body jolts as I feel the stinging sensation in my upper arm, the coldness of a liquid entering my bloodstream. I rebel against Buttercup, freeing my arm finally.

I drop to the ground as my legs prove to be too weak to withhold my weight.

"Banks–" I fall forward onto the palms of my hands.

I grip the grass, trying to focus on my breathing as everything begins to warp and slow down. I'm trying, I'm trying so fucking hard to fight against it. But, I can't.

My body slumps to the ground as it consumes me.

Chapter 24

Devon

Okay.
   What.
      The.
Fuck.

To think myself and my team used to pride ourselves on being steps ahead, I'm officially taking it off of our radar.

Not one part of this 'plan', has gone to plan.

If were wanting to take Banks out, it has to be now. The team *must* be aware of this drastic change.

I don't even want to consider the latter, if they don't act now. It will mean we're on a one-way flight to some batshit rich island in the middle of the ocean, with no contact, no wi-fi and sure as hell, no team.

"Lorenzo, put her in the car. The jet is set to leave the tarmac in the next half hour." Jesse orders.

Chapter 24

I nod my head and stride towards Rhea's limp body on the grass, her face relieved of the stress and anxiety. I can't deny that she looks sensational whilst she's sleeping, she worries too much.

I know her game, I know the front she places on herself to appear preppy and free.

But, especially now, I know the anchors she tried so hard to fight against. Her past, the abuse, her escape, is all detrimental to the way she carries herself. Why she is so determined to maintain her positive energy, she wants to uplift people to her level so she can tell people things do get better. If anything, I utterly and truly admire her. She has the strength and courage I never did.

I pick up her body, her arms flailing downwards, along with my heart. Her noticeably thinner frame, is weightless within my grip. It pains me to see her be treated this way, to see a glimpse of what she potentially endured during her relationship with the psychopath. He will get his due diligence.

"Please, be careful with her." Banks says to me.

I almost stop in my step at his words, they almost come across as giving a shit about the girl he just had sedated.

"She's precious." He continues.

Barely nodding my head, I seethe with anger, frustration and torment.

If anything spared Rhea of this physical and emotional warfare, I'd take it. If he genuinely cared enough about her well being, so she would never have to suffer, I'd bow down, let him have her. It wouldn't be for him, for her. She deserves every ounce of goodness in this world.

I really can't tell if this is my own insecurity with what happened to Isabelle, my inability to protect her or save her from the evil in the world, or if it is my genuine affection towards her. Either way, I'm infatuated, and I can't help it.

I place Rhea across the backseat of the SUV, attempting to strap her in with all three seat belts.

"Oh, come on Lorenzo. Did you have to place her in the middle bay? Now it's just awkward for those of us who have to climb in through the trunk." Jesse says.

Honestly, if I wasn't here on a job, and protecting Rhea, I'd have taken his jaw off, to avoid hearing his constant yapping. I've had better company with a chihuahua.

Not bothering to respond, I dip my head at him, I can't risk being caught out from my accent, or lack thereof.

Pulling myself out of the car, I glance back at the visual of my love, incapacitated and vulnerable.

"Are we ready?" Banks appears within my visual, his smart appearance a juxtaposition of the entire situation.

None of this is professional. Every part of this operation he has is fully illegal, the woman he has captured, the weapons he holds and the 'off the books' traveling.

If there's anything I know about Banks, it's that I need to be careful. He is not the usual submissive type, he's smart, he's observant and apprehensive. Regardless, whether he trusts his bodyguards or not, it's every man for himself.

"Banks, you sure about this?" Jesse says, not a hitch in his voice.

"Are you questioning my integrity?" Banks scowls at him.

"Nah man, I just wanted to make sure that things were going as planned, you know, with Rosie and shit." He tries to rectify.

"Jesse, if you have an issue, I suggest you fucking out it now. I have Lorenzo and Nathan, perfectly capable of doing the job without questions, here you are. Asking questions about *me*." Banks spits at him, flexing his jaw.

"Come on, you know I didn't mean it like that." Jesse shakes his head.

"Consider yourself, discharged from service." Banks says straightly.

"You're joking, right?" Jesse laughs dryly. Me and Nathan look at each other, not able to gauge each others reactions.

"Do I look like I'm joking, fuck off Jesse." Banks growls, his demeanor changing drastically.

"Get rid of me, and it will be your death wish." Jesse deadpans, puffing his chest out, like it matters.

"I'll add it to the list, cheerio Jesse. You proved as useless as your references stated." He snarls, igniting Jesse.

Jesse begins to strip of his armor, huffing as he does so.

Within a split second, Jesse is on the floor with Banks on top of him. I can't tell whether I should intervene, with Nathan's fixated stance, I decide against it.

Banks grabs him by his clothing and drags him across the lawn, traipsing over Rhea's conditioned plants.

Jesse fights back, thrashing at Banks' grip on his clothing and trying to kick him away, each action failing.

"You've been a pain in my ass since I hired you." Banks spits, spluttering over his face. Jesse grips and nips at his wrists, desperate to free himself.

Then, he hangs him over the surface of the pool. I hadn't even realized I'd followed suit with Nathan's movements until now, and I can't tell whether I'm anxious or thriving over the demise of Jesse Wolfe.

"Sink or swim, Jesse" Banks grits, his body tense and solid as he holds the entirety of Jesse's weight on his biceps.

"Fuck you, Banks." Jesse growls.

Wrong answer, man.

Banks dunks his head under the water, the thrashing and splash of the bubbles, soaking Banks during his sanctification.

About a minute passes before Banks yanks him free of his torture, allowing his lungs to be blessed with oxygen.

"I'll ask again, Jesse. Sink or fucking swim." his voice is murderous, unforgiving and bloodthirsty.

"You're fucking crazy you kn–"

His voice is drowned out with a split second of gargling, and then splashing. Clenching my back teeth together, I turn my head away.

It's one thing to be in this business and put a gun to someone's head but, it's a completely different ball game to murder someone with your bare hands.

My eyes settle upon a bed of flowers, I wish I knew which kind. I've managed to gauge a base knowledge, courtesy of Rhea, anything further than that is lost with the wind.

A sickening feeling rises in my throat as the persistent bubbling noises fade away. Gradually angling my head towards the pool, I purse my lips and inhale deeply through my nostrils.

Banks shoves his lifeless body away, the haunting sounds of the water, alive and thriving.

"Lorenzo, call your guys to clean up this mess. We need to be moving." He shrugs himself off and shakes off his soaked hands.

My guys? Shit.

"And now, my suit is all wet. Brilliant." Shaking his head, he turns away, walking back towards the car.

Nathan follows after him and I take that moment to 'call my guys'.

I dial Pete, not exactly sure what I'm about to ask of him.

The call consists of trying to concisely update him on the new agenda, and the, unfortunate, expiration of Jesse Wolfe. Within less than a few minutes, I had an actual idea of what my next moves are.

There's a reason that Pete is the lead operator for us, he is more than qualified and excellently smart. Not to deny that I'm also very well curated, but the difference between me trying to figure out this

Chapter 24

news over a few hours and Pete, the width of a phone call is all it had taken for him to formulate an entire new strategy.

Feeling freshly confident, I return to my mission, to Rhea.

Chapter 25

Rhea

Groggy and disoriented, I shift my body and frown at the pounding sensation within my skull.

I take a second to think about the potential circumstances that I'm about to open my eyes to. Devon, Banks, spontaneous vacation and sedation.

"Aha, I have to agree. That is the most fun part." Banks' voice pierces my ear drums.

"You know, I've never actually cared too much to make myself appeal to the female population, they've always just been there. Helpless and wanting." A deep voice chuckles.

Who the fuck is that and why is his attitude towards women so completely, degrading?

"I've had my fair share of those kind, and boy, they are *hard* work." Banks' confident tone grates across my skin.

I flinch my eyes open, focusing in on the two men sat diagonal to

Chapter 25

my… Jet seat?

Oh fuck, no.

"Morning, sunshine. Now that was an awfully long nap you've had there." He smiles at me, smugly.

I use my abdominal muscles to pull my slouched body, upright. I'm in an uncomfortable pair of jeans, covered in soil and a tee with no jacket. My arm hairs are raised but I can't figure out if it's the temperature of the cabin, or the fact I'm in close proximity with Banks and his minion.

Speaking of minions, where is Devon?

"I need to use the bathroom." I stand from my seat, about as graceful as a baby deer, gripping the seats along the aisle as I find my way to the toilet.

It's then I notice Devon, the seat behind me, his helmet still planted firmly on his head. I can't imagine that being very comfortable, but it's better than exposing his true identity.

I can feel my back burn with his gaze, a blanket of protection. I've come to the realization of how safe I feel in his presence, it's like I just know he'd jump in front of a bullet for me. Well, I could be way off course and he'd be the one pulling the trigger, but I like to think my judgment is of better standing.

I pull open the door and slide inside, the artificial lighting buzzing to life. I lean over the sink and splash my face with water a few times to try and wake myself up more. My eyes trail upwards, taking in my gaunt appearance.

Fuck, I've struggled with an eating disorder before but, I didn't ever think it could get this bad. My eyes are sunken, my skin barely has a pleasant complexion anymore and my, once soft, features are sharp and pointed. My fingertips graze along my jawline, pushing and prodding, figuring out the new dimensions of my face.

It's insane to think of the similarities between this moment and the one on my first flight with Devon. And, then the differences.

I groan and try to plot out in my mind what the fuck I'm meant to do, how we're meant to escape from the grip of Banks and his controlling measures on a remote island. We can't just go full Tarzan-style, can we? Maybe not, I probably wouldn't even last a week.

I feel so fucking useless right now, and guilty. Guilty that Devon is only here because of me, his poor princess that needs saving from her evil step-mother. I know what Banks is capable of, I don't want Devon to suffer as I have.

Putting on my big-girl shoes, I unlock the bathroom door and saunter out with my head held high.

I pass by Devon, barely passing him a look.

"I need some help, with um… with lady problems." I cringe.

Banks and Buttercup are playing cards, adjacent to each other and a whiskey in tow.

"Lorenzo, duty calls." Banks throws a look over at Devon and nods his head towards me.

Instantly, he's up and out of his seat.

"You can deal with the slack, seeing as though you were the last to join the team." Banks returns to his hand, pondering his next moves.

Perfect.

I angle my body around Devon and walk back towards the other end of the jet, as if I'm needing a change of clothes. I push open the door to, what I assume to be, the bedroom.

The room is pristine, glamorous and untouched. The leather and glossy lining to everything makes it appear much more luxurious than it is, it's a small bed – queen size at best.

Devon follows behind me, his heat propelling through his armor and swarming my body. As soon as I close the door, I do exactly what I promised myself I wouldn't do. I pounce.

I am lost.

Chapter 25

No, lost insinuates that I'm not where I belong.

My lips against his is exactly where I want to be, our frenzied tongues are battling for freedom, but not from each other. My nose bumps against his helmet and I reach my hand up to tug it from his head, revealing his devastatingly handsome face.

His hands grasp and pull at my hips, my body flush against his.

Oh, God. I don't know how to stop, I don't want to stop.

This feels so *right*. My breath is virtually non-existent as I'm throwing my entire being into this kiss. I need him. I want all of him.

"Fuck me." I pant, only withdrawing my lips for the split second it takes to say the words, smashing my lips against his.

The lack of contact has me reeling, my body aches.

"We can't." He tries to speak against my lips, but my excelling need for him overpowers his ability.

I never want to remove my lips from him, the lightening strike of emotion and pleasure he excels within me, has me desperate.

"Please," I moan, the volume barely above a whisper.

I grind my hips into him, his rock hard erection proving everything I already knew. He wants me.

Or…not?

He pulls away from my lips, setting his hands on my shoulders to push some distance between us. I feel like a dog being pulled away from his bone. If he wants to treat me like a dog, fine. I pucker my bottom lip and widen my eyes, offering my best 'puppy eye' look.

"Oh, come on, Rhea. Don't look at me like that." He turns his head away, looking at the ceiling.

I continue to pout.

He lets out a sigh and then leans down to retrieve his head gear, not daring to meet my gaze.

"What's wrong?" I push, his demeanor drastically different to five seconds ago.

"Look, Rhea. This. *Us.* Can't happen right now."

Someone better find me a fucking parachute because I'm about to pull the jet door and free-fall to my death.

"It's not that I don't want it to, it's just–"

"No. It's fine. I get it." I twist my words, hoping they come out as stern as I intend.

"Rhea, you don't get it, I'm on a job. I need this to stay prof–"

"Like I said, Stark. I. Get. It." I snap.

He flinches at the use of his last name, his 'professional' title. I let his 'saving' me, cloud my judgment. This was a job for him, a mission that would have happened regardless if it was me, or not. I could be back in Atlanta right now, comfortable and plodding along with my usual duties, feeding the kittens and bitching with Fizzy about reality TV. He would still be here, onto Banks.

It's a bitter pill to swallow, but it's true. None of this is about me, it's about Banks. I just coincidentally ended up in the mix, the timing was a little skewed.

I tighten my lips as Devon stands completely still, stunned.

"I need you to move, so I can get out." My voice is barely my own, it's sinister.

"Rhea, please. Just give me a chance to explain this–"

"I will fucking scream and have Banks murder you with his bare hands." I dare. He squints his eyes at me, his frame becoming larger, somehow.

"Is that meant to intimidate me, Rhea?" He cocks an eyebrow.

"Think of it more as, foreshadowing." I smile arrogantly, confident that I've won this battle.

Before I can even take another step or say another word, I'm thrown backwards against the wall, his grip tight around my throat. My eyes are wide and my oxygen supply quickly depletes.

His eyes, usually dark brown, are virtually black.

Chapter 25

"You wanna say that again?" He growls, his hot breath fanning over my face.

My gaze is fixated on his exposed teeth as he spits his words at me. He brings his face closer to mine as I grip onto his thick wrists, my pathetic attempt of fighting back. I don't know if this is some sort of trauma response, but I'm pooling between my legs right now.

His lips graze my ear lobe, his teeth bared and nipping at it.

"The only time you'll fucking scream is when I pin you down and fuck you so hard you can't remember your own fucking name." He snarls.

I'm officially butter. I've melted in his hands and I'm dripping from his fingers onto the floor below. Unable to do anything else, I taunt him further.

"Never." I choke back to him.

He presses his groin against me, the solid length teasing and sparking the firework inside of me. It may not be the fourth of July, but I'm about ready to explode.

"You want to test that theory, little dove? I'm so fucking ready to implant my own seed into you, never mind your own little garden you have in your apartment."

I *love* this.

Whatever the fuck is going on right now, is fueling my fire more than any flammable liquid ever could.

He nudges his nose against my cheek and I turn my head away from his, trying to avoid the contact, just to charge up his determination.

He grips my jaw with his right hand, twisting my face to his, the entirety of my body becomes combustible, aching for him to grant me the reason to burn.

"It's a real pity that you're so fucking beautiful, Rhea." His comment throws me off guard as I try and process his words.

"Because right now, I want to thrust into your body so hard that I could tear it apart, limb by limb."

His grip tightens around my neck, the buzzing sensation dances around my head, like it really may be the fourth of July.

My vision begins to darken, the stars litter my vision and a euphoric feeling spreads from my head, down to my fingertips. It's almost like I'm paralyzed, I've lost the ability to move my limbs, but the only thing I can focus on right now is *him*.

"I already know you far too well, Rhea. I know exactly, what the fuck, you like. You want me to suck on that soaking pussy and drive you into the oblivion of pleasure I can offer you." Oh fuck, please.

I'm incapable of even answering his question right now, my head is in the clouds above, he sounds so distant.

He presses deeper into my neck, the pressure behind my eyes almost unbearable.

"Threaten me with that bastard again, and you really will feel the weight of my wrath." He releases his grip from my neck and I slump down the wall, intoxicated with his torment.

Most people, sane people, would run. I want to stay in the burning building, allow his flames to consume me, lick at my skin and scar me permanently.

"Get the fuck up from the floor, Rhea. Go back out there with your head held high, you're a fucking Goddess. Start acting like it." He shakes his head and honestly, I want to rise up on my knees and become the Goddess he says I am, blessing him with every miracle that my mouth can offer.

"Get the fuck up, little dove."

Hm, I'm a fan of this nickname. No idea where he got it from, but I'm begging for him to continue calling me it.

I take his advice, rising to my feet. I don't meet his face, or anywhere near. His frame is tall and masculine, I am small, frail and weak.

"There you are." He begins to smooth out my hair and t-shirt, my

Chapter 25

neck tense and throbbing from his vicious, sensual grip.

"Perfect. Fucking perfect." He scans my entire body, focusing mainly upon my face.

My insides are back flipping, somersaulting and inside out. How does one continue with life, knowing that they're completely infatuated and lusting after their secret savior? Regardless if I make this out alive or not, he gave me the passion and drive to carry on during the days since we reconnected.

The circumstances, not ideal, are the only reason I haven't fully disconnected with the real world, yet. Call me selfish, but I'm fucking glad he's here.

"I have one sentence of advice for you, that is all." His tone sends shock waves through my system, he has a plan.

"Do not, under any circumstances, put on the oxygen mask."

I scan his face, anxiety and confusion spread across my own.

"There is no time for questions but, just know, do not put the oxygen mask on. It doesn't matter what you hear, just don't." I nod my head, completely unaware of what it is I'm agreeing to.

All I know, is that I trust Devon.

Call me naive, call me stupid, but I will not spend another second longer being under Banks' orders.

Chapter 26

Devon

The alarms sound. The panic begins. Except, I'm not panicking.

The oxygen masks drop, Banks and Nathan reaching for them as if their lives depend upon it. *Ha.*

I focus on Rhea, making sure that she doesn't fall into temptation, following suit with her captors. She angles her body towards me, her eyebrows etched with worry and confusion.

I nod my head at her, the seriousness of my face obvious.

Banks and Nathan are adjacent, their eyes wide with worry and concern.

"Rosalie, mask!" Is all I can make out from Banks' muffled voice.

She stares intently at Banks, a fierceness in her eyes. This is all part of our plan. But, the part I don't expect, unfolds in front of me, before I can stop it.

Banks removes his oxygen mask, darting towards a stubborn Rhea.

Chapter 26

I watch on as he pulls the mask downwards and over her face, she fights him. I'm fixated.

"Put the fucking mask on, Rhea!" He screams.

I'm taken aback by the use of her name, her new name. His movements are slowed, his eyes are droopy and I realize that it's taking effect. The nitro oxide tank has done it's job, but I didn't think that Banks was stupid and caring enough to fight for Rhea's life, risking his own. Not once, has he glanced in my direction.

Nathan is completely unconscious, he's slumped in his seat with the oxygen mask attached to his face. Rhea is kicking and screaming at Banks, avoiding the mask at all costs.

Why I haven't been able to move, I don't know. My hands shake erratically as I try and conjure up the strength to move, to discard of Banks. I fight. I push my body up, the shakiness of my hands, unwelcoming to the actions I'm trying to commit to.

"Take your fucking hands off of her." I growl, gripping Banks' shoulder and yanking him backwards.

He falls easily, the nitro oxide clouding his defense.

"Devon!" Rhea shouts, before I hear it.

**

Excruciating pain. My shoulder. Agony. Burning.

I'm slumped further down the aisle, my legs completely useless as I try and comprehend the agonizing sensation spreading across my upper body. I can't move my arms. I'm rendered useless. I demand my eyes to remain open, despite the desperate need to close them. I've been in this situation before, I'm no rookie.

He fucking shot me. In my fucking shoulder. I use all of my strength to try and prop myself up higher, adjusting my gaze upon the predator. Or, so I thought.

It's then I see her legs, spread apart and a defeated Banks in the center of them as she towers over him.

"Do you know how much you've fucking hurt me!" She screeches, my heart splitting in two.

"You had no right to do it in the first place, and you thought you could do it again. You came into my life, Rhea's life, and wanted to implant yourself deeper into me." She's crying, her voice is hoarse and painful.

Watching her take back her freedom, has the pain in my shoulder seem insignificant.

"Rosie, it's not like that." Banks voice is different, he's fearful. Something I have been yet to hear.

"It's Rhea!" She screams at him, her back muscles jolting with her movement.

It's then I understand. I can tell by her angle, by the defensive tone of Banks, that she's aiming a gun at him.

Yes, little dove. Take control.

"I fucking loved you, you senseless asshole! You fucking *ruined* me!" I don't need to see her face to know it's streaming with tears right now.

I'd give anything to jump up and comfort her, hold her until she knows that I'm here for her, but this is for her. She needs this.

"Darling, I didn't mean it. I promise, I love you!" Banks words lack the devotion she's looking for.

She doesn't need a useless pig like him, she needs someone like me. Someone who worships the ground she walks on, values her incessantly and loves her with every part of my soul.

I jolt at the sudden shock wave of sound. The obvious tell-tale that she's made her decision, that she's had enough.

Chapter 26

She stills. Banks stills.

Holy shit.

She did it.

She shot Banks.

Straight through the fucking cranium.

Fuck.

"Rhea?" I manage to find my voice again.

She doesn't respond.

Her position stays exactly as is, Banks unmoving and cold. She needed her revenge, she needed to take control of her life again, without knowing that Banks could be lurking around any corner.

"Rhea?" My voice is softer this time, but the pain still evident.

She turns to me, her face splattered with red specks of Banks. Her face is picturesque and frozen in time.

"He's dead." She whispers.

I glance back at the obvious hole in Banks' skull and nod my head.

"He's dead." She repeats, this time a little louder.

I shift my body, trying to alleviate the pressure and pain in my shoulder. Despite my brilliant body armor, unfortunately, shoulders are unprotected. Of course, Banks knew that.

He didn't want to kill me, he wanted to warn me.

Sadly for him, a warning is all it will ever be.

"Little dove." I begin, her face completely stuck and her eyes glistening under the cabin lights.

"No." She whispers, glancing at the wall and then the window.

"It's okay." I try to add some sort of reassurance, that she isn't wrong for what she did.

I pull myself upright, the blood from my wound trickling downwards, using my arm as it's canvas. Before I barely get to my feet, Rhea sinks to her knees, dropping the silver pistol to her side. I launch towards her, wrapping her within my frame, not caring if I soak her in my blood. I pull her head in tight, kissing her scalp softly and shushing her.

She doesn't cry though, she's still. Stiff.

"Rhea?" I pull back and hold her face in between my hands, both of them covering her expanse.

Her blue eyes glance up at me, completely blase. She isn't here, she's disappeared. I know too well the feeling of the first time you pull the trigger, the first time you end a life, even if it's to save your own or someone else.

"Sh, little dove. It's okay, I'm here." I pull her tightly against me, her frail body shrinking into me.

I smooth my hand over her hair as she releases her pain, allows me to feel it with her, numbing the agony in my shoulder.

I've failed once before at protecting someone I loved from the heartache, from their suffering and torture.

This time, I'm here; present and prepared to welcome it with open arms.

Chapter 27

Rhea

Days pass by in a blur. I don't remember what it feels like to live, to function and have normal concerns. Instead, I'm plagued with memories, the sound and the sight of it. His face flashes through my mind so much more than I want to admit. Banks. My first love. His panic and fear. His eyes, cold and still. The smell of his blood. The taste of it.

I scrubbed myself in the shower a thousand times, but it's not enough. It never will be. I took away a life when it wasn't mine to take. I became God for a moment, I held his life between my fingers and I let it go.

Too many thoughts have floated around since then, each of them putting me at the forefront. It's the opposite of what I thought of at the time. I thought I could do it and finally be free, feel like justice had been served.

Instead, I'm an empty shell of a person. I have no satisfaction from the crime I committed. Instantly, the regret swarmed around me like a colony of bees. I was their prey, the sugar-coated bait waiting for the sting.

The sting never came.

Quite the opposite actually, it was nothing. The bees tried to invade, to take what I had left. Little did I know, they didn't have much to take.

I refused any help, I don't want it. Don't deserve it.

I'm a murderer. A cold-blooded murderer. A criminal. I want to turn myself in, admit the inhumane acts and have my punishment presented to me harshly. At least, in handcuffs I may actually feel something.

Fizzy was relieved when I returned, but she couldn't make sense of any of it. She apologized profusely, telling me she should have paid attention, been there for me and noticed a creep in the bar.

None of which, matters to me anymore.

That was someone else.

Not me.

I'm a fucking murderer. Evil, sadistic and twisted. Exactly what I was trying to avoid. But that's exactly how things were with me and Banks, we brought out the worst in each other. We battled till the end, somehow I ended up being the worst.

I'm back at square one, or even less than. My mind is tormented with my entire life story. Every one of my mistakes, weaknesses and negative attributes are heightened.

The good is clouded, whisked away in the hurricane of trauma.

I don't deserve any of the good, I'm exactly the person Banks said I was, I proved it a week ago.

I'm deceitful, impulsive and stupid. I wouldn't have shot my ex-lover right in the glabella if I wasn't.

I suppose we can surprise ourselves sometimes, when we despise

Chapter 27

the person who hurt us so much that we become them in the end. All to *win*.

None of this feels like a win. To win, means to celebrate and be proud of your actions, I deserve to rot in a prison cell for the rest of my life.

I pull my knees deeper into my chest, my hoodie swamping my entire frame. When was the last time I ate? I can't remember.

I can barely drink water these days, filling my stomach with anything gives me the nauseous feeling that I had immediately after… you know. Everything reminds me of that moment, the crack of thunder, the feeling of the metal handle in the shower, the push of a button. It's all sadistically wrapped around my life.

I wish it was like the movies, like I got my sweet revenge and went on with my life, thriving and reveling in the fact it was *I*, that ended the villain.

How can I be happy?

How does this work?

This isn't in my genetics, I'm not made for this.

For the heartache, the struggle, the pain.

I'm in despair, I'm a lost cause. Nothing in this world can help the way I'm feeling. It doesn't link to anything specifically, the sadness eats away at your being.

I'm sat here with tears trailing down my face, without a reason. Without a solution.

I've fought too many battles, too much emotion and suffering. It's like waving the white flag, surrendering to my demise.

It's tragic, in so many ways. To think, I could have been happier in an alternative life. This didn't have to be me. Unfortunately, it was.

I'm an empty shell of a person with no true meaning in life, no family and no friends.

Life can be so artificial, to the point it isn't worth it anymore.

Eventually, you want to give up on the parts that are false. It turns out, that is my entire existence.

How should one feel?

How should I continue, knowing that I don't hold the value that others do?

Everyday, is a struggle. A task. An assignment.

What was I placed on this earth for?

I have yet to find out, if ever.

The emptiness within me is too much, I don't know where to place it.

Do I continue the rest of my life, waiting for the place to make itself obvious?

None of this is easy, I can't continue my life with no direction. I've tried. I beg, I beg for the world to give me some sort of sign that I am present.

Pinch me.

Typically, one learns from their mistakes. I don't. I tear out the page as if it never happened and keep making the same mistakes.

I'm tired.

I am so fucking tired.

Taking hold of the picture in my drawer, holding it up in the light, I pour upon the only picture I have of me, my mother and father. The parents I never had a chance to experience.

I focus in on the little girl, with her hair braided and the pristine appearance. I was loved, so cherished that when the world robbed me, I was left empty.

Cracks.

The girl that begged to be loved, to be cherished once again.

My eyes are heavy after two bottles of wine, the hollowness barely concealed with the toxic liquid. The only thing that makes me feel these days…

Chapter 27

In some ways, I think it was why I'd stayed with Banks for so long. After our honeymoon period, things plateaued. I loved him, I really did. We were picturesque, desirable and ideal.

Until the first time.

The first time he laid his hands on me.

It shattered something within me, something that can never be fixed. Will never be fixed.

I lost a part of myself that day, the part of myself that held my confidence, my hope in life that things can get better.

Until it continued.

Then, it became less about me, more about him. I changed how I reacted, watched his signals and his triggers. This meant I avoided him in those times, became fearful of the clock. I didn't know when it was time to let go, I didn't have chance to consider it. My mission was to continue to wake each morning, not plan my escape. I became the background character, my emotions a seasonal appearance.

I didn't know how it felt to feel anymore. I was idiotically numb. To numb my pain, meant to lose myself in the process.

Help me. I cried.

My tears attempted to wash away the bruises, but failed.

It resulted in myself becoming traumatized, living in a state of limbo.

The knock on the door has my heart in my mouth, my body flinching and tense at the sound and volume of it. I try and curl tighter into a ball, sinking my head against my knees. I close my eyes and the darkness of it provides an odd comfort.

The rapping at the door sounds again. *Go, the fuck, away.*

I couldn't even answer the door if I wanted to. Thanks to Devon, the door is entirely metal and steel, so I can't touch the handle without having a, full-blown, meltdown. Fizzy isn't here either, so it looks like the door is going unanswered.

The sound of the locks clicking causes my eyes to pop open, the visual of the hairs on my legs significantly close to my eyes.

I hear the door push open and the shuffling of some bags, then a deep groan. *Who?*

"Rhea?" He calls out. I sink deeper into the couch, avoiding being seen.

"Rhea? Where are– Oh. There you are." Devon's voice softens towards the end, relief entangled with it.

I don't bother to move, to look at him.

He, makes it worse.

He, reminds me.

He, saw me do it.

The warmth of his touch almost has me leaning into it, but I was tempted by the devil before. This time, I'll bite the devil's hand off before he tries to feed me with it.

"Little dove, come to me. Please." His voice is strained and his thumb grazes over the nape of my neck, igniting shock waves and goosebumps across my body.

I sigh, lifting my head.

He freezes at the sight of my face, his mouth parted and his eyes wide. Thanks, I know I look like shit, what can be expected of someone who has just *killed* another?

"Rhea... This– Look, you need serious help."

You think? I roll my eyes and place my head among my knees, not caring to be a welcoming host.

His hands grip onto my knees, forcing them apart. My eyes trail up to see he's changed positions, crouching in between my legs and looking up at me.

Swallowing harshly, I follow the crease in between his brows, down his sharp nose and eventually to his full, kissable lips.

"Please, just let me help you, Rhea. I hate to see you like this, not for my sake, but yours. You mean a lot to me, I can't let you slip away from me. I've been in your shoes many a times, what you're going through is tough, trust me. But listen, okay? It gets better. Life gets better. You have spent far too long being afraid of a man like Banks, it's time you learn to *live* again." His lashes flutter as he speaks, his dark hair tousled and unkempt.

"Let. Me. Help. You." He demands.

"You can't." My voice is barely above a whisper, it's scratchy and broken.

"To hell I can't!" He snaps, gauging my attention once more.

"You are fucking strong, Rhea. What you did? Yeah, fine. It was awful for him, truly. But I watched it. I seen what happened. I watched a woman stand up and take back what was rightfully hers. He stole your life long before that moment, and you grew a pair of wings, Rhea and you flew. You became alive again, you had more right in this world than any one of us. You deserve to be happy, you deserve to be loved and cherished in ways that never have you feeling less, only more. So I'm going to ask again, but I'm not really asking. Please, let me help you." His eyes are lined with water, lips trembling and jaw tight.

I sit, stunned into silence. I've never had anyone fight for me like this, to care about me more than I care about myself.

He reaches up, lacing his fingers through mine and squeezing them.

Slowly, I begin to nod my head, not quite sure what I'm agreeing to. His shoulders slump and it's then I take in the fact his shoulder is still bandaged up under his t-shirt. Somehow, I'd forgotten that detail, despite it being the fuel I didn't know I needed.

Seeing Banks hurt him, seeing him do what he's done to me from an outsiders perspective, gave me the final push.

It made me realize how much I cared to protect Devon, how much I wanted to hurt Banks for hurting him.

I've tried to tell myself over again that the reason I shot Banks was purely for my own sake, to punish him for everything he ever did to me. I didn't expect a mitigating factor to be my overprotective nature of Devon, the thought of anything happening to him had me kicking the gun out of Banks' hands and claiming it as my own.

"Thank you." Devon sighs, entangling his right hand in my hair, pulling me towards him.

Our foreheads meet and the connection throws me back into the plane, in the bedroom. How badly I wanted him, how much I craved his affection and touch.

It's like the floodgates have opened, I'm an open book. He has this effect on me like no other, the ability to wrap around me like ivy, nestling himself deep into my skin. Deep enough that it cannot be removed, shouldn't be removed.

His lips graze against mine, softly asking for permission, to let him in. Little does he know, he's already the one who holds the key to my heart.

Chapter 28

Devon

She presses her lips against mine and my entire world explodes like an atomic bomb. I'm stunned from the feeling of her tender touch, the torturous slide of her wet tongue against mine as I fist her hair tightly.

She lets out a sweet moan, the sound wrapping around my heart and tugging. Without breaking the kiss, I stand up, pulling her with me. She instinctively wraps her legs around my waist and I release her hair, cupping her ass cheeks.

I smirk against her, the feeling of her bare skin under her hoodie leaves little to the imagination. Fuck, yes, little dove. Practically running to her bedroom, I hold her in my grasp, desperate to give into our temptations. I've wanted this for so long, *too long*.

Kicking open her bedroom door, I take in her room, her bed sits unmade and messy. *Perfect.* So, I'm not going to do too much damage, then?

I let go of her ass and she loosens her legs, dropping to the bed. Without even having to say anything, she removes her hoodie, exposing her beautiful breasts. The pink nubs are pointed and begging for my touch, the cold air kissing and teasing them. I pull off my t-shirt and as I reach for my jeans button, she wraps her small hand around my wrist. Or, tries to.

She pushes my hand away, her innocent eyes, surrounded by dark circles, look up at me. Rhea is so devastatingly beautiful right now. She is broken, completely shattered. I intend to pick every piece up and be the glue that holds her together, placing her back on her pedestal.

She tugs at the button and shuffles my jeans downwards, along with my boxers. My cock springs out, almost hitting her in the face. Her eyes are wide and her mouth parts.

"Everything okay?" I ask, cupping her jaw slightly as I tower over her.

"Yeah… it's just– wow." She pants, glancing between my face and my dick.

"I always thought Banks wasn't packing." I grin, earning an eye roll from her.

"I'd rather not talk about the guy I shot, whilst I'm about to put you in my mouth for the first time," She pleads.

"Touche." I laugh, which quickly ceases as she encapsulates my cock with her warmth. Jesus.

She moans as she swirls her tongue around my length, my eyes fluttering closed at the euphoric sensation. I have thought too many times about this moment for it not to be completely dreamy. I'm completely submissive to her Godly mouth, letting her take me for everything that I am.

My hand finds its way into her hair, grabbing and fisting as she takes me deeper, her mouth doing her best to accommodate my size.

Chapter 28

She swallows deeply, taking every inch of my restraint along with it. The suction has my eyes rolling and my hips pushing, her gags filling the air.

"Rhea, yes. Take all of me." I breathe, rocking my hips to meet with her movements.

The vibrations from her moan drive me insane, pulling the ecstasy from my cock to the rest of my body.

I peer down at her hollowed cheeks, her fluttering eyelashes and her swollen lips, each and every part of her, tragically beautiful. I pull back, unable to cope with the budding orgasm that I was about to submit to. Her mouth pops and a string of saliva pulls away, her stunning blue eyes watery and wide.

Licking my lips, I run a finger over her chin, dragging the drool and bringing my finger back up to her mouth. She sucks on it eagerly, her eyes remaining fixated on mine. I swallow harshly and take a moment to appreciate her.

"Tell me to stop." I beg, worried that she isn't going to be able to deal with what I'm about to do to her.

"Never." She smirks, the sweetness in her face cursing her dirty mouth, reminding me of the moment we shared on Banks' jet.

I lean forward, lowering my hand to her neck and taking grip under her jaw. She follows along easily, her head falling back and her eyes closing.

"The things I'm going to do to you... Hmm. They're are going to have you wishing that you were never saved." I purr, nipping and biting along her jaw.

The soft smile on her lips has me reeling.

I apply further pressure to her neck, trying to gauge her reaction. She's been through a lot and I don't want to push her to the limits she can't face.

Lowering her to the bed, I place my thighs either side of her and pin her in place. My cock rests upon her stomach, the wetness from her mouth allowing it to glide along her smooth expanse of skin.

"Stop being so fucking fragile." She grits, her jaw tensing above my hand.

I pause, my eyes burning into her closed ones.

Maybe I am being too careful?

I tighten my grip to her neck, leaning down and nipping her bud between my teeth, something I've been fantasizing about since the day she turned up to our flight with no bra on.

"Stop treating me like I'm damaged goods." She shivers.

My eyes roll into the back of my head and a smile spreads across my lips, my deepest desires coming out to play.

"Damaged goods, huh? Is that what you think you are?"

I lean back and spit onto her chest, causing her eyes to burst open. She looks at me and squints them at me, a playful look on her face. So, my little dove likes it dirty, just like her mouth?

Keeping one hand pressed on her neck, I use my other to angle my cock between her tits, rubbing along the spit puddle between them.

"Oh, my sweet little dove. You won't be damaged goods until I'm finished with you." I thrust between her plump breasts, pushing my cock between them and gripping them, pushing them further together.

She whimpers, her mouth parting and her hands trying to dive to herself.

"I don't fucking think so, Rhea. I am the only one who touches you, not even yourself." I growl, gripping her wrist and pinning it above her head.

"You've never experienced being fucked like I'm about to fuck you. That sweet innocent face is going to be wiped from your personality Rhea, no more fucking fragile shit."

I push my hips forward, angling my cock so its at her mouth. She

Chapter 28

obeys, opening wide as her eyes pour into mine, begging for me to ruin her. I push the tip in, her teeth grazing over my head slightly, the sting and pang of sensitiveness only encouraging me.

Driving my full weight into it, I thrust my cock into her mouth as it glides down, surprisingly easy.

"That's it little dove, relax." I continue to have my way with her mouth, her choking and gagging only making it feel better.

The constant pulse and tense of her throat, gripping around my cock has me spiraling.

Her wrists try to resist my grasp as I push all the way in, her body flexing underneath me whilst she takes me to the clouds above. This is the fucking paradise I've been searching for my entire life.

My cock twitches at the high that's building and it's about to cascade me into an epitome of ecstasy as she swirls her tongue around my base whilst I'm balls deep into her throat.

I yank my cock out last minute and explode onto her face, the stars behind my eyes spread across my vision.

I finally conjure up the courage to open my eyes, peering down at her flush face and her tongue that is stretched out, lined with my cum. *Jesus fucking Christ.*

"Weren't expecting that?" She purrs whilst swallowing and licking her lips.

No, little dove. I wasn't expecting my innocent little Rhea to be a fucking animalistic beast in the bedroom. Hoped? Abso-fucking-lutely.

I grab her by her hair and pull her further onto the bed, shoving her thighs open with my knee, no resistance. I need her, I need to taste her and ruin her.

Pulling back, I sink my mouth over her glistening pussy causing her to cry out. I press my hand onto her stomach as my tongue dances around her sweetness, lapping up every bit of earned juice.

I hum against her and she raises her hips, chasing the high as I push her flat against the bed with my hand, sucking and nibbling at her swollen nub, teasing her with my tongue. I love the way her moans sound and the way her body writhes, pleading for me to grant her the pleasure. Over my dead body. She will cum when I want her to.

I slip my index finger into her, curling it upwards slightly. She fists my hair and I push firmer on her stomach, not wanting her to move. I swirl my tongue around her, figuring out exactly what she likes, pumping my finger agonizingly slow.

"P–Please." A whimpering mess is exactly where I want her.

I want her to know the only person who makes her pussy feel this good, is me.

She tries her best to ride my face, attempting to buck her hips against me. Denying her once again, I build up to the perfect finale. I press my tongue in deeper, inserting another finger and increasing my pace.

She is so fucking wet for me. If I didn't have any self-control, I'd be balls deep inside of her right now. But, I've fantasized about this for too long, I'm not about to let this be over within a few minutes. No, I've wanted to have her legs over my shoulders since the second I met her.

Feeling her tighten around my fingers, I focus to keep my pace, proving difficult from how much I'm reveling in the fact she's coming because of me.

"D–Devon. Oh, God. Don't–don't stop." The sound of her moaning my name causes me to plunge a third finger in, curling them at the perfect angle.

She cries out, her body thrashing underneath my as my tongue flicks at her clit, not applying too much pressure but enough to help her to run and jump off of the cliff.

Her body slacks beneath me and I take that as my opportunity. I push forward, her legs already resting upon my shoulders makes it easier. I press in the tip, not being able to hold myself back. She's so fucking divine, perfect.

I look down at her face, her cheeks a lively shade of pink and her eyes glazed over, barely open. I push in, the warmth of her welcoming me with open arms.

"Fuck, Rhea." I moan, drawing out my words just as I hit the halfway point.

She's small, I don't think she can take all of me without it being pleasurably, painful.

Her hands reach up to try and relieve some of the pressure I'm putting on her, but I press them down to the mattress in a swift movement. My knees are curled underneath me as I fill her to the hilt, she tries to push away from me with all of her strength.

I lean forward, bringing her knees close to her face as I pepper her with tender kisses, beginning to move slightly.

"Such a good girl." I whisper and she nods slightly, indicating she's ready.

I don't think she knows what's coming, but I'll thank her for her enthusiasm later.

My hunger for her only grows with each tiny taste I get, making me want to devour her like a buffet.

She is the expensive and desired seven-course meal, she is no measly three-course. She offers anything you'd want and everything in between. She is missing nothing, she is captivating and deserving of only the highest praise. I am no Michelin-starred chef, but I'm about to devour her as if I have any clue about what a woman as exquisite as her, needs.

My impulse takes over as I plunge into her, the primal need to take her, becoming the only thing that controls me.

Her slickness allows me to ride her with such ease, her finger nails digging into my shoulders alongside her calves. I shift forward, pressing into her more as she wails at the pressure building within, her walls clamping down on me.

I have dreamed of this moment, and it doesn't come close.

This is so much more than my brain was able to conjure up, her body was gifted from the God's above.

Her body begins to shake as I slow my pace, dragging each thrust out slowly and then diving back inside.

I peer down at her face, appreciating every little sound and face she makes. I never want this moment to end.

"Tell me… Rhea." I breathe.

Her blue eyes spring open and they take a moment to focus on my own, a lazy grin lines her face.

"You're my God, Devon." She moans.

Not what I was going for, but even better.

I lean my head down and take her nipple in my mouth, my other hand leaving her hip and finding my way to her clit. She flinches as I draw circles around her, pinching slightly to heighten her sensitivity.

I feel my balls begin to tighten, just as she does again.

We're both a hot and sweaty mess, completely enthralled in each other and nothing in the universe could suffice this moment.

"My God, Devon." She cries out, as our worlds completely shatter into each other.

I pull her to me, trying to catch my breath, my eyes squeezed tightly together so stars are dancing around my vision.

I withdraw myself, laying down beside her. I stare up at the ceiling, mesmerized and stunned all at once.

I've never experienced an orgasm so intense, it burned me to my core.

It's like everything I've ever done until now, has been wrong. This, *this* is what they talk about. In movies, in books, in dreams. I place

Chapter 28

my arm under my head and angle my body closer to hers, she lays with her eyes closed, her nostrils flaring slightly.

"Is everything... okay?" I lean forward and nudge her cheek with my nose.

A random pang of anxiety washes over me, she hasn't spoken since we finished and I'm praying I didn't push her too far.

She inhales deeply, then turning to meet my eyes.

"Everything, is perfect." She smiles.

Chapter 29

Rhea

He looks at me like I'm the most precious jewel in the box. He can't take his eyes off of me.

I've never felt valued in life, never felt worthy, and here he is. Devon Stark, offering me it all on a platter. A very stunning and chiseled platter, I might add.

Laying here, side by side, with him is what girls dream of. The man who will worship your body like you are his queen, prioritizes your needs over his own and making sure that you know how much you merit his existence.

"You are so God damn perfect, do you know that?" He reaches a hand up, moving parts of my hair out of my face, gently grazing my skin in the process. My body tingles from his touch alone, his words allow my body to slowly heal.

"Devon... I– Thank you." My eyes flicker between his, the grin on his face making me melt completely.

"Don't thank me yet, little dove. I'm not finished." He smirks, intertwining his fingers with mine.

"What's with the 'little dove', anyway?" I ask, the curiosity getting the better of my hormonal instincts to let him have round two.

We gaze lovingly at one another as his thumb swipes across the top of my hand, the rhythm soothing.

"Well, I suppose it was meant to reference us, in some way. I know a lot about your past with Banks, it's awful you've had to go through that. You didn't deserve any of it. I think, I wanted to call you something that was symbolic, seeing how much you like the symbolism of plants." He chuckles, I smile in correspondence.

"As much as I love your name, Rhea. The circumstances around why you had to change your name were tragic, it wasn't your choice to change your name. So, Rosalie. In honor of your love for plants, your original name and then mine. You became my little dove. D and V for my name, O and E for Rose. Together we make the dove, the freedom that you deserve so much." He finishes, biting his lip.

My eyes are welling with tears and I release his hand, bringing it up to my mouth in an attempt to conceal the sobs.

"And you say you're not one for romance?" I laugh, whilst crying.

"Maybe, I'm just… for you."

Cue the wails, I can't control them. It's like everything he does or says is crafted so perfectly, so much meaning between his words.

"This is…" I begin.

"Amazing? Perfect? Sensational? Orgasmic?" He tries to finish.

"Too good to be true." I frown.

He sits up abruptly, pulling me up with him. He kneels down before me, his face aligning with my stomach as my legs dangle over the edge of my bed.

It's then I see the disastrous mess of my room, the embarrassment flushes upon my cheeks.

"Rhea, you need to listen to me now. I'm only going to have this conversation with you once, and once only." He grips my hands, a fierce look in his eyes.

I nod.

"You need to wash him away, Rhea. He's gone. He isn't here to torture your mind for any longer. But, I'm here. I'm here to help you pick yourself back up and put you back together. You need anything at all, you just ask. I don't know if this is some fucked up game of fate, but we met each other for a reason. Everything that has happened has built up to this. I know, you probably won't understand this, but I'm willing to try. I think, I need you just as much as you need me." His eyes are wide and looking for a response in mine.

"But, Devon. I just– I'm not well." I break down, my body shrinking inwards.

As much as I want us to skip off into the sunset together, I have a few things that hold my anchor.

He begins to speak but I cut him off.

"You don't need me, I'm a burden. I have so much to figure out, so many issues and it isn't fair to place it all on you. As much as I hate to admit it, I am fragile." I grimace at the word, hating it's hold over me.

"You are not fragile, Rhea. You've been hurt. Far too much for one lifetime. But I'm here to take away the weight of that hurting, I'm here to lift that anchor and allow you to breathe." He winces at the end of his sentence, turning his head away so I can't see his face.

I reach forward, placing my hand on his broad shoulder. He turns back to me, his face pained and screwed up.

"Devon what–"

"No. I've had to deal with this before, Rhea. I fucked up. I didn't do what I was supposed to do and I didn't stand my ground. Not this time. This time, I'm not taking no for an answer." His voice is stern and convincing, enough so I'm ready to submit.

Chapter 29

"Okay." I relax my shoulders, dropping my arms to my sides.

"Okay?" He questions, wanting a second confirmation.

"Okay." I smile as he dives forward, throwing me backwards onto the bed.

He litters me with kisses all over my face, trailing them down my neck and across my chest. My legs tighten around him as he adds more fuel to the fire. Keep me burning, Devon. Keep me burning until the day I finally perish.

Chapter 30

Devon

Walking out of her apartment was one of the hardest things I've had to do in a long time. I wanted to stay in the bed with her day and night, cherishing every sweet second with her.

But, duty calls.

Or in my case, *the boys.*

It's been a few weeks since we last met up, especially since Ever had back to back motocross races. I swear that boy doesn't sleep. Then again, neither do I.

I put my Range Rover in park, evaluating the last twenty-four hours. I feel like a featherweight, like everything that has been pulling me down has finally lifted.

I climb out, making my way towards the entrance of Billy's, the familiar comforting smell of tobacco and alcohol invading my nostrils.

Chapter 30

Reed and Blake are already seated in our usual booth, Ever either at the toilet or not here yet.

I slide in alongside Blake, taking note of Reed's glass of soda.

"Whoa, whoa. Dude, what's gotten into you?" Blake pulls his head back, trying to get a better view of my face.

Him and Reed both peer at me, like I've walked in with a sharpie cock on my forehead.

"What?" I furrow my brows, taking turns in looking at them as they gawp.

"You… oh my *fuck*!" Blake fist pumps the air.

"You fucked? Didn't you?" Blake continues trying to gauge my emotions.

I look at him deeply, trying to mask over any tell-tale signs. I thought it was well hidden, apparently not.

"Devon got laid." He sing songs, Reed chuckling into his glass of soda.

"I– Okay, fine. Yeah, I did." I bow my head whilst the pair of them 'whoop' and cheer, clinking glasses.

I've only been celibate for almost a year, around the time I became sober. The pair came hand in hand for me. If I was going to kick one bad habit, I thought it'd be easier to do them both at the same time. It wasn't.

"So bitter Devon is gone?" Reed asks, cocking his head.

"Oh, no. That's just Devon." Blake jokes, earning a scowl from me.

They engage in small talk whilst I pull open my phone, texting Ever to see where he is.

"You guys heard from Ever, at all?" I ask.

"Nah, he's been pretty busy, or so I've heard." Blake rolls his eyes, taking a drink of his beer.

Blake is so laid back it's unreal. I wish I had the ability to just take each day as it comes, without a worry in the world.

"So…" Blake makes googly eyes at me and I'm cringing.

I figured they'd pick up on some different vibes, but I'm not ready to share with them about Rhea, yet. She's mine for the moment, I want to revel in that fact. I've always been quite private about my personal life anyways, so they're not going to expect me to be an open book now.

"Nice try, Blakey." I flip him off and one of the bartenders saunters over, her low cut skirt and crop top leaving little to the imagination.

"Boys! It's been a while." She drags out, fluttering her lashes at us.

Blake chuckles into his beer bottle as me and Reed glance at each other.

"Hm, Blake. You weren't laughing when you had me crouched over your face." She spits, narrowing her eyes at him.

"Seriously? Her too?" Me and Reed snigger, trying to cover our faces to avoid the awkward encounter.

"What do you mean, her too? There's others?" She gasps, looking between us.

"Oh, boy." I sigh, trying to move out of the firing line.

She leans down, grabbing Reed's soda and throwing it directly at Blake's face, his eyes squinted shut and his lips pursed. Both of us can't help but let out a belly laugh, Blake obviously fuming.

She struts away, flipping her brunette hair over her shoulder. It's then, our laughter ceases.

Ever is stood behind where she was, his face twisted and his lip trembling. Blake shoves me, trying to get me out of the way so he can get to Ever. I oblige eagerly, sliding out.

I watch as Ever turns away, the back of his denim jacket seems to be the only thing I see of him these days.

"Ever, wait up!" Blake shouts, almost sprinting after him.

I stand there, unsure whether or not to follow them. I can't tell if this is an Ever problem, or something more private between them.

Chapter 30

They've been so off lately, I'm sure it's why Ever hasn't been coming to any of our meetings.

"What's gotten into them?" Reed says as he hops over to the bar, asking for some blue roll.

"No fucking clue, but it can't be good." I take some of the blue roll from him and begin to dry off the soaking table.

"I'm just glad it didn't hit me, I wouldn't exactly want to explain to Indie why I ended up being swilled by some random chick." He laughs dryly.

"Same here." I laugh along with him, ordering two more sodas for us.

I slide back into the, now dry, booth. Reed looks at me, as if he's wanting to ask me something.

"What?" I roll my eyes.

"Nothing, just, happy for you." He chirps, shrugging his shoulders.

A group of men walk in, far too loud for the usual Wednesday night atmosphere. I cast a glance towards them and immediately my stomach drops.

What the fuck is *he* doing here?

Chapter 31

Rhea

I kiss goodbye to Doc and Dopey, their tiny heads nuzzling into my cheeks as I do so. Gemini couldn't be less interested, I think she's been more than accommodating to her seven kitties, she deserves a break.

We have Sleepy and Bashful left. Grumpy, Sneezy and Happy went to their new homes this morning, all separately.

I'm glad that Sleepy is one of the last to go, the extra day with him means he gets more attention and I get my final snuggles without the others getting jealous.

"Thank you, we'll take really good care of them." The lady says, her knit jumper and leg warmers in the middle of summer are slightly jarring. But, at least the kittens will stay warm.

"Please keep us updated with them, if you would?" I grin, closing the kitten carrier with them both inside.

"Mm-hmm." She nods, reaching down to grab the kitty cage. I'll

Chapter 31

take that as a polite no.

"Bye bye kitties!" I pout my bottom lip and lean down, waving to them one final time.

She turns away, leaving my apartment through the barricade of a door. Fizzy is due home any moment now, we have a catch up long overdue.

I swipe up on my new phone, the home screen ordinarily bland and absent of my usual apps. I bide my time by downloading and installing my social media. Maybe changing my Apple ID password two weeks before being abducted was a stupid idea, meaning I can't gain access to my backup storage.

Maybe, a fresh start is exactly what I need?

Fizzy stumbles through the door, shopping bags in tow. Hm, maybe I really should start picking up my slack and doing a spot of grocery shopping.

"Fizz?" I stand up from the couch, shakily.

She jumps, releasing the bags and they clatter to the floor.

"RHEA!" She squeals, darting towards me and diving on top of me, sending us crashing down onto the couch.

We laugh and giggle as she hugs me tight, kissing my forehead.

"It's so good to see you as yourself again!" Her words hit a lot harder than she intended them to. Don't we know it, Fizzy. Rhea is back.

"We have so much to talk about, so much gossip to fill you in on!" She's about to burst her seams, she hasn't even closed the door yet.

"So much, Fizz. I've missed you so much. I'm sorry, things have been so hard lately and–"

"Nonsense! Don't apologize, I've missed you far too much, more than I want to admit." She pouts her lip, laying her head on my chest.

She raises up and down with my every breath, her hair smells pleasantly of coconuts.

Her eyes trail back to mine, then along my neck.

"What the fuck, is that?" She screams, bolting upright.

I blush, trying to readjust myself so I'm sat higher up.

"This, is why I wanted us to have a catch up!" I prod my finger into her side, her body spasms as she tries to fight me off.

"Oh my God, my best friend is so in *love*!" She sings.

When I got back from the ordeal with Banks, I tried to shut everyone out. Well, I did.

Fizzy tried so hard to help me, leaving me meals and iced water at my door every morning, knowing I couldn't face getting out of bed. I told her minimal details, but I couldn't face knowing what I'd done, so I kept her out. Now, it's time I owe her an explanation.

"Fizz, I need to tell you some things. About what happened..." I chew on my fingernail, unsure how to begin.

"Does this conversation require wine? I've brought wine." She points to the bags on the floor.

"Hm, hopefully they were strong bottles." She giggles, drawing a long-missed laugh from me.

She sits down with one leg underneath her, the other leg pulled up to her chest as she places out mugs on the coffee table.

I grab mine, taking a large gulp out of it, trying to conjure my thoughts into a rational order.

"Damn, is it that bad?" She leans forward, trying to make eye contact.

I nod, swallowing more wine. The taste reminds me of the night with Banks, the night I discovered Devon was there for me. My sweet savior.

"Oh, come on, Rhea. You're acting like you've killed somebody." She jokes.

My eyes lift slowly, meeting hers. Her laughter begins to cease as her jaw drops open.

"You've got to be fucking with me." Her smile versus my stone cold

Chapter 31

face.

"Oh." She looks downwards, now gulping the wine in a similar fashion to me.

* * *

We make it through two bottles of wine by the time I've finished explaining everything to her. I swear, her fake tan seems to have disappeared over the course of the conversation. Her skin is now a sickly white.

"So… yeah. That's why I've been MIA." I smile bashfully as Gemini jumps up, curling in my lap.

"Well… *fuck*." She breathes, her eyes still bugging out of her head.

I don't blame her. A lot of shit has happened, and technically I'm a murderer now. You'd think I was crazy, telling people about what I've done. But, I trust Fizzy with my life. She was the first person I met after escaping Banks' grasp, and we have that connection that I will never be able to shake.

"So… Um, what now?" She asks me, I can understand her curiosity.

"I think Devon is serious, about us. He makes me feel like nobody ever has, he's so dreamy, Fizz. I'm falling, hard." I cringe, drinking my wine in the mug.

The living room is lit up by the fairy lights, the boho theme in full force.

"I'm all for him, I met him when he brought you here. He is dreamy. But, what happens with his line of work. Like, I get he's a pilot part-time but, he seems to be doing some pretty risky shit." Her face is etched with concern.

"Yeah, it isn't really something we've discussed. We've just been trying to deal with what's just happened first." I get the vibe that something's off with her, it's not like Fizzy to be super serious.

"Maybe, you should discuss those first. Before jumping head first into a potential snake pit." I deepen my stare into her, scanning her features.

"What's that supposed to mean?" I prod.

"I'm just saying, Rhea. Someone needs to look out for you, the last time you jumped at something without thinking, it got you holed up with your psycho ass ex." She continues.

I'm dumbfounded. Speechless.

"I'm sorry if this is coming across as harsh… It's just– *God*. You don't know what it was like when you just disappeared. I thought it was my fault, I pulled you to the club and that was the last I seen of you for weeks." She sniffles, wiping her nose on her sweater arm.

"I'm sorry Fizzy, I didn't see it that way." I whisper, dropping my chin to my knees and closing my eyes.

My life constantly feels like its push and pull. One step forward, two steps backward. It's a game I keep playing, and losing.

Chapter 32

Devon

I burn my eyes into his back, his group of friends cackle and howl at something he's said. Each one of them is built like a brick shithouse, the opposite of him.

"Excuse me, Reed." I slide out of the booth, taking a deep breath and straightening out my long-sleeve top.

My military boots seem to thump under my feet as I make my way over to him, each one heavier than the last.

I tap his shoulder. The rest of them drop silent, focusing their attention on me.

He turns, scanning me once before turning back around.

I clear my throat. "Tommy." He ignores me.

"Tommy." I repeat, flexing my jaw and rubbing my hand over it, beginning to grow more irritated.

"Fuck off, Devon." He spits, barely twisting his head to the side.

Fine.

I shove the back of him, catching him off guard.

"Get your sleazy ass out of here, this isn't your turf." I grit through my teeth, his presence unwarranted.

His guys step to the side, trying to puff their chests out, as if it matters. I see Reed move out of the booth and head towards me in my peripheral, my gaze fully attended to my brother.

"Oh, come on, Devon. Don't be like that. I'm just here for a quiet drink in my friendly neighborhood." He smirks, his speech slightly slurred. Brilliant.

"I'd prefer if you'd leave." I state.

He turns away to his group, mimicking my words and pulling faces whilst they all howl with laughter. He's wearing a white tee, imprinted with images of playboy bunnies, their nipples starred out.

"Some of us still enjoy life, Devon. Not all of us are bitter over a suicidal piece of pussy." He cackles whilst my fists ball at my sides.

"That's enough." Reed, steps forward, honing in on Tommy.

"You got one of your bitches to speak for you? Tsk, you're just as pathetic as she was. You know, her cunt was pretty fucking tight, I can see the –"

I throw my fist forward, hitting him directly in the nose. The force behind it nearly throws me off balance, his body crashing backwards into his group.

The bar erupts into carnage, the sounds of scraping chairs, glass smashing, girls screaming.

I'm grabbed by the biggest guy, he tries to get me in a headlock but I counteract with an elbow to the stomach. He keels over and I grab his head, slamming it down on my knee.

I glance to the side to see Reed fully engaged with punching another guy. It's like everything is happening in slow motion, but all at once.

Tommy gets up, charging forward and hitting me in the brow bone. The buzzing sensation has me thrown, I feel the blood trickling almost

Chapter 32

instantly. The motherfucker is wearing a ring.

He shoves me backwards and I collide with a table, him coming down on top of me.

"You fucking sorry piece of shit!" He screams at me, his fists pummeling into my face. I grab at his collar and bring him down closer, raising my knee into his groin. Hard.

His body tenses and I shove him off, he falls backwards from the table. I pull myself up, prepared to take on the next guy that's about to give it his best shot.

We all jolt, then freeze, at the sound of a gunshot.

"All of you! OUT!" Margaret screeches from behind the bar.

Oh, shit.

Everyone begins to scurry, Reed lets go of the guy beneath him, giving him one last kick before turning to me. His nose is bleeding and his fists are bruised, but other than that, he looks fine.

"Sorry, Madge." I bow my head and she nods at me curtly, before gesturing to the door.

Reed follows after me, the adrenaline pumping through my body. My hands shake incessantly as I try to curb the fury.

"What the fuck, Devon?" Reed seethes, shaking his hands.

"Don't fucking bother, seriously." I shake my head as I storm over to my car.

"Don't tell me to not fucking bother, man! I'm your bro. Talk to me!" He shouts, his footsteps quickening to keep up with mine.

I stop when we get to my car and he shoves my shoulder to face him.

"I wouldn't fucking do that if I were you." I grit at him, the anger still coursing through my veins.

"Or what? Huh. Or fucking what, Devon? I had your motherfucking back in there, no questions asked. And you wanna tell me to keep out of your fucking business?" He growls, shoving my shoulder once again.

"I didn't fucking ask you to."

"Exactly the fucking point! You didn't have to ask! I was there for you without having to have a reason. You're a fucking idiot if you think it'd be any different." He shakes his head, turning his back on me.

I close my eyes, inhaling deeply.

"Reed." I say. He continues to walk away.

"Reed!" I shout louder. He continues walking.

I groan and roll my head, forcing my feet to pivot in his direction. I break into a jog, his head start keeps him ahead.

He stops and snaps his head to me.

"You don't have to be such an ass all the time, Devon. We're here for you. Look, I know you don't ever want to be indebted to us, but I'm indebted to you. In so many ways. You saved me, and my family. There isn't anything I can do that would match up to that, the least I can do is be someone you feel open to talk to." He shoves his hands in his jeans pockets, chewing on his cheek.

He's right. I am so closed off all of the time, I've forgotten how to feel. I've left my friends in the dark, all because I wanted to stop feeling at all. And now, well, I've began to feel again. It's not all that bad.

"You're right." I whisper, looking down.

"I'm sorry?" His head picks up.

"I said, you're right." I say a little louder.

"Sorry, one more time?" His face pulls up into a lazy smile.

"Fuck off, Reed." I chuckle, playfully shoving him.

"It's not every day that Devon Stark tells you you're right. I want this one for the memory books." He winks.

"See you at AA?" I ask and he nods in return.

We give each other a bro hug and go our separate ways, another

Chapter 32

warm feeling of relief washing over me. What is it lately? All of a sudden, I'm an emotional wreck.

I think Rhea has reintroduced me to all of these foreign feelings that I've pushed down for so long that I'm in a total overload.

Rhea.

A smile forms across my face as I decide to pay her a little visit before I go home.

Chapter 33

Rhea

"What the fuck?" I whisper-shout.

It's like 11p.m and Devon is stood at my front door, bloody and horny.

"You should see the other guy." He jokes, but I don't laugh.

"Where have you been? Oh God, are you hurt anywhere? Devon! Your shoulder!" I take notice of the blood that's seeped through, perfectly over his bullet wound.

I yank him inside by his arm and plant him on the couch whilst he tries to fan me off.

"I'm fine, Rhea. Chill." He says lazily, spreading out across the sofa.

I rush to the kitchen, pulling open drawers and cupboards, searching for some sort of first aid kit.

"Oh hey, kitty." I hear Devon pine over one of the cats, probably Sleepy. He always cozies up with whoever is on the couch.

Taking a washcloth, I pick up the bottle of vodka, seeing as though

Chapter 33

were not kitted out for men to show up in the middle of the night, bloody and bruised.

I climb over the couch, sitting directly on his hips and leaning over him, scanning his face for the damage.

"It's all artificial, don't stress, little dove." He grips my forearms, pulling me down to him.

I pull back, lifting the vodka and his eyes grow wide.

"Oh, um. Yeah, we should probably talk about that." He shuffles backwards, proving difficult from my position.

Huh?

"I'm an alcoholic, in recovery." He deadpans. I shake my head, confused what the hell is going on.

"What?" I furrow my brows, my lips parted.

"I hope that's not a deal breaker, cause like, I really like you." He smiles sheepishly, his hands resting on my hips.

"No, of course not. I just– I wasn't expecting it, is all." I blink a few times, trying to process the information. There is so much I want to ask.

"How long? Have you been sober, I mean." I ask.

"I get my one-year chip, on Friday." He beams, proudly.

"That's amazing! Wow, really. It's incredible." I smile down at him, his poor face is swollen and shiny, the blood dried around his eyebrow.

"I guess I shouldn't ask you to swig this before I clean you up?" I joke. He shakes his head, his perfect smile lines popping.

I tip the vodka onto the cloth, then begin to dab at his eyebrow. He hisses slightly, the sound of it warming my insides. *He's in pain, Rhea. Stop it.*

Leaning forward, I lift my hips slightly to get a better angle. He watches my every move, his eyes trailing along the expanse of my body.

"You should probably take this off." I gesture to his long-sleeve shirt.

"Hm, only because you're asking, baby." He smirks, earning an eye roll. He's so fucking charming.

I lean back whilst he sits forward, yanking it up and over his head, then laying back down. I run my fingers over his abs, the softness of his skin glistens under the fairy lights.

His concrete grip wraps around my wrists as he pulls me forward, the position has me falling onto him, his lips ready and waiting to catch mine.

The second we make contact, the world ceases to exist.

It's me and him.

The sun to my moon.

The yin to my yang.

He kisses me with such passion, it fills my heart up with every positive emotion known to humanity.

His hands rise from my hips up my back, spreading across my shoulders and back down again.

I feel how badly he wants me beneath my pajama shorts, the thickness of it too much to deny.

The lights flick on and we freeze, our panting becoming apparent.

"What the– Argh!" Fizzy screams, throwing herself backwards and nearly hitting into the kitchen counter.

"Oh my God. Oh my God. My eyes. They're burning!" She squeals, covering her eyes with her hands and wandering about aimlessly.

I let out a small giggle and peck Devon once more, sliding off of him. I throw the daisy pillow onto him so he can try and mask his raging hard-on, whilst I tend to my best friend.

"I swear, I didn't see anything!" She rambles.

I grab onto her wrists, pulling her hands away from her face but her eyes are still squeezed tightly shut.

Chapter 33

"I just wanted a bottled water, you know? My mouth was so dry and if I'd have known I'd have never– Oh God. Why didn't I just go back to sleep? Argh!" She groans.

"Fizz, nothing was happening." I try to reason with her.

"Yes. Yes there was. I seen it. That wasn't nothing!" Her eye peaks open at me.

"Just– Just get me a bottled water, I'll leave you two love-birds to it." She grimaces, glancing a side eye at Devon.

I open the refrigerator and grab her the water, placing it in her open hand.

"Happy?"

"Nope, still scarred for life." She whines.

I shake my head, giggling and shoving her away.

"Go on, little miss nosy."

She walks away, not daring to look up again.

Once her bedroom door closes, I walk back over to a solemn looking Devon.

"I think, for tonight, it's best that you head home." I smile coyly, not wanting him to take it personally.

"Yeah, you're probably right."

"But, I'm returning to work on Friday." I grin at him, proud that I am gaining some normality again.

"Bummer. I'm not working Friday." He sulks, grabbing his shirt from the floor and slipping it over his head. I admire the way his muscles tense and flex as he does so, the beauty of them only making this harder.

"What about Saturday?" I ask.

"Um, I have a meeting. With the guys." He says nervously.

"The guys as in…?" The undercover vigilante guys.

"Yup." He offers me a half-smile and I return it, feeling defeated that we're not going to see each other for a little while.

I've enjoyed being with him so much over these last few days that it feels too hard to say goodbye, not knowing when I'll be seeing him next.

I stand up, walking him to the door.

"So, how's the door?" He smirks down at me, the cheekiness evident.

Shaking my head I lean up, pressing my lips against his.

"Goodnight, Devon."

"Sweet dreams, little dove."

Chapter 34

Devon

My hands shake as I sit in the doctors office, the anxiety crippling me.

I hate any sort of environment like this, being surrounded by so much death and sorrow. People are either ill, dying or dead.

It's like I can smell it along the bleach washed floors, the harsh lighting and the pitiful glances.

This, however, is routine. I thought it'd be best to get my wound checked up on by an actual professional, rather than being my usual stubborn-self. Something I'm having to force myself out of.

I swing my legs, trying to distract myself.

The door opens and the older man walks in, carrying an iPad and a coffee.

"Oh, sorry. I didn't realize you were here already!" He laughs. I offer a tight smile in response.

"Right, give me a moment and I'll pull up everything I need." I take note of his name, Dr. V. Rivers.

I flex my hands, the adrenaline causing them to stiffen slightly, whilst I wait.

"So, as per the information you've provided, you received a bullet to the right shoulder around ten days ago?" I nod.

"And... you haven't received any medical assistance, professional medical assistance, for this wound?" I nod again.

"May I ask how the bullet was removed?" He takes a sip of his coffee.

I purse my lips and give him a 'look'. He nods in correspondence.

"Okay, lets take a look then, shall we?" He stands up and I slip off my t-shirt, wincing slightly at the movement.

Rhea was right, I should have gotten it checked out two days ago when she insisted, I'm learning to stop being so stubborn.

Dr. Rivers pulls back the dressing, peering intently at it. He pulls out a marker pen and begins to circle around the wound.

"Okay, now. Mr Stark, do you have any family history of any conditions?" He asks.

I furrow my brows. "No, why?"

"Shall we check your movement? With the wound of course."

I nod in agreement, not quite sure of the vibes he's giving off. Anyways, he's the professional.

"Stretch your arms out in front of me, tell me if you get any pain."

He stands up from his chair, appearing in front of me.

I do as he says, lifting both of my arms. I shake my head from the minimum amount of pain, the movement relatively easy.

"Hold it, for a moment." He taps his pen against his mouth, eyeing me carefully.

I glance around the room, the walls littered with random biological posters and advertisements for smoking cessation meetings.

Chapter 34

"Interesting."

I drop my arms, turning to him.

"Interesting?" I retort.

"Mr Stark, have you suffered any other trauma to your body, besides this event?"

I swallow harshly, his tone beginning to concern me. I feel that this is no longer about the bullet hole in my shoulder.

"I was in the military, suffered with PTSD and anxiety and got discharged. That's about it." I thin my lips offering a curt smile.

"We thank you for your service." He bows his head at me and I offer my usual 'thank you'. This isn't new to me.

"If it's okay with you, I'd like to run some tests. There's just a few things I've picked up on that I'd like further clarification for." His pen continues to tap against his lips, the movement almost hypnotizing.

"Sure." I shrug.

* * *

After I left the doctor's office, I couldn't help but feel uneasy. I didn't like his concern, for something unbeknownst to me.

I'm to return in a week, for some scans and what I think, are blood tests. He assured me not to be concerned, until he gives me a reason for concern. I'm content with that, for now.

I think it's time I visit my mother, it's been over a week since I last came to visit for lunch and I'm missing her a lot lately.

Holding my usual flowers and a bottle of wine in one hand, I knock thrice. She opens the door quickly, genuine surprise on her face.

"Devon! My gorgeous boy!" She leans forward and wraps her small arms around me, the scent of her providing me with the safe haven for all things bad.

"Mom, I missed you." I lean down, placing a soft kiss upon her cheek, noticing a new lipstick shade on her lips.

"That color looks gorgeous on you, Ma" I smile as she taps her hand against my chest and shaking her head.

"Come on in, you're in luck. I've just baked a new recipe, Gordon's lemon tart, it's meant to be the best!" She sings with pride, her love for Gordon Ramsey shining true.

I don't remember a time where she didn't watch his cooking shows religiously, she even met him once. I've never seen my mother bat an eyelid at another man, but when it comes to him, she's a love-struck teenager.

I follow after her, walking through the hallway that only weeks ago, was too hard to stomach. Now, I walk through with ease. Rhea really has made my life so much better, in ways that I am still continuing to discover.

Setting down the wine and flowers on the counter-top, my mother pulls the lemon tart out of the refrigerator, the crystal cake stand I bought her three Christmas' ago is still pristine.

"Now, I haven't had chance to make the raspberry coulis yet, but I'm happy to sneak you a little slice." She rubs her hands together as she begins searching for her cake cutter.

Admiring her passion, I take in the effort she's placed into her presentation of the tart, the raspberries are beautifully ripened, each of them positioned perfectly.

She fusses for a while, insisting she can't find it.

"Relax mom, I'll find it." She's becoming more flustered, and she deserves a break. She offers me a small nod before stepping aside.

Walking over beside her, I walk over to the drawer that she usually keeps it in, knowing the layout of the kitchen religiously.

Sitting there, shining and polished, is her engraved cake slice,

Chapter 34

another gift from me.

"See, just relax mom. I've got it." I laugh and turn to her with it my hands, but seeing her face has it clattering to my feet.

"Mom!" I dash forward, clutching onto her as her pale body slumps against the kitchen counter, my heart tearing in two.

Her body is weak and she looks up at me, her eyes wide.

"Mom, what's going on. Mom, tell me." I choke, the bubbling of my tears overwhelms me, drowning out her face.

She clutches onto me with all of her strength as I pull her into me, whilst pulling my phone out of my pocket to dial 9-1-1.

"Mom! Look at me! Stay with me!" I cry, pressing the phone to my ear as my chest aches, the worry pierces through me like a javelin.

"9-1-1 what's your emergency?" The woman asks.

"My mom– she– I think she's having a heart attack." I sob, barely able to form my words as I cradle my entire world within my arms.

"What is your location, Sir?" The sounds of the keyboard tapping in the background heightens.

"2593 Chestnut Grove, Buckhead." I peer down at my darling mother, seeing her in immense pain.

I would do anything to save her right now, anything at all.

"Requesting a unit to your address immediately. Does the patient have a pulse?" I wince at her words, but it doesn't exclude the importance of them.

Pressing two fingers to her neck, I find it, thrumming away far too fast for my liking.

"Yes, too fast. It's far too fast." I begin to count the beats in my head, knowing this kind of information will be vital.

"Mom, look at me, look at me!" I scream as her eyelids begin to flutter closed.

She grasps onto my hand tightly, her mouth unable to conjure words, her touch telling me everything I need to know.

"Don't you dare." A tear rolls down my chin and drips off onto her face.

"Don't you dare, Veronica Stark. You look at me right now, and you fight." I demand, not being able to allow her any mercy right now.

She squeezes my hand once and I silently pray that it was her agreeing with me. My brain swirls, time becomes insurmountable, each passing second is too long.

"How long?" I shout, the phone still held to my ear with my shoulder.

"Three minutes." The respondent tells me.

"You hear that? Three minutes mom. You can do it, Ronnie." I sniffle, gritting my teeth and pulling her body further upright, my legs either side of her. Pressing my lips to her temple, I hold it. Her skin is clammy and pale, her blinking is gradually slowing and every one of them, holds my fears. That each time she closes her eyes for a brief second, that they may not open again. That it may be the last I will ever witness.

I shower her with kisses all over her forehead, brushing her hair from her face and cuddling her tightly, never wanting to let go. Afraid, that if I do, she will disappear.

The sirens sing in the distance, my hope beginning to grow that everything will be okay, everything will work out.

"Mom?" Her hand goes limp in mine.

"Mom!" I howl, her lips part as my anxiety becomes far too real.

I lay her flat onto her back, inhaling sharply through my nostrils and rolling up my sleeves.

Not today, mom.

You are not going to die on me today.

I begin chest compressions, my extensive training coming to brilliant use, but for the most tragic of circumstances.

Shutting off my emotions, I imagine that this is one of my comrades.

I won't be able to give her the strength she deserves if I consider her being anything but, someone to save from death.

Forcefully, I continue the chest compressions, alternating between mouth to mouth and then back to the compressions.

The sirens of the ambulance ring loudly, the fire in my gut fueling my actions as I ensure all of my fight, goes into her.

"Come on." I grit, my breathing becoming harsh and labored.

The front door to the house bursts open, I don't stop.

The sounds of scuffling feet carry down the hallway.

I'm not losing her. No more loss. Please.

"Sir, please step aside. We are here to help, we will take over." A member of the EMS crouches down beside me.

Sweat beads across my forehead as I don't dare to stop, not even for a second.

"Allow me, to takeover." His hands come up beside me, level with my own.

My stubbornness almost has me shoving him away, insisting he doesn't have the determination to keep her alive like I do.

But, I do what Rhea would do.

I step aside.

He takes over instantly and begins barking orders at the other EMS crew, the stretcher then lays beside my mom as they figure out the best way to transition her.

Sinking into the corner of the kitchen, I pull my knees up to my chest, wrapping my arms around them as I watch the chaos unfold around me.

The shock absorber is pulled out, whilst they do their best to challenge the inevitable.

I can't do this again. Not her, not my darling mother. Please, God. Let her live.

Please...

Chapter 35

Devon

I stare at the blank wall. My throat is dry, but I don't care enough to swallow.

Sitting here, completely emotionless, numb and bitter.

I wish I knew a way to keep the evil of this world away from those least deserving of it.

How can it be fair? That those with the purest of souls and the biggest hearts, end up suffering so much.

First Sarah, Bella's mom, then Bella, then Rhea, and now... my mom.

I wish I could hold the power of justice in my hands, so that I could deliver it to those who are more than deserving of the pain. It makes sense why I've joined the group I have, just to have an essence of what that is like.

But today, today feels like none of it was worth it.

None of the efforts I've given to making the world a better place,

Chapter 35

has paid off. Because, the world deems it necessary to repay me in ways that are completely unjustified.

My mother, my darling, loving, sweet mother, lays before me, unconscious and her life hangs on by a thread.

The doctors have no idea when she will wake up, if ever.

They told me that I have potentially saved her life, that without my 'quick thinking' and 'quick acting', she wouldn't have stood a chance.

I'll take the gratitude once she is awake and telling me like I'm her gorgeous boy again, wearing her usual apron and smiling at me with her pretty lipstick on.

Her lips are an unnerving gray. They were chapped at first, not anymore. I made sure to get her some lip balm and I've been applying it repeatedly, knowing that she would have hated to see them in such a way.

If there's anything that I can do, it's to keep my mom, as my mom.

Just because she's in the hospital does not mean that her standards should drop, I mean I've already paid for her private suite but all of that is inconsequential to me. As long as she is getting the ace treatment she deserves, then I'll do what I can in the meantime.

A soft knock disrupts me, startling me from the wall I've been locking at as if it were a piece of art from the *Louvre*. I swivel my head to see a sorrowful looking Rhea, a collection of flowers wrapped in brown paper in her arms.

"Hey..." She says softly.

"Hey," I reply, then bow my head towards my mother.

"I– I heard what happened, I just– I thought I could come here to keep you company for a while." Her voice is timid, nervous.

After I don't respond to her, she continues, "I'm so sorry, Devon. I can't imagine what you're going through, I– Sorry." Her words fade out, but it wasn't as if I was really listening anyway.

I can't think about anything else at the moment than the constant beeping of my mother's heart monitor, the sound that reassures me she's still here, the heart I tried so desperately to keep beating.

She shifts and I hear the door close behind me. Part of me wishes that she'd have disappeared behind the door, but part of me wants her to stay. I'm so torn, at the moment it feels like everyone around me suffers, everyone close to me ends up being hurt, and I don't know if I can place Rhea in the firing line, risking her too.

My eyes sink closed as I feel her small hand rest gently upon my shoulder, her touch instantly relaxes my entire body. My muscles loosen and the tension in my chest seems to ease, all through the simple gesture.

"Devon," she whispers.

I blow out a heavy breath, building up the courage to look at her again. I can't.

Knowing what I need to do makes everything so much more difficult, but it needs to happen in order to protect her, to save her from my destruction. She's been through enough with Banks, she doesn't need me adding to her trauma.

The last thing I'd want is to place her in harms way again, not after everything. She deserves better, someone who can give her a safe life, safe from the darkness that seems to follow me wherever I go.

"Rhea—" I find myself choking up, unable to formulate the words that are constricting my heart.

"It's okay, you don't have to explain anything to me. I'm here, for you." She responds sweetly. Too sweet. Too caring. Too deserving of better.

Inhaling through my nose again, I conjure up the strength to speak, despite how dry my mouth has gotten, "Rhea," I begin.

She steps to the side, laying down the flowers she brought. I wince even just looking at them, knowing how much meaning is behind them. I have no doubts that she picked each and every flower from

Chapter 35

her own garden, with their own meanings. That's Rhea.

The most kindhearted soul, always searching for the greater-good.

Once again, I'm struggling. She has this effect on me, this kind of aura that warps my senses, draws me in, the scent of lavender, the warmth from her proximity. It almost hurts, I feel my heart bleeding for her.

But, I've got to let her go.

"She looks beautiful, peaceful even."

Glancing up, I finally take her in as she sits beside my mother, grasping onto her hand. My heart swells at the sight yet my brain is ashamed. Ashamed that I've given Rhea false hope.

She said it herself, that she was too mentally unwell to date and I related to it. Here I am, I've done exactly what I said I could never do again.

"Rhea… I– You should go," is all I manage.

The only view I have of her reaction is from her side profile, and even that is enough to destroy me. Her eyes slowly flutter closed, her grip still entangled with my mother's.

For a while, we are silent. Still.

I'm prepared, prepared for her to explode on me, tell me how much of an ass I am for leading her on, for promising her the world and barely giving her a week of my time.

The lump in my throat becomes too hard to swallow, the silence eating away at me with every passing second. Say something, Rhea. Please.

Offering a curt nod, she raises my mothers hand to her mouth, leaving a gentle kiss before letting go completely.

The kisses that are meant to be shared with me, the kisses that I swore I could never have enough of.

"Please, you've got to understand–"

"It's fine." She responds, her voice as timid as a mouse.

She's about to walk out of that door with the last shred of humanity I have left in me, and it's all my fault.

I was expecting her to fight against me, her usual feisty self to tell me to stop being so stupid, that she doesn't care about my feelings and she selfishly wants me anyway.

My eyes are trained on the same blank wall, my only comfort in this morbid room.

"Good bye… Devon." She mutters, slipping past me and out of my peripheral vision.

The pain in my chest intensifies, my heart cries for me to turn around and tell her not to leave, to pull her into my arms and never let her go. Yet, my brain is the loudest of them all, screaming at me to let her go, let her live her life away from the danger, the danger that is me.

The sound of the door opening and closing shreds me inside out, my heart feels like its about to burst out of my chest and run after her, even if my legs won't.

"What have you done?" I whisper to myself.

Chapter 36

Rhea

As it turns out, it is impossible for someone like me to be loved. I'm not meant for the good guys like Devon, my purpose in life will always draw me back to the dark side.

I struggle to hold back the tears as I leave the hospital, but it's not like anyone would care anyway. If there's one thing that I've always been aware of my entire life, it's that no one cares about helpless little Rosalie.

Maybe, things would be better if Rosalie is no more.

Reaching for the exit, my heart pounds and everything begins to feel like it's too much. My head swims as I try to concentrate on something else, something that will distract me from this pending storm in my mind.

A group of guys blocks my exit and I don't have the patience to be nice anymore. What's the point?

"Can you guys move out of my way?" I scowl, almost about to

charge through them.

They turn to me and scan me up and down for a moment before I continue, "You do realize that this is a hospital and you're blocking a very important entrance, for people who need access more than you inconsiderate dicks." I snarl.

"Whoa, are you okay?" The blonde guy asks.

"Perfect! Everything is fucking perfect!" I grit, just wanting to get some fresh air before I self-combust in this hallway.

"You sure, you don't look okay?" The guy with the leather jacket on challenges.

"What is this? Twenty-one fucking questions?" I snap.

"Damn, you sure you're not on the run from here?" Leather jacket guy proceeds to interrogate me.

Everything is building up, I am about four seconds away from becoming part of the artwork on these walls.

"Look, ignore him. You okay?" A guy with piercing blue eyes looks down at me with genuine concern.

"I was, until three ignorant jerks decided to interrupt my day!" I fume, but then pause.

Distraction.

This is the distraction I asked for. The tension in my chest and the pounding in my heart is considerably less.

Looking back at the three men in front of me, I drop my shoulders a little, admitting a partial defeat.

"You wanna sit?" His accent shines strongly.

Exhaling, I nod as he offers his arm towards the bench in the hallway. Dragging my feet, my body exhausted from the whirlwind of emotions, I practically throw myself onto the bench. Sighing in relief, I lean my head back against the stark white walls as I close my eyes.

"Move over."

Chapter 36

"No, you move over."

"Ever, move your ass over and let me sit the fuck down."

"I don't wanna squash the poor girl, just squeeze in."

"I'm not gonna fit in that tiny space, Ever, stop being a pussy and move over."

"Blake I swear–"

"Enough!" The guy still standing hisses, drawing my eyes open as I focus on him.

"You know what, I'll just fucking stand. Enjoy the seat, dick." The leather jacket guy huffs.

What is with these fucking maniacs?

"My names Everett, but everyone calls me Ever." The guy sat next to me offers out a hand towards me.

I stare down at it for a few moments before pulling my hand out of my hoodie pocket and connecting it with his.

"Sorry, if it's a little– sweaty…" I cringe, knowing I've had my hands balled in fists for the last few minutes.

"Nah, don't sweat it. No pun intended." He offers a lazy smile, his white teeth contrasting with his tan skin.

"Your accent?" I ask, genuine intrigue lining my words.

"Ah, Aussie." He smiles.

"Why'd do you get to go first? I swear you just love to hear the sound of your own voice." Leather jacket guy jabs at Ever.

"Then what's your excuse?" I say, raising an eyebrow towards him as he turns his gaze on me, narrowing his eyes slightly.

"You're barking up the wrong tree, little lady," he scoffs, folding his arms across his chest.

Whoever this guy thinks he is, needs to back the fuck off. I'm in no mood for other people's curt responses.

"Shut up, Blake." Ever scowls at him.

Ah, so leather jacket guy is Blake.

"Come on guys, enough babysitting. We need to get to Devon." Blake blurts, but I'm not even offended with his comment.

My breath hitches at the sound of *his* name.

"Yeah, Blake's right. Come on, Ever." The blue-eyed guy nods agreeing.

"Reed–" Ever begins.

"Sorry, we're here for a friend and he really needs us right now, it's nothing against you." Reed points his words towards me.

Clenching my fists, I plaster a smile on my face, "Of course! Please, don't let me keep you. Your friend obviously needs you, go."

"Well, it was lovely meeting you…"

"Rosalie." I finish.

"Bye, Rosalie." Ever says, as the other two offer me a wave, leaving me alone in the hallway.

I can't lie, it hurts like a motherfucker to have Devon shut me out. But, it hurts so much more knowing his door is open for others.

Suck it up, Rhea.

You've dealt with worse, this is just another bump in the road, of many. I stand up shakily, using the fuel of my anger to keep me energized. People pass by me, without a care in the world.

No one cares, Rhea, my mind taunts.

Striding towards the automatic doors, I let the outside air fill my lungs with a newfound understanding of the world. An understanding that the only person who should care about me, is me.

Chapter 37

Devon

"Devon! We bring goodies!" Ever chirps as he comes in with a handful of snacks from the vending machine.

"Not hungry." I turn away from them and return my eyes to my mother, her body completely still.

"Do you have some kind of off switch?" I hear Blake hiss at Ever.

I swear, those two never stop bickering. I'm just glad that they're back to their usual selves.

"What Ever was meaning to say, is we're so sorry man. If there's anything we can do, just let us know." Blake pats my shoulder twice before sitting down in the seat Rhea had.

"She'll pull through, Devon. If she's anything like you, she'll come out of this even stronger." Reed pats my shoulder twice too, then stands against the wall with his hands clasped together.

Two arms lace around my neck and pull me tightly against their chest, the embrace warm and comforting.

"I'm sorry, Devon." Ever says into my neck as he cuddles me.

I pat his forearm and he releases me, joining beside Reed and leaning with one leg propped up on the wall.

"Thanks guys, it means a lot having you here. I'm just hoping you can take my mind off of it for a little while," I sigh, leaning back in the uncomfortable chair, my back begging for forgiveness.

"Well, we've got just the story," Ever begins.

"Ugh, God. Ever, you never had the hots for a girl before?" Blake taunts him and Ever shuts up, looking away from Blake.

"What?" I say, my eyes dancing between the three of them.

"Ever here, tried to hit on some batshit crazy girl just before we got in here. It was pretty fucking embarrassing to be honest." Blake shakes his head, a dry laugh following.

"So, I'm off the radar for what? Twelve hours. And Ever finds himself a new girl." I tsk as I thank them internally for taking my mind off my mom for longer than five seconds. If there's anyone who can do it, it's these guys.

"You're just sour because she ate you up with your own insult." Ever grits at Blake.

"She did not." He fires back.

"She kinda did." Reed weighs in.

"Who?" I ask, confused what all the fuss is about.

"Rosalie." Ever responds, a slight grin on his face.

The blood drains from my face, knowing exactly what kind of jab she's tried to throw by using her old name.

"Devon?" Reed furrows his brows and lowers his head to try and catch my gaze.

Refusing to look at any of them right now, I train my eyes to remain on the floor, each gray speckle on the contrasting white surface, becoming the most interesting thing in the world.

"Oh, shit." Blake trails off.

Chapter 37

If this were any other situation, I'd be eating up the fact that Rhea wiped the floor with Blake, knowing he's the most witty out of the lot of us. Right now, it feels more like a sucker-punch to the gut. She's been gone for no longer than an hour and I already feel like I'm missing half of me, the half of me that I loved more than this half I'm left with.

"That was her wasn't it?" Blake asks, and I'm lost for words.

Admitting it was her, not the hard part. Confirming that she was mine, and now she isn't, ruins me.

They won't get it, nobody will. No one knows what it's like, to see so much pain and suffering surround one person to the point you keep your walls sky-high, with metal barbed-wire at the top so nobody can get inside.

At this point, I'd prefer if someone just locked me away for good to spare everyone else from my destructive tendencies.

With the way my life is, I wouldn't be surprised if my relationship with the boys is another ticking time-bomb.

"Yeah." I say bluntly.

The room remains in silence, the only sounds that can be heard is the continuous beeping of my mother's fighting heart.

"Are they from her?" Reed points towards the carefully crafted bouquet of flowers, a mixture of lavender and dandelions positioned perfectly within the brown wrapping, sealed with a twine bow.

I don't even have the strength to continue talking about her, so I simply nod.

"That was… nice of her." Blake's words come out as more of a question, probably confused how to approach me at the moment.

I know they're completely in the dark about everything with Rhea, and I kept it that way on purpose. Stuff like this is so much simpler to deal with when you can keep it all inside of your own mind.

But of course, like fate just wanted to bait me further, she had to somehow get mixed up with the boys on her way out and leaving an impression big enough for them to not forget her. Not that I'm surprised. I think she has that effect on everyone. She most certainly did with me.

"And… yeah. We're all a little lost here, Devon." Reed confesses, his voice treading on egg-shells.

Lifting my head to meet their faces, "It's not the time, nor the place, to be airing out my issues with Rhea," I respond bluntly.

"I thought her name was Rosalie?" Ever cocks his head at me, his eyebrows furrowed.

"Long story," I sigh, my brain beginning to ache from the torturous events in the last twenty-four hours.

"We've got time." Reed steps forward, peering down at me as if I'm some sort of injured road kill.

"Well, I don't." I respond, twisting my body so that I don't have to face any of them, focusing my eyes upon my mother.

Once again, the silence warps around us like a persistent fly, irritating every one of us but there isn't anything we can do about it. Normally, I would involve the boys, seek their advice. This time, never. What happened between me and Rhea, stays between me and Rhea.

"Look, I know things are tough right now, but if there's anything you need to say to her, you need to say it. Before it's too late." Blake says, and I see Ever's head fire towards him, his eyes settling upon our dark and mysterious boy.

Blake has so much more to him than meets the eye, he gives off the impression that he's completely dark and mysterious, but that's just surface level. Behind the mask, he's completely down to earth, straight to the point and pretty fucking obnoxious. Yet, he's perfect like that. We know what to expect with him, his attitude, his random input and his strong opinions.

Chapter 37

"You're one to talk." Ever says to Blake, alerting me to the obvious newfound tension in the room.

"What's going on between you two? You've been at each other's throats since we got here." Reed asks before I get the chance to.

"Nothing." Blake clips, Ever turning his head to peer at the opposite wall to him.

"Guys, I'm just glad you're all here, for me, and for my mom." I wince at the end of my sentence, still in a state of disbelief.

"Always."

"Of course."

"Without fail."

The three of them respond.

The fact I have these three, the guys who give me a shoulder to lean on, a mind to speak to and a body to cuddle, gives me hope.

Without Rhea, things will be difficult, but manageable. I was Devon before Rhea, and I will remain as Devon after.

Chapter 38

Rhea

"Are you not supposed to be at work?" Fizzy asks, packing up a bunch of crackers and bananas.

"Nope." I deadpan.

"Oh, sorry... Are you okay?" She turns to me, dropping the crackers onto the counter-top.

Dragging the throw closer to my chin, I turn further away from her, focusing my attention on the TV.

"Fine." I clip, trying to extract the memories of him from my mind.

"Is Devon coming over to see you today?" Fizz's words pierce my chest with the sound of his name.

"No."

"Oh, I see... Is everything okay?... With the two of you?" Her hands don't continue to pack her lunch for the day, I can almost feel her aqua eyes burning into me with every passing second.

"No."

Chapter 38

"Do you need me? If you need me, I'm here. Anything you need, Rhea. I'm here."

My eyes begin to well as I grip onto the fluffy blanket, twisting the material as I try to mask my emotions.

My knees flex as I tuck them further into me, my breath unable to contain itself anymore. The gasp that escapes my lips overrides any answer I could have possibly given.

"Oh, babe." Fizzy says, before I hear her shift from the kitchen and into the living space, her gym leggings coming into my view.

I don't have the effort to even look up at her face, already knowing it's stained with a sympathetic look. I didn't have to endure this when I escaped from Banks, I had basically no friends, no family, no one.

Now, I have other people who will pick up on my downfall, someone else to consider whilst I endure being heartbroken, for the second time.

I'd be lying if I said I thought me and Devon were *it*. But, I thought it would last longer than a measly few weeks.

Felicity lifts my legs by the ankles, lifting them up and sitting down, propping my legs back over hers.

"Don't let it ruin you, Rhea." She sighs, rubbing her thumb over my ankle.

"I won't." I moan, stretching my body from the position I've been stuck in from the last few hours.

"Okay, I'm sure Indie won't mind, shit happens. I'm taking the day off." She confesses, pulling out her phone.

"No, don't." I rush, not expanding further on the matter.

"Rhea, stop it. Sometimes, you treat me like I'm just some stranger that you live with, but I'm not. You think I don't know that every one of your bed sheets has a flower that is representative of the month? You think I don't know that you purposely don't use the air-fryer because you don't believe there is a difference between that, and the oven? You think I don't know you listen to your true-crime to go to sleep on a night? You think I don't know that you wear the same pair of Chucks every Friday because they bring you 'Good Luck'? Rhea, I'm your best friend, don't shut me out." She finishes.

My mind is plagued with guilt, from the idea that Fizzy is merely a stepping stone. I've found it difficult to attach to anyone, since *him*. But, exactly what I needed was right under my nose. It wasn't getting my three-stripes, it wasn't being with Devon, Christ, it wasn't growing the garden on my balcony.

It was appreciating the life I've been gifted, the people that choose to care about you, the people that intentionally want to make your life better without causing you some level of emotional damage.

"Fizz… I– Thank you." There are no words better to describe how I'm feeling right now.

"Enough, Rhea. This isn't some sort of favor. I'm your best friend, start treating me like one. I'm not some fragile piece of china that you need to protect. Offload to me, rant to me, give me something. Stop holding it all in."

My chest constricts, my eyes flutter closed as I grip tighter onto the blanket, unable to conjure up the words of how much she means to me.

The quiet atmosphere is comforting in a way, allowing me to process everything she's said to me as she sits cradling my feet.

"Indie is covering today, I'm yours now." Fizzy says, shifting slightly.

"What? Isn't she like, about to pop?" I ask, gathering the information Fizz has told me over the past few months.

"She's not that far along, she can still do classes." She admits, not making my inner conscience feel any better.

"I'm yours, all day, baby." Fizz jabs at my side and I kick my legs in response, barely able to mask the impending giggle.

"What did you have in mind?" I ask.

Chapter 38

"The world is our oyster for today, Rhea. Anything you want." Her brown eyes bore into me, waiting for an answer.

"Hm... What about a girly cocktail night? I'd love to just drink obnoxiously expensive drinks and talk shit about anything and everything." I confess.

"Oh, Rhea. Now you're speaking my language." Her face spills into a wide grin as her shoulders slump slightly, probably relieved I still have some sort of life within me.

Just as she's about to get up from the couch, I dig my heels into her to prevent her from moving. She looks up at me quickly, her hair flicking with the movement.

"What?" She looks at me quizzically.

"I just wanted to say... I really do love you, Fizzy." The smile on my lips is weak, but not from the lack of emotion, more the lack of defense behind my words.

"I love you too, Rhea." Her gorgeous freckled face lights up as she squeezes my ankle in a comforting way.

"Let's head out and have the best girls night we've ever had!" She raises her arms in the air as she stands up, my legs dropping off the couch as I'm half hanging on.

"Get your lazy ass up, girl. You really need to explore my new wardrobe that I've purchased whilst you've been M.I.A." She pulls on my arm, trying to heave me out of my slum.

* * *

"You sure this isn't too revealing?" I pull at the dress hem, trying to force it down further than the material will allow.

"You look hot as shit, as always." Fizz bumps her hip with mine as we walk further down the street, the sounds of our heels clacking against the sidewalk.

I wrap my arms around myself as the wind whirls around us, nipping at our skin, igniting a layer of goosebumps across my body.

"Bit chilly tonight, aint it?" Fizz's teeth chatter obnoxiously.

"Just a bit. Sucks that we decided to do this in the middle of November." I cringe, unsure why neither of us bothered to bring out a coat despite our lack of clothing.

"Ugh, just hurry up. It's only a little further." She encourages.

The echoing of our heels bounce off each side of the street, the pace now slightly increased. The speed also helps the blood pump around my body, encouraging warmth.

My eyes draw in on the cute cocktail bar, 'Luna Moon' shines in neon cursive letters. The exterior of the building is littered with an array of floral decor, much to my liking. It gives off a homely atmosphere, welcoming and comforting. Empty tables and chairs sit outside, but the inside is bustling with customers. I suppose that's expected for the weekend.

Fizz enters the bar first, holding the door open for me as the heated air welcomes me with open arms. I drop my hands from my upper body and instantly feel at ease, the sounds of some indie artist plays softly in the background.

"This is a real steal, Fizz. How did you find this place?" I ask, looking around in amazement at the flower wall, large golden mirrors and hanging yellow light-bulbs. The choice of lighting means the room looks as if it's hazy, but glowing.

"Oh, Rhea. I have so much to bring you up to speed on." She laughs, shaking her head as we line up at the bar.

To our delight, the cocktails are on a two-for-one offer, meaning that instead of splitting the round, we double up. I choose porn star martini's, a classic and a favorite. Fizz opts for strawberry daiquiri's,

Chapter 38

insisting it's the best one she's ever tasted.

Once we find a table, we sit adjacently to each other, two cocktails in front of us. The bass of the music heightens the further into the bar we are, an array of 'girl power' quotes sit inside of thick golden frames, adding to the already feminine atmosphere.

"This place is stunning, I can't believe we've never been here before!" I half-shout over the music.

"Well… I kind of came here… on a date." Fizz blushes and sinks her face behind one of her cocktails, taking a rather long sip.

Picking my jaw up from the table, I lean forward with intrigue, "Tell me more!" I smile, my grin being genuine for the first time in a while.

"Okay… Um. Right, get over yourself, Fizzy. So, we went on one date. But, I'm obsessed. Like, crazy in love, Rhea. He's so handsome, charming and oh god, he's so funny!" She babbles like a love-sick teenager.

If anything, I'm watching on in awe, loving every second that she feels this unique happiness.

"How did you two meet?" I push, taking a drink of my cocktail and almost moaning as the flavors invade my taste buds.

"At work. But, he doesn't work there, he actually came by looking for Indie and of course, I was there and not Indie. We spoke a few times whenever he came by, and then one time, he came in asking for *me*." She giggles and claps her hands giddily.

My mouth drops open again, dramatically and excitedly. This side of Fizzy is the best, when she gets so enthusiastic about something, the world falls at her feet. Whoever this guy is, he is one lucky man.

"And then?…" I encourage.

"He asked me on a date, and he brought me here. Can you imagine my face when a guy brought me to the most feminine bar in the city! Of course, I'm not being sexist but it just gave me good vibes that he didn't take me to some trashy place or super over-the-top restaurant." She fans herself whilst she rambles away.

"Is he, related to Indie or something?" I question, honing in on the fact he was always there to see her.

"Yeah, kind of. It's her brother in law." She answers, grabbing her hair and positioning it over one singular shoulder.

"That's gotta be exciting, does Indie know about it? Seeing as she is your boss and all?" I cringe, imagining myself in the same situation.

"She was there when he asked me! She was more than encouraging of it, telling me how much of a good guy he is. Eek! Can you believe it?" She is almost about to burst out of her chair with how much she is bouncing up and down, "Six months ago, we were both jobless and single and now– Look at us!" Her eyes grow wide as she can't stop the words tumbling from her mouth.

"Shit, fuck, shit. Ignore me, ooo I can get a little bit too excited sometimes, can't I?" She bites her lip before draining the rest of her cocktail, presumably to stop her from talking some more.

"It's fine, it's not like there isn't a huge elephant in the room right now. I may as well spill." I roll my eyes and heave a breath, trying to psyche myself up to talk about *him*.

"Ugh, where to start, where to start? So, everything was fine, we were amazing if anything. I went to work and nothing untoward had happened, until I returned. I heard through Rick, another pilot, that Devon was taking some time off due to a family emergency. I heard that it was pretty traumatic, his mother suffered a heart attack, and he'd not left her side since. I thought I was doing the right thing, I picked some of my flowers from the garden, the ones symbolizing health and recovery, and visited him." I close my eyes and take another deep breath, the next part of the explanation is going to be the hardest.

Fizzy looks up at me with worry in her eyes, the brown irises dance between both of my blue ones, searching for answers.

"So… when I arrived, lets just say, he wasn't best pleased to see me. Can I say that, if he didn't really look at me? I dunno, but yeah. Um– He asked me to leave, so I did." I try and evade the more morbid thoughts that followed afterwards, not wanting to ruin the night.

"Oh… Well, shit." Fizzy slumps back in her chair, her eyes blinking rapidly.

"I don't know if he meant for good, or at that time but, it didn't make me feel so good. I just wanted to be there for him, you know? Like he was there for me." I chew on my inner cheek, submitting to the pain to stop any tears from forming.

"Yeah, no. Don't think you're at fault, Rhea. You did what any significant other would. Hell, you were just being nice." She continues, shaking her head in disagreement.

"Apparently not. Or, I thought we were more than what we were. Or are? I don't know. This is all so fucking stupid." I grit, annoyed that I have no clue what the pretense is.

"And he hasn't contacted you since?" She asks.

"Nope." I deadpan, taking a long sip from my cocktail.

"Are you going to do anything about it?" She toys with the coaster on the table, flipping it between her fingers.

"Nah, I'm not too bothered anyway. It's fine. It was a fling, shit happens." I lie when in reality, my heart is splitting further apart from every word that I've just spoken.

"I'll go get us some more drinks, my choice this time!" Fizzy sing-songs as she stands up, taking her purse with her.

I smile and nod, finishing off my drink and taking notice of the prints on the wall.

Almost choking on the liquid in the mouth, I read, *'They tried to bury us, but they did not know that we were the seeds'*. The irony of the quote and the matter of the metaphor fills me with confidence, the words complement my soul.

My eyes follow the rest and I giggle at the one that says, '*Less DePresso, more espresso*', that one I need to focus on religiously.

The ache in my chest reappears when I read the words of the third one, '*Behind every strong woman is herself*'.

The word '*strong*' takes me back to that room, the moment Devon said it to me, the idea that he seen me for who I was, I felt like the only girl in the world at that moment. And now? Now, the word makes me feel sick to my stomach, sick at the fact he used that word so absentmindedly, but it meant everything to me.

"Okay, so this is strong but I kinda feel like you need it tonight." Fizzy laughs, carrying over a dark colored cocktail in a tall glass, mint leaves sticking out of the top.

"And this is?" I scan the sweating glass suspiciously as she places two of them onto the table in front of me.

"Long Island iced tea, baby!" She sways her hips as she returns to the bar to collect two more of them.

When she returns, I lift the glass and give it a sniff to gauge the alcohol content in it. Instantly, my nose burns with the musky smell of whiskey; I feel like I could get drunk from the smell alone.

"Jesus, what the fuck is in this?" My eyes grow wide as I analyze the pretty glass.

"Um… Just a little vodka, gin, rum, tequila, something else and cola. Oh, and I asked for a shot of whiskey in there too because, why not?" She lifts her drink, preparing to 'cheers' with me.

I groan and pick up the ice cold cup, raising it to her height.

"To girls night!" She cheers, clinking her glass with mine.

"To girls night!" I laugh, as we then proceed to drink it.

I almost choke on the intense burning in my throat, complemented by the sharp flavor of mint. Aside from the crazy whiplash it's just given my brain, it tastes pretty good.

Tonight is definitely going to be *wild*.

Chapter 39

Devon

The agony is different this time.

Before, I thought she'd ditched me, couldn't give a shit about me, or didn't like me.

This time, I know.

This time, it was me who pushed her away despite our inevitable connection. Between the different time periods, there has been death, love and destruction.

I'm sure that everyone thinks I'm going out of my fucking mind for telling her to leave, even I think I am. But, there is a greater meaning at stake. Her welfare.

I couldn't guarantee that I could keep her safe from the dangers that come with being involved with someone like me, and I care too much to let anything happen to her again.

Part of me wishes that she was like most other girls, where she cried and fought me to stay, instead of holding it all inside. But, that's incredibly selfish of me and completely idiotic because she's perfect in every way, I admire her for being who she is and the strength she holds.

I suppose all of this was bound to warp around my heart the first time seeing her since then, knowing that any second she's going to enter this cockpit, similarly to our first meeting. Only now, the animosity between us isn't a level of flirtatious banter, it's pain.

Removing my blazer, I hang it over the back of my chair as the sweat begins to pool at my lower back.

Is the air-con not working?

I lean over to Rhea's side and start pressing a few buttons, knowing I'm not used to being on this side of the controls and hoping that I somehow press the right button.

"Ahem, what do you think you're doing?"

I freeze at the sound of her voice, the sternness within it almost has me smirking. *God, I've missed her.*

"Nothing." I respond and retreat to my side, avoiding her eyes.

In my peripheral vision, I see her sit down, her blonde hair shines in the autumnal sun.

"Any reason for the tardiness this morning, Miss. Jensen?" I raise an eyebrow, finally allowing myself to breathe in her beauty.

Her head doesn't fire towards me as it normally would, she turns it agonizingly slow. Her bright aqua eyes glisten as she scans my face, my deep brown challenging hers right back.

"Sorry, I spent the night out of town, I didn't expect the traffic on the way back into the city." She beams at me before turning her head away.

I gulp harshly.

She… spent the night… out of town…

My mind races, my heart thumps at the thought of her being with someone else last night, knowing now, exactly what is beneath that

Chapter 39

uniform of hers. That uniform that… *Oh, boy.*

My eyes trail down her exposed legs, the short skirt is hiked up her thighs, revealing far too much for my body to handle.

Shifting my eyes straight ahead, I feel a bead of sweat drip past my temple and I reach up to wipe it away quickly, before the evidence is noted.

She knows exactly what she's doing, wearing the same skirt that had me drooling over her before, before I found out the sounds she makes whilst I'm tongue-fucking her.

"Captain Stark!" She snaps.

I whip my head to hers, confused at her outburst, "What?" I ask.

"I said, how many crew are on board with us today?" She says, annoyance in her tone.

"Oh, um. There's seven." I swallow, my throat dry from knowing exactly what she tastes like beneath that skimpy piece of material.

I grip onto my thigh firmly, trying to distract myself from her with anything possible. But, it's even her scent, the pheromones that she emits are taunting me like a kid in a candy shop.

"This is co-pilot Rhea Jensen, flight E392, preparing to taxi in nine minutes." She speaks, the deepest undertones of her voice crawl under my skin, embedding itself and not letting me go.

"Hey, Rhea. It's James, nice to have you onboard today. Lining you up for runway four." A masculine voice responds.

I cock my head, biting on my inner cheek before I say something that I really shouldn't.

"Oh, hey James! Thank you *so* much!" She replies, and I'm almost ready to bend her over and show her exactly where that tone gets her when it's used on anyone other than me.

Oh, Rhea. This is one fucking dangerous game you're playing.

"Everything okay, Captain?" She bats her eyelashes at me with a pathetic fake smile.

"Perfect." I grin back, bearing teeth.

She nods and sticks her nose back into the pre-flight checklist, analyzing the statistics for everything.

I glance downwards and can already see the outline of my traitorous body part, ignoring my wishes for him to stay quiet. Leaning forward to mask it, I try my best to complete my own checklist without becoming distracted by the most fucking divine woman sitting beside me.

"One second, I forgot something." She says, as my eyes follow her body standing up from the chair.

She doesn't pull her skirt down like she did religiously last time. If anything, she walks with a wider stance so it rides up higher, sitting just below her plump ass.

Closing my eyes, I take in a heavy breath as my chest aches from the sexual tension in the air. This level of teasing is completely untoward, considering the circumstances.

My eyes snap open at the sound of her contagious giggles through the open cockpit door. I angle my body so I can see directly through the gap, and she's speaking to a member of the flight crew, a *male* member.

This plane is about to burst into flames from my own internal body temperature. I can't cope being in this close proximity with her for the next nine hours, knowing I can't have her. *This is actual torture.*

"Rhea!" I shout, gaining her attention.

She scowls at me and says something else to the guy, then stomps her way back to the cockpit.

"What?" She snarls, the fury dances in her eyes as she stares at me.

"What's the weather forecast?" I ask, a lazy smile plays on my lips, earning a huff from her.

"Really, Devon? Can't check it yourself?" She groans, slamming the cockpit door shut.

Chapter 39

She called me Devon for the first time this flight, I'm counting that as a win. She thinks that she can play me, tempt me and make me jealous? *I don't fucking think so.*

Rhea is about to have my name engraved on her permanently, in a way that makes a tattoo seem like a whiteboard marker.

Chapter 40

Rhea

Yup, I've gone a little bit fucking crazy.

I couldn't fight the anxiety before coming into work today, hence why I was late. The only way I could do it, is by psyching myself up and putting on an entirely different persona, and acting like the bad bitch I have buried deep down inside of me.

Cue the formulation of operation *'Destroy Devon'*.

I want to make him fucking squirm under my gaze, I want him to feel every lustful emotion known to mankind, and have him begging for me to stop.

After the night with Fizzy, it became apparent that I wasn't going to take no for a fucking answer.

He's going to want me in ways he never thought possible, he's going to be imagining every single position that my body can contort into, all whilst giving him a pleasure that only I can emit.

Even now, he can barely remove his eyes from me as I twist my body purposely, angling it so that he can scan the revealed skin of my thighs. It feels like sweet fucking victory.

"We're at twenty-thousand feet, Captain." I say in the most sultry voice I can possess.

The Adam's apple bobs in his throat, a sheen of sweat lines his forehead and if he thinks he's being coy about the bulge in his pants, then he's sorrily mistaken.

I'm eating this up.

"We're at thirty-thousand feet, Captain Stark." I practically moan, his eyes shift to mine.

It's kinda sweet, seeing him trapped like a deer in headlights, not sure what to do with these bodily responses. He flicks his eyes away, his jaw flexes and his hand finds its way into his hair as he tugs slightly.

"You pulled my hair in a similar fashion." I smirk, selectively averting my gaze.

"Oh, we're at thirty-five thousand feet, Mr. Stark." I giggle, leaning back and pushing my chest out.

The silence from him is exciting, like I'm waiting for him to burst his seams and let the waterfall flow. It's invigorating.

"Initiating cruise control." He almost mumbles, speaking through gritted teeth.

"Cruise control initiated," He whispers, hanging his head and removing his headset.

Tactically, I remove mine and reach my arms into the air, stretching my body outwards and letting out an obnoxious moaning sound, the air-con fanning over my nipples causing them to harden through my white shirt.

Without even having to look at him, I know he's watching. Despite the cold air blowing at me, my skin burns under his watchful eyes, feeling them dance all over my body like a laser.

"Something interesting caught your eye, Mr. Stark?" I taunt, pulling my hair tie and letting my hair cascade around my shoulders.

"Interesting? No. Captivating? Yes." He responds, daring to challenge me in a stare off.

"Hm, I wish I could say the same…" I tease, loosening the tie around my neck, "Is it just me or is the temperature in here, just *so, fucking, hot*." I pant, fanning myself.

"Fucking sizzling." He speaks, his voice strained similarly to his pants.

With a victorious smile playing on my lips, I undo the first button on my shirt, the thrill of his eyes scanning my every inch, has my heart thumping ferociously.

"Rhea…" He whispers, and I don't bother to look at him as I continue onto the second button.

"Rhea." His voice is pained, but full of excitement.

When my fingers graze the third button, about to expose my cleavage, he snaps.

"If you want any hope of landing this plane and not having me tear you limb from limb whilst I fuck you incessantly, I suggest you stop what you're doing right now."

Now, he's got my attention.

I drop my hands and slowly turn my head to meet the squinted eyes, his veins protruding out of his neck as his forearms remain locked, his grip on the chair disgustingly unforgiving and merciless.

"Is that so?" I raise an eyebrow and toy with my hair, twirling it around my index finger and spreading my legs slightly.

"You see, Captain. A little dove once told me that I was a fucking Goddess, and fortunately, or unfortunately for you, I've started to fucking act like it." I bore my eyes into his, allowing him to see the fire behind them as I fill my body with so much confidence, I'm sure I'm flying well above this jet.

His knuckles flex as his hands hold onto the chair as if they are any sort of saving grace.

"I've been told my entire life how worthless I am, told how to act, who to serve and under someone else's commands. But, not anymore. Now, I'm going after exactly what I fucking want."

With this statement, his face erupts into a sly grin as he shakes his head, but still maintaining our intense eye contact.

Seeing him look so devastatingly gorgeous only confirms the way I feel, more.

Devon Stark is exactly who I fucking want, and Devon Stark is exactly who I shall fucking have.

"Perfect. Fucking perfect." He whispers, igniting the same goosebumps over my body as he did the last time.

Despite my persistent crave for his touch, I can't deny the overpowering tug on my heart from this moment. We are so incredibly fucking matched, it's incomparable to anything I've ever felt before. This connection between us is not lust, it's complete and utter fucking insanity.

I'm only sane when I'm around him, within his proximity I can breathe easier than I ever have in my life, he permits me the ability to live.

He twists his body so that he's facing me head on, tucking his knee up to rest over the arm rest. His shirt pulls at his muscles and wraps around them like cellophane, outlining every sinful shape on his body.

His tan skin contrasts with his white, short-sleeved, button down, his stubble has grown since I last saw him, making him appear even more masculine than his frame allows.

Despite our seven-year age gap, his experienced body only attracts me more, knowing that each and every line has been on this earth longer than I have. It's invigorating.

Not being able to cope with the intense feeling swirling in my gut, I decide I need to take a moment alone in the bathroom before I do something that could lose me my pilot's license.

"Where d'ya think you're going?" He growls, his dark eyes drawing in on my mid section.

"I–"

He yanks my hips towards him, his grip sizzling through my skirt as I almost topple right on top of him.

"Devon! What are you–" My mind turns to mush as he runs his nose up the middle of my stomach, the slight pressure tickling and taunting me.

"Devon, stop–" My head drops back as my jaw opens whilst his teeth graze over my hardened nipple through my shirt.

The sensitiveness of them causes my legs to buckle slightly, overwhelmed with the pleasure from the bare minimum.

He wraps his huge arms around my thighs, pulling me flush against his face as he yanks my tucked-in shirt from my skirt. The second his lips make contact with my stomach, I'm littered with goosebumps from his cold and wet lips against my hot skin.

"Oh, Devon," I pant as my eyes roll around in the back of my head, his hands gripping my ass through the skirt as he nips and sucks above my navel.

The phone in the cockpit rings out, startling us from our intense embrace. I stumble backwards, lost for words as his eyes skate up to my face as he wears a smug look.

Yanking my shirt down and into my skirt, I reach for the phone, pulling it to my ear.

"Hello?" I say, entirely unprofessional and breathless.

"Rhea? Hi, yeah we have an emergency on-board, a woman has entered into a premature labor." Erin ushers, her voice full of concern.

My eyes grow wide as I turn to Devon, "We need to make an emergency landing, where is the closest airport to here?"

We're currently en route to Sao Paulo, Brazil.

Chapter 40

"It's looking like Miami is our closest, but we will have to turn back we're just crossing over the Atlantic." Devon picks up his headset, channeling in to the Miami air traffic control.

I tap my foot impatiently, waiting for a response as Devon discusses timings and runway plans.

"We're able to circle back around, coming from the south towards the airport. Yes– Mm-hmm– Yeah, got it." His face is stone cold serious.

"We're preparing for an emergency landing in eight minutes, they'll have the EMT team waiting and ready to come on board." He reiterates to me.

I repeat the information the Erin and she thanks me, before we both put the phone down.

Turning quickly, I sit back in my seat and place the headset back on as we prepare for our first emergency landing together.

"You wanna take this one?" He asks, not looking at me but ensuring the plane is circling successfully, out of the flight path of any other jets.

"Um, yeah." I laugh full of confidence, glad that I'll get to add to my portfolio of landings.

He shakes his head with a slight smile on his lips, placing his aviators back on as the sun pierces our windshield.

He looks every bit as gorgeous as he did the first day I met him.

Chapter 41

Devon

"Okay, I'm deciding to discard of half of fuel tank, we were filled up with twelve hours worth of flying, it's going to be too heavy to have a sufficient landing if we carry it with us." Rhea begins thinking hard, working out the math side of the landing.

"So, that would mean we must dump at least twenty-thousand gallons of fuel, leaving us with twenty-thousand gallons remaining which is approximately... one-hundred-and-thirty-six-thousand pounds of fuel." She mutters to herself, to my amazement of her brain working at this speed.

"A Boeing seven-four-seven weighs around eight-hundred-thousand pounds with four-hundred passengers on board, and a full tank. Minus the one-hundred-and-thirty-six thousand pounds of fuel, which brings us to a total of six-hundred-and-sixty-four-thousand pounds." She continues, I don't dare to interrupt her brain

Chapter 41

at work.

"No, that's too much." She looks at me with wide

"We're gonna have to dump at least, another quarter but we're still going to be at a heavy load." She looks to me for reassurance and I nod my head, enjoying the smarts of this incredible woman.

"Okay, perfect. Let's do this." She cracks her knuckles in front of her and gives herself a little shake down, before taking control of the yoke.

* * *

Rhea lands the plane with perfect precision, ticking every box within my own expertise.

A pilot being able to land a jet this size under normal circumstances? Brilliant.

A pilot being able to land a jet this size under emergency pressure? Outstanding.

It's starting to eat away at me that somehow, she can still stop the plane earlier than myself and any other pilot I have worked with, military and commercial, even with the extra weight.

I'm a little jealous, just a little.

We stop at the end of the runway, allowing the the EMT team to escort the pregnant passenger off the flight and straight to the nearest hospital.

Rhea slumps slightly in her seat, looking mentally drained.

"You did great." I mumble, half not wanting her to hear me.

"What did you just say?" Her head whips so fast, her blonde hair shakes behind her.

Rolling my eyes, I repeat, "You did great."

"Oh, Devon. You do know you're never going to live this down, don't you?" She laughs, the creases around her eyes shine prominently. This look suits her.

"I know," I accept.

She just looks at me, her smile slowly fading as we battle for dominance in our eyes, neither of us submitting to defeat.

"So, what now?" I bait.

"What do you mean?" She looks at me quizzically.

"Well, you've saved the day, saved the lives of the passengers on board and gotten us to safety. We're stuck in Miami until further instruction, how about you go on a date with me?" I propose, with a smile so wide it gives me jaw ache.

"Devon, are you seriously asking me on a date right now?" She gasps, her hand raising to her chest as she looks around at the pretend people, a shocked look on her face.

Rolling my eyes, I nod my head, knowing she's doing this on purpose to try and make me uncomfortable. But, I've never been more comfortable with anyone, like I am with her.

"I'd be honored, Captain." She salutes me with a cheesy smile, her cheeks glow with a pink undertone.

It's about time I put myself out of my misery, and give into exactly what I want. And, that's Rhea Jensen.

* * *

Knocking at her hotel door, four rooms left of mine, I step back with a bouquet within my sweaty hands. I can't deny that I'm actually feeling pretty fucking nervous right now, this is the most platonic action I've ever committed.

Chapter 41

Going on a date.

The sound of the bolt unlocking has me quivering in my dress shoes, my knees growing weaker by the second.

It swings open to reveal the most breath-taking woman I've ever seen, her hair let loose and around her bare shoulders, a cute pair of mom jeans and a cream colored corset top.

It's completely different to how you'd expect a woman to dress for a date, normally they'd have pulled out all of the stops and spent hours debating which outfit to wear. But, that's not Rhea. What you see is what you get, and it's nothing short of perfect.

"You look– Wow." I shake my head as if what I'm seeing in front of me isn't real.

"Oh, stop. I literally had nothing else to wear." She shrugs me off and proceeds to locking her hotel room door, putting the key fob back into her bag.

"These, are for you." I shove the flowers forward, after almost forgetting about them. They hit her straight in the chest and the paper crumples, a few stray petals falling free.

My arm retreats quickly, "Shit, sorry. Um, these are for you though." I cringe, unsure why the fuck I'm acting as if I don't have a single brain cell to my name.

"They're beautiful, I love the combo of the white roses and the peachy carnations. Mmm." She takes them from my hand and brings them to her nose, giving them a strong sniff whilst smiling.

Devon, you did good. Momma would be proud.

"Oh, I should probably pop these inside, actually." She laughs, grabbing her key fob out of her bag and disappearing through the hotel door.

I sway from one foot to the other, my mind running rings around me, debating what to say next, if asking her platonic questions isn't the vibe we're going for, if I'm even good enough for her.

"What's got your face so twisted up?" She angles her head slightly, analyzing me.

"Nothing, nothing at all." I plaster a huge smile on my face to reassure her.

"Great! I also got you a little something…" She begins, and before she makes any further moves, my heart fills with warmth, knowing exactly what it is.

Our ritual.

"Okay, so I don't know if this is some fucked up twist of fate, but I got you these…" She hands me two packets of seeds, which I take with eagerness.

Peering down at them, my eyes grow wide when I read the titles of them.

White Rose.

Carnation.

"Are you kidding? Are you sure you just didn't bring an entire greenhouse and you wanted to be kinda sweet?" I raise an eyebrow at her, to which she shakes her head and letting out a small giggle.

"No, honestly. This is fucked, right?" She gestures to the seeds and I begin to laugh alongside her.

"So fucked." I reply.

* * *

"Mr. and Mrs. Stark, please be seated this way." The waiter escorts us to our table as me and Rhea share a disgusted look between us.

I do the gentlemanly thing, and pull her chair out, allowing her to sit before me.

Taking my own seat adjacent to her, my palms are lined with sweat

Chapter 41

so I wipe them on my pants, hoping to alleviate my anxiety as they shake incessantly.

"Did you hear him? *Mr. and Mrs. Stark.*" She mocks, pulling a face and putting on a silly voice.

"With the ways the stars have been aligning lately, I wouldn't say he was that far off." I respond as Rhea grimaces, scrunching her nose adorably.

"Where is Devon Stark, and what have you done with him?" She jokes, picking up the drinks menu in front of her.

The candlelit dinner in front of us is definitely too fancy for our liking, but I couldn't resist. You only get a first date once, and I wanted this to be special.

"Hm… Call me ignorant, but all of this is in French." Rhea says and I avert my eyes from her stunning face to the mediocre-looking menu, unable to read any of it myself.

"Yeah… Probably should have looked at that before I booked…" I sigh, attempting to translate any of the words.

"Ah, I know this one, *Champagne.*" Her eyes light up like a Christmas tree, winking at me at the same time.

She is honestly everything I could ever want, her bubbly personality but so incredibly outspoken, doesn't take shit from anybody and is so different from anyone I've ever met before. Mom would absolutely love her.

"Champagne it shall be, little dove." I smile at her as she folds the menu, her cheeks balling into rosy apples.

"So, to what do I owe the pleasure of this, all expenses paid, business meeting?" She leans forward on her clenched fists, her elbows resting lightly on the table. I'm enjoying seeing her face under this setting, the candlelight gracing her face with warm shadows.

She is sensationally beautiful.

Chapter 42

Rhea

"This *date*, kindly paid for by *Titan*, is actually for us to get to know one another, start fresh and be normal. And of course– my apology for the way I reacted when you came to see me at the hospital." He explains.

I nod my head agreeing, my chin bobbing on top of my clasped hands. We're interrupted by the waiter, requesting for our drinks order, to which Devon orders a crisp cold bottle of Champagne, in a bucket of ice.

Oh, he's really pulling out all of the stops tonight. And, I'm eating up every single second of it.

"So, Stark. What d'ya wanna know?" I lean forward further, his chocolate eyes focus on my lips as I speak.

"Lets start off simple, what's your favorite color?" He asks, I almost groan at the boring topic of conversation.

"Blue, what's your favorite sex position?" I smirk, not caring about ramping up the heat factor.

Chapter 42

If he thinks, after what happened in the cockpit today, that there is any chance we're going to spend the night learning what each other's star signs are, then he's on a date with the wrong girl.

"Alright then, hmm... I'd say I'm a sucker for reverse cowgirl." He admits, his eyes slightly glazed over.

I would bet my entire years earnings, that he's imagining that with me right now.

"Nice, I actually prefer the magic bullet." I look around the room, not caring to maintain eye contact whilst he digests my words.

"Mm, yeah. That's a good one." He agrees.

"You know it?" I ask, surprise in my tone.

"Do I know it? Ha-ha, Rhea. You really do make me laugh." He says smugly, shaking his head at me.

I think I sometimes forget he's seven years my senior, and when he looks like a God under that clothing, it doesn't surprise me he's well-educated in the bedroom department.

"Maybe, you could show me a trick or two?" I reply, just as the waiter brings over the champagne, the bucket of ice may as well have been thrown over our heads from the interruption.

"Would you like to try, Madame?" The waiter says with a strong French accent, but I can't tell if it's fake or not.

I love that they consulted me for my opinion, rather than my 'husband'.

"Of course!" I smile in correspondence as he fills my flute part way with some of the liquid.

Sipping it gently, I let the bubbles sizzle on my tongue for a moment and then wash it away, allowing the slight burn to entertain my throat.

"It's beautiful, thank you." I nod and place the flute back down as he fills it up further, then proceeding to fill Devon's, but I instinctively put a hand over the top of it before he gets the chance to.

"He– Uh..." My words are lost before me, unsure how to phrase it.

"No champagne for me, thank you. I'll just take an iced water." He smiles up at the waiter, and he whisks away, leaving the bucket of ice with the bottle in, on the table.

"Does that ever get really awkward? Like, does it make it more difficult when I'm drinking?" I ask, for some reason not holding back.

"Yeah, it can be. Especially when shit gets tough. But, right now? No."

I bow my head, trying to mask the obvious blood rising to my cheeks from his divine smile.

Everything about him, comforts me. Whenever I'm around him, he makes me feel so free, like I could conquer the world with him by my side. It's this insane God complex, being invincible and powerful all at once.

"I do have an interesting question for you, something that I've been meaning to ask but, of course, things between us went a little pear-shaped." I let out a dry laugh as the waiter sets down a glass bottle of water and a crystal cup with ball of ice inside.

"Do ask." He prompts, adding the water over the ice.

"Those guys... I kind of met them at the hospital, after... you know..." I'm tip-toeing around the situation as I don't want to trigger any of our feelings about that day.

"Ah, the boys." He lets out a chuckle into his glass as he takes a sip, our eyes meeting over the rim.

"The boys?" I angle my head to the side, waiting for him to provide an explanation.

"Yeah. They're pretty much my brothers. We're solid as a rock, the ride or die type. Take a bullet for each other, got each other's backs, you know?" He's smiling fondly as he speaks, the words coming out of his mouth have me grinning back at him, to the point my cheeks ache.

"Tell me more," I insist, loving that this is a side of Devon I am yet

Chapter 42

to be introduced to.

"Okay, so there's Ever. Total golden retriever energy, can pretty much get along with anyone, wouldn't hurt a fly unless the fly hurt him, or someone he cared about. He's into motorbikes, he actually set me up with mine–"

"Yours?" I whisper-shout, trying to avoid capturing the attention of surrounding diners.

"Yeah?" He looks back at me, his head slightly pulled back in confusion.

"You have a motorbike?" I ask again, needing the clarification.

"Yes. I own a bike, that has two wheels and a pretty fucking neat engine." The arrogance drips from his words as I cross my arms over my chest.

"Interesting." I deadpan, hoping he will continue with the story of the boys.

"Anyways, before I was *rudely* interrupted, I was saying that Ever participates in the Atlanta Motocross, we attend every year and other events, as long as we aren't busy. He's the most single guy I've ever met, barely showing an interest in anyone."

I listen intently, picturing Ever from our interaction on the bench at the hospital.

"Then there's Reed, he's the newbie, or so we say anyway, it's more of a running joke at the minute. We're no less brothers just because he hasn't been here for as long as the others. He's married to Indie, and they have two kids, well one and one on the way–"

"You're kidding?" I whisper-shout, again.

"What this time, Rhea?" He sighs, rolling his eyes.

It turns out, I can't sit listening without my mind working in overdrive, putting together the pieces of the puzzle.

"Fizzy, you know, Fizzy?" I begin.

"Yes, Rhea. I know Fizzy."

"If you keep rolling your eyes at me, Devon, they'll get stuck." I stick my tongue out at him and he almost, very nearly, rolls his eyes at me again.

"Anyway, she works for this big-time ballerina, Indie Thorne, and she's pregnant and holy shit! I think that's the same person." I gasp, hoping that Devon is following along.

"Yeah, probably." He shrugs, not gauging my excitement.

"You can be such an ass." I grumble.

"You know, you and Ever would get along just fine." His eyes crinkle at the corners as his pearly teeth shine.

"Oh, we do, actually." I chirp.

"So I've heard." He drops his head to the side, the smile lines on his face deepen as he looks up at me.

"What's that supposed to mean?" My eyes grow wide.

"Oh, nothing. Just the boys, being boys."

Scowling slightly, I encourage him to tell me the rest about them, "And… the other guy, the miserable tatted guy?" I laugh lightheartedly as he does.

"You mean, Blake? Yeah, he's going through a bit of shit at the minute, but he's a good guy. At surface level, he can give of the impression he's closed off, disinterested and quite frankly, a moody asshole. But, once you break through that surface, he's like an iceberg. There's so much to him that you can't see with the naked eye. He's quite fascinating."

"Yeah… I don't think he likes me all that much." I scratch the back of my neck awkwardly, remembering his distaste to me.

"I doubt that, Rhea. You're so fucking likable, too fucking likable." He jokes, gaining a side smile from me.

"Ah, yeah. So, I'm actually Reed's sponsor, we attend AA meetings together every Thursday, albeit when I'm working. We're quite similar in a lot of ways, I could practically smell the alcoholism on him, and I don't mean literally. He looked exactly how I did, before I made the decision to go sober." He pauses for a drink and I debate asking him the question that's eating away at me.

I suppose tonight is about getting to know one another, "Why did you get sober, like what gave you the push to finally do it?" I cock my head to the side and pick up my champagne flute, taking a sip.

His hands freeze, mid-drinking. I watch as the Adam's apple in his throat bobs up and down, but he's not drinking anything anymore.

Shakily, I set my drink down, hoping I haven't pushed him too far. The last thing I want is to corner him and have him put his walls back up again. This is the most free I've seen him since we met.

"It's okay, if it's too sensitive to talk about. We can talk about it another–"

"No, it's fine." He grits through his teeth, his hands shaking as he puts down his glass.

Whatever it was, has him incredibly worked up. I don't know what to prepare myself for. I almost flinch from the outburst of his breath across the table, the force behind it blowing directly at my face.

"Her name was Isabelle, but we called her Bella." He begins, and for some reason my stomach sinks.

I can't understand my emotions at the moment, I'd never really considered Devon having previous girlfriends, sexual partners - yes.

"We were best friends since childhood, grew up as neighbors, our mother's were joined at the hip." He continues, his knuckles shining white as they lay upon the table.

Me? Frozen to my seat, too paralyzed to blink.

"Her mother died when we were younger–cancer. She had a pretty bad run in with mental health, struggled and spiraled constantly with depression, she'd taken numerous overdoses, self-harmed, any of the warning signs, she had it."

Is it ridiculous to be secretly disliking her in my head right now?

I'm also getting a bit pissed off that she was mentally ill, like myself. I can't quite make sense of it, but this feeling is gnawing away at my insides.

"We kind of, um, liked each other at one point. And, one thing lead to another and–" His voice fades out as I avert my gaze to the floor, focusing upon the intricately designed carpet.

Why does this seem to grate on me more than anything else? Than anyone else? I'm not a jealous person, I can happily think about Devon sleeping with other women, well, not happily.

For some reason, this Bella girl rubs me the wrong way. Please God, I hope we never cross paths.

"...she hung herself, that night." He finishes, his eyes slightly glazed as he blinks rapidly.

It's as if my prayers were answered. I need to be careful not to be smug about it right now, he's sat across from me, obviously in pain.

Come on, Rhea, she's not around anymore, she isn't a threat. Only to herself.

My eyes widen with the thoughts of my inner conscience, astounded at the words that are throwing a party in my brain right now.

"Oh, I'm so sor–" My words are interrupted by the fit of laughter I break into.

Oh, my, fucking, God.

I can't stop it.

My eyes are shining with tears as I sit here, belly laughing at the fact he's just told me his childhood best friend killed herself.

What the fuck is wrong with me?

I can't look at him.

But, I do.

The expression on his face is unreadable, shocked? Maybe.

Without saying anything else, I rise from the table and practically

Chapter 42

run to the bathroom with my hand over my mouth, trying to physically gag myself from making this any worse. If that's even possible.

Chapter 43

Devon

What the actual fuck is going on right now?

I'm at a loss for words.

Rhea, my sweet, kind and loving, Rhea, has just erupted into the biggest laughing match I've ever witnessed.

Over my sob story, about Bella.

If she'd have giggled, that can be passed off as a nervous laugh. But, to laugh in such a way, is barbaric.

Not knowing how to respond or act when she returns, I dial Ever.

"Hey Ever, bit of a fucking weird situation here."

"Go on." He prompts.

"Well, I'm on a date with Rhea–"

"Aw, sweet. I love Rhea." He whoops and hollers.

"Not the time, Ever."

"Sorry, carry on."

"Anyway, the conversation got real deep and she asked about my

Chapter 43

sobriety. Well, more specifically what instigated my sobriety, so I told her."

"Ooo, damn. How did that go? I hope she didn't cry, it's never easy hearing your guy was in love with someone else." He sucks in a breath as if it is painful.

I don't know whether to correct him that I wasn't actually *in* love with her, I had love *for* her but I wasn't *in* love with her.

"Yeah, that's the thing. She didn't cry."

"Surely, that's a good thing, no?"

"She started laughing, hysterically." I deadpan.

The line goes silent.

"Ever?"

"Yeah, still here. So… she just… started laughing?" He asks.

"Yup."

"Not gonna lie, man. That's kinda funny." I hear him chuckle slightly down the line.

"It is not." I pout my lips.

"Kinda is." He argues.

"What am I even meant to say to her?" I panic.

"What d'ya mean? Where is she?"

"She's in the bathroom, she literally darted off because she couldn't stop herself from laughing."

"I knew I liked her from the moment I met her."

I can practically hear him talking through a grin.

"You're fucking crazy, I've called for some advice and all you're doing is telling me how this fucked up situation, is making you like her more!" I groan, frustrated that I'm no closer to figuring out how I'm meant to handle this.

"Try Blake, he might be better than me. Sorry, D." He sighs.

I agree with him and say my good bye's, dialing Blake next.

"Sup, Devon?" He says instantly.

"I've spoken to Ever, he was no help. Please say you can help me." I beg, then repeat the same story that I've just told to Ever.

"Aha, Devon that's pretty bad ass." Blake says.

I close my eyes, my hands clenching around my phone.

"I'm just gonna try Reed, thanks you dick." I end the phone call, the sounds of Blake's laughter echoing in my ears.

Please, Reed. Give me some sort of moral advice here.

"Hey, Devon. Everything okay?" Reed's voice speaks through the phone.

I repeat what happened, and to my delight, he doesn't say anything close to what the other boys said, he actually offers me a silver lining.

"Okay, so this sounds like I'm out of my depth here. I'll put you onto Indie."

Repeating the story for the fourth time in the last five minutes, Indie listens intently.

"Devon, did you say that Rhea struggles with her own mental health?" She asks, her voice considerably higher pitched than the guys.

"Yeah."

"Hm, have you considered that she's desensitized to situations like this? Like, I don't know, death or suicide. I'm just taking shots in the dark here." She says, igniting a light bulb in my head.

"Thanks Indie, you've been a great help. Reed promised you a back massage by the way, gotta go, bye." I end the phone call quickly, nervous that she's going to be back any second.

I need time to think this through, rearrange my thoughts and feelings.

Okay, so of course, Rhea struggles with her own mind, her emotions. What if... what if her bodily response was to laugh, as she was triggered.

She's desensitized to it, sure. But, what if her coping mechanism,

Chapter 43

is to ignite a laughter within herself, so fierce she can't control it.

It would make sense, to counteract the negative emotions in her mind, you can't feel depressed whilst laughing so uncontrollably.

As if my body can sense hers, my eyes shift to the entryway of the bathroom as her thin frame begins to weave through the tables towards me.

Shit, Devon.

Get your words figured out, *now*.

She doesn't make eye contact before she sits down, her entire body is still, her shoulders tensed.

"Rhea–"

"Devon–"

We both let out a dry laugh at the awkwardness.

"You go," I insist.

She takes a heavy drink from her flute, draining the contents and setting it back down.

"Look, I am so sorry for that... outburst. I don't know what came over me, I really am sorry for what happened, it must have been tough. I just... I don't know what happened, if I'm being honest." Her head remains bowed, her hands fiddling in her lap.

Leaning across the table, I reach for her hand and she obliges, lacing her fingers through mine.

"Show me that beautiful face, Rhea." I say softly.

Her chin slowly raises, her eyes trailing upwards until they meet mine, a slight smudge of makeup sits underneath her lower lash line.

"It's fine, truly. I get it, if anything, I'm just kinda glad you didn't cry, not that I expected you to, or that me being with another girl would upset you, or her dying–"

Rhea cuts off my rambling, "Devon, it's okay. You don't need to explain anything, I'm the one with the weird feelings, not you." She jokes.

"So, we're cool?" I ask.

"Fucking great." She smirks in response.

"Is this a weird time to kiss you?" My voice is timid, nervous to reconnect our lips for the first time since we parted ways.

"Not at all," she urges, bringing her face closer to mine.

Pushing myself forward, I use my free hand to caress the side of her jaw, appreciating her beauty from a closer proximity.

Her eyes flutter closed as my thumb slides across her smooth skin, her cheeks begin to tense as her lips tighten into a small smile.

My breath fans over her face as I near her, my heart drums loud enough to hear it in my ears, blocking out anything else in the room but me and her.

As my lips touch hers, she releases a tiny breath and I use the opportunity to slide my tongue along her lips, but not in an aggressive way. I touch her soft lips with my tongue so delicately, they feel like silk.

She pushes her lips against mine, solidifying us as one whole.

Pulling away, I keep my face close to hers, searching her dilated pupils to confirm that she is experiencing everything that I am.

Who needs alcohol? I would rather get drunk on this loving feeling.

Chapter 44

Rhea

Skin.
 Teeth.
 Tongues.
Hands.
Hair.

He pushes me up against the elevator wall, my legs instinctively wrap around his waist as he sucks on the sweet spot on my neck.

My hands tug on his hair as he kisses along my collarbone, his tongue wetting any part of my exposed chest.

"This… is taking… too long…" He pants, in between nibbling on my skin.

As if he was in control of time, the elevator 'dings', announcing we've arrived at our level.

I hop down from him as we grip hands, both tugging at each other as we race out of the double doors, laughing and giggling.

The sounds of our harmonious laughter echo along the hallway, just as he corners me against the wall again, unable to keep his hands off me.

"God, Devon." I moan as he licks along my jawline, sending vibrations directly to my inner thighs.

I take off into a sprint and he's hot on my heels, reaching for my waist and pushing me up against the wall again.

"I can't get enough," He laughs into my neck, sucking and pulling at my skin with his teeth.

My legs almost weaken from the pleasure that rolls through my body every time his lips make contact.

With firm hands against his chest, I push him away and I pivot on my ankle, darting towards our room.

"Your room or mine?" His deep voice vibrates through me.

I squeal as his arms capture me, lifting me to the point my legs are no longer on the floor.

My tummy flutters as I feel his rock hard abs against my back, tensing whilst he swings me around.

"Put me down!" I gush, kicking my legs in the air as his burly thighs brush against my ass.

"Never," He snarls into my ear, the lust drips from his lips.

I reach my hand back, entwining my dainty hands in his locks of hair, tugging as his lips rest in the crevice of my neck.

Just as we near his room, I expect him to put me back on my own feet, but he doesn't.

Instead, as smooth as you like, he retracts the key fob from his pants pocket and scans us into the room, kicking the door open with his foot.

I've never felt more safe or protected than right here, in his arms.

The motion-censored lights spark into action, igniting his suite through the spotlights.

His room is different to mine, larger of course, with an extra living

Chapter 44

room.

But, I barely have time to be nosy as he whisks me straight into the bedroom and throws me onto the bed.

My hair fans around me as I stare at him, then decide to lean up on my elbows for a better view as he removes his clothes.

"You're pretty fucking ripped, aren't you?" I eyeball him and lick my lips, scanning him from head to toe.

"Why do you sound surprised?" He fakes a hurt expression whilst slowly unbuttoning his dress shirt.

"I'm surprised that you find the time to work out." I confess.

"Touche." He chuckles as he pulls his shirt apart, revealing the defined abdominal muscles, each one chiseled to perfection.

The sounds of his belt unbuckling has me pooling between my legs, watching him move and flex, the veins in his arms protrude through his tan skin.

"You might wanna hang on to that…" I bite my lip as his hands pause, his belt half-way looped through his pants.

"Is that so?" He cocks his head and looks at me hungrily.

"Mm-hmm," I moan, throwing my head back and pushing my chest forward, feeling his eyes devour me.

Startled, I scream as he yanks on my ankle, pulling me towards him as he stands above me. I notice he's now only wearing his boxer briefs, the material barely able to restrain his girthy length.

My hands rush to my jeans buttons, but he grips my wrists, raising them above my head.

"Allow me," he purrs, kissing along my jaw and down through the middle of my cleavage, until he reaches the tip of my jeans band.

My eyes follow his every movement, my chest rises and falls at a rapid pace, almost blocking my vision of him.

His eyes flick to meet mine as he opens his mouth, teeth bared and tugs at my jeans, his jaw flexes and his lips tighten as he pulls the material away from the button.

Holy fuck.

Releasing my wrists, his huge hands tear at my jeans, shuffling them down my legs before discarding of them somewhere on the floor.

"Mm, did you choose these specifically for me?" He licks his lips and tugs at the string of my thong, the purple lace suits his skin tone better than my milky one.

"You know, it's a shame you didn't indulge when we were thirty-five thousand feet in the air," I tease.

His eyebrow raises as he looks at me expectantly.

"Lets just say, I was feeling a little… free." I giggle as I twist away from him, exposing my behind.

"You went commando?" He growls, leaning down and pressing wet kisses up my thighs.

"Something like that…" I breathe as my eyes flutter closed.

"I think I might actually quite like you, Rhea." He whispers, his lips hovering above my skin to the point I can feel his lips graze me when he speaks.

"Is that so… Captain Stark," I moan, barely able to construct a sentence with his hand slowly tickling my inner thigh.

The corset top I'm wearing begins to loosen, meaning he's finally began to unravel me, in more ways than one. The adrenaline fires through my veins as my body begins to shake with anticipation from the slow build-up.

When his hands are finished, they find themselves around the back of my rib-cage, rubbing slightly and pulling at my skin, causing my eyes to roll. They work into my shoulders, and then up my neck as he positions himself over my thighs, just behind my ass.

The inner of his thighs are warm against the outer of mine. I think I could stay here, forever.

His hands pause as he readjusts them beside my head, and I feel his body lay over mine, encasing me within his masculine frame. My head is turned to the left, so he brings his face down over mine, kissing my nose gently.

It's then I feel him, *it*, solid against the crease of my ass line. The size of it makes it pretty hard to ignore.

"Everything about you, is utterly fucking perfect."

I shift underneath him as his words vibrate through me from his chest to my back, the pectorals of his body pressing into me.

"Utterly fucking perfect." He mutters, drawing back from my face.

The bed dips and I'm assuming he's back to his original standing position.

Rolling back over, he stands with his hands on his hips, his boxers now at his ankles.

My mouth begins to salivate, seeing the godly body before me, each part of him crafted so inexplicably flawless.

Is the air-con on in here? It can't be.

The second his legs begin to move towards the bed, everything stops moving at a slower pace, it's as if someone has finally hit the play button.

His hands are everywhere, my hands are all over him, in his hair, at his hips, around his neck, on his abs, as we kiss each other with such a passion.

Nothing could stop this from happening, we're both entirely enthralled in one another.

Our teeth clash, our tongues collide as we pant, sweat and grab.

His kisses leave my lips as he leaves a trail of them down to my lower abdomen, pausing just before my slither of pubic hair begins.

His eyes flicker up towards me, his lashes float so effortlessly as he sinks his tongue inside of me.

My eyes roll to the back of my head and my hands grasp onto the bed sheets either side of me, gripping and pulling on them as his tongue swirls around my clit.

The intensity of the sensation has my body twitching, pulsating and writhing around, but his strong hands hold me firmly in place, clutching onto my thighs as he pulls me closer towards him.

It's so much, just so much intense pleasure. Almost too much, but not enough, all at once.

My moans bounce off every wall in this suite, to the point I'm sure the entire floor can hear me. But, I couldn't give a fuck.

The moment his teeth graze me, I'm done for.

The orgasm explodes through me, rocking every single nerve-ending in my body as I cry out for mercy. My entire body has been shaken to its core, my body quivers and my hands are in his hair, probably yanking out a decent handful of it.

Even whilst I'm taken to heaven and back, he continues kissing my clit, each touch causes my body to spasm as my orgasm continues for as long as I've ever experienced.

"Devon…" I moan, twisting my head from side to side as his finger dips inside of me.

"Fucking dripping." He growls, proceeding to sink onto my clit again.

"Oh, oh my God." I pant as my body almost immediately builds up to orgasm number two.

"That's it." He hums against me, once again turning up the magnitude of sensations that are dominating my body.

Forcing myself to pull my eyes open, I peer down at him to see his eyes have never left my face. The look within his intense stare screams how much he wants me, his eyes are almost growing lazy from how drunk he is on my pussy.

I have never seen anything so fucking attractive in my life, having Devon Stark eating me out, completely lost in serving me orgasm after orgasm.

Chapter 44

The burning in my lower abdomen intensifies, and I make it my mission to orgasm exactly where I am right now, staring into the eyes of the most beautiful person that exists.

Chapter 45

Devon

My tongue twists and flicks her clit as she pulls on my scalp, to the point it stings. But, it only turns me on more.

Her legs begin to shake as I increase a finger, and the pace.

Come on, baby. Shower me with your honeydew.

Her blue eyes begin to close and I can see her fighting against it, her eyebrows turn downwards while she tries to hold my gaze.

My tongue continues to taste and tease her just as I see her meet the impending oblivion.

Her head falls back, unable to contain the strength to hold herself upright as I begin to suck on her, delivering her the most intense orgasm on a silver platter.

She rocks her pussy against my mouth, unable to hold herself still from the shock waves of pleasure jolting through her body, her moans ceasing to quiet whimpers.

Withdrawing my fingers, I prop my knees on the bed, grabbing her thighs to pull her body downwards to me.

"Devon… I–" She begins, but I place my index finger over her lips.

"That was just the beginning." I smirk, towering over her with my cock floating in between her thighs.

Her tiny fingers trace the outlines of my face, her eyes entranced with following the route of her fingers. They graze over my lips, my nose, my eyebrows, my forehead.

"Are you counting how many lines I've got?" I pout, my forearms either side of her head, holding me up.

"I'm just appreciating you." She whispers, her hands don't cease.

My heart flutters from her words as I peer down at her, the innocence shines within her face but the pain acts as a shadow behind her eyes.

I know everything she's been through, more than I should. But, that's before I knew she was Rosalie, or Rhea. I'm not sure which way around it should be, considering I met her as Rhea.

As I'm looking at her, her eyes begin to shine, but not in a good way.

"Rhea…" I cup her face with my hand, concern etches in my face.

"I just–" She cuts herself off, swallowing harshly.

"Stop." I murmur, using my nose to catch the tear that has managed to escape from her.

"I just can't believe, you're here, right now, with me." She lets out a strangled laugh and the tears free-fall, the force of gravity causing them to roll down the side of her head and into her hair.

"You don't know how lucky I am, to even know you, Rhea…" My voice trails off as I press my lips to her cheek, her wet lashes fluttering closed.

"My little dove, Rhea." I mutter against her lips as her hands hold onto my back, her legs shifting and I feel her graze against me, the wetness of her is obvious.

Reaching between us, I grab onto my cock, positioning it against her clit and she hums against my lips in correspondence.

Rubbing her slightly, I press downwards, just the tip slides through her crease and my body shivers with the divine sensation.

She wraps her legs around my hips and pulls me into her, my cock sliding in with minimal resistance, until I'm about half-way.

I make several small thrusts, pushing myself a little further each time to ease her body into it, the warmth of her providing a homely comfort.

Our breath begins to grow ragged as my pace and depth increases, we try our best to continue kissing, but it's grown messy.

"The magic bullet, huh?" I smirk down at her, unraveling her legs from my body and pushing them in front of me, pinching them together.

She wears a lazy smile through hooded eyes, her lips swollen from our frenzied kissing.

Placing her closed legs over one shoulder, I bury myself inside of her to the hilt, her moans growing louder as I remain sat up, thrusting into her over and over. Her reactions drive me crazy, everything about her is exquisite, she's fucking captivating.

Feeling myself this far inside of her, watching her mouth open and close as she tries to handle the size of me, has me in rhapsodies of bliss.

"Destroy me," She gasps, her body writhing beneath me.

Without even thinking about it, I part her legs and loop her calves over my forearms, then grip onto her wrists pulling her up to me. Her arms wrap around my neck as I hold her at her hips, pounding her with the insatiable need to give her every part of me.

"My God," She whines just as I sink my mouth around her hard nipples, my hips bucking at a rapid speed.

Her blonde hair floats as she drops her head back, her eyes

beginning to roll. Flicking her nipple with my tongue, her calves tense on my arms, her body becomes harder to hold as she stiffens, her pussy clenching around me.

"Tell me how good it feels, baby," I growl, my teeth bared.

"Like fucking ecstasy," She grits, pulling her head up to meet my eyes.

"This is it for me, this, *you*." I breathe as my own head falls against her chest, feeling myself begin to come undone.

"I– I can't." She cries out, her body thrashes against me whilst my cock buries itself inside of her.

This is where I am going to *stay*.

"Come for me, now!" I roar, just as my orgasm shatters through me, annihilating anything but the euphoric venom that pulses through my veins, feeling myself spill inside–

SHIT

Yanking myself out of her, my eyes scan hers for her own realization.

If anything I'm more confused than ever, I've never made this mistake before, I was completely enthralled with the moment, wholly obsessed.

Releasing her legs, she sinks against my chest, her face and hair slightly lined with a layer of sweat.

"You okay, baby?" I whisper against the top of her head, kissing her hair softly.

Feeling her cheeks ball against my chest, she replies, "Better than ever."

We stay like that for a while, enjoying being wrapped around each other, the aftermath of our orgasms making everything more relaxing.

If I've done anything right in my life, it's to be here now, holding her within my arms.

She is *everything*, there isn't anything I wouldn't do to ensure it stays this way.

Chapter 46

Rhea

My chest heaves as I reach the wall, my legs burning with determination from running.

Securing my fingers through the holes of the trellis, I climb, higher and higher until I reach the top.

One glance down, I can see them, close behind.

Come on, Rhea.

You're almost there.

Swinging my leg over the wall, I prepare to jump from the other side, but startle to see I'm now stood on a cliff-edge.

What the? My head swings around, trying to understand my new surroundings, looking for a way out.

But, that's when my eyes land on *him*.

Banks.

My stomach drops and my legs weaken, terrified to see his villainous face, the murderous grin spreading wider as if he can smell my fear.

"No," I whisper, but my voice is inaudible.

"Rosie," He taunts, singing my voice and taking a step forward.

Instinctively, I back up a step and flinch as I hear the gravel beneath my bare feet fall from the near edge.

"I told you, I warned you," He shouts, his hair sticking to his forehead from his sweat.

"I've come to take you home, where you belong." His voice haunts me.

"No, Banks." But my voice is rendered useless, no sound comes out.

"Did you really think you'd get away from me? It's me and you Rosalie, until the day we die." He growls, the smirk never leaving his face.

He continues to step closer to me, my heart thumps out of my chest and the anxiety shakes me to my core.

"You don't deserve anything good, Rosie. You're a useless whore, no one is ever going to love you, but me. Look at you, you're fucking deluded!" He begins to cackle and it echoes around the entire cliff edge.

Peering over the edge, the wind blows aggressively almost taking me with it.

"You're permanently scarred with me, no matter how far you try and run, no matter how much you want to forget me. I will forever be in here." He pats his palm above his bare chest, just over his heart.

I shake my head, the tears flowing freely.

"The only way you can get away from me, is for this–" He taps his heart again, "to stop beating."

I refuse to believe him, but he barely stands five feet away from me now, his usual aftershave invades my nostrils.

"Jump, Rhea." He baits, tilting his head towards the drop behind me.

"Do it." He orders, his teeth bared and his face scrunches up.

Before I get a chance, he shoves my chest, throwing me completely

Chapter 46

off balance as I topple over the cliff.

My chest burns from my screams, my body desperately tries to grip onto something, anything as I'm free-falling to my death.

"RHEA!"

My eyes burst open and my chest heaves, the tears have flooded my face, my throat aches.

I've went from being completely numb to being completely overstimulated within a matter of seconds. Everything is too much, I'm freaking out.

"Stop," I plead as his face hovers above mine, his hands wrapped around my cheeks whilst he peers down at me looking completely terrified.

"Rhea." His voice is softer, gentler, now.

He doesn't deserve this, he doesn't deserve any part of this broken shell of a girl. He deserves someone who has their shit together, someone who can give him the world and more, someone... who is not *me*.

Bolting upright, he falls backwards, a shocked expression on his face. I throw the covers from me and begin grabbing my clothes from the floor, putting them on as fast as my body will allow. All whilst he follows around after me, tugging on my arm, begging me for an explanation, calling my name.

None of which, I can give him.

I have nothing left to give.

"Just stop!" He screams at me, his hands pull at his hair as he looks at me painfully.

Releasing a sigh, I shake my head.

"So this is it, huh? You spend the night with me and you're just gonna up and leave, no explanation, no good bye?" He spits, his eyes lined with tears.

If I wasn't completely broken, it might have changed my mind. But, I'm far too familiar with being hollow, that nothing seeps in anymore.

"Fuck you, Rhea. Seriously. Fuck you!" He shouts and then grabs the fruit bowl from the counter top, throwing it at the wall behind me.

My body flinches, but my mind remains calm.

"You think that I want to leave?" I twist my words, narrowing my eyes at him.

"You think that I want to be this fucked up?" I cry, the pull in my chest causes me to almost choke on my words.

"You deserve someone better, Devon. Fuck, you deserve the fucking world! And... I– I can't even offer you an ounce of it. I'm not right, Devon. I'm not right, *for you.*" I sob, my arms wrapping around my upper body.

He looks at me with his face screwed up, his nose running and his fists clenched.

"I'm sorry, Devon. But this, this ends here." I say, blinking back the tears.

"What? What is it, that I can't give you?" He cocks his head, taking a step closer to me, "and don't give me that fucking bullshit, *it's not you, it's me.*" The anger vibrates through his words.

"But, it is *me!*" I demand, my knees buckling slightly.

"It's what I can't give you..." I whisper and he turns his back to me, the tanned skin tight as his muscles flex with the movement of his hands dragging over his face.

"I'm sorry..." I say, turning and opening the door.

A hand above me slams the door shut, his body caging me inside of him, pressing me to the door.

"I'm not satisfied with your answer, *Rosalie.*" He growls into my ear, causing my stomach to flip.

Turning around, I try to place my hands on his chest and push him

Chapter 46

away but my effort results in nothing. He doesn't budge.

His hands remain on either side of me, keeping me locked in place, beneath him.

The darkness in his eyes translate more emotion than his words ever could.

"I let you go once, it's not fucking happening again."

"But, Devon–"

"No, Rhea. You listen to me. You're. Not. Fucking. Leaving." He orders, the confidence in his voice almost has me believing him.

"Tell me what it is you want from me, I'll give you it. Here–" he drops to his knees before me, completely stark naked, vulnerable and unguarded.

The sight itself would have any woman at her own knees, but I'm not like other people. I'm not normal.

He grasps onto my hands and looks up at me through his dark eyelashes, his lip trembling slightly and his hair disheveled.

"Rhea, *please*. Let me in, don't push me away. I'm not Banks, I'm not one of the demons you're fighting. I'm Devon. *Your* Devon." He pleads, pulling on my hands as he begs before me.

"This isn't fair on you, I can't give you–"

"I don't want the world, Rhea. The world can go to hell, what I want is *you*. I don't want things to be fair, I want to carry some of the weight you wear on your shoulders, I want to be the person you turn to when you're upset, I want to be the person who carries you when your own legs can't. Please, Rhea. Don't leave."

Every word of his speech runs deep, almost like he holds the key to unlock the cage I placed my own heart inside of. He's slowly twisting the key, releasing the pressure of it being contained for so long.

To see him being this unguarded, so completely open with me, has every part of my body wanting to stay exactly where I am, with him.

I'm struggling, badly.

But, he still wants me, for who I am, flaws and all.

With my mind made up, I drop to my own knees, still holding his hands.

He falls forward, his arms wrapping around my entire frame and his head falls into the crevice of my neck as his body shakes, his hands vibrate on my back.

"Thank you…" He whispers, and my heart is officially set free.

Chapter 47

Devon

We walk hand in hand out of the airport, pulling along our small carry-on bags but it feels completely weightless within my grip.

Everything feels different, I'm no longer walking around with a chip on my shoulder, but with Rhea on my arm. It's perfect.

"When will I see you next?" She asks, her pilot cap sits slightly angled on her head.

"Tomorrow, I'm taking you out." I grin at her, whilst she looks at me excitedly.

"Is that so?" She jokes, raising an eyebrow.

"Well, that's only if the first two in line decline the offer." I wink and she shoves against me with her shoulder as we walk to the airport staff car-park.

"In that case, I'll happily duck out of the race, I'm sure they're more worthy of you anyway." She says with a cheeky smile.

I shake my head and bump my hip against her, insinuating I know exactly what she's trying to get at.

"Not cool, Rhea." I pout, pretending to be hurt.

"You're a big boy, Stark. I'm sure you'll get over it." She laughs and it draws me back to the time I broke into her apartment for a 'welfare check'.

If only us then, could look at us now, walking hand-in-hand and completely obsessed with each other.

"This is me," She says, stopping at a red Mini.

"Cute." I tip my head at the car and she rolls her eyes, unlocking the trunk and throwing her case in.

"I'll pick you up tomorrow, at seven." I tell her, pushing her up against the side of her car.

"I'll be ready for eight." She giggles and I let a lazy smile appear on my face as I bow my head to try and level with her height.

"Don't miss me too much–actually, please do." I chuckle, pressing my nose against hers.

"I'm sure I will," she mocks, closing her eyes.

I press my lips to hers, the sweetness of her vanilla lip balm invades my senses and my pulse quickens whilst my brain buzzes with delight.

She's the fucking best addiction I could ask for.

"Bye." I say, pecking her lips again.

"Bye." She replies, pressing her lips to mine.

"Bye." I laugh, kissing her again.

"Bye." She smiles, kissing me.

"Bye." I can't stop kissing her, I don't want to part ways.

"Bye." She does the same, I don't think she wants to either.

Stepping back, breathless, I release her hand. She nods her head and climbs into the drivers seat whilst I take hold of my carry-on.

Walking towards the motorcycle section, I find my black bike sitting there, looking like every man's childhood dream.

Popping the trunk open, I throw in my carry-on and pilot hat, retrieving my helmet and strapping it on my head.

Chapter 47

I put on my gloves and then step into my overalls that I had tucked away neatly in the box.

After locking the trunk, I swing my left leg over the seat, gaining my balance before kicking off the stand.

Flicking the switch, the bike roars to life, vibrating through my inner thighs.

There's nothing better than the adrenaline rush you get whilst riding, it's the best thing Ever introduced me to.

I release the brake after putting the bike into gear, slowly pulling away from the parking spot.

***

Entering this house no longer feels as lonely as it once did, the walls don't echo, or at least I don't hear the echoes anymore.

Leaving the carry-on in the entrance doorway, I walk past the console table and pause when I see the red light flashing on it, indicating a voicemail.

I hesitate for a moment, but then proceed to press the answer machine.

"Hi Devon, this is Dr. Rivers here. I noticed you didn't attend your scheduled appointment with us, for the additional testing. I strongly advise you to re-book this appointment at your earliest convenience."

Oh, shit, yeah. I was meant to go to that, but after what happened with Mom, I was a bit of a loose cannon.

I'll sort it later.

As I begin to pivot away from the phone again, the answer machine carries on.

"Hello Mr. Stark, this is Dr. Ellen from the cardiology department at Piedmont Hospital. We would just like to make you aware that your mother has began to show fantastic signs of recovery."

My hands fall forward onto the console, my eyes close as I take in deep breaths of relief.

"She is currently in the stupor stage, meaning she has been waking up periodically and does respond to stimuli, but she falls back into a state of unconsciousness regularly. I know that you're a fairly busy man, but I thought it best to give you an update."

For once, I'm feeling genuine relief. Things are starting to come together, finally being put right. The weight of the world is being lifted from my shoulders, one small step at a time.

Standing back from the console table, I begin to unzip my overalls so that I can get more comfortable and enjoy a relaxed afternoon before going to visit mom.

The stomps of my heavy boots cease when I enter the living room, the vision of the person I'd least expect, sits on my couch as if he owns the place.

"What the fuck do you think you're doing?" I snarl, capturing his attention.

"I tried the safe, couldn't figure out the code, so I was left with no option but to wait here for you. Trust me, I don't wanna be here as much as you don't want me here." Tommy says, stretching his arms along the back of my six-thousand dollar couch.

"How kind of you." The sarcasm lines my words as I walk further into the room.

"Let me guess, you need money?" I tut, shaking my head.

"Well, yeah. Mom is obviously off the radar for a while so I've had to put my differences aside, and come to you." He whines, as if mom having a heart attack is an inconvenience to *him*.

"You know, I think if you'd taken a moment to give a shit about anyone else but yourself, then maybe, just maybe, I'd consider to help you," I spit at him, my fists clenching with fury, "our mom is sick, Tommy. Real fucking sick. You couldn't even give her the time of day to be there for her."

"Look, you don't know what I've been going–"

"Tommy! This, this is the fucking problem. It's always me, me, me, and I'm fucking done. We're done cleaning up your messes, you're *thirty* for fucks sake! Get your fucking life together, I'm not bailing you out anymore." I shake my head, throwing my bike gloves on the counter top.

"You've had it so fucking easy, compared to me," he mutters, putting his head in his hands.

"Enough of the fucking pity party. This show's over."

I go back to my backpack in the hallway, pulling out my wallet and grabbing a collection of one-hundred dollar notes. Returning to the room, I throw it at his sorry looking ass.

"That's it, Tommy. Take the money and just–" I swallow harshly, "just don't come back." My voice is pained, I'm disgusted that this is how we've turned out, this relationship between us is so toxic, I can't do it anymore.

He scrambles to pick it up and has the audacity to begin counting it. Letting out a hasty laugh, I turn my back to him, not wanting to spare him anymore of my time than he's already taken.

"Devon, this ain't enough."

Stopping in my step, I slowly crane my neck towards him, my eyes narrowed viciously.

"You have some fucking nerve, Tommy. You've broken into *my* home, you walk around this city as if the world owes you a favor. But, it owes you *nothing*." I grit, anger beginning to overpower my mental battle to remain calm.

"I wouldn't ask if I wasn't desperate–"

"You're always fucking desperate! There's always some other fucking reason why you can't step up to the plate and be a man! Our mother, the woman who gave you life, *almost died*, Tommy!" My voice breaks, my lip trembles.

"Fuck, I know! You think it doesn't affect me? Just because I don't fucking show it, doesn't mean it doesn't hurt in here." He points to his heart, his forehead shines with a layer of sweat.

"Honestly, I don't trust a word that comes out of that fucking mouth. You'll say whatever you want, to get what you want. That's you, Tommy. I have no interest in being your brother at all, that ship sailed a long fucking time ago," I laugh dryly, "but the person who I care about most of all, doesn't deserve this. She deserves to have a son who makes her proud, a son that shows up and takes care of her instead of draining the life from her!" I finish.

"She's got you for that." He replies, burning his eyes into mine.

"She's got two sons, Tommy. Not one."

"I'm a fucking mess, okay? Is that what you want? For me to sit here and admit how much of a fucking waste of space I am!" His voice is raised now, the veins in his neck pulse with his torment.

"Do something about it. Go out there, get a fucking job, get clean, be someone. Be the son that she deserves." I keep my voice low and firm, trying to assert my dominance.

"It ain't that fucking easy, man." He laughs, sucking in a breath through his clenched teeth.

"I'm giving you a chance here, Tom. Make it right. It's not too late."

He groans into his hands like a petulant teenager being told he needs to clean his room.

"I'll give you the money. As long as, you promise. You promise

Chapter 47

mom that you're going to change, to get better. You visit her, in the hospital. You rebuild the fucking bridges you burned, and most of all, you get clean." I demand.

He looks up at me with wide eyes, "Yeah, of course–"

"I fucking mean it, Tommy. No more fucking around with that shit, you'll wind up dead before you know it. I don't trust any one of those guys." I confess as I turn on my heel to go to my safe.

"Yeah, no, honestly, Devon. I will." He says to me, as if his words are anything to believe.

Sighing, I disappear out of the living room and walk into my dining room to see the picture frame already pulled out from the wall, the safe exposed to the open from Tommy's attempts earlier.

Keying in the code, I unlock it, twisting the handle and pulling the door open.

I begin to grab a handful of cash when a sudden explosion of pain sparks from the back of my head.

Instantly, I drop to my knees from the impact, my vision compromised as the stars dance about in front of me. Turning to the force of the impact, I see Tommy standing over me, a baseball bat in his hands. *Where the fuck–*

"Sleep tight, pretty boy." He snarls, before raising his arm and striking me across my head again.

Everything shuts out, the world becomes a blanket of darkness.

Chapter 48

Rhea

Looking down at my two kitties, I rub their ears as they purr in satisfaction, their eyes closing slightly.

"I'm gonna miss you both, so much." I pout, counting down the minutes till the guy giving them a new home is arriving.

I'm not ready to part ways with Sleepy and Bashful and I don't think they are either. It's like we're sat in mourning, knowing that their inevitable departure is nearing, just like it was with their brothers and sisters.

Fizzy had to take over the vetting for these two, I became far too particular in the search for the person I wanted to adopt them. As Felicity put it, *'you're declining everyone in the hopes people will lose interest, so you can keep them for yourself'*.

Subconsciously, yeah. She's right.

I want nothing more than to keep them both with me, but I'm not being realistic by doing that, I don't have the time in my schedule to raise them.

"Rhea, where did you put Sleepy's favorite toy, the fluffy bunny

Chapter 48

one?" Fizzy shouts to me from, what I presume is, her bedroom.

"Is it not in the basket? That's where I always put it." I respond, seeing Sleepy tilt his head up at the sound of his name.

"If this is your desperate last attempt of keeping him, it isn't going to work!" She says, pacing into the living area, the two starter-pack baskets in her arms.

"No honestly, Fizz. I haven't seen it." I insist.

"Where is Mr. Muffy, Sleepy?" I coo, placing my hands around his tiny head.

He stares at me with his wide eyes, the amber color reflects under the lights as Fizzy flips over cushions and gets onto her hands and knees looking for the bunny.

"Got it!" She cheers, pulling out the bunny from beneath me, under the couch.

Sleepy darts from my lap onto the floor and grips onto the bunny with his teeth, pulling and gripping onto it with his full weight.

"Let go, Sleepy! Please," Fizzy says, trying to resist his efforts.

I watch as he fights against her and I can't help but wonder if this was his way of trying to remain here, to hide his Mr. Muffy where we can't find it.

Poor Sleepy.

The doorbell rings out, signifying the arrival of their new owner. My heart sinks slightly and Sleepy lets go of the bunny, jumping up onto my lap and nuzzling into me. I stroke him for a while, leaving Fizzy to sort out the logistics.

Bashful trots over, nudging his nose into the side of my leg and wrapping his tail around my arm.

"I'm sorry guys," I whisper, drawing them both in close for our final snuggles and good bye's.

Felicity walks around the couch and looks down at me with a sorrowful expression, and I just nod in response, allowing her to take them from me.

I shift my eyes to the window, seeing the reflection of them leaving through the window is enough to make my eyes water.

Yeah, most people probably think this is pathetic. But I take pride in the fact that my pets mean so much to me, they are like my children.

I peer at the clock on the wall, to see I have around two hours to get ready for my date with Devon, and that really does fill my entire body with excitement.

It couldn't have came at a better time, something to completely distract me and to be able to spend more time with him. He really does bring balance to my chaotic world.

***

Officially, I'm an *idiot*.

Somehow, I've ended up with Devon's carry-on case, meaning he has mine.

Luckily, Fizzy saved the day with letting me borrow some of her makeup, I wonder if Devon has noticed yet?

He's a guy, there is no way he's even began to unpack that thing.

I'm waiting patiently in the living room, as if I'm not counting down the minutes till he arrives. Fizzy fishtail plaited my hair whilst I put on a layer of makeup, I also threw around six outfits at her because I couldn't decide what to wear.

After some deliberation, we settled on ruby red satin dress, laced up across the open back and revealing a fair amount of cleavage.

I have no idea what kind of date he has planned, but I wanted to show that I can make myself look pretty, even when I feel ugly inside.

"Would you like a cheeky glass of wine before you head out?" Fizzy asks, whilst she raises an eyebrow at me.

"Um, no. I'm gonna pass... I'm sort of, choosing to go teetotal." I tighten my lips into a harsh smile whilst Fizzy's eyes bug out of her head.

"What? Since when? Why?" She gasps, looking at me as if I've completely lost my marbles.

"I just, I think it's for the best. I've been shown that life can still be adventurous and fun without it, so... why not?" I laugh dryly, knowing Felicity will strongly disagree with me.

"You impress me more and more everyday, Rhea." She sighs, pouring the wine into one mug instead of two.

Peering back up at the clock, I see it strikes seven and my stomach fills with butterflies. The anticipation of him knocking on that god-awful door he put there, has my head swimming.

It feels crazy to look back on that day, to remember the innocence between our interactions but unable to stay away from each other.

Not much has changed really. We still try and irritate one another as much as possible to try and see who can get on the other's nerves the most.

Clearly, he's trying to do that right now by being *late*.

My eyes stare at the clock, my body almost flinching every time the hand moves a fraction.

Come on, Devon.

Maybe he'd taken my words literally, thinking I actually won't be ready until eight.

Yeah, that'll be it.

***

Okay, Devon.

You're officially pissing me off.

"Where's Mr. lover boy?" Felicity asks as she sits at our small dining table, her head in her phone.

"Not here." I deadpan, wearing a scowl on my face.

"Have you tried calling him? Maybe something has came up." She tries to reason with me, but the last thing I'm seeing right now is sense.

"Do I look desperate to you?" I retort.

"Um, yeah. Kinda." She shrugs, lowering her face back to her phone.

"You're not helping, *Felicia*." I snap, knowing how much she hates when I call her that.

"Hey! I'm not the one who has stood you up!" She fires back, narrowing her eyes at me.

"I haven't been stood up! He's just late." I grumble, rolling my eyes back to the clock.

Based from the original plans, he's an hour and forty-five minutes late.

I debate for a while in my head, not sure whether or not to call him.

Will it make me seem desperate? What if he has a perfectly reasonable explanation, and I'm completely overreacting.

Overriding my anxiety, I dial his number.

It doesn't connect, going straight to voicemail.

I bite on my nails, deliberating my next steps. I don't know where he lives, so that's out of the equation–

My bag.

My carry-on has an AirTag in it.

Using my phone, I load up the app to track where my bag is and see it ping a location in Buckhead. *Bingo.*

"Okay, crazy Rhea is coming out to play." I rise to my feet and place my hands on my hips as my confidence radiates.

Nobody ghosts Rhea Jensen.

***

Chapter 48

Using my GPS to the location of the AirTag, I drive across town.

Mr. Stark has a lot to answer for. It doesn't take much effort to send an excuse through text, even if he didn't have the balls to say it to me.

Completely blanking me as if I don't exist? Yeah, not gonna happen.

I drive along the freeway, the roads are dark and empty compared to the usual traffic conditions.

Switching the radio station, I bop along to *'Push It Down - L Devine'*, singing the lyrics a little louder with the angry emotions swirling through my body.

As I've been driving, I haven't realized that the AirTag has moved, until now.

"Huh? What the fuck are you doing, Devon?" I speak my thoughts aloud, watching my GPS shift to a place on the outskirts of the city.

Whatever.

Turning the music louder, I decide to enjoy the drive instead. It's not often I get to drive unless it's for platonic reasons, like work.

The directions lead me to a gas station. I drive my car onto the gravel, slowing down enough so that I can scan the surroundings.

A dim yellow light flickers above the store, the gas pumps seem ancient. I swing my car around and park it next to one of the pumps.

I swear, if I find Devon having a cheap hook-up with some sleazy whore, I'm about to blow the roof off this place.

Getting out of the car, I slam the door shut behind me and notice how silent the outside is, compared to the music I was blaring. *Oops.*

I'm grateful that I swapped my heels to a pair of chucks before driving, especially now I'm on this uneven gravel surface.

Crickets sound in the distance and I whip my head around left and right, unable to see past the exit of the gas station due to the night sky and lack of street lights.

Devon's car is no where in sight, or his bike. But, if I was with a skank, I'd be trying to hide it as much as possible too.

Honestly, I don't take him for a cheat but finding him here is raising alarm bells in my head.

I don't bother to get my purse from the car, I'm intending to be in and out. Whatever explanation he's going to give isn't going to be good enough for me, I have no reasoning to stay.

Walking towards the entrance of the store, my eyes notice the pickup truck parked alongside the building. I'm almost tempted to ask the owner of it for a ride, I'm a sucker for old Chevy's.

The doorbell above me rings out as I push open the door. A musky smell of cigarette smoke invades my nostrils and I find myself scrunching my nose with disgust.

Nobody stands behind the counter and the only thing I can hear is the crackling sound of an old radio, playing country songs.

This is giving weird vibes.

Where the fuck is Devon?

"Hello?" I call out, wondering why the door is open if it is closed.

I startle at the opening of the door to the left of me, labeled with 'Staff Only'.

A viking looking man enters my view, his eyes scanning me from head to toe. I tap my foot and stare at him back, with just as much determination in my fiery gaze.

His greasy hair is scraped back into a disheveled bun, his skin looks dirty as if he's been working in a coal factory and his beard is in disarray, completely untamed.

"Can I help you?" His deep voice vibrates through me, making me jump.

"Uhh…" I twist my face and go to turn around, looking back at my nearest exit, when he speaks again.

"What's a girl like you doing in a place like this, at this time of

Chapter 48

night?" He narrows his eyes and me and steps forward, his clunky boots almost cracking the floor tile beneath him.

"Uh, I– I think I'm in the wrong place," I gulp, my eyes unable to focus on anything as they scan around for potential weapons.

My breathing rate quickens and I notice my chest rising and falling harsher.

"You think?" He cocks his head and pulls a cigarette from a bronze metal case, placing it between his lips.

He uses a match to light it and he takes a slow drag, keeping his eyes on me whilst he blows the smoke at my face.

I let out a nervous laugh, "Yeah… I think I'm just gonna–"

Pivoting on my heel, I dart back through the exit at the speed of lightning.

Okay, well I need to get the fuck out of–

I charge straight into something hard and it knocks the wind from my lungs.

"Woah, watch it whore." They growl.

Standing back, I look up at the guy before me.

Why does he look strangely familiar?

"Sorry I'm just– Hey! That's my bag!" I furrow my brows at the bag in his grip, able to see my name written in cursive on the tag as it dangles freely.

"Out of my way." He demands and I refuse to budge.

"That is my bag." I declare.

"And, you're in my fucking way. Now move, before I have to move you myself." His dark eyes challenge me and his inky curls contrast to his mean looking face.

"You got a problem here, Tommy?" Another guy follows up behind the one holding my bag.

"Yeah, this dumb bitch is blocking my way." He laughs as the other guy joins him at his side.

The guy next to him is coated in tattoos, from the top of his bald head and down to the tips of his fingers.

"Like I've already said twice, that is my bag. Now, give me it." I stand up straighter and scowl at the pair of them, my impatience growing into anger.

I have no idea how these guys have managed to gain possession of my bag, but that's besides the point.

"She's pretty fucking feisty considering we could probably break her in half without having to lift a finger." The bald one laughs, speaking to the other guy as if I'm not standing right in front of them.

"You know, you look pretty fucked up considering you've spent all that money on those tattoos, such a waste." I counter.

"Oh, honey. What else can that mouth do besides talk back?" The curly-haired guy laughs, leaning his face forward.

Ugh, misogyny at its finest.

I pretend to cry, putting my hands over my face and letting out exaggerated sobs.

Through my fingers, I see them glance at each other looking smug.

I let my sobs translate into a hysterical laugh behind my hands, waiting for the perfect moment.

After they look at me again, they return their eyes to each other with confusion across their faces.

Instantly, I grab the curly-haired one in front of me by the shoulders, bringing my knee forward directly into his groin. He lets out a startled howl and I twist my ring around my finger so that it's pointing directly upwards. Clenching my fist, I throw it at the bald guys face, aiming for his eye.

The curly-haired one remains keeled over, clutching onto his prized possession as the bald guy stumbles back from my impact.

All I'm seeing right now, is *red*.

I'm probably not the hardest hitter, but hopefully the ring tore into

Chapter 48

his flesh.

I pull the ribbon from my hair and get behind the bald guy, looping the ribbon around his neck and dragging him backwards so he loses his balance.

He falls to the floor and I tighten my grip on the ribbon, yanking it tight to restrict his airflow.

The curly-haired one turns to see me trying to choke his friend out and he charges at me, knocking into my side and sending my body hurtling across the floor.

I gasp for air, winded from the impact.

If there's one thing I can't stand more than toxic masculine men, it's misogynistic men.

Rising to my feet, I head to the trunk of my car and pry it open whilst the pair of nut jobs conjure a plan.

If there's one thing I've learned from having a psychotic ex who kidnapped me, it's to always be prepared for the inevitable.

You bet your ass I've bought myself a gun.

But, where's the satisfaction in that?

My hand slides over the gun case and I grip onto the wheel wrench, intended to change a spare tire, which I can also do.

Slamming the trunk shut, I wield the wrench in my right hand and storm back over to the two junkies.

"For the third time, you've got my motherfucking bag." I growl, standing over the pair of them with the metal bar raised above my head.

"You're fucking crazy." The curly-haired one shakes his head, laughing in disbelief.

Having lost all of my patience a while ago, I strike him across the face with the wrench and his body falls back onto the gravel. He groans in pain, disoriented.

"Are you going to make me ask again?" I raise an eyebrow at the remaining guy.

"Just take the damn fucking bag." The bald one gasps, holding onto his throat and looking up at me with wide eyes.

"Thank you. It's all I asked for." I smile at him, skipping over him to retrieve the bag.

"Oh, a tip for the future guys. Never underestimate a woman." I chuckle, swinging the carry-on at my side.

It's only when I get to the car, looking back at the waste of oxygen, that I see the guy from the store.

He's leaned against the wall with his boot propped up behind him, taking the same slow drags of his cigarette. His dark eyes burn into me from across the way with a small smirk on his face.

He taps his nose with his index finger twice, turning his back on the injured pair and going back inside of his store.

I let a small laugh escape my lips and I get inside of my mini, throwing the bloody wrench onto my passenger seat and the bag into the foot well.

Thank God, for leather seats.

Chapter 49

~~~~~~~~

Devon

I sit up in the bed, wincing as my ribs ache.

I've been at our base since yesterday, having Pete check me out.

"How you feeling, soldier?" Dan says to me as he pops his head into the medical room.

"Like I've been beaten with a baseball bat." I hiss, readjusting my position.

"Yeah… I heard that's what being beaten with a baseball bat feels like." He cringes.

Shaking my head, I avoid a laugh to spare my three fractured ribs. "What time is it?" I ask, my voice still croaky from sleep.

There are no windows in this underground bunker, so I have no concept of time. I've slept mostly, whilst being here.

"It's about ten." He replies.

My stomach pangs with hunger, "Any chance there's some breakfast on the room service?" I joke.

"Nah, sorry, man. Wait, you eat breakfast in the evenings?" He looks at me puzzled.

"What?" I counter, looking at him just as puzzled.

"You said you wanted breakfast?" He points at me, slipping further into the room.

"Yeah... Is that not normal?" I furrow my brows.

"Man, how hard did he hit you? Nobody eats breakfast at ten at night." He laughs.

Ten... at night.

"Shit, how long have I slept?" I gasp, throwing the covers from me and almost ripping out my IV.

"A while. Did you know you talk in your sleep?" He tries to continue the conversation but the only person at the forefront of my mind is Rhea.

"Where's my phone?" I ask desperately.

My bare feet drop to the cold flooring and it elicits a shock wave of pain through my body as my muscles tense from the weight on them.

"I think it's in your locker, I'll get it. You stay there. I'm sure Pete said you need to stay in bed for a while, give your body some rest." He advises as he exits the room.

Fuck.

Rhea is going to think I've stood her up for our date, fuck.

I feel so guilty.

The door opens again and Pete walks in with my phone in his hand.

"You're looking eager to get out of here." He laughs dryly.

"You could say that." I huff, reaching my arm out to take the phone from him.

Switching it back on, my phone lights up with a missed call and messages from Rhea.

Pete continues to talk about making sure I heal, give my body a break and don't do anything strenuous. I dial Rhea, mid conversation.

"Hey, Rhea. I'm so–"

Chapter 49

"You've got a lot to answer for, buddy." She deadpans.

"I know, I know. I'll explain everything. Just– just come by my place. Tonight." I plead.

"Hm, I don't know. I might be busy, or I might have plans. I haven't decided yet." She says, the sarcasm in her voice makes me smile.

"*Rhea…*" I reply, dragging out her name and lowering my voice.

"Okay, okay. Don't beg. Send me you're address and I'll swing by. No funny business though." She speaks boldly.

"Fine, fine." I agree, without meaning it.

"See you soon," She ends the phone call.

"So, that's who has you so preoccupied lately?" Pete angles his head, looking at me with a smirk.

I don't respond as I don't even think there's a point.

"So, Devon's finally off the market?" He says as he walks over to the cupboards in the room, retrieving the equipment to remove my IV and bandage me up.

"I was never on the market." I respond snarkily.

Pete turns around and shakes his head at me as he takes my forearm in his hands.

"She really must be something, to break down those walls." He mutters.

In a lot of ways, Pete has been somewhat of a father figure to me all these years. He's been the one to pick me up when I've passed out drunk somewhere out of town, drawn me back to reality.

Without him, I don't think I'd have survived. I sure as hell wouldn't have been able to stay sober. Pete came to the first few AA meetings with me and supported me whenever I struggled. He was kind of like my unofficial sponsor. And now, I'm giving Reed the same respect.

"She came at me with a fucking wrecking ball," I reply, letting out a painful chuckle.

"I'm happy for you, son. Truly. You deserve a bit of light in your life for everything you've done for humanity." He says whilst bandaging up my arm after he removes the IV cannula.

"Thanks Pete." I clip, shifting my body to try and stand up.

"Take it easy for a while, I've got you covered for the next mission," he says.

"No, no need. I'll be there. This is… minor." I tell him, gritting my teeth as I stand up.

"You've done enough, Devon. It's time you had a break and focus on yourself for a while. You've met someone, she deserves all of you. Don't make the same mistakes I did." He winces, blinking frequently to avoid betraying his front.

I tighten my lips as my mind focuses on exactly what he's talking about. Pete's wife gave him the ultimatum that we all dread, choosing between continuing this side hustle, or his marriage. Pete couldn't give this up, he was enthralled in saving the world and putting the men who deserve it, in the ground.

"Are you sure?" I ask, nervous to take the back seat for a while.

In a lot of ways, I'm glad he's suggested it. With my mom being sick, I'd love to be able to take care of her when she returns home. Of course, being able to spend time with Rhea is a huge bonus.

My skin tingles with the knowledge of being close to her soon. The thought of touching her soft and delicate skin whilst my lips graze hers, awakens the spirit within me to a new level.

"Positive. Now, get yourself home. Be on your guard for that mongrel of a brother you've got. He's a nasty piece of work." He places a tender touch to my shoulder, careful to avoid my injuries.

We bid our goodbyes and the guys cheer me out of the building, each one of them glad to see me on my feet again.

The only person at the forefront of my mind right now, is Rhea.

Chapter 49

***

Getting out of the car was a lot more difficult than I thought it would be. Being sat in that position for a while did absolutely nothing for my rib cage.

I barely have time to enter the house before headlights flood the driveway of my house, signaling Rhea's arrival.

Deciding to wait outside for her, I lean against the door frame of the front entrance to relieve some of the pressure from remaining upright.

Her door slams shut and she storms over to me, with a scowl evident on her face. I furrow my brows and flinch as she throws something at me.

If it wasn't for my ribs, I'd have bent down to pick it up, checking it out for myself.

"What's that?" I wonder.

"Look, I don't have any fucking idea what you've gotten yourself into– What the fuck has happened to you?" She gasps, raising her hand to her mouth as she staggers back.

"Like I said, I'll explain." I bite.

My eyes travel over her delicious outfit, a stunning red dress that accentuates her boobs perfectly.

"This for me?" I gesture to her outfit.

She groans and picks up the object at my feet, passing by me and taking my breath with her.

It's quite a sight, to finally see Rhea on my home turf. Everything about her is homely, and I can't wait to bury myself inside of her.

Closing the front door behind me, I follow after her into my living room. I flick the lights on and the curtains begin to automatically close, on their evening schedule.

"Real fancy." Rhea says, watching the curtains draw closed.

Now that she's captured my attention under the light, I notice a lot more than I did in the darkness outside. Yes, her dress is red. But, so are the speckles over her forearms.

"Rhea... what the–" I begin.

"No, Devon. You don't get to ask questions. I came here for your explanation. Now, explain." She demands, folding her arms across her chest and making her breasts pop out further.

My brain is pulsing with confusion and angst as to why she's littered with blood.

"Devon." She prompts.

"Okay, fine. My brother, he broke into my place. Beat me up with a baseball bat and stole a lotta cash." I spit it out, not caring for details as my mind is far too preoccupied with the wonders of her.

"So, where have you been? Have you been in the hospital?" She gawks, her guard dropping slightly.

"Nah, the guys patched me up pretty good. A few broken ribs, nothing major." I try to mask the seriousness of my injuries and the extensive amount of painkillers I'm on.

"Well... shit. Where's your brother now?" She asks, her fingers graze over her messy plait.

"No idea." I sigh, slumping against the pillows of the couch, and then readjusting myself again to stop myself from crying out in agony.

My eyes fall to the object she brought in with her, the bag...

"Rhea. Where the fuck did you find that?" I ask, my pulse thrumming in my neck with anxiety.

Surely, Tommy didn't rob me just to ditch it somewhere.

"Funny story, actually." She starts with a quiet giggle, but I don't laugh.

"So, I'm sure you know. This is my bag–" she gestures to the bag. "Well, I have an AirTag in it. When you didn't show, I was *pissed*. I intended to use the tag to track you down, you know, give you a piece

Chapter 49

of my mind or something…" She trails off, looking at the wall behind me.

I'm vibrating with anxiety, waiting for her to tell me why the fuck she has blood on her.

"I tracked my bag down to some dodgy gas station outside of town, I thought you'd… I don't know." She cringes.

"Thought I'd what?" I push.

"I thought you were meeting someone…" She finishes.

Struggling to hold back a laugh, she fires her eyes into mine, daring me to even try it.

"Anyway, a guy was there and he had my bag, this bag. I didn't really have a choice, I asked for it back politely and they mocked me. Both of them. I was a girl on my own, of course I was scared and intimidated but I couldn't let them know that. I was so angry already, and they just continued to kick me where I was already hurting." She rambles.

"Rhea, what are you saying?" I sit forward a little more, clasping my hands together on my thighs.

"I kind of, gave them what they deserved. They were awful and made suggestive comments and I think in some way… I was triggered." She bites her lip and looks away from me.

"Rhea, what did you do?" I say, my voice sounding rushed.

"Kind of, attacked them." She mumbles, my ears straining to hear her.

I blink. And again.

She… attacked… *them?*

Guys.

More than one.

"Is this some sort of fucked up joke?" I laugh in disbelief.

My eyes settle on the bag at her feet, and it clears every one of my doubts. She must be telling the truth, or how else would she have the bag?

"Do I look like I'm here to crack jokes?" She fires at me, narrowing her eyes.

"Fuck. What do you mean by attack?" I ask, unsure whether they're still breathing or not.

"The bald guy, I punched him and choked him out. The curly-haired one, I kneed him in the groin and hit him with my wheel wrench. Across the temple." She looks down, unable to meet my gaze.

Curly-haired.

Tommy.

"Shit, were they alive?" I ask, unsure why I'm not more bothered about her giving Tommy some of what he deserved.

"Yeah, I didn't kill them. Christ, what kind of girl do you take me for?" She baits, offering a slight smile with her words.

I shake my head at her, everything in my body screams how proud I am of her. Rhea has never been weak, she's always been the strongest girl I've ever known. She continues to prove me right every single fucking day.

"Honestly, Rhea…" I whisper, letting my smile dance on my lips.

"What?" She looks at me with a raised eyebrow.

"Nothing." I grin, feeling my heart swoon for my crazy girl.

There is nothing and no one who is like her, she drives me insane.

"Okay. Well, that's that, then. I guess I should be leaving." She thins her lips and pats her bare knees before standing up.

I rush to get up and suck in a harsh breath from the stabbing sensation around my ribs.

"You got somewhere to be?" I angle my head, staring at her deeply.

"Maybe I do." She teases, her gorgeous face splits into a smile.

"Somewhere other than right here, with me?" I take a step closer to her, the smell of her perfume wafts around me.

"Definitely somewhere other than here." She pouts her lips and my

Chapter 49

eyes flick to them, admiring the pucker.

"With someone else?" I ask, closing the gap between us.

"Anyone but you," she says, practically breathless as my body begins to shield hers from the lighting in the room.

I reach my hand upwards and cup her jaw, her body melting slightly with the simplest of touches.

"Anyone but me. Is that so, little dove?" I pant, leaning my face down and placing a tender kiss on her jaw.

Her body ignites underneath me. Her skin ripples with goosebumps over her arms and chest. I can only imagine how pebbled her nipples are right now.

"Nobody… but *you*." She breathes, her eyes fluttering closed as I litter her neck with my kisses, swirling my tongue onto the sweetness of her skin.

I use my other hand to reach around her back and place it on her ass, sealing our bodies together.

Groaning into her mouth, my body aches for her. It needs her.

Fuck, I need her.

Chapter 50

Rhea

There's not a bone in my body that isn't longing for Devon Stark. My entire being is consumed by him.

He works his hands around my thighs and as soon as I feel him squeeze them slightly, I jump. A hiss escapes his mouth and his teeth bite down onto my lip to the point I feel a slight sting.

Pulling away, my eyes struggle to focus for a moment, "What was that for?" I say whilst trying to get a better look of his face.

"Sorry, just a bit weak still," he replies, looking like he's holding in a breath.

"You know, I'd have never thought there would be a day when I kick someone's ass and you get your ass kicked…" I tease, averting my gaze to the distance.

Devon nicks my neck with his teeth whilst letting out a deep growl.

"You're pushing your luck, Rhea." He warns, his tongue swirling along my jawline.

My body shudders for a moment before I let a mischievous smirk spread across my face.

Chapter 50

"Poor Devon, he needs his girlfriend to come and save him from the big bad men." I moisten my lips with my tongue and narrow my eyes at him.

Slowly, ever so slowly, he retreats from my neck to make eye contact with me.

"Hm, girlfriend?" He lets a lopsided grin take over his initial scowl.

Fuck.

We've never clarified the terms of our relationship and I'm out here placing a label on myself that we've never discussed.

"I didn't mean–"

"Is that what you want, Rhea Jensen? To be my *girlfriend?*" He raises his eyebrows as he continues his fierce stare.

I feel my ears burning from embarrassment and I pull my bottom lip between my teeth as the anxiety builds.

"Rhea, little dove," he whispers as he takes one of his hands away from my ass, curling his index finger underneath my chin to raise my face.

"For us, there is not an ounce of simplicity. I don't have to ask the question because I don't require an answer. You're *mine*, Rhea." He looks at me with such adoration.

Everything between me and Devon is so different to anything I've ever known. I've never been able to communicate with someone so much, without the need for words. Being with him, being *his*, warms a part of my soul that I thought was long forgotten.

"I'm yours," I murmur, feeling the lump in my throat to stop myself from tearing up.

"As much as I've loved this heart to heart. I really hope you didn't think you'd get off lightly with your devious comment." He says, nudging the tip of his nose into my cheek.

I plaster a wide grin on my face to match my sparkling eyes as my core burns with anticipation.

"I think it's about time you see what I've really got in store for you. Oh, it's going to be anything *but* careful," he snarls, taking my bottom lip between his teeth. "You're my girl and I'm going to show you exactly who you belong to when you run that sweet little mouth of yours."

I lose my breath as I'm flipped from being upright, to my back on his living room rug within a matter of seconds.

"Devon," I pant, feeling slightly disoriented from the rush of blood to my head.

"My girl," He mumbles, kneeling and planting wet kisses all over my bare thighs.

Every time his lips make contact with my skin, I feel every nerve-ending in my body shake and tremble with pleasure. My hands find their way to his hair and the familiar feeling of him ignites the shock waves within my heart.

My Devon.

"Mine." He grits.

My eyes begin to roll in my head as I feel his teeth sink into my inner thigh. The sharp pain heightens my sensitivity, eliciting goosebumps across my body.

He hasn't even begun and my body is already in complete submission, alive and roaring for him to take me for everything that I've got.

His fingers trail up the outer of my thigh and trace across until he's level with my panties.

As if I'd been electrocuted, my body jolts the moment his finger grazes over the silk material protecting my sweetness. Without even having to check, I know I'm completely soaked from the satisfied smirk he wears.

My clit is begging to be touched again, I'm swollen and desperate for him to relieve me from this torturous anticipation.

Chapter 50

His finger slides over my clit again and I cry out as my legs shake slightly. The build up is killing me, I'm losing my patience.

His face lowers to me and I push the back of my head further into the rug to prepare myself and keep my body still.

Expecting to feel his fingers or his tongue, I gasp when his teeth clamp onto me through the silk. All kinds of pain and pleasure roll through my body at once, my heart thrums violently in my chest as my breath is lost to the world.

He kisses me slowly, his lips masking over the outline of my clit as he teases and pulls at me with his teeth. Everything is too much, but not enough.

"Devon, *please*..." I cry out as his mouth envelops my clit, but my frustration from the material between us almost has me kicking him away so that I can finish myself.

It's fucking *agonizing*.

His huge hand smooths over my stomach and pushes down to try and resist my body from writhing underneath him. Devon loops his finger around my panties and tugs them to the side. The cold air mixed with his hot breath feels like it's very own tornado, like it's about to rip through me with no care for the damage it leaves in its path.

And I'm about to become a fucking storm chaser.

Focusing my attention to him, he looks up at me with almost black eyes. Without breaking our stare, he hollows his cheeks and spits onto my clit. I shiver from the contact, the smallest touch is almost enough to tip me over the edge.

Devon's tongue slides through his lips and he dips his head to me, I hold my breath.

"Holy... *fuck*." I moan as his tongue glides over me in one long stroke.

My nipples are bursting through my dress as I feel the pleasure roll through each and every one of my nerve endings.

"Tell me, Rhea. Tell me how fucking incredible you are." He hums against my pussy, his tongue delivering me to the devil himself.

Through the sounds of my panting and gasps, I try to conjure words, "I'm– I'm incred– *Oh*."

"Come on, Rhea. Speak to me, baby." He smirks, inserting a finger into me with his spare hand that isn't restraining me.

"I'm– *fuck*. I'm so fucking– *GOD*." I squeeze my eyes shut as my body shudders with complete euphoria.

His fingers caress my inner walls, curling to the exact spot that breaks me apart. My arms flail outwards, trying to grip onto anything and everything as my back begins to arch. The orgasm racks through my body with such a force my entire brain buzzes and the sounds of anything but my screaming is blocked out.

It is complete fucking bliss.

Devon's lips kiss my clit over and over as I lay here, completely shattered from within. He could do absolutely anything he wanted to me right now, I would never stop him.

His kisses continue up my thighs and he uses his hands to pull my dress up my body. I raise my ass to make it easier for him, lifting my arms up with the little energy I have left in my body.

"My sweet, sweet, Rhea." He murmurs against my stomach, trailing over my navel with his wet lips.

My tits are fully exposed, my nipples pointing upwards to the ceiling as the cold air heightens their sensitivity.

I almost frown once his lips leave my skin but when I see him standing above me, I'm in a state of complete infatuation.

He removes his white t-shirt and it's the first time I've been able to see the damage from his brother. The purple bruises line his entire left side and it looks like he's been hit with a truck, not a baseball bat.

Looking at him injured and pained has me wishing I hit that piece

Chapter 50

of shit more than once with the wrench.

"Looks bad, huh?" He cocks his head at me as I close my mouth, unaware I'd even let it open.

"Don't think that this artificial damage will have me going easy on you…" He grins at me, unbuckling his belt.

Licking my lips, I prop myself up on my elbows to get a better view of him. I bend my knee and sway it slightly, taunting him with the view between my legs.

"On your knees." He demands, removing the rest of his clothing.

Pursing my lips, I obey.

My ass sticks upright in the air and I part my legs slightly, feeling my juices from earlier leaking down my thighs.

I hear him moving behind me and I angle my head to see him better. My breath escapes from my chest when he leans over me, gripping onto my wrists and pulling them behind me.

My face rests on the rug beneath me and my back arches further to accommodate for this new position. The cold straps of leather loop around my wrists, binding them together. He yanks on the belt and pulls it as tight as they'll go, almost to the point of being painful, even when I'm still.

"Look at my goddess. Completely and utterly fucking perfect." He whispers behind me.

I try and clench my thighs together as his words cause more heat to pool at my core. I'm throbbing for him to touch me, please me.

"My Rhea. Bound and waiting for me like a fucking good girl. Just beautiful." He grips onto my hips and I lean back into him, begging for him.

"Please, Devon," I moan, patience not being my virtue.

"Patience is a virtue, darling." Taking the words right from my mind.

He positions himself behind me and everything becomes slower, the sounds of my thumping heart echo inside of my ears and my palms sweat with excitement.

Just when I think he's about to unify us, he leans over so that his lips are level with my ear.

"I love you, Rhea *Stark*."

Chapter 51

Devon

Her head twists to the side and I take the opportunity to sink myself inside of her. The encapsulating feeling of her warmth annihilates any ounce of pain in my body as I become overwhelmed with contentment.

"Devon…" Rhea pants, her golden hair falls to one shoulder as she tries to look at me.

Without thrusting, I pull her by her restraints so that her back is flush against my chest.

Reaching my head around the side of hers, I place tender kisses on her soft cheeks.

"Yes, my love?" I mutter against her skin, pushing myself further into her. She hums in agreement and pushes her ass further into my crotch.

"I love you, so fucking much." She whispers, nuzzling her cheek into me.

Everything I've ever done, everything I've lived for, the mistakes, the torture, the agony of my life, has all built up to this moment.

She is my life. She is the air I breathe. She is the most fucking sensational woman to walk this planet. Her hips rock against me, drawing my attention from my inner conscience to my physical being. I kiss her shoulder once before lowering her body back to the floor with the leather belt, her ass still pointed upwards.

"Now, let me fucking show you what love looks like," I growl.

Looping my wrists around the spare leather, I lean forward on my knees and begin to thrust into her. *Hard.*

Her pussy grips me tightly, squeezing me as if she never wants to let me leave. And that's one of the promises I ensure to keep. I draw myself out completely, then slam back into her as her hips move to meet mine. The rhythm is slightly off but right now, we're both completely lost in desire. Rhea shoves her ass back against me, almost knocking me completely off balance.

"Devon?" She says, breathless.

"Yes, darling?" I reply.

"Let me– *Oh.* Let me take control." She moans.

I stop thrusting, stilling inside of her. With a lazy smile, I withdraw from her and pull her up by her leather straps.

One of the thousand things I love about Rhea, is her power. She does not back down from a fight, she is a determined, stubborn, and fierce woman. Like all of us, she has her down moments. But, I intend to be the one to straighten her crown every time it slips.

I didn't get the opportunity to save Bella before the darkness consumed her, but with Rhea, I'll die making sure that she has all of the light that she deserves.

I untie the buckles, letting her have free reign.

"Hands." She demands at me.

"Hands?" I cock my head at her, narrowing my eyes.

"In front, like this–" she gestures with her wrists together in front of her.

Chapter 51

"Oh, Rhea. So you want *full* control?" I raise an eyebrow expectantly and she lets a shy smile appear.

"Mm-hm," she agrees, nodding her head.

I allow her to have her moment, placing my wrists together as she binds the leather around them. As soon as they're tight enough, she stands up. My eyes follow her, scanning her godly body.

Her small foot presses against my chest and shoves me backwards, laying me flat on the floor. She places her legs either side of me and lowers herself down, gripping the base of my cock with her right hand.

I lay back in satisfaction, watching her completely dominate me. She positions me at her entrance and lowers herself gradually, placing both of her hands on my chest for support.

My hands remain on my stomach, the buckle pressing into my skin slightly.

"Look at you…" I pant, analyzing the way her body looks perched over me with her breasts pressed together by her arms.

She begins to move her hips and I slide in and out of her with ease, drowning in her love potion. Her eyes flutter closed as she grinds against me, deeply and her legs shake with every movement. The way she grits her teeth has me staring at her in complete awe and infatuation.

There is nothing she could do that would change the way I feel about her. I've seen her at her worst and I'm ecstatic to even imagine her at her best.

"My God, Devon." She throws her head back as she rides me, the flexing of her abdominal muscles glisten with a layer of sweat under the warm lighting of the living room lamp.

Her nails dig into my pectoral muscles and I clench my fingers whilst my body overloads with delight. Watching her face twist and pull, seeing the pleasure she is giving herself using my cock, elicits a newfound pleasure of being the submissive.

I've normally preferred to be the one with the control but with Rhea, I'm unruly and wild. Something only she can bring out in me.

Her head drops forward again as her hair hangs freely above me, casting shadows across her face. Her eyes open hazily and I get to see her stunning blue eyes, her pupils completely dilated.

"You're so goddamn beautiful," I whisper, feeling my heart pull at the words.

Rhea lets a soft grin form on her face as her eyes begin to roll, her moans reverberating from every wall in this house. This is where they belong, and this is where they'll stay. With my cock buried inside of her.

The second I feel her tighten around me once again, I'm surrendering to my body's ache. Her body vibrates as she shatters completely, and I'm about to fall head first after her.

"Rhea, I'm gonna–" I try and buck my hips out of her but she slams herself back down onto me with a force, determination written across her features. Unable to stop my battle with nature, I succumb to the whirlwind of ecstasy exploding through my personal barrier.

For a moment, everything is silent and I'm in a state of complete serenity, lost within the kingdom of Rhea.

The world is righted, the moon is shining and the birds begin to sing.

It's *her*.

She's the only way to restore balance within my world, and I will spend every second of my life ensuring she knows exactly that.

***

Copious amounts of sex, noodles and orange chicken later, we've finally managed to retreat to my bedroom.

Chapter 51

I sprawl out on the bed, completely naked. It's obvious that now the adrenaline has left my system, my muscles throb painfully.

Whilst Rhea is in the shower, I lean over and open my bedside drawer to retrieve some of the Oxycontin I was prescribed for my shoulder wound.

I tip a bunch of them into my palm and knock my head back, allowing them to fall into my mouth and chewing them so I can feel the effects faster.

Feeling the instant diminish of pain, I let my head fall into the plush cushions so my body can finally relax fully.

Closing my eyes, my mind begins to race along with my heart as the chemicals work their way around my system.

Somewhere far away, Rhea enters the room in just a towel but my eyes feel too heavy to keep fixated on her.

Everything becomes quiet, my breathing slows and I slip away into a painless unconsciousness.

Chapter 52

Rhea

Twisting away from Devon's sleeping body, I stand up from the bed, looking for something to throw on over my exposed body. I walk over to his closet, pulling open the top drawer of the dresser to look for something along the lines of a t-shirt.

Finding nothing but boxers, socks, and gym shorts, I focus my attention to the rest of the closet. Another chest of drawers sits in the back corner, underneath his pilot blazers. Trying my luck again, I pull open the middle drawer first.

Bingo.

I shuffle around to try and find one at the bottom rather than a newer t-shirt, my hand falls onto a box. *Huh?*

Parting the clothes, I pull the box out and notice the childish engravings littered around the exterior. It's the size of a jewelry box with a wooden encasing. 'D + B' is engraved into the center.

Curiosity killed the cat. It might well kill me too.

Clicking open the flip lock on the box, I open the lid and stare at the contents.

Chapter 52

My body stills.

The first thing my eyes rest upon is a singular image of a girl, with dark hair and pretty green eyes. She looks young, maybe eighteen? She smiles at the person behind the camera, complete infatuation and admiration written within her features. My stomach twists at the thought of Devon being the one behind the camera, imagining another woman looking at him like that. Like how *I* look at him.

Flipping it over, I read the words written in red sharpie, clear and bold.

'*My Bella*'

Um, so this is *her*.

As much as she isn't a threat-because she's dead-it doesn't make it any easier to see he still holds onto memories like this, of Bella. Sitting down with the box in my lap, I place the photo on the floor and continue to work my way through the rest of the box.

A collection of memorabilia fills the small box, movie tickets, concert tickets, a heart locket necklace and two folded pieces of paper. Sorting through the numerous pieces, I look at the movie ticket for '*The Notebook*'.

Are you fucking kidding me? They went to see The Notebook together?

How fucking *romantic*.

I take hold of the locket and part it with my finger nails, revealing the faces of a much younger looking Devon, with braces and his cute smile. And then, that bitch.

Isn't this just *adorable*.

Closing it, I drop it to the floor and delve into the folded paper, realizing quickly it's a letter. Reading the first line, my heart stops.

'*To my only love, Devon,*'

Is this?

It can't be.

But it is.

This is her *suicide note*.

Well fuck me, if this isn't about to get juicy.

My eyes scan the paper greedily, translating from one paragraph to the next as my heart beats just as fast as my eyes move.

To my only love, Devon,

If you're reading this I just want you to first know, none of this is your fault. There is nothing you could have done to save me, to prevent me from succumbing to my darkness. In fact, you've been the only light in my life, Devon. I want you to know how much you mean to me and the impact you've had on my life. You kept me fighting another day, and I've been here seven years longer because of you.

I've been drowning, fighting to keep my head above the water for you, only you. But, I've grown tired, D. I can't keep my legs kicking for any longer, it's been seven years. It's time that I let my body rest and release you from my weight.

Everything that you've done for me is more than I could have ever asked for, I didn't deserve your love. Nothing about me is worthy, I drag you down whenever I'm around you, I can see it in your eyes. I see the pity, but I know you love me too much to let me go.

So, I've made the decision for you. It's time I let you live, without my constant burden.

I called you tonight.

I know you'll be wishing that you answered, wishing that you could take back time so that you could save me again, and again. But I wasn't calling to tell you what I'm going to do, I was calling to tell you how much I love you. You'd have been none the wiser if you'd have answered or not, so please don't blame yourself for any of this.

You kept me fighting, Devon.

You will forever be my only love, and I'm more than content with dying, knowing that I've experienced what it's like to carry the love of Devon

Stark. And, in my heart it will remain.

I'm so sorry I'm leaving you behind, but promise me one thing. Promise me, you'll find your great love. Promise me, that you'll love her like you loved me. She will be the luckiest girl on the planet.

I'm sorry. I love you.

Bella x

Surprisingly, I can't contain the emotion that seems to be pouring out of me right now. I cover my mouth with my hand as I struggle to make out the words on the paper through the tears blocking my vision.

They're falling at a rapid pace and my chest aches from trying to contain my sobs.

I did not expect to feel like this.

Strangely enough, I resonate with every single one of her words. I feel connected to her in some way, with knowing exactly the type of person Devon is, I can only imagine how special he made her feel.

He kept me fighting too.

It's in his nature, in his DNA, to be a love so great that it keeps your heart beating for longer than you can allow yourself.

My bitterness has ceased, my jealousy has vanished and my insecurities have faded. It feels like I've bottled up all of my feelings and projected them onto this girl, as if she wasn't an actual existing person. But these words have made her more real than I could have ever imagined.

She, was like *me.*

Folding the paper on the crease, I pick up the next folded piece of paper.

My heartstrings pull at the handwritten letter, seeing it begin with 'To Bella,'.

This is Devon's response.

To Bella,
I'm sorry it's taken me this long to do this.
I haven't read your letter.
I don't think I ever could.
I've been in pain, a lot of it. My nights have been restless, my dreams have been torturous, and my heart has ached for you since you left. I quit drinking, I'm seventeen months sober, seventeen months since you left and took a piece of my heart with you. It's taken a lot of strength to be able to write to you, to put on paper exactly how I'm feeling. But I've found something, or someone, whose given me that strength.
Her name is Rhea.

I stop reading, my eyes growing wide as I stare at the blank wall of the closet.

He hasn't read her letter.

He has written to her, about *me*.

Now, I feel like I'm overstepping my boundaries. Reading a letter written by somebody you don't know, can be considered invasive. But, reading a letter written by your… *boyfriend*, is definitely invasive.

This feels like reading his diary.

However, curiosity is like a love language of the mind.

Since you've been gone, I couldn't open my heart to anyone or anything until she came along. You would have loved her, Bells. She has this energy that I can't explain, she is uplifting and when I'm around her it feels like I can conquer anything.
She's so fucking strong.
In some way, Bella, it feels like you've sent her for me. Since I've known her, the dreams have stopped, the tightness in my chest has eased, and I feel like my life can continue.
I will never forget you Bella, you will always hold a special place in my

Chapter 52

heart.
 All my love,
 D x

I clutch at my chest and shrink away into a tight ball as my body shakes from being completely overcome with emotions.

Within those words, I feel his struggle and his release all at once. This letter for him, was him letting go and accepting that she is gone. The final stage of grief. I feel so incomparably honored to be the person that helped him along the way.

Sniffling and wiping my tears from my cheeks, I place everything neatly back in the box with care and compassion. As much as I've invaded this portion of his life, I'm glad I did. It's helped me see things from a different perspective, a selfless one.

I pop the box back in its place, underneath the older t-shirts. Taking a plain white tee from the top of the folded pile, I put it on and it drowns me, covering down to mid-thigh.

Closing the drawer, I decide to wake Devon up with breakfast in bed. It's the least I can do after what he's been through and knowing he's been there to pick me up every time I've fallen.

***

Halfway through cooking eggs, my gaze falls to the his huge backyard. My eyes scan the expanse of it, imagining how amazing it would be to have a garden this large and the potential for all kinds of new exotic plants that I could grow.

My breathing stops.

My heart clenches.

It can't be, can it? It's as if every nerve-ending in my body is exploding from surprise and thrill all at once.

Under the glistening winter sunlight, sits an entire glass-walled house. *A greenhouse.*

I turn off the cooking hob and place the pan to the side, my bones exploding with the urge to explore the pretty building in the yard. Too eager to put on shoes, I pad bare-footed across the lawn with my arms wrapped around me from the cold breeze.

As I've gotten closer, I can see how new and perfect the greenhouse is, not a speck of rust in sight. Pushing open the door, I step inside and the warmth hits me instantly, encapsulating my ice-cold body.

The entire greenhouse is lined with plants and flowers of all kinds, a blur of colors and greenery. It's absolutely beautiful.

My feet shift slowly as my hands trail along the petals and leaves of each plant, my brain buzzing with excitement from knowing every single plant in here. I'm in awe at the presentation and decoration of the entire building, from the real wood shelving compartments, to the huge glass centerpiece of white roses.

Everything inside of me is bubbling and bursting with joy.

Almost hidden by orchids, a bookcase sits in the corner towards the back. My eyes scan the collection of books, all dedicated to gardening.

A giggle passes my lips as I read, '*Gardening for beginners: Children edition*'.

The basket on the middle shelf holds all kinds of seeds, but the familiarity is not a coincidence. These are the seeds *I gave him*. He kept every single one of them. I don't know how much more my heart can take today, I'm in a state of complete tranquility.

Devon Stark is the sweetest, most loving guy I've ever met. I've never known someone to be so genuinely selfless and kindhearted. The incessant need to see him overrides anything else, I need to be with him right now.

I am completely saturated with his love.

My feet move quickly and my heart thumps with every step as I

Chapter 52

race into the house and up the stairs.

I need him.

Entering the bedroom, he still sleeps soundly where I left him, his lips slightly parted. He looks like an absolute dream.

"Devon?" I whisper, nearing the bed and not wanting to wake him up aggressively.

He doesn't stir.

"Devon, baby." I place my hand on his arm and flinch my hand back from the coldness of his skin.

My brows pull inwards and my smile drops from my face.

"Devon." I say, a lot more firmly.

I pull on his good shoulder, shaking him with a force.

"Devon!" I scream at him, as his body rolls towards me with no resistance.

Everything in my world crumples at once.

My entire purpose in life is pulled from beneath my feet.

My hands continue to shake as I dial emergency services.

The time between the phone call and the arrival is a matter of mere minutes.

But it may as well have been hours, days.

I fold into myself as I watch them burst into the room with their equipment, checking his pulse, blood pressure and shining a torch in his eyes.

The eyes that hold my soul.

The body that carries my love.

The person who is my reason for existing.

Chapter 53

Rhea

I can't sleep.
   I don't sleep.
   The birds don't fly.
The clouds stop moving.
The world holds its breath.
I refuse to breathe.
Everything is insignificant, but *him*.

Chapter 54

Rhea

I sit at his bedside, clasping onto his cold hand that has now grown sweaty from my own. My heart lays here beside him. The monitor provides me a comfort, listening to the beating of his heart, confirming he is still here, still fighting.

"Were you aware of Mr. Stark being prescribed opioids?"
"Do you know how much Oxycontin he had taken?"
"Was Mr. Stark a regular drug abuser?"

All of these questions, but no answers.

My head is spinning from the torturous conversations with the doctors, asking me about his opioid overdose. I had no idea he was even taking oxy, never mind taking too much of it. He's not a drug user, that isn't Devon. He would never.

But, I can't help my mind wandering to places that I don't want to go to.

What if he was?

It's impossible. There is no way Devon was suffering with an addiction like that right under my nose.

I think about the past few months, the gunshot wound in his shoulder and the beating from his brother. Both of which contribute to the reasoning of him taking Oxycontin.

Only Devon knows the truth, and I'm hoping with every part of my body that we are going to get to hear that truth. The nausea in my stomach rises from the thoughts of if I wasn't there with him, of ways this situation could have been agonizingly different.

The only person at the forefront of my mind right now is Devon and his recovery. I can't even begin to think otherwise or I'll fall down the rabbit hole I won't be able to get myself out of.

Without Devon, I am nothing. He is half of my heart and we all know what happens to someone who loses half of their heart.

I'm so lost in my own mind that I don't hear the door open.

"So, we meet again." A harsh voice sounds from the doorway.

My body flinches from the sudden interruption and my eyes cast upon the dark figure in a full black outfit.

"Nathan…" My voice breaks, barely audible as my heart thumps aggressively.

The hairs on my body stand up as if trying to create a defensive barrier around me to protect me from the monster lurking in the shadows. He drawls out a smug laugh, closing the door behind him and sealing us together inside. In an instant, I'm hyper-analyzing the room and looking for escape routes, potential weapons and the emergency call button.

"You know, it's a real shame about what's happened to your little boyfriend here–" he angles his head to the side whilst he peers at Devon in the hospital bed. "Opioid overdose? Pretty common, not suspicious at all…" he smirks.

My stomach drops as I look at Devon, my breath becoming shaky and strained.

Chapter 54

"Did you really think you were going to get your happily ever after, Rosie?" He laughs, throwing his head back as his shoulders shake.

Rosie.

I can't escape it. Him.

"Banks is dead. You don't need to fight for his corner anymore." I argue, not wanting to engage with him for any longer.

"Oh, don't we know it. Thanks to Mr Stark, Banks is no more, meaning I'm out of pocket." He shakes his head, scowling.

He thinks Devon killed Banks.

"This is about money?" I retort, furrowing my brows.

"When is anything ever not, Rosalie. This last mission was meant to be my big payday for all of us and I'm talking *millions*." His eyes almost flash with dollar signs as he gazes at Devon like he is a magnet.

"As it turns out, your boy here is worth a hell of a lot. He's pissed off some very rich people who want him out of the picture, for good." He continues.

My guard instantly rises, my protectiveness for Devon radiates through the touch of our hands and I hold it a little tighter.

"You'll never get a chance to touch him. You have no idea what he's capable of." I fume, determined to stand my ground and throw him off.

"Oh, but my sweet Rosie. I already have." He plasters a huge smile across his face before turning around and leaving through the hospital door.

My chest rises and falls heavily and it feels as if I've been winded, as if Nathan took all of the oxygen in the room away with him. So Devon's overdose, was in fact… *Nathan's* doing.

I let go of Devon's hand and lean over in the chair, placing my elbows on my knees and dropping my head into my hands. I try and contemplate how the fuck I'm meant to deal with this.

He's already struck once, and he could have killed him easily if he wanted to. But, he hasn't. He came here as a warning, to get under my skin and show that he has the control and the power. All whilst Devon is lying here suffering. And, for actions he didn't commit.

It was me.

I'm the one who shot Banks.

If anyone is going to pay for it, it's going to be me, not Devon.

Chapter 55

Rhea

After returning home, I packed a few bags of clothes and stuffed them in the trunk of my car along with my weapons of choice.

The next time Nathan comes across me or Devon, it will be his last. I'll make sure of it. Devon saved my life, and it's about time I return the favor.

Entering Devon's hospital room, I startle at the presence of his three best friends.

"Rhea!" The blonde, Ever, cheers.

He walks over to me and wraps his huge arms around me, pulling me into his chest.

Is this guy ever not in a happy mood? I absorb his hug and breathe in his scent, as fresh as the ocean breeze. He smells like sunshine. *Quite fitting.*

"Honestly, we can't thank you enough. If you hadn't have been there, I don't know what–"

"Lets not get onto what if's. I'm just glad he's safe." I say, stopping

Ever from going down a dark route.

Pulling away, I glance over to the rest of the guys and that's when my eyes settle upon a beautiful dark-haired woman. She looks heavily pregnant, like she's about to burst at the seams.

"Hi, I'm Indie! You must be Rhea, I've heard so much about you!" She gushes, waddling closer to me and reaching for a hug.

We make an awkward attempt at it as I laugh nervously, considering the huge bump between us.

"Yeah? I've heard a lot about you too, especially from Fizzy." I reply, rolling my eyes.

"Fizz, she's amazing! She's been an absolute God send for me these past few months, as you can probably tell," she laughs, gesturing to her stomach.

I smile in response and look at the moody boy at Devon's bedside.

"Blake, let Rhea sit." Reed says, knocking his shoulder with his elbow.

Blake looks at me with a scowl and tightens his lips before standing up. He motions to the chair, completely overzealous.

"No, no. It's fine, I've practically been here since he arrived. By all means," I offer a curt smile but Blake turns his head away, looking out of the window instead of at me.

I have no idea what I've done to offend this guy, but he clearly has a distaste for me. I can't control the ignition of my short fuse, barring everything that's going on. I'm not in the mood for mind games and I'm most certainly not in the mood for little Blakey boy to be throwing his toys out of the stroller.

"What the fuck is your problem?" I throw my words at him with as much force as I can conjure, causing the room to fall into silence.

Everyone is bouncing their eyes between my face and the back of Blake's head. Slowly, he turns his head with his eyes narrowed as he burns from the inside out, threatening to take me down with him.

Chapter 55

"You don't remember me." He states plainly, pulling the breath from my lungs.

Remember him?

What is this guy on?

"Blake, I don't have a clue what you're talking about." I cross my arms across my chest and angle my head, staring him down.

Instead of replying, he glances at Devon before twisting on his heel and heading straight out of the room, slamming the door on his way out.

"What the fuck?" My eyes follow after him before scanning the rest of the shocked faces in the room.

"You should probably…" Ever begins.

"Yeah. I'm going." I snap, turning to follow after the guy acting like a hormonal teenager. I leave the gawking faces behind me as I break into a slight jog to try and find Blake and which direction he was heading. As I turn the corner, the elevator adjacent to me reveals an angry looking Blake, leaning against the back mirror.

"Blake!" I shout, capturing his attention.

His dark eyes look upwards and the second he spots me, he begins jamming the button on the elevator.

I set off into a sprint to try and stop him from blocking me out of the elevator as the doors begin to close.

Not on my fucking watch.

He holds fierce eye contact with me as the vision between the two of us narrows, the doors almost shut.

I stretch my foot forward, causing the doors to bounce back open. Plastering a wide smile on my face, I step inside of the elevator, directly beside him. He huffs in response and turns his head away.

Leaning in front of him, I press the ground floor button and then return to my original spot. Once I'm sealed inside with him, I start.

"Can you spare me the bullshit, Blake. I don't understand what I'm supposed to remember, give me a break." I sigh, leaning back against the mirrored wall.

He lets out a heavy breath and runs his fingers through his jet black hair.

"Rosie–"

My eyes grow wide, "Don't call me that! Where the fuck did you hear that from?" I fume, confusion and anger whirling around in my brain.

"It's me, Blake, your *brother*."

Without having chance to process anything, the elevator jolts to a stop and the lights above flicker before shutting off completely.

"Great." I mutter, looking up to the ceiling and praying for someone to remove me from this cell with an absolute nut job.

The emergency lighting springs to life, illuminating the space in a vibrant red.

"Rhea, did you hear what I–"

"Yes! I heard what you said and I have only one thing to say in response. You are absolutely insane. Now, I wouldn't mind if you'd step out of the way of the control panel so I can actually call for some help." I snap, irritated with his ignorance to us being trapped within the elevator.

He obliges and steps aside, allowing me to press the emergency call button.

"Hello, Peidmont hospital security speaking."

"Hello, I'd just like to *kindly* inform you, the elevator has stopped working and I have somewhere I need to be. If you could let me out, that would be *incredible*." I say.

"Ah, we're on it. Engineer said around an hour. Sit tight." He responds and the emergency call cuts off.

"Honestly, you'd think someone was out to make my life *hell*, just to have a giggle at how pissed off they can make me." I groan, slouching

Chapter 55

down the wall and tucking my legs up in front of me and wrapping my arms around them.

"Rhea, I don't know what to say… I don't understand." Blake says from above me, his voice trailing off at the end.

Turning my head upwards, I look at him as best as I can considering the luminous lighting.

"Blake, whatever or whoever you thought I was, you're wrong. I'm an only child, my Grandma raised me when my parents died, and here I am. Pretty simple, no room for errors or in this case, a secret brother." I deadpan, hoping he will just get the idea out of his head.

At the moment, my priority is Devon and putting Nathan out of his misery. I don't have time for any slip ups or time-wasting, Nathan needs to pay.

"What do you mean your parents died?" He looks at me quizzically before sitting across from me, fanning his long legs out in front of him.

"Bit of a shitty question, but they passed away when I was five, house fire," I tighten my lips and look away from him, a mixture of anger and grief warps its way around my mind. "Funnily enough, they shouldn't have even been in the same house together. They were separated, my father must have came over for whatever reason and they left a candle burning. I was spending the night with my Grandma whilst they burned to death in their sleep. Pretty morbid." I cut off my voice, not wanting to express any emotion.

Growing up without parents and a Grandma who passed away when I was sixteen meant that I had to grow up rather quickly, I had to mature and learn the cruel realities of life. Especially since I leaned on Banks back then. Look how far that got me.

"Vince Rivers?" Blake asks, looking down at his clasped hands in his lap.

My ears prick at the sound of the name I hadn't heard for so many years, to the point it sounds foreign.

I grow suspicious, or concerned, "How do you know that?"

"Because, he's my father too." He deadpans, maintaining intense eye contact with me, his dark eyes contrasting with my lighter blue.

I analyze him, like really look at him. His light skin tone, his black hair and deep brown eyes like my father, my contrasting blonde haired blue-eyed self, identical to my mother.

"It's impossible..." My voice escapes me, tracing my lips with my finger whilst being deep in thought.

It seems incomprehensible to imagine my father having another child, I'm so used to being an only child, to being alone. In some ways, I want to cling to the idea that I'm not on my own in this world, that I have a blood connection with someone who is still living and breathing.

"It's really odd, you being here in Atlanta. You're from Texas, right?" He asks, stunning me at his odd knowledge of my background.

I don't need to say any words, I don't think my traumatized brain could come up with anything that makes sense right now.

He continues, "Our father, your father, met my mother during a work trip. He's a doctor and a pretty successful one at that." I draw my brows together in confusion at his words. "When my mom told your father she was expecting, he'd offered to pay for everything and make sure that she was comfortable. Of course, he was married to your mom at the time, but you didn't exist back then. Vince maintained a relationship with me, flew me out to Texas whenever he had the chance. He told your mom everything, and your mom insisted that he was to ensure that he held that relationship up, prioritized me. And, when I was around three years old, you came along."

This doesn't feel real, none of this information seems realistic or anything like the life I remembered, the life I had known. This is distorting my sense of reality, what I knew my background to be.

Chapter 55

"Of course, we grew up together periodically. Whenever I came to stay, we got to play happy families. We were everything you'd expect from being siblings. I loved you Rhea, you were, *are*, my baby sister. I just didn't know you still existed, until now."

I can't even interrupt him, my thoughts are playing catch up. With the house fire, it explains why I'd have no evidence, no family pictures to remember except the one I hold close to my heart. The only last 'living' memory I have of my parents.

"When I found out what happened with the house fire, Vince told us that both you and your mother tragically passed away. I was heartbroken, lost and grieving for my missing family."

Wait.

"What do you mean 'Vince told you'?" I angle my head towards him, my movements ever so careful.

"I don't understand the question." He looks at me with just as much confusion as I'm looking at with him.

I stay silent, running through every irrational thought in my brain, going over every word he's said.

"You mean to say, Vince... is alive?" My voice breaks as the lump in my throat becomes too hard to swallow, the tightness in my chest grows with every passing second.

"He's more than alive, Rhea. He's here, in this very hospital. He's Devon's doctor."

He confirms everything that I hoped he wouldn't, that my father had in fact, survived. Not only was he alive, the motherfucker left me to my grandmother, with no care for my well-being. I moved in with Banks when Grandma passed, meaning I endured all of the suffering, the beatings and the torture for no fucking reason.

Standing up abruptly, my head spins and I try to right myself, holding onto the wall for support, "I need to get out of here." I rush the words out.

Blake stands up, his face is pale but his attention is fixated entirely on me, not himself.

"Rhea, it's okay–"

"Would you just shut the fuck up for a minute?" I snap, my head throbs with pain.

Turning away, I begin to repeatedly press the emergency call button. I just need to get out of this fucking elevator that I'm trapped in with some bat-shit fucked guy who is telling me my father is alive and he is my long lost brother.

Nope. Nope. Not today.

"Maintenance."

"Get me the fuck out of this elevator before I climb up the shaft myself." I demand, gritting my teeth.

"Apologies, Miss. They're almost finished, you'll be out in no time. We aint looking for no lawsuit." He argues, to my distaste.

A hand touches my shoulder and I immediately flinch from the contact, my protective instinct kicking in.

"Woah, what's that about?" Blake pushes, his voice becoming stern.

"Nothing." I grumble, twisting my shoulder out of his gentle touch.

Something I discovered after being with Banks and his ways, is if I'm not expecting to be touched, no matter how tender, it will always raise alarm bells in my head.

"Rhea." His voice warns.

I am not ready to have this conversation right now.

He steps closer to me and my legs buckle slightly, preparing to run. I've dealt with far too much shit in this lifetime, my body has it's own defensive reflexes. It's uncontrollable.

Before he gets a chance to push any further, I get it over with. "Yes, previous abusive ex-boyfriend. Over and done with, it's whatever." I play it off, hoping it will stop any of his pending questions.

"Who? Who the fuck is it? I'll kill–"

Chapter 55

"Already done." I mumble.

He pauses, his breath catching.

I swear you can hear the crickets in the distance. Fiddling with my fingers, I bow my head. I don't care that he knows, Devon obviously trusts him and if anything, it makes me trust Devon more. The fact that he hasn't spilled anything about what we've been through, even to his best friends, says more than words ever could.

"And now, Nathan is gonna make sure Devon's going to pay for it if I don't get out of this goddamn fucking elevator!" I screech, kicking the metal doors in front of me.

"You know, I'm growing tired of these fucking coded answers, Rhea. Just fucking speak to me." He steps beside me, peering down at me with a cold look in his eyes.

Folding my arms across my chest, I stare back equally as cold, "It's too long of a story, Blake. I'm not really interested in catching you up on the past sixteen years of my life. It's not pretty."

Before he has a chance to counter, the elevator sounds and the doors spring open, letting in normal lighting. The red was starting to feel a little Carrie-esque.

I bolt out of the doors and rush through the hospital with Blake quick on my heel.

"Rhea– just wait!" He sounds after me, but I don't care to have any deep and meaningful conversations.

Everything has reignited, like my life had pressed pause for the time in the elevator and now it's playing, my anger is *back*. Nathan.

The cunt is going to pay, one way or another.

Chapter 56

Devon

"Where is she?" I ask Reed and Ever, not being able to see my love.

"Her and Blake had a little tiff, not sure really. She bolted after him." Reed answers, looking at me with concern.

"I need to see her," I wince, attempting to sit up but my head feels fuzzy.

"What you need is to rest, she'll be fine, she's with Blake." Reed presses his hand onto my shoulder, sitting me back against the plush cushions. Throwing my head back, I stare up at the ceiling in frustration. I have spent far too long in a bed lately, it really is pissing me off.

"Oxy Devon? Really?" Ever tuts, shaking his head.

Immediately, I swivel towards him with my eyes narrowed.

"What the fuck do you mean?" I fire at him, confusion wallowing in the shadows.

He takes the seat beside the bed, looking at me with sympathetic eyes. "The Doc said you had an overdose on oxy, what the fuck are

Chapter 56

you doing taking that? You already had an addiction to alcohol, and you think you can pop the most addictive prescription drug without an issue? Not fucking cool, Devon."

I don't think I've ever seen Ever so angry, in all my years of knowing him. He cares so much, sometimes too much.

"I'm sorry, Ev–"

"Sorry doesn't cut it. You could have fucking died man. Dead. Fucking gone. And then what?" His voice cracks and he lowers his head to avoid displaying his watery eyes.

Seeing him like this is tearing at my heart, pulling and refusing to let go. Even though I didn't take oxy in any attempt to overdose, it doesn't change the fact how careless I've been. Of course, I'm an addict. And of course, I've managed to OD on pills. I don't blame them for having this perspective.

"It won't happen again." I mutter, not wanting to try and give myself any excuse.

It shouldn't have happened, point blank.

"Too right it won't." Reed agrees, looking at me with the same fierceness that Ever had originally.

Man, I've really put them through it, haven't I?

Our attention is captured by Blake as he storms through the hospital door, fury written across his face.

"All of you, out. Now."

With a mixture of expressions, the guys obey. Once again, I think this is new for Blake too. I've never seen him appear so goddamn fucking furious.

His gaze remains fixed on me and I can't help but wonder what the fuck I've done that's warranted this response. It can't coincide with the reason I'm in the hospital, right?

When the door shuts, he wastes no time. "Nathan. Tell me who he is."

My lips part, struggling to find the words as my brain tries to conjure how he knows about him and why he wants to know.

"*Now*, Devon!" He screams at me, the impatience eating him.

"Fuck, okay. He's a guy from one of my operations, I don't understand why–"

"And how is he linked to you and Rhea?" He doesn't falter.

Now he's got my attention, "He was the partner of a very dangerous guy, a guy who we eliminated. I really shouldn't be telling you this or it could get you involved in some shit you don't want to be involved in." I explain.

He lets out an exasperated breath, rubbing his hands across his face and revealing his wrist tattoos. "She's after him." He states plainly.

"Who?"

"Rhea." He shakes his head, gritting his teeth.

Instantly, my alarm bells are ringing, my heart quickens and my legs are throwing themselves over the side of the bed.

"Where the *fuck* is she?" I growl, pulling the tubes from my arms and looking around the room for my clothes.

"I said, where the *fuck* is my girlfriend?" I scream as the panic begins to take over.

For a while now, we've been hunting Nathan down. He managed to escape from the plane and out of our hands, meaning we knew he would come back eventually. But, what we didn't expect was for Rhea to fucking walk into the lions den with her head held high.

Sometimes I just want to shake that woman and ask her if she has a death wish. Her God complex really can obscure her judgment. Does she not realize or care to remember that I have an entire team equipped to deal with matters like this, to protect us? But of course, Rhea wants to handle it herself.

She is strong, but she can be fucking naive.

"She didn't say anything, she just said she wasn't going to let you

Chapter 56

pay for it, and left." Blake says.

Whilst I fumble in a travel bag that Rhea must have packed for me, I pause. "You. Let. Her. Leave." I repeat.

"Have you met Rhea? There's no stopping that woman." He argues.

Yeah, in all fairness, he isn't wrong.

I remove the hospital gown, standing in all of my glory whilst Blake turns his head away. Slipping a t-shirt on, a pair of sweats and trainers, I switch my phone back on and dial Pete immediately.

Rushing out of the hospital room, Blake follows behind, trying to keep up.

A nurse startles at my sudden outburst, "Mr. Stark, you really shouldn't be–"

"Don't bother." Blake answers for me.

"Pete, it's Devon. I know this is my personal cell but it's an emergency." I breathe, entering the staircase to the ground floor.

My body sweats and my co-ordination feels off, but I have her face imprinted in my mind, fueling my every step. I felt like this the last time, when I thought she'd disappeared for good. It's soul-destroying, this anxiety.

"Devon, what is it?" He asks, full composure and professionalism lining his voice.

"Nathan. Rhea has gone after him. I don't know what he did to get a rise out of her, but it's working." My voice is breathless by the time I reach the bottom of the stairs.

Racing down eight flights of stairs after recovering from an OD is tough, with the added pressure of the love of your life being in danger, it's a whole new ball game.

"We'll get right on it, where are you?" He asks concerningly.

"I'm at home, just peachy keen to get my girlfriend back on our turf."

The last thing I need is another person against me, trying to deter me from leaving.

As we exit the hospital, I see Reed and Ever perched on a bench in deep conversation. They startle at the appearance of me, looking at Blake for some sort of explanation.

"He's gone fucking feral. Don't bother to stop him." I hear Blake shout to the boys behind me, my feet burning into the pavement to get closer to the cab station.

"I'll drive you!" Reed's voice sounds, but I'm too involved with my conversation with Pete to acknowledge him. Pete explains to me that he can track Rhea's whereabouts using her cell and to head straight to the bunker to suit up for action.

There is simply no time to waste, this is happening and I can't even fucking think about the consequences of us not arriving in time. For some odd reason, I always knew Rhea would be the death of me, and my heart is about to jump right out of my chest.

We bundle into Reed's car with them asking me a million and one questions, which I leave unanswered. My leg bounces uncontrollably as we race through the highway, dodging traffic build up and slow drivers.

"Fucking move!" Reed screams a few times, I appreciate his urgency.

With the use of the GPS, we managed to save some time by avoiding busier roads and screeching to a halt outside of the dusty warehouse.

Bolting out of the car, I hear the boys try their best to keep up with me despite their lack of an invitation. An eruption of nausea invades my senses and my mouth begins to water but I can't tell if it's from the OD or the fact Rhea has been so fucking stupid.

Once we're underground, I witness the chaos of every single man in our operation suiting up and loading our weapons. I'm guessing they've found them.

Chapter 56

"You guys just wait here, we've got this." I say to the boys.

"Devon, this is Rhea. We're here to help." Blake insists.

I look him up and down, scanning his body, "Have you ever held a gun in your life?" I fire at him.

If he wants to give it the fucking big'un, he better know how to enforce it.

"Well, no but–"

"Blake, enough. Just leave it to the professionals." Ever tugs on Blake's leather jacket and Blake instantly softens, slumping his shoulders.

"What about me?" Reed cocks an eyebrow, knowing I know he can handle himself after his situation with Allie and Scott.

"Just, whatever. I don't have time." I sigh, twisting on my heel and rushing into the Armour station.

After being suited up with bullet proof vests, cargo pants and combat boots, I'm almost ready.

"Sounds like your girl got herself in a little bit of trouble again?" Dan smirks at me as he leans against the door frame.

With everything going on, my fuse is shorter than a fucking tea light candle. Less than a second later, I have Dan shoved up against the locker room wall with my teeth bared in his face.

"Don't fucking joke, Dan. You know better." I spit, throwing him back against the wall as I release his top.

"Not cool, Dan." Killian shakes his head as he walks past us.

The atmosphere is tense, each and every one of us is stone-faced and on a mission. This is what it's like before we commence an operation, it's strictly professional and about protecting lives. Jokes are banned.

Reed passes through with his suit on and his helmet in his hands, his biceps on display in his tight black tee. "Anytime for you to flex." I mutter under my breath, knowing the standard dress code is long-sleeved.

It's probably a good job I didn't follow suit with Reed, because I'd put him to absolute shame. I'll let him have his moment.

Blake waits outside of the room looking deep in thought.

"You okay?" I shout to him, grabbing his attention as he looks up at me startled.

He enters through the doorway and beckons for me to follow after him, which I do.

"I need to tell you something, it's about Rhea." He begins, and I'm instantly drawn into the conversation. I nod for him to continue.

"Well, I should have probably told you. At first. But, I just couldn't believe it, it took me a while to wrap my head around it and I thought she was purposely not wanting to acknowledge me considering our past but–"

I groan, "Don't tell me you've *fucked*. Blake." I grit through my teeth, feeling the anger beginning to explode behind my eyes before he has chance to argue.

"No! *Fuck*, no. She's– She's my *sister*."

If my brain wasn't already about to self-combust from the situation, it's definitely about to now. "What?" is all my mind can come up with.

"Well, half-sister. Her dad is my dad and so on. It's a long story but I just wanted to say, I really care about her. Please, please bring her home." He pleads, looking the most heartfelt and genuine that I've ever seen him.

Blake has never been an emotional guy, his emotions are normally locked away with a key that is buried at the bottom of the ocean. So this, is a surprise at the very least.

"Of course. She's coming home." I assure him, resting my gloved hand on his shoulder and patting him twice.

He tightens his lips into a crooked smile and nods before leaving

Chapter 56

me and returning to Ever's side. I appreciate him telling me, but I can't mentally comprehend it at the moment. Not with the head space I need to get myself into.

I purposely haven't followed up with Pete about what's going on, where she is or if there's anything I should know about. The only way I'm going to be able to remain calm and not shoot the entire fucking place up, is by treating it as if this is a non-context mission. Like I've been given an order that I must fulfill. Right now, I'm a soldier, just like the rest of us.

"Line up!" Pete's voice bellows, hinting it's almost time to go.

I grab my helmet and leave the locker room to meet with the rest of the group.

"As you are all aware, we have Nathan Hunter on our radar. He has came out of hiding today and has struck up a deal with a woman, Rhea Jensen." I chew on the inner side of my cheek to stop myself from bursting with questions and not to shank Rhea for making a deal with the devil.

"We discovered that they are to meet in a bar on the outskirts of town, Billy's Bar." And with that, I see one of the men in the group twist his head towards me, and I know it's Reed.

Why the fuck has it gotta be Billy's for fucks sake. That's our happy place.

"The clock is ticking and they meet at six P.M. Dan has already hacked into the cameras on the exterior of Billy's so we can monitor their movements whilst we are on route. I'm sure you're all aware of Devon's connection to Rhea, but this is a professional mission and the take down of a violent criminal. I expect nothing less than absolute composure. Anyone found to be out of control of their emotions will be removed from this mission. Do I make myself clear?" Pete finishes, his eyes burning directly into mine.

I clear my throat, "Yes, Sir."

"I said, do I make myself clear?" Pete asks again, his voice becoming more stern.

"Yes, Sir!" We all shout in unison, earning a delighted nod from Pete.

And with that, we split off into our designated groups, leaving my emotions behind.

Chapter 57

Rhea

I'd be lying if I said I wasn't fucking terrified of what's to come. Since I agreed to meet with him, my mind has been trying to sum up how I've gotten to this point in my life, dealing with some of the most dangerous men on the planet.

Of course, I keep getting the same answer. Banks.

I thought ridding him from existence would at least put that portion of my life to rest, but here I am. Dealing with his messes once again.

If I had the money to pay Nathan off, I certainly would. It'd have made things so much easier and straight forward. Instead, I'm having to somehow overthrow someone who kills and kidnaps for a living. Devon saved me from Banks, now it's my turn to save him.

I'm driving to Billy's Bar outside of town, my trunk full of contenders for my weapon of choice. *If* I need them.

Has the thought crossed my mind that I might not make it out of this alive? *Absolutely*.

I'm not dumb enough to think that this is going to be easy and I'm going to get my happy ending, it's never worked like that for me. Life hasn't been too kind, so why would I expect anything different now?

I doubt my success so much so I decided to put a few thoughts on paper. My last words if you will. The last thing I'd want is Devon to think I did this because I didn't care to spend the rest of my life with him, I'm doing this because I want him to spend the rest of his life *alive*.

Reading the letter from Bella, him saving me and his impeccably kind nature, he deserves it. He deserves to have someone save him for a change, to set him free from the demons that are chasing him.

My eyes begin to well with tears at the thought that I may not see him again, I may not touch his skin again or press my lips against his and feel the warmth of his breath against me.

I truly resonate with Bella, with the ability to die happy knowing that you'd experienced a love so great, the love of Devon Stark. He is precious and must be protected at all costs and in some ways, I'm honored to be the one who has the power to protect him. He is my one true love and even if I'm not worthy enough of his love, I hope he knows just how much I love him.

Parking in the gravel outside of Billy's, I unfold the neatly folded letter on my passenger seat.

My love,

This is the kind of letter that is too hard to write, where words can't actually explain what I'm feeling. I'm hoping it's a letter that you will never have to read, but if you are reading this then the inevitable has happened. I'm dead.

Oh, Devon.

Devon, Devon, Devon. Did I mention that I love your name? Did I mention that I love your smile? Did I mention that I love the way your tongue dips out of your mouth when you're reading? Did I mention I love

Chapter 57

you?

I love you.

I know you're ~~mad~~ ~~furious~~ *enraged with my decision and you won't understand why I did it but this is what I'm here to explain, there are a few things I need to get off my chest.*

1. *I'm sorry.*
2. *I love you.*
3. *You deserve the world, you protected me and saved me in my times of need and now it's my turn to save you, baby. It was Nathan, he did it. He swapped out the dosage of your oxy pills as a warning, a threat.*
4. *I read Bella's letter. I know this is a huge breach of privacy and you're probably going to be annoyed with me but I just want you to know, you need to read it. Bella sounded amazing.*
5. *I would never regret dying for you.*

Please, Devon. I'm asking you this and only this and I don't want any excuses. This request has come from your dead girlfriend, it'd be shitty of you to ignore it. I want you to start living your life for you, you've played your role. You've saved and bettered so many lives, the world owes you so much in return and we thank you for your service.

But, it's time to step down soldier.

Baby, I love you so fucking much. I love the way you look at me as if I am the only person worthy looking at, I love the way you make my body tingle when you're around.

But, we were never going to get our happy ending, were we?

Take this from me, you can't save everyone. Especially those who don't want to be saved.

I love you Devon Stark, until we meet again.
Rhea Stark

Shit. I'm crying *again*.

Wiping away the tears with my jumper sleeve, I look at the clock on my dash reading 17:42 P.M.

No harm in showing up to your funeral twenty minutes early, right?

Picking my courage up out of the gutter, I exit my car on shaky legs, leaving my folded note on the drivers seat of my car. It's fully addressed to Devon so I'm hoping that if things do turn sour, the letter will reach him.

I scan the car park and notice only one vehicle, a blacked out GMC. He's here already. As I load my gun in the trunk of my car, the hairs on the back of my neck stand upright. The feeling of being watched overwhelms me to the point I feel the need to look around. My eyes dot around the area, searching hopelessly for my knight in shining armor, the man who saved me last time. Only this time, I know for certain he isn't coming.

Pucker up, Rhea. It's just going to be you and your pretty pink pistol running the show.

The smell hits me first, the muskiness of the stale smoke and beer and only the sounds of my entrance can be heard. The bar is empty.

Or so I thought.

A long and slow clapping begins from behind the bar, followed by a smug looking Nathan.

"Rosie– Rhea. Sorry, can't get used to the name change. Not that it matters after I'm done with you." He offers a wink which almost causes me to gag.

Thump-thump-thump.

The sound of my heart is all I can hear as it pounds against my chest, begging to escape and run from the predator.

"Nathan." I nod my head, trying to keep my voice stern and confident.

Chapter 57

"It'd be rude for me to be standing behind the bar and not offer you a drink. How about a straight vodka with a side of Rohypnol? For old times sake, of course."

I narrow my eyes at him, "Just a bottle of bud is fine." I grit through my teeth, taking wary steps towards the bar. Nathan turns away and grabs a bottle of beer from the refrigerator.

Where the fuck is the owner of the bar?

"You know, I didn't know what to expect after hearing Banks thirst after you for years. It was a pleasant surprise to see you in the flesh." He pushes the beer bottle towards me after I analyzed his every movement, making sure he didn't have the opportunity to slip anything in my drink.

I pick up the bottle and chug, letting the icy cold liquid refresh my dry throat, "Good to hear." I press my lips together into a thin line.

"Such a shame about Banks. And Devon. Rest in Peace." He does some sort of holy ritual, ending with his hands in the praying position before drinking the remainder of his straight whiskey.

I bite on the inner of my cheek to stop myself from losing control, to stop him from baiting me into action. Calm, cool, collected.

"Can we just get to the point of the deal. I didn't come here for some sort of friendly chat." I say before drinking more of the beer, my throat feels incredibly scratchy.

"Sure, take a seat." He gestures to the table behind me.

I offer a curt nod but allow him to move first, my eyes burning holes right through him as he walks. The last thing I want is to be caught off guard.

"Ladies first," His cocky grin makes a reappearance which only aggravates me more.

"I'm sure the last thing on your agenda is manners, Nathan. Just sit the fuck down." I snarl, flicking my chin to the booth.

He shakes his head with a chuckle but obeying my command. I

take the chance to sit across from him, feeling the weight of the pistol in my jeans back pocket as I angle myself so I'm not actually sitting on it. After all, I want easy access.

"I've done some digging around, spoke to a few guys on the darker side of the world and we reckon that we can cut you a deal. But, I don't think you're gonna like it."

I wait with bated breath as he slouches back with his arm draped over the back of the booth.

"You. In exchange for him."

That's it?

"Deal." I say without a second thought.

"Woah, woah. You haven't heard the rest of it yet. We've had confirmation that someone wants a taste of you, someone who is a little close to home, someone who really wants to make you pay." He continues, messing with my head.

"The notorious, Viktor Steele."

The blood in my veins freeze over, stilling with the oxygen inside of it as everything slows down and my lungs refuse to inflate again.

Banks' father.

Chapter 58

Devon

My heart is as cold as ice, my finger remains hovering over the trigger of the gun, my body as still as a statue.

Focus and attention. This is purely another mission with a target that must be taken out.

"Men, eleven o'clock." Pete speaks through the ear pieces.

I shuffle on my stomach to angle my scope to the correct position, watching a fleet of black SUV's swarm the car park of Billy's.

Closing my eyes, I let out a weighted breath and clench my jaw as I inhale through my nose and perfect my aim on the new arrivals.

"Looks like Nathan brought company." Someone says through the ear piece, jarring my insides.

Rhea, baby. What the fuck have you done?

All of us are lined up along the hill opposite Billy's, with our snipers presented in front of us.

I can't even begin to describe how difficult it was for me to stay positioned, watching Rhea exit her beloved Mini with a frown on her face. She was absolutely fucking terrified, the same as when I seen her with Banks.

It took every part of my willpower to remain routed to this spot and not sprint down the hill after her to save her from entering the bar, I'm under Pete's orders. I had to sit here and watch the love of my life waltz into a snake pit in a desperate attempt to save me. My heart fractured in that very moment, tearing me in two and exposing every loving feeling that my heart has managed to hold onto. It spilled out and now I don't know what to do with it. I need my Rhea to come back, to come home.

The thought of a world without her in it has my head completely spinning and my blood simmering. All of it, makes me sick. To think I'd ever thought I'd lived until I met her. Boy, was I wrong.

She has shown me how it feels to have someone around you that makes you breathe easier, someone who helps you appreciate waking up every morning, someone who makes the hours in the day never seem long enough.

I haven't had enough time, I'll never have enough time with her. But to lose her now, would be the greatest loss of them all. After everything she's been through, after everything she's survived, she deserves a saving grace.

"Holy shit..." Pete says, and my attention is focused on the bodies exiting the vehicles in front of Billy's.

Within a few seconds, my confidence plummets from being in the sky to six feet underground.

"That's Viktor fucking Steele. *Alive.*"

Chapter 59

Rhea

"Lucky enough for you, he wanted to come and pay a visit before going through with his transaction. He wanted to... how can I say this? *Try before you buy.*"

My stomach swirls with anxiety as I hear the door behind me open and a bustling of feet whilst they make their way into our view. The graying of his hair and the bitterness of his face makes me regret ever thinking I could manage this on my own.

Why didn't I think that there was someone bigger than Nathan pulling the strings on this shit show?

"Rosalie, *darling.*" Viktor's voice drawls, sending a scurry of bugs across my skin.

"Mr. Steele." My voice is no longer the courageous tone it once was.

"Please, call me Viktor." He says as he hands his bodyguard his thick black coat, revealing his pristine tailored suit. Some things never change.

I don't even want to begin thinking about how he is alive, he's a very powerful man with the means to fake his own death. After all, he is one of America's most wanted.

"Nathan, would you excuse us?" He says as if he is asking a question. But with Viktor, it's never a question. Your heart would no longer be beating if you were to deny him.

I shift in my seat to position my ass further away from the newfound audience, to at least try and hang on to my measly pistol. As if that would stand a chance now.

Nathan is replaced by Viktor and the rest of his crew exit through the bar doors, leaving me and Viktor in our own social bubble. Everything about this feels wrong, the uneasiness in my bones only increases with every passing second.

"When I found out that Banks was shot and killed, I wasn't surprised. I knew that he was flying too close to the sun, and he got burned. Happens to the best of us." He begins, the topic of Banks sending shivers down my spine.

"I know all about your little boyfriend and his little vigilante team. Devon, Pete, Dan, Killian, the list goes on. I'm sure you're also aware that I know Devon didn't kill Banks. I know it was you."

I still in my seat, not even daring to blink away from his milky blue eyes and his leathery skin.

"If I'm to lay all of my cards out on the table Rhea, it's that I couldn't care less that Banks is dead. What I care about is that I now have a business that is unable to operate until I find someone who is honorable enough to take over, allowing me to pull the strings from behind the curtain. I wanted to make you pay, but by doing this, it's to my advantage." He continues, stirring the pot.

"I don't understand what you mean." I reply.

"Well, as fate would have it, you would manage to sort out a bucket load of problems that I had before, when I make you the CEO of Steele Arms Weaponry–"

Chapter 59

My ears fail me and the sweat begins to bead on my forehead as he continues to explain the situation, but I can't fathom the thought. This is worse than death, this is worse than torture. This is purely keeping me alive to be at his service, at his discretion to use whenever he pleases. To be the forefront of Steele Arms Weaponry.

"–It makes it even better because you come with a built in shield. It solves my 'vigilante' problem, because we both know Devon would never be able to hurt you. If anything, he'd become a protector for you, from a distance of course. I can't have any sort of corruption on my hands."

"I–I can't. Just–just kill me. Please. Don't make me do this." I beg, throwing my entire guard down and bubbling up in front of him. He can't make me do this, but *oh* he fucking can. That's the worst part. I agreed to the deal, before I knew what the deal was.

Stupid, *stupid* Rhea.

He lets out a harsh laugh, baring his pristine white veneers, "Rosalie, it would serve me no purpose to have you killed. After all, you were by Banks' side during his take over, you're not new to any of this. Especially after you seem to gravitate towards it in some form." He raises an eyebrow, hinting at Devon.

"I agreed to this to save Devon's life, he doesn't deserve any of this. He didn't kill Banks, it was me. So I deserve to be punished. An eye for an eye." I plead, uncertain of how this has come to me begging to be murdered.

"Oh, darling. Don't you see? This was always the intended outcome. Devon was a scare tactic to get you to agree to our deal, we were never going to hurt him. He's as useless to us as road kill. You, on the other hand, are destined to suffer. You always have, little orphan Rosie. Don't bring down a guy as good as Devon, don't taint him with your wretched being. Now that would be more cruel than what I'm doing, at least I'm sparing the world from your toxicity." His words grow more vicious with every breath, tearing at my scabbed wounds with his talons.

"No one wanted you, no one wants you. Even Devon, you were his pity project, darling. To save him from the guilt of losing his true love. Do yourself a favor and allow me to give your life some sense of purpose, a true meaning to the reason you're still existing." My scabs are now open and bleeding, pouring with no means to stop.

"Banks shaped you into a good little girl, with a few thrashings here and there. I'm sure that can be arranged if you're feeling a little uninspired for your new role." He smiles at me again, stunning me into silence despite my mouth moving in an attempt to fight my case.

Shifting in my seat with the uneasiness of the situation, the metal cylinder in my back pocket digs into me, reminding me of its presence.

Act, think later.

Devon's charming face flashes across my mind, giving me the last bit of fight I needed to commit to my actions. *Oh, the familiarity.*

With everything that I thought I knew, everything that I thought I'd learned, I didn't know everything.

And that, was that Viktor Steele was faster than me.

Chapter 60

Devon

"They've been in there an awful long time, are you sure we shouldn't make a move?" Killian says, his gaze unmoving from the crowd outside of the bar.

Each one of us is targeting a different person, Nathan being my target. My finger trembles on the trigger, the eagerness of wanting to pull it and end the smug son of a bitch.

"You okay?" I hear from beside me, and I shift slightly to see Reed's eyes looking at me fiercely through his helmet.

"Fine." I grit through my teeth, turning my attention back to Nathan.

We hear the sound first as it ricochets through the hills around us, vibrating through our bodies and most significantly, piercing through my heart.

I don't even need to hear Pete's command, I'm already ten steps ahead as my feet bolt me into a sprint down the hill. The sound of the two gunshots echoes in my head with every footstep, the alarm bells sounding in my head as the relentless thumping of my heart assures me that somehow, I am still alive.

The crew in front of the bar scramble inside to attend to the commotion and the only image that is playing in my mind is Rhea, injured. Or worse, dead. If it wasn't for the absolute fucking rage boiling through my body right now, I'd have collapsed from the agony in my heart.

Having left my sniper behind, I swing my assault rifle from my back and grip it so tightly I'm afraid it may shatter into a million different fragments.

I instinctively duck my head when I hear the soul shattering sound of another gunshot and I'm refusing the chance to be sick all over myself.

"Please, God," my mind screams repeatedly as I come upon the bar doors.

To think I've come full circle, in the bar that holds so many happy memories for me, may end up holding one of the most devastating memories of all. It will be the death of me. Without Rhea, there is no Devon.

She is my fucking sun, moon and stars.

Just as I push open the doors, I can smell the copper of spilled blood and the burning haze of a gun barrel. My pulse increases tenfold as my knees begin to weaken, seeing her blonde hair peeking from the corner of the booth, the sight burning into my eyes as a memory I will never forget.

The next few seconds happen so quickly, I don't think my brain is consciously aware of what my body is doing.

All I see is blood, skin and teeth as I let loose of all of the composure, the rage and the despair.

I'm pounding into faces with my fists, kicking teeth out, breaking jaws and snapping bones. Anyone who comes into contact with me, does not leave with a pulse. Every single one of them becomes

Chapter 60

completely unrecognizable as I feel my fists connect with their nose, hearing the squelches and the cracks of their fragile faces. Even then, when they can't fight anymore, when their bodies are limp and broken, my combat boots take over.

The sole of my boot is thick-too thick-I want to feel every fucking inch of their skulls crushing into the wooden floor. I want to tear out their eyeballs with my teeth and set every inch of their body on fire, to burn in the hell of a world they've created.

"Devon!" Someone shouts, but my brain doesn't care.

My fist slams again–again–AGAIN.

"DEVON!" The voice grows louder, but ignorance is bliss.

The sounds of the bar are quiet except my labored breathing and the sound of bone crunching whilst I continue to pummel this good-for-nothing fucker into the ground.

"STAND DOWN SOLDIER!" Pete's voice restores my blurry vision, clears my foggy mind and has me releasing my clenched knuckles.

I blink a few times, staring down at the piece of meat attached to a black suit below me.

Not feeling satisfied, I take off my helmet and keel over, spitting directly on the mush pile. The sweat beads down my forehead, dripping from my nose onto the floor.

Turning on my heel, I face the rest of the men who stare at me with blank expressions, their bodies covered in blood. It's then that everything makes sense, the reason for my outburst, the reason for my complete insanity.

Reed stands a few feet away from me, holding my entire world within his arms, her face covered by her hair.

"The ambulance is barely a few minutes out. She still has a pulse but she's been shot, in the stomach. She's lost a lot of blood and–"

The blood drains from my face, standing and staring at her, staring at the lifeless body of Rhea Jensen. The clocks stop ticking, the sun stops shining and the world holds its breath as my mind registers the visual in front of me.

"Baby..." My voice breaks.

Everything stands still as I take a shaky step forward, a fraction closer to my little dove with the broken wing. Her white cami is soaked through with blood as Dan applies pressure to her abdomen, staring at me with absolute fear. And that is fear from a soldier, who has seen the brutal repercussions of war.

We've carried home our brothers with missing limbs and bullet wounds, but with war you have some sense of forewarning. This, *this is different*.

"Baby, no–no..." I shake my head in disbelief.

Each and every soldier in this room is being taken back to the front line, the PTSD is slowly unraveling in front of our very eyes as we carry one of our own back to base. Except this time, we don't have a medical crew waiting on hand.

"No, no, no, no–"

I attempt to form words but the immediate heartache in my chest permits me from doing so, enough to give me the feeling of being asphyxiated. The beads of sweat on the back of my neck dare to move against all odds, compared to the frozen stature of everyone else. We don't know what the fuck to do.

My insides swirl and the intense nausea cascades over my senses as my knees buckle beneath me and everything turns black.

Rhea's mistake.

Our mistake.

My mistake.

Chapter 61

Devon

2 Weeks Later

I sit beside my mother, admiring the way she smiles at her crochet blanket, which is four days in the making. Her hands move quickly as she keeps her eyes trained on the T.V in front of her, her small legs propped up on the reclining arm chair I got for her.

"I can't believe how good it feels to be home, to be back in my familiar surroundings." She says, letting her grin widen as she glances around the living room.

"You don't understand how incredible it feels to have you home, mom." I reply, watching her take in every breath independently.

"Oh, stop it. Do you really think I'd have gone anywhere when I hadn't gotten to meet the woman who finally melted my darling son's heart? We all knew you swore off love, so she must be someone special." She raises her eyebrows at me, making a comment about the fact she still hasn't met Rhea.

"You'll meet her soon, ma."

Mom woke up from her coma ten days ago, right when I was discharged from the hospital. I couldn't have timed it more perfect, I didn't want her to worry about anything, especially with her recovering from a heart attack. If she knew what I did in my spare time, I'd no doubt give her another one.

After the Billy's bar situation, I collapsed from being severely dehydrated and not finishing my course of medication for my oxy overdose. But it was nothing they couldn't solve.

We tried to get in contact with Tommy after mom woke up from the coma, insisting he needed to come home, but he's off the grid since Rhea gave him a run for his money.

I let a lazy smile play on my lips from the memory, of how different life was only a few weeks ago. And now, now everything is changed. Nothing can ever be the same.

Rhea was rushed into emergency surgery the second she arrived at the hospital, or so I've heard. I was unconscious, being treated by other doctors whilst my other half was battling for her life in an operating room.

I've tried to have a more positive outlook, to view things in life in a different perspective and appreciate each day as it comes.

Speaking of Rhea, I should probably go and see her. I only saw her yesterday but since everything happened, I can't keep myself away from her.

"Mom, I'm gonna head out but I'll be back for dinner. I'll make your favorite, tomato soup!" I tease her, knowing she's on a special diet for her heart.

"Very funny, we can't all be as young and thriving as you are." She retorts, shooing me away.

Chapter 61

I walk along the pathway, admiring the beauty of the trees and the freshness of the winter air. Tucking one hand in my coat pocket, I pick up my pace to get to the exact spot where we meet.

"I'm back, baby. I promised you I wouldn't be gone for long." I grin as I lean down and press a kiss to her pretty little face. "I brought you these–" I lean down and place a perfectly crafted bouquet of white roses and carnations against her headstone.

"It's quite chilly today, isn't it?" I rub my hands together and cup them around my mouth, breathing onto them.

"My mom is eager to meet you, I know we never agreed to any formal parent introductions but I thought I'd ask for your permission first." I say, setting myself down on the ground around the freshly filled soil. As if she is answering my question, the sun peaks through the clouds, casting a ray of sunshine directly over me.

"I'll take that as a yes?" I chuckle, staring at the gravestone in front of me.

My eyes scan over the engravings, reading them for the hundredth time, but it will never be enough.

Rhea Stark
To blossom means to grow
To fly we need to spread our wings
Fly high, little dove

"The boys are coming tomorrow, they struggled a lot, losing you. As have I, but I don't truly feel like I've lost you. I feel you all around me, wherever I go." I bow my head, feeling my chest begin to ache with that feeling I've grown all too familiar with.

Grief.

"You have no idea of the impact you've had on the world, Rhea. And, the impact you will continue to have. I was going to keep it as a surprise for Christmas, but I may as well tell you now, I can't keep it to myself anymore."

I reach into my pocket and pull out the printed out copy of the lease, with the picture of Billy's bar on the front.

"Me and the boys have decided to buy the bar–" I audibly gulp, struggling to picture the bar as it once was and not as a war zone. "We're bulldozing it, and turning it into a flower store, dedicated to you, little dove." I place the paper onto the vibrant flower bed, taking one of the decorative rocks to hanker it down.

"*Rhea's Roses*, we've named it. It's a nod to both your past and your present because no matter what, I want to remember every single part of you. And I hope to God that I don't forget a thing." I let out a small sigh as I take a few moments to soak in the happiness bubble that only she can give me.

I know when she's here, I can sense her presence, I smell her strawberry shampoo all around me.

A tear escapes my hold and I wipe it away quickly, swearing that this is the last time I'd let her see me slip. When I'm with her, she only sees me for the Devon she knew, the happy and loving one. She doesn't deserve to see when I suffer.

For a moment, a fraction of a second, I feel her arms wrapped around me as if the world was never so cruel. As if the world didn't tear her from my life and leave me completely empty on the inside, again. As if she truly were beside me, comforting me and drawing me out of the bad places my mind travels to when she's not around.

"White roses and carnations, great choice," I hear behind me, startling me to turn towards her voice. A mixture of disbelief, pain and joy washes over me as my eyes cast upon the most beautiful woman I've ever met.

My throat threatens to close as I try to say her name, "Rhea."

I've obviously gone completely crazy from my grief, I've never been

Chapter 61

great at managing it. You'd think I'd be a pro with the experiences I've had. But regardless, my tears bubble up at the insane visual my mind is conjuring up.

She sits down quietly beside me, crossing her legs before saying, "I brought you something."

My breath hitches at the memory, our beloved ritual that I'll never get to experience again. The action that broke the ice between us but the thought that made me fall in love with her.

She retrieves two crumpled packets from her back pocket and straightens it out in front of me. Every one of my heart strings tugs as I watch her with complete adoration, praying that this moment never has to end. Despite knowing that absolutely none of this is real, it doesn't make it any less beautifully tragic.

"Okay, so I don't know if this is some fucked up twist of fate, but I got you these..." She hands me two packets of seeds, which I take from her reluctantly. Only because I didn't expect to be able to actually touch them.

My mind buzzes with the significance of her words and the irony that this exact situation happened before. On our first 'real' date.

White Roses

Carnations

It takes me a moment to be able process everything, to drink in her beauty as well as the kindness of her innocent heart. She didn't deserve this, none of us do.

The words fall out of me before I can stop them as my tears flow relentlessly, "I'm so sorry baby."

Her face softens as she aligns her body with mine and her arms embrace me in the warmest of hugs. I sink my face into her chest and allow myself to break, to let out everything I've been holding in for the past two weeks. The absolute torture of my heart being ripped from my chest and there was not a single fucking thing I could do about it.

Her hand winds through my hair as her other hand strokes my back tenderly. Her voice shushes me whilst whispering 'it's not your fault' and 'it's okay' over and over.

And, she holds me like that for a long time, for what feels like forever. The comfort she provides me is incomparable to anything or anyone else, it's me and her.

Devon and Rhea.

Without Rhea, there is no Devon.

Chapter 62

My body throbs with pain as I attempt to turn over but I'm restricted by something. Instantly, my eyes spring open and I realize all at once that I'm no longer in the graveyard with Rhea's warm embrace, but I'm back in the hospital.

"Devon!" A group of voices rush and my eyes cast upon a very tired looking Ever and Blake.

I flinch at the volume and the sudden movement of their bodies as my brain struggles to focus on them entirely.

"Blake, go and get the doc!" Ever says as I close my eyes again, wishing for less of a migraine. Just let me fall asleep, allow me to speak to my little dove again. *Please.*

Dr. Rivers, my usual doctor, strides through the door with a concerned look etched within his brows, making him appear older than usual with the extra wrinkles.

"Devon, we're glad to have you back with us–" He begins, but my interest waivers back to being in the comfort of my own mind, the self-soothing of Rhea still being here. The odd thing about grief is your mind tries to grasp onto their being even if it means rendering you completely insane. But, I'll take insane if it means getting one more second with her.

Two fingers snap in front of my face and I startle my attention back to him, "–Devon? Are you listening?"

I nod slowly but let my gaze linger on the pained expressions of Blake and Ever.

"Where's Reed?" I ask and notice how unbearably dry my throat is when I erupt into a coughing fit. They scramble towards me and offer me an array of drink options, far too many to comprehend right now. I take the closest one to me and begin to twist the cap, noticing the way my knuckles ache incessantly. That's when I realize the huge gauze that is wrapped around my hands, preventing me from getting any further with the bottle.

"You've fractured several bones in your hand, allow me," Dr. Rivers offers, taking the bottle from my grasp and proceeding to open it with ease.

I take back the drink and guzzle it eagerly whilst the rest of the room watch me with beady eyes, analyzing my every move.

"Well?" I raise an eyebrow whilst setting the drink onto the hospital table.

"Indie went into labor, so he's still here but on a different ward. Lets just say that she wasn't best pleased when she found out he was in the middle of a blood bath whilst she was timing her contractions." Ever cringes.

Ever stands closest to me and Blake stays in the shadows with his head down, not wanting to engage with me.

For the next hour, Dr. Rivers asks me a load of questions about my reflexes, my muscle tone and my anxiety tremors. He told me how whilst I was unconscious, he was able to run the tests he'd been bugging me about for the last few weeks.

If I thought my situation couldn't get any worse, it did. He took samples of my brain and spinal cord fluid, checking for a specific

Chapter 62

protein known as alpha-synuclein. It all sounded like a bunch of jargon to me at first, but I soon came to hear about the meaning behind it all.

The test results came back positive, and it turns out I have early onset Parkinson's disease, which explains my 'anxiety' tremors. They aren't anxiety linked at all, they are PD tremors. After all, I'm not as invincible as I thought.

To me, none of this even matters. I couldn't care anymore, I have no reason to be so bothered about being in prime shape when I'm going to spend the rest of my life wishing I had just died with her.

"On the good side of news, your mom is awake." Ever says with a wide grin that could give the Cheshire cat a run for his money.

I tighten my lips and cock my head to the side as the confusion overtakes any other thoughts playing in my mind. "What do you mean *'she's awake'*, I've literally just been at home with her..." My voice trails off as I try to make the situation make sense.

All of us stare at each other, exchanging glances continuously but not one of us saying a word.

"How hard do you think he hit his head when he went down?" Blake whispers to Ever, but it's loud enough so that I can hear.

They snicker before returning serious again. "Honestly, we thought you'd have been a lot more eager to ask about her. We didn't want to bring it up first but... you've been awake for two hours now and not one word. If that isn't a red flag that you've fucked up your brain, I don't know what is." Blake folds his arms across his chest and scans me up and down as if he is looking for some sort of injury he should be aware of.

"Like I said, she's at home." I bite, growing agitated with their snide comments.

"Not your mom, Rhea." Blake answers back with a pointed glare.

My breath hitches and the lubrication from the drink earlier proves pointless with the mention of her name. I give myself a few moments before stomaching the courage to respond to him with the pain swirling inside of my aching heart.

"Rhea… She…" I audibly gulp, not able to physically speak any longer.

"–is fine." Ever finishes for me.

My head snaps up, my eyes grow wide with shock and fear all at once. The last couple of weeks play over in my mind like a movie, reciting every traumatic and torturous moment that I've been through. Waking up to find her gone, the funeral, my mom, and visiting her gravestone. All of it has my head spiraling until I'm dizzy, with nausea accompanying it.

"But–but, she–she–"

"She is fine. She's been coming around for the past twenty-four hours but she is still pretty weak. Taking a bullet to the gut will do that to ya." Blake sighs, displaying his own level of pain.

"I– I don't understand. She's gone. She–" My lip trembles uncontrollably as my heart thrums with hope, clinging on to every one of their words with trepidation.

Ever moves first, stepping around Blake to wrap me in a tight hug, something I wasn't aware I needed until I'm squeezing him back twice as hard. Physical affection isn't my forte but right now, it's my lifeline.

"She's perfect, Devon. Well, as much as you can expect from someone recovering from a gunshot wound. But, it's Rhea. You didn't think she'd give up that easily do you?" He chuckles into my neck as his blonde curls brush against my cheek.

"Alright love birds, move over." Blake sighs, dodging around the bed to bring join into the cuddle.

When I think I couldn't be happier right now, we almost pull away when we hear the door open but are immediately comforted by who

Chapter 62

it is.

"Missing someone?" Reed asks, raising an eyebrow as we all laugh and he strides over with pride.

The four of us are awkwardly trying to hug despite it being impractical with me being in a hospital bed and the three of them leaned over.

"Poppy Breckenridge, seven pounds and six ounces of perfection," Reed mumbles as we all revel in delight with his news.

"Congrats man!"

"Fuck! Congratulations!"

"Congratulations daddy Reed," I wink and he rolls his eyes at me before thanking us.

He shows us photos on his phone of the cutest newborn with thick dark hair and then little Willow meeting her for the first time. Indie is infatuated with her, which warms my heart so much with knowing how bad they deserve to be happy, after everything they've been through.

In a weird way, it ignites a foreign feeling within me, something I didn't think I'd ever experience. Broodiness. Of course, I have absolutely found the woman I want to spend the rest of my life with, but kids? That's something that I haven't ever thought of, my lifestyle hasn't particularly ever been 'child friendly'. But now? Now, it's something that is one hundred percent on my radar, and I'm not getting any younger. I'm thirty-four in a few weeks and maybe it is time that my interests took a turn for the calmer, sweeter things in life. And, every single part of it I want it to be with Rhea by my side.

That, I know for certain.

"Guys, I might need your help with something..."

Chapter 63

Rhea

In some crazy twist of fate, I'm still here, my heart is still beating and I've never been so fucking pissed at myself. That I chanced everything, that I thought in some insane spur of the moment anger, I could take this on independently.

So yeah, I've been humbled in the best way.

Leaving the hospital was hard, but living with the anxiety from being shot is harder. I'm full-time back on Ezra's schedule and running with a new diagnosis. Something that does explain my irrational behaviors, my impulsivity, my God complex as well as my 'end of the world' thinking when things go wrong.

Borderline personality disorder.

At least I'm not unhinged without reason, I suppose. I'm going through intense cognitive behavioral therapy to unravel why I am so emotionally out of control, and learning how to channel those emotions.

Seeing Devon for the first time since the 'incident', was tough. I had mentally prepared myself to never see him again, to literally fucking

Chapter 63

die for him. What I didn't prepare for, was to survive and deal with the aftermath.

And let me tell you, as much as he was absolutely thrilled to see me, he was just as fucking pissed at me. As he should be.

We've both been working through our own shit, with Devon being diagnosed with Parkinson's and me having BPD. The best part is that we've had each other to rely on for that support, we've leaned on each other to get through the hardest parts and it just makes me even more completely in love with him.

I never got a chance to thank Devon for the greenhouse, or technically saving me. But the biggest thank you, goes to Blake. Knowing that he was the one who told Devon about Nathan, was a shock for sure. But, it proved to me that he does in fact care for me.

"You ready?" Devon walks into our bedroom wearing a black button-down and dress pants. My eyes scan over his body through the mirror reflection as I finish up with my makeup routine.

Every time I see him, my body pulses with adrenaline as I think of every way that I want to have him because it will never be enough. "Do I look ready to you?" I smirk, fumbling in my makeup bag to look for a nude gloss.

He steps up behind me and the smell of his cologne warps around me, the masculinity of it makes me clench my thighs together. His index finger reaches out and tugs on the shoulder of my silk robe, letting it fall to expose my bare skin.

I try to act disinterested and preoccupied when in fact, I'm fucking soaked just from looking at him.

His breath fans over the nude skin and I'm almost moaning from this alone, imagining his hot tongue swirling inside of me. It will never be enough, I can't get enough of him, ever.

"You know, I prefer when you're not ready anyway," he says and the deep huskiness of his voice has my eyes falling closed from the way it reverberates through my body. Every single moment that I'm with him, all of my senses are on high alert. Like they are so aware of his presence, nothing lets me forget how he makes me feel. It's exhilarating.

"*Devon.*" My voice warns as his eyes connect with mine and I notice the exact darkness in his eyes, the lust dancing through them as he looks at me hungrily.

"I'm meeting your mom for the first time, we *can't* be late." I hum as he leans down to kiss the sweet spot under my earlobe, knowing full well it's my weakness.

His deep laugh sounds into my neck, "I'm sure she wouldn't mind, not if it meant we could give her a grandchild." He nips at my earlobe and I roll my eyes, knowing this is the hundredth time he's mentioned this lately.

"Devon, *stop it–*" I moan as he slips his hand in the front of my robe and cups my breast in his hand, rolling my nipple between his index finger and thumb.

He shakes his head antagonistically as he pulls apart the robe to expose my entire upper body to him through the mirror reflection.

"Do you realize how fucking beautiful you are?" He purrs into my ear, staring at me deeply as we communicate entirely through the mirror.

I gulp, feeling my own body beginning to surrender to his touch, ignoring my brain screaming, PRIORITIES!

His hand slowly retreats from my breast and he trails his finger further down my abdomen, to the part where I feel the need to crawl inside of myself and hideaway.

"Do you remember what I said to you, Rhea? When we had our first kiss?" He begins, as my breathing becomes ragged from all kinds of emotions, not just lust.

"I said you were so fucking strong, and that's exactly what this

Chapter 63

represents, baby." He whispers as his fingers slightly graze over my scar, the skin still slightly raised and purple. His lips begin sucking on my neck whilst he touches me carefully around the scar, maintaining eye contact with me.

"And one day, this amazing body will carry our children and I will make sure that every day you know how fucking strong you are. This scar is just a permanent reminder of your love for me, of your strength and your courage. I can't wait to see the love you will have for our future children." He continues as I sit compelled with his words, letting them warp their way around my heart.

"I'll always be here to make sure that you know that Rhea, until one day, you finally believe it. Until you know the immense fucking power you hold." He growls, spinning me around on the chair so my back is to the mirror and I'm met with his strained pants.

There hasn't been a single day when he hasn't made me feel worthy, he serves me a constant reminder of how incredible I am. He gives me so much confidence that I really feel like I can do anything that I set my mind to.

"Now let me fucking worship you before we go to dinner."

I bite my lip and spread my legs slightly to allow him to step closer, raising my hands to meet his belt buckle. I remove it slowly as he peers down at me, waiting in anticipation. Eagerly, I hand him the belt back, giving him my silent permission of what I want.

He smirks before taking it from me and I raise my wrists to him whilst he loops the leather around them, securing it as tight as the belt will allow. I get onto my knees and spread my legs wide with my bound wrists in between, waiting for him to position himself in front of me. His pants drop and he pulls himself out, already throbbing and dying to be sucked.

My mouth salivates just from looking at how much he wants me, the evidence hard and clear.

His hand cups under my jaw and he jerks my head back so my eyes meet his as he runs his thumb over my lips.

"Open up for me, little dove." He says as I obey with ease.

I open wide and stick my tongue out. My eyes remain fixated on him as he slaps the tip of his cock against my wetness, giving himself a little tease before he thrusts into my mouth firmly. I gag a little when it hits the back of my throat and my eyes begin to water, but my throat hums in desire.

"I fucking love dominating you my sweet girl." He pants as he pulls himself out slowly before plunging himself back into me deeply. I shift on my knees feeling myself become more needy. Even the cold air is giving my clit a naughty tease.

Every time his cock enters my mouth, I tease him with my tongue and rub along his veins as the silkiness of his skin glides over with ease.

"Fuck, I need you, now." He moans, retreating from between my swollen lips.

"Where do you want me baby?" I ask, dying for him to fill me completely.

He grabs onto the top of my hair and pushes me so that I'm face down onto the carpet with my ass sticking upright.

"Holy fuck, this is a view," he says and I turn my head to see where he is looking. It's when my eyes meet his in the mirror behind me that I see all over his face how completely infatuated with me he is.

He gets onto his knees and slides his hands up and over my back until he gets to my ass. His cock rests above my head when he spreads me apart and his breath becomes heavier. A finger slides over my clit and instantly my body jolts in surprise and pleasure.

"So fucking wet for me."

My hips rock naturally as he allows a finger to dip inside of me and my entire body begins to burn with desire. All I want to do is give

Chapter 63

into him, to give him everything he has ever wanted, everything he has ever deserved.

I am his, solely and wholly.

The mindset of giving myself to him entirely catches me completely off guard as my body propels me into an orgasm, all from the thought of letting him have me completely.

"Devon, yes. My answer is yes…" I say, breathless but loud and clear. His fingers slow and I listen to his heavy breathing, giving myself something to focus on other than the elephant in the room.

He leans back on his knees and I use my restrained hands to push myself up and off the ground to be able to look him in the eyes, to gauge his reaction. With the weight of gravity, a tear rolls down my left cheek and I flinch from the raw emotion. I can't even hide it, I can't wipe it away. But, *he* does.

He wipes away my tear with his thumb as he cups my jaw tenderly, with his eyes racing across my face searching for regrets, searching for any hesitation. Yet, none of it arises.

It's an unspoken love between us, something that is written in a place far beyond our reach. It's comforting, it's our safe space, it's just me and him.

I peer into his deep brown eyes, looking at each and every marking on his face, the indents of his smile lines, the small scar through his right eyebrow, his thick and framed lashes. I have never been so utterly and completely infatuated with anybody but the man sitting before me, looking back at me with the exact same expression.

Every passing second without him makes me homesick, every passing second with him is my saving grace.

Carefully, he begins to untie the belt around my wrists before looping my arms around his neck as he lifts me onto his lap. Without breaking eye contact, he sinks himself inside of me, bare and naked.

His head juts down to my level as he aligns his lips with mine, the sounds of our breathing matches as our chests rise and fall with so much emotion swirling between us. It feels as if our hearts are binding as one whilst we wait patiently, allowing me to adjust to him and for us to silently consent to what we're about to do.

I lift myself slowly whilst I drop my forehead to his, feeling my heart swell completely with the intensity of our love. The intimacy doesn't falter as I begin to move rhythmically on him with his hands pressing into my hips to support me.

Our moans tumble out together, the beauty of being with him like this makes me realize, this is what *making love* feels like. It's so *real*.

We don't speak words, we don't look at anything but each other as my body moves on him, blessing us both with the euphoric connection between us. My eyes threaten to spill over with tears again from how powerful our bond is, everything we've been through; the times we've loved and almost lost, the times we've fought and fell back together, the demons we've battled together and won.

There isn't anyone else I would want to share this with, than *him*.

Devon's face begins to change as his lips part, his eyes begin to glaze over but he holds them on me, never breaking the contact as he pulses and spills inside of me. Our moans coincide as my own body links up with his, with the most earth-shattering climax that causes my legs to weaken. But he holds me, he keeps me upright with him, letting me ride out my own pleasure with his help.

My head drops to his shoulder as we sit together, panting and equally stunned with the monument of our intimacy. It's calming but relieving all at once.

"I love you, Rhea," he whispers into my hair as he places a kiss against me.

My eyes flutter closed as a lazy smile forms on my face, "I love you, Devon."

After a while, Devon reminds me, "Now, let's go and meet mama

Chapter 63

Stark."

***

"Oh my God! Devon! She is absolutely beautiful!" The cutest woman with wispy white hair gushes toward me with her arms wide.

I smile deeply and welcome the embrace with ease, the smell of her perfume already comforts me and I've known her for barely a few seconds.

"Thank you, Miss Stark!" I reply before she bats at me insisting I call her *Ronnie*.

"I wasn't lying, what did you expect when your son is such a stud?" Devon teases before stepping forward and pulling his mom into his arms. The action is so sweet and wholesome that it solidifies exactly why Devon is the way he is. And it's all thanks to Ronnie Stark.

Devon hands his mom the custom basket I put together, filled with a bunch of gardening supplies and of course, my favorite selection of flower seeds. She accepts them gracefully with a wide grin, eagerly scanning the contents of the basket.

"Come, sit, sit–" Ronnie says, stepping aside to allow us into her home.

We step into the hallway and I clutch my bag awkwardly, knowing that first introductions don't usually turn out too well for me. My eyes land upon the decorated walls, the framed pictures that display different era's of life of Devon. And *Bella*.

If I'd have seen this a few weeks ago, my jealousy would have been enough to turn my mouth sour. But now, it's comforting to appreciate that they were a such a big part of each other's lives.

Already, I'm feeling secure and my nerves have dissolved into the floor beneath me with the warm welcome from Devon's mom. I don't know what I was so worried about, she is the epitome of Devon's brighter side. And, it makes me love her all the more.

Devon grips onto my hand firmly and pulls me through his childhood home towards the dining room that opens up into the kitchen. I take note of the delicate ornaments displayed on the shelving, all impeccably dusted and intricately placed. My mind spirals back to living with my grandmother for the early years of my life, after my parents passed. Or simply, my mother.

I'm comfortable with Blake, I've acknowledged that everything he told me is true when I sat through Devon's appointment with him, staring directly in the face of Vince Rivers. Of course, he stared back. Without a single care for who I was. But that just proves what it's like for a parent who purposely left their child, I could be anyone. Yet, to me he was everything to me, I could never forget his face. So, that was the day that confirmed for me I had no interest in trying to force a relationship with someone who could be so cruel. I've gotten this far in my life without him, what is the need to complicate things?

It's quite sweet to have Blake by my side, to have a blood connection with someone when you have ran your entire life alone. I'm excited to learn more about him, especially now when it doesn't feel like he hates my guts.

"I hope you don't mind, but I got you a little something myself–" Ronnie says as she begins rifling through the cabinets in the kitchen. Instinctively, I step up to help her look for whatever she's trying to find.

After a few moments, she glances behind me and makes eye contact with what I presume to be Devon and the room falls silent.

"Is everything okay?" I ask her tenderly, as my head turns back towards Devon for his recognition but my eyes drop downwards, to see him crouched on one knee as the physical form of admiration.

Chapter 63

Instantly, my hand jets to my mouth to cover my gaping jaw, a whirlwind of emotions swallows me whole.

"Rhea…" He begins, his voice as gentle as I've ever heard him which stirs a bubble in my throat.

"I couldn't have done this without you meeting my mom, and I know it's only been a mere few minutes but that is still even longer than I wanted to allow. I can't wait any longer to make you mine." He says and my eyes soften at the edges as my heart thrums obnoxiously in my chest.

"I always told you I wasn't one for the heart stopper kind of loves, but you've made my heart stop, beat and fucking explode. I've never met anyone who can make me feel ten different emotions all at once, until I met you. You are the one who makes me want to believe in marriage, in spending my life committed to you and making you the happiest woman on the planet. All I want is to do life with you, whatever that may look like. I know that I'll wake up every morning thankful that you were brought into my life and that you're by my side. I love you Rhea, please would you give me the honor of being your husband?" He finishes, and I'm already frantically nodding my head as the word 'yes' spills out of my mouth uncontrollably, as if my own brain didn't have a say in the matter.

Nothing feels more right, nothing could compare to being in this moment with the man who saved my life, the man who continues to give me a reason to keep fighting another day.

He slides the ring onto my finger and I don't even care to look at it, it doesn't matter to me. He is all that matters.

I fling my arms around his neck and dive on top of him as he falls backwards, letting out a hearty laugh. Ronnie claps and celebrates behind us and I almost forgot for a moment that she was here, but I'm glad I remembered before I was about to thank Devon in every way possible.

"I love you so much! I can't believe I'm going to be *your wife!*" I gush, placing kisses all over his cheeks as my body buzzes with delight, reveling in the thoughts of belonging to him forever, as he will to me.

Epilogue

1 Year Later

Rhea

I shake the sand from my hair, listening to the sounds of the beach waves crashing against the shore. The sun graces me with it's warmth as I wrap the towel around my body, the post-swim breeze trying to nip at my body.

"I'm going to head back to the villa and get cleaned up for dinner!" I shout over to Devon, grabbing his attention. He turns his head and I focus on the way the sun carves out every outline on his body, adding to his glowing tan.

"I'll come and help you!" He shouts back with a mischievous grin on his face. He leaves the boys playing volleyball as they all whine and complain at him being a total wet wipe.

The second he begins walking towards me, the moment we lock eyes, I feel the gravitational pull on my entire body. Like we are two magnets, not able to resist each other even if we wanted to. It's our nature, the way we were made.

"Look at you, my stunning wife." He beams with pride, loving being able to finally call me his.

"And you, my handsome husband." I counter as he nears our deck chairs, kicking sand with him as he walks.

In a swift movement, he scoops me up in his arms and brings me close to his chest, the heat radiates from him and comforts me all at once. *Home.*

"Devon!" I squeal in excitement, thrashing my legs and throwing my head back in laughter. He leans down and takes my lips in his, the saltiness of the ocean invades my mouth as we entangle ourselves together. His tongue slides inside of my mouth effortlessly as a rush of heat spreads across my entire body, a reaction only he can warrant.

"Lets enjoy some more of this post-marital bliss, Mrs. Stark." He smiles against my lips, not breaking our contact as he begins to walk with me back towards the beach house.

With every moment that passes, our kisses grow more ravish and aggressive as the need for each other intensifies. He plants me straight onto the dining table that we ate from only this morning with all of our close friends and family around us.

"Devon, what if they come back?" I pant, trying to push his shoulders back but it proves useless.

"What if?" He smirks with a slight shake of the head, tugging at my bikini bottoms.

"No, *sand*." I mutter against his lips as he attacks me with his luscious kisses, "Shower–" I mumble before he scoops me back up and I wrap my legs around his waist.

His hands flow through my hair and he grazes my scalp with his fingertips, making my eyes roll from the sensation. Even the slightest touch from my darling husband has me shaking to the core.

Devon turns on the shower head as soon as we're inside, with me still looped around him like a koala bear.

"Devon! It's freezing!" I scream, trying to duck out the way of the jets streaming down all over my body.

"It'll warm up, little dove." He winks, before dropping me to me feet and pushing me back against the wall. He tugs at the strings of my bikini bottoms and they drop to the floor quickly with the weight of the water. His lips burn my skin with every tender touch as he plants them all over my thighs and up my stomach.

He pushes my legs apart and places one of my legs over his shoulder as he goes in for the kill, his mouth devouring my most sensitive body part.

"Oh, God." My jaw slackens as my eyes flutter closed, feeling his tongue delve into the places he is so familiar with, the places he knows are my sweet spots. My hands find their way to his hair, gripping it in between my fingers to try and hold myself together even though he is trying his hardest to completely unravel me.

"Forever mine," he growls, the vibrations from his deep voice tingle from my sex up to the rest of my body as it encapsulates me into a puddle of pleasure. He takes satisfaction from my shaking legs as he pins me in place, not even retreating for air as he tongues me to my orgasm.

It blows through me like a hurricane as my entire body spasms and my moans howl through the bathroom, drowned out by the splashing of the shower.

Before my body comes down from the skies, he stands up and grips my ass to hoist me onto his waist. My legs wrap around him with ease as he plunges inside of me, drawing me tight. We both hiss at the extreme sensation overload as we connect together as one, the unification of our souls as we entangle together physically, mentally and now, *legally*.

As of less than twenty-four hours ago, I became Mrs. Stark and Devon has made it his mission to prove to me in every position possible, how much I am his wife. There hasn't been a single second of us being married that I have taken for granted, I have reveled in every moment of belonging to him.

The shower sprays over us both as we hold onto each other, almost as if we're fearful that the other would disappear if we were to let go. I mean, we can't be blamed considering the insanity of the beginning of our relationship.

Our bodies grind into one another, drunk on the delirium that he sends my mind spiraling into. Him and only him. Forever and always.

I moan as my back begins to arch and my legs grip his waist, squeezing him to try and hold myself steady as I unravel before him.

"My wife, forever," he pants as his fingers press into my hipbones, holding me in place whilst he drives into me over and over, delivering us both to our rapturous peak. The word *'wife'* bounces around my head like it's my own national anthem, and I would never have associated myself as being patriotic. But, my God, I want to hear that word for eternity. I want it to be carved into my soul forevermore, it sounds more fitting to me than my own name.

My limbs weaken as my orgasm takes over the function of my body, I can't do anything to stop it, not that I'd even want to. My screams don't cease as he delves into me deeper, sending me soaring into the clouds above as if he really is taking me to heaven and back. My nails dig into his back muscles as he holds me tighter against the tiled wall, the sounds of our synced moans shatter me from within and solidify that we are entirely designed for each other.

His teeth clamp onto my shoulder as I feel his body grow rigid, his thighs stiffening underneath me as his pace slows, drawing himself out and plunging back inside of me. My eyes roll when I feel him come undone, expelling his cum inside of me, for probably the thousandth time.

Epilogue

He stills as we hold onto each other, fighting the urge to stay interlocked like this forever. If I could, I would. He slowly withdraws from me but adjusts me on his hips so that I'm higher up on his defined abdomen.

His lips press against my chest as he mutters over and over how in love with me he is and my heart swells.

I hate to interrupt the moment, but… "Devon, I need to lay down." I remind him and he groans before nodding his head, flicking his wet dark curls out of his face. See? I knew I was right with him having curls when his hair is wet. He drops me to my feet and I stand up on my tiptoes to give him a sweet kiss on his juicy lips.

"Get your ass on that bed and don't move, I'll head down and get us a drink," He slaps my ass as I turn to walk out of the shower. On my way out of the bathroom I loop the white fluffy towel around me and hop onto the bed, laying down so my face is pointed at the wall. I place my legs vertical on the wall, allowing my wet hair to soak into the luxurious four-poster bed.

Devon wanders out of the room and I angle my head to stare out of the balcony window. The warm breeze blows the thin linen curtains and they float in the air with such grace, looking almost hypnotizing. The sun shines brightly and the smell of the salty ocean air envelops me in a calming, relaxing atmosphere. I don't even notice as my eyes flutter closed, the time difference between Hawaii and Atlanta obviously catching up with me.

* * *

I'm being shaken awake gently as his tender voice coaxes me out of my slumber, "Rhea, baby…"

I smile with my eyes still shut as his finger traces lines over the softer parts of my face. I moan as I turn my head away, desperate to return to dreamland. He lets out a quiet laugh before leaning closer to my ear and whispering, "You need to take the test baby, it's the fourteenth."

I pout my lips feeling the overwhelming sensation of anxiety, knowing it's that time of the month already again. If it wasn't already obvious, me and Devon have been trying to get pregnant for almost a year now, with no success. It wasn't anything I had comprehended, struggling with fertility. I assumed I'd be just like everyone else, I'm young and generally healthy, I didn't think that it wouldn't come to me easily.

I track my ovulation religiously, we know exactly which days are my most fertile days and the days that, if pregnant, are my testing days. Not including today, it's been eleven negatives and zero positives.

I started on fertility hormones around three months ago now, after consulting with a private fertility doctor about our issues. Devon insisted that I receive only the best course of treatment and that this was only the beginning of the 'VIP' treatment I would get as being his wife. Of course, I'm filled with gratitude but almost twelve months down the line, it's become mentally and physically exhausting. Especially when I keep seeing no results from our hardworking efforts.

"Just let me sleep, baby. I'll do it in the morning," I whine, rolling over to hide my face from him.

The guilt eats away at me month by month, knowing how desperate he is for me to be pregnant with his child, but I keep failing. My body has failed me and continues to fail me, robbing me from something that so many take for granted.

I'd be a lot more eager to take the test if I actually felt any different, if I had suffered with some symptoms like I'd convinced myself multiple times prior. It became old real fast, each time became more

Epilogue

disheartening than the last to the point that even if I felt any different, I wouldn't get my hopes up.

It's looking more likely that in the coming months, we may have to venture into the world of in vitro fertilization, which is a whole new ballgame of mental and physical strain.

Nobody talks about the pressure to fall pregnant naturally and easily, and nobody listens when it doesn't happen that way. We got tired of pretending like there wasn't issues, that it would just take time. Which it will, but it's also not guaranteed.

Devon scoots in behind me, pulling my body into his and encapsulating me inside of his burly arms, providing me my protective comfort. I smile against his arm as I prop my head onto it, enjoying the musky scent of his aftershave and salt water.

"Where is everyone?" I mumble sleepily.

He kisses my shoulder blade before speaking, "They're having a movie night with the projector in the lawn, if you want to join them?" He suggests but I shake head, enjoying the snug feeling of being inside this huge bed.

"You should go and join them, I'm fine just here." I encourage, leaning down to place my own kisses on the back of his hand. He tightens his wrap around me and shakes his head into my back as I feel his hair tickle me lightly.

"You should, I'm not going anywhere, we invited them for a reason. Go and have some fun, my love." I smile, even though he can't see me in the darkness of the room. The moon illuminates a section of the room and it is like having my own natural lamp from mother nature herself.

"But I want to lay here with you, you're so snugly," he insists, pressing into my ass with his growing hardness. I roll my eyes and try to escape from his grip, letting a soft giggle escape from my lips.

"I don't think so, Mr. I'm still recovering from earlier. My mind may change by the time you come back..." I tease as he groans behind me. I love knowing how much he wants me and how he can't keep himself away from me for longer than a few hours, he's so inexplicably perfect.

"Fine, fine. But, don't expect me not to wake you up with my cock inside of you. I'm holding you to your words." His deep laugh swarms around me and it delights me to hear the musical sound erupt from his chest.

He pulls me so that I'm flat on my back and I instinctively wrap my arms around his neck as he leans over me, the darkness of his features shadowed by the moon.

"I look forward to it, *husband*." I grin, never getting bored of saying it.

"I bet I am more, *wife*." He says as he kisses me deeply before pulling up and leaving me in the center of the huge bed, his absence already making me feel partially empty. It probably isn't normal how much I feel like I'm missing a part of me whenever he leaves, but it makes me all the more excited to see him when he gets back.

It's the same with work, now that I am officially a First Officer and Devon is no longer my mentor. We generally fly separate now considering that we're both on the same level, but Devon has remained part-time whilst I am full-time. Devon decided it was best to part ways with the team, especially now that they fulfilled exactly what they'd set out to do but he meets up occasionally with them for old times sake. He insisted on remaining part-time originally because we were expecting to be with child before long, and he wanted me be able to still have the career I'd worked so damn hard for. It only solidified how I'd made the best decision by choosing to have children with Devon, with him putting me at the forefront of his mind so I can still have my career and him be the primary parent.

But, that's Devon for you. Always making sacrifices to better the

Epilogue

world for everyone else around him. God, I love that man.

My mind continues to chase around with the bliss of my life and our family and friends that surround us, the one thing I'd always wanted in life. The urge to pee becomes unbearable and I conjure up the strength to climb out of my cocoon of comfort.

My feet pad across the warm wooden flooring as I entire into our private bathroom, connected to our room. As I sit on the toilet, I ponder whether or not I should get it over with, in my own privacy. At least then, I don't have to see the disappointment on Devon's face for what feels like the hundredth time.

I pull open the cabinet drawer and grab the zip locked bag with all of my 'fertility' items inside. My fingers push through the boxes of medication, the ovulation tracker and the diary of dates until I come upon my new arch nemesis. The pregnancy test.

I tear the blue wrapper and silently curse at the amount of money we've spent on buying the digital ones but Devon, once again, insisted that we buy only the 'best'. I sit with the test in between my legs and finally relieve myself, pulling the test out midstream and placing the cap back on. I place it on the counter top and finish up, pulling on some pajama shorts and washing my hands.

The digital screen displays the egg timer that I've stared at for far too many minutes than I want to admit. I tap my foot impatiently, then proceed to look at myself in the mirror.

I lean over with my hands rested either side of the sink as I peer into my own blue eyes, seeing the entire history of my life flash before my eyes. This situation, right now, has come full circle.

The numerous times I've stopped and looked at myself in the mirror at different stages in my life and how entirely contrasting each time has been.

My eyes wander down the front of my torso, settling upon the pink scar on my stomach. I purse my lips as I touch it tenderly with my fingers, tracing the outline of it as Devon does almost daily, reminding me of my strength.

A beeping sound draws me out of my thoughts as I dare to take a glance at the stick that holds so much of our longing hearts. But, my mouth dries when I see something entirely different to every other time, something that proves all of this wasn't for nothing. My eyes fill with tears as a shaky hand rises to cover my mouth. The heartache, the destruction, the turmoil, was all worth it.

'Pregnant'

A huge thank you!

Thank you so much to each and every one of you who have rode alongside Devon and Rhea on their turbulent journey, I hope it was worth it!

I hold Rhea very close to my heart and I relate to her on so many levels that she felt almost natural to write, I couldn't resist but to give her a happy ending! And what better way to do that than for it to be with our sweet soul, Devon.

This couple will absolutely be one of my favorites in my author journey and I hope you'll stick around to see glimpses of them in Book Three!

About the Author

Jordyn Ellery is the author of the 'Billy Boys Series' which includes titles such as 'Retribution' and 'Redemption'.

She is a dark romance author and loves to include morally gray characters as well as plot twists. Jordyn is a huge fan of romantic suspense and gritty love stories. If she isn't writing about the most loveable hated characters, then she's reading about them.

Follow Jordyn on her socials: @jordyn.ellery to keep updated on new releases!

www.ingramcontent.com/pod-product-compliance
Lightning Source LLC
LaVergne TN
LVHW012031070526
838202LV00056B/5467